THE GEMINI PROJECT

by Ian Moran

This book is sold subject to the condition that it shall not, by way of trade or otherwise, be lent, re-sold, hired out, photocopied or held in the retrieval system, other otherwise circulated without the publisher's expressed prior consent in any form of binding or cover other that that in which this is published and without a similar condition including this condition being imposed on the subsequent purchaser.

Double Scotch Publishing
Box 62, Salmon River,
Nova Scota

First Edition (A0130)
First published – 2024
© John and Lorraine Moran, 2024
Typeset in Salmon River
Printed in Halifax, Canada

Library Cataloguing in Publication Data
Moran, Ian
   The Gemini Project
   1.   Fiction
   2.   Science Fiction
   3.   Distopia

ISBN 979-8-3255826-84

*Play, laugh, eat,
sleep, repeat.*

For Lorraine, who reminds me
everyday to seek the child within.

Contents

	Prologue	1
1.	The Academy	5
2.	An Interview with the Doctor	18
3.	Doctor Osler	21
4.	Father's Day	48
5.	The Tunnel	63
6.	Visiting the Library	74
7.	An Interview with the Doctor, con't	94
8.	Generations	99
9.	A Plan to Survive	116
10.	The Betrayal	137
11.	Road Trip	154
12.	The Birth and Death of Youngstown	165
13.	On the Road Again	175
14.	New London	198
15.	And the Cradle Will Rock…	236
16.	Like Father, Like Son	251
17.	Enlightenment	272
18.	Easter Eggs	274

Prologue

Fire. Another synapse provided a burst of electrical impulses, which formulated into a question in the adolescent's brain. The seventeen-year-old's voice contained a slight tremble that went unperceived by the doctor. The boy did not intend to be profound; he just wanted a simple answer to a simple question.

"How did we get here?"

Dr. William Osler, who considered himself an above-grade amateur philosopher, would have been very bored with such a mundane question if it had been asked by one of the other boys. However, he was fascinated by this particular student's rapidly developing cognitive abilities. He was also slightly stoned. A question about the shaping of society could be exactly what he needed. After the previous night's conversations, Dr. Osler surmised that the boy wanted to understand how man evolved its social system to become what it was today. A simple, but excellent, question. Dr. Osler had grown to appreciate that the boy always allowed him the leeway to provide detailed background in his answers, leaving only the question of where to start. Keep it simple, he thought, but also flood the boy with a good dose of truth.

"Throughout history, there have been four basic societal structures in play. Four doctrines that have been struggling to be the one real truth that will rescue mankind."

This was Dr. Osler's attempt at simplicity.

"We started with the doctrine of religious rule, where the guiding light was provided from above. Then came the ruling despot, which was sometimes in harmony with, and sometimes in conflict with religious rule. Like it or not, for most of our history, these two dogmas are what we have lived under. Democracy was a latecomer to the game, and it really only gathered steam when democratic countries became rich. Then a few political theorists created a fourth doctrine: nothing gets inherited, and people get rewarded based on their value to society. That sounds like a really good idea, until you add man into the mix."

Dr. Osler didn't pause to gauge whether his audience was keeping pace with him (and the boys were used to that). He was self-indulging, formulating much of his diatribe as the words spewed out. The doctor had fed the youth a paucity of information for years, but now the boy's desire to learn puts more demands on the conversation. Under the influence of the hallucinogenic, a domino of thoughts came tumbling from the doctor's mouth. The two other boys that were there, paid little attention to the soliloquy. Over the past few months, the doctor had provided facts and opinions on everything from modern art, to science, to philosophy. Tonight's diatribe on politics was the easiest for him to extend into one of his rants, and even easier for the other boys to ignore.

"As a young man, I believed that everything had played out to its natural resolution in the 20th century," Dr. Osler continued. "Kings had lost their kingdoms, and the odd self-proclaimed despot had effectively succumbed to their own greed. Even religious reign was on the decline. That left a battle between the theorists that believed communism was the answer, and those that believed in the power of democracies."

A pause. Not to compose his thoughts or gauge his audience's attention level, but for a quick inhale. The two other boys had already lost interest and they got up to head to a checkerboard. Losing some of his listeners did not bother the doctor, but he did sense confusion in the remaining youth's expression. Nevertheless, he persisted. He was attempting to fill in knowledge gaps, without stopping to ascertain what the gaps actually were.

"Then, out of virtually nowhere, communism suddenly ended in Russia. It really felt like the great experiment was just a theory that failed, and democracy had won the day."

The Gemini Project 3

In the dimly lit room, Dr. Osler sat in a maroon leather wingback chair and squinted through the slits of his half-closed eyes. His occasional glance at the boy wasn't to ensure he was being comprehended … it was to make sure the boy was still there. Across the room on a matching sofa, the young adolescent sat below a half-filled bookshelf, staring intently back at the lecturer.

'Where is this going?' the boy thought. 'What does Russia mean? Is he ever going to answer my question, or is he just going to prattle on?'

Dr. Osler took another quick inhalation of his 'antidepressant' and continued in his slow cadence.

"Even the Bolsheviks had to admit that democracy had won the doctrinal beauty contest. But wait! There were still wars, and where there is a war, there is usually either a religious or materialistic objective. And, despite the sham elections, Russia had left communism not for democracy, but to fall back under the rule of a despot. Then the democracies started self-destructing with their own would-be despots pulling their countries back to authoritarianism. Some even imploded under the desire to remain outside of a global economic union. Reliance on your neighbour is not something that comes easy to us.

All of this spawned from an era of manipulative intelligence, with truly little intelligence injected into the equation, so then we …"

Dr. Osler glanced briefly through his eyelids and saw that the boy's expression had succumbed to bewilderment.

"Are you following me? Or do I need to go over some more of the history again or delve into the part that technology investments played?"

"You're not answering my question. I mean, how did *we* get *here*, me and my father."

"Oh," Dr. Osler softly muttered, his words frozen in his head as he slipped into a soma-induced introspection. The boy wasn't being philosophical at all. He had asked the right question, but the doctor had been giving the wrong answer.

"You and your father … that's a bit harder to explain."

He couldn't explain it. There was no way to explain to a boy why his father would want him dead. What are the acceptable motives for killing one's son? In a way, it was related exactly to what he had been trying to explain to the boy. Society had evolved to make this proposition acceptable, but how to make this make sense? Then the doctor smiled. He took amusement in knowing the punchline to one of the greatest historical jokes: what had pulled down the great states of the twentieth century? It wasn't war. It wasn't global warming. It wasn't a global pandemic. He believed it was the success of healthcare. Healthcare caused the bankruptcy of publicly funded systems, private systems and the goddam insurance companies.

When Dr. Osler first arrived at the Academy, he was given the usual warning about having any personal discussions with the boys. However, he no longer interacted well with the other doctors at the school, so telling students a few anecdotes about his own life experiences was a justifiable mental release. Now however, he had to explain why a failed healthcare regime led to a society where this boy's father would kill him, the same way his father had killed the boy's older brother.

"You know your father is a doctor, right?" Dr. Osler asked, unsure of where to take the conversation.

Osler paused in exasperation, while Jan waited intently for the doctor to gather his thoughts.

"There's just so much you don't know yet ..." Dr. Osler said as he let his thoughts tail off.

"I know that if I do nothing, I die. What if I kill my father, would I be allowed to live?"

It was mid-August, and the doctor knew that the plan for the 17-year-old boy would see him dead in less than two weeks.

1. The Academy

The students lived on the school grounds and collectively lived an extremely isolated existence. Life at the Academy meant only seeing the school staff and the other boys. Four times a year the students were visited by their fathers, but beyond that, there were very few outside connections for any of them. The net effect was that most of the boys had absolutely no concept of the state of affairs in the world outside of their school. In their daily routine, there was no scheduled discussion of current affairs, just a timetable filled with sports, gym, meals, rest and of course a regular meeting with one of the doctors.

At The Corpo Academy for Development, very little mental development was encouraged. Physical development was not only the core curriculum of CAD ... it was the only item on the syllabus. Any cognitive advancement that did occur, would be serendipitously developed through an informal osmosis. Most of the elite doctors didn't talk to students outside of the conventional environment, but Dr. Osler liked to sit and talk with the boys. He didn't talk 'to' them as much as he talked 'at' them, ignoring the responses that were relatively immature. However, earlier that year, he discovered that one student was eager to learn and actually asked meaningful questions.

Jan was 17 years-old and he suffered from hemochromatosis, a condition signified by too much iron in his system. The extra iron meant that he required less sleep and was more active than the other boys. The inherited disorder, known informally as 'the Viking disease', could eventually damage his liver but was very manageable if treated. The treatment was simply a regularly scheduled phlebotomy, a blood letting to temporarily reduce the amount of iron in the patient's circulatory system. The remedy hadn't changed much since a doctor prescribed leeches in the 1800s.

With far too much iron in his system, Jan found it challenging to cope with any lax schedules. Wednesdays were the worst. The mandatory sleep-in time for Wednesday was 11 a.m. It was difficult for Jan to sleep past seven o'clock. He would lie in his dormitory bed, trying not to squirm, trying not to wake his roommate and of course, trying his best not to allow the slightest thought to enter his head. His only chance to fall back to sleep was to suppress thinking. With great regularity, his mind wouldn't let him slumber and instead it wandered to thoughts of what it was like where his father lived, or who invented the game of soccer, or how does someone become a doctor. He usually awoke at least two hours ahead of his school roommate.

Jan often fantasized about a life outside of the Academy. He had an analytical mind but had very little to apply it to. Corpo was not a place that would develop a student's ability to apply logic or reason. Instead of mathematics and sciences, the student's daily programme adhered to a strict regime consisting of various physical activities. The only deskbound education was based solely on the requirement to understand the rules of a sport or game. The Academy believed that sports and exercise were all that the students needed to prepare them for their life. Sleeping in, lots to eat, plenty of spare time, plenty of workout time, no academic studies ... the Academy should have been every boy's dream. For Jan, it was just life as he knew it.

By the time he reached the age of 17, Jan maintained the statuesque physique of a young man. An athletic young man. As a product of the Corpo Academy, he knew little about the realm of politics, governments, or finances, let alone about art, music, or romance. The only members of the opposite sex that Jan had ever seen were the two female nurses that tended the students, and a

The Gemini Project 7

glimpse of Nurse Rossignol would do very little to excite an adolescent mind. Jan had been raised by a squad of trainers, coaches, nurses and, of course, doctors. He lived a life of game playing and sports as far back as his memory would take him. And Jan was good at it. The blossoming youth excelled above his classmates in most sports, particularly water sports and gymnastics.

Although they didn't use the expression, Jan and Dixon Gémeaux had been best friends since they first met. Dix had been Jan's roommate for the past three years. Standing beside each other, Jan and Dix made an impressive duo. They were both well built and had handsome features. Dix was taller, broader and heavier than Jan, and yet somehow it would be very apparent that he was less of an athlete. Where Dix was slightly overweight and slightly pear-shaped, Jan's physique was more chiselled and better proportioned. Jan was a blond, blue-eyed boy of Scandinavian descent. Dix had unusual brown eyes with an undertone that was almost orange, together with chestnut hair, slightly olive skin and DNA from any of a number of Southern European countries. Very often at the Academy, roommates were not only the same age in years, but were also born in the same month. Jan was born on August 24th and Dix was born on the 28th.

This year their birthday celebration was anticipated to be the best one of their lives. Not only would they celebrate their renaissance, but they would celebrate it together, or at least in the same week. The renaissance was the final celebration at The Corpo Academy for Development, which marked the end of their time at the school and the beginning of a new life ... a life together with their fathers. To Dix the renaissance represented the conclusion of an old life, one he would miss, but to Jan it was the beginning of a new life, one that brought new opportunities.

Despite all the anticipation, neither boy knew exactly what form the renaissance celebration took. Jan pointed out to Dix that it wouldn't be like a Solstice party as there wouldn't be other boys invited. Besides, you could never hear any party noises coming out of the hall during any of the older boys' renaissances. The older boys had headed to Renaissance Hall in the evening of their 18th birthday and the next day their belongings would be packed into one box and shipped off. Occasionally, some of the older boys had been spotted a day or two after their party. They were laughing and smiling as they boarded the shuttle that would take them away from the Academy.

Dix told Jan that he didn't need to understand what form the party would take, just that there would be a grand party and that it would be in his honour.

On that particular Wednesday morning, in early June, three months before his 18th birthday, Jan lay in bed awake. He contemplated the transformations that would come along with his renaissance celebration. In the glow of a deep indigo light, Dix continued his tenth hour of sleep. Jan lay quietly with his eyes closed. He knew that he would not be able to go back to sleep unless he could stop thinking about the potential held in his new life. Jan wondered if his father would attend the party and take him directly to New London immediately after the festivities. He looked around his dorm room and thought about whether his new room, in his father's residence, would be as sparse as his current accommodations. He didn't begrudge his current environment as there was everything he needed, he just wondered if there would be a little more of him reflected in his new bedroom. Everything Jan knew about his future life was based on his own fantasies.

The light in the room slowly shifted to a warm tangerine as the 11:00 a.m. wakeup horn sounded. Two long blasts and Dix immediately woke, sat upright in his bed as if programmed to wake up and he began to talk about that day's activities. The sports for Wednesdays were field hockey and tennis.

"Right, here's how we're going to win this thing today," Dix stated. "If I'm selected as captain for the hockey team, I'll pick you first. If you're captain, you pick me. If that fat-ass Jet is captain, let's both hide at the back of the pack, so he doesn't pick us. Deal?"

In individual competitions in the school, Jan often finished in the top three. In team sports however, much to his coaches' dismay, he was less of a standout. He would all too often selflessly make a pass to allow a teammate the opportunity to score a point. This was especially the case when they played field hockey. The superior player, Jan would pass even if he had a better chance of scoring. Usually when Jan passed to a weaker player, after the game Dix would point this out as a mistake, as if his expert sports knowledge were required for the post-game analysis. However, when Jan passed to Dix, if Dix didn't score, he would never suggest that Jan shouldn't have passed to him. Dix would find some other reason why he failed to score.

The Gemini Project

Within minutes of wake-up, all the boys of the Academy hurriedly got changed out of their pale blue elastane sleepsuits, then went for a quick wash-up to start the day. Jan and Dix didn't need to shave. They were both at the peach fuzz stage in facial hair. Once ready, the boys proceeded to the dining hall for breakfast. Breakfast was always big but was also always extremely healthy. No bacon and eggs. The boys had never seen bacon or eggs. Instead, they had yogurt, whole wheat toast, all bran cereal, and lots and lots of fresh fruit.

The school grounds consisted of a vast campus with 20 low-level buildings, 17 of which were currently functional. The buildings by and large had a retro design making them appear as if they were built in the 19th century, however many of them were less than a decade old. The only buildings with an exterior that did not have the feel of brown chiselled stone and mortar, were the Administration Building and Renaissance Hall, both of which sat in contrast with their sterile atmospheres created through a mesh of green glass and steel. Even the outside of the dormitory looked like it was centuries old. The buildings that the boys used most often, the velodrome, the swimming pool and the new gymnasium were all built within the last five years. They were specifically designed to provide a nostalgic feel such that the boys' fathers would relate to their own high school days. However, the fallen structures of their fathers' youth had been authentic and there was very little that was authentic in the construction at Corpo.

The extensive dining hall was functionally located next to the boys' residence. The building's pleasing external aesthetic sat in contrast to an interior that was markedly stark. The large dining area was contained by high walls that were undecorated by posters or paintings. The walls were straddled with thick wooden beams that conjured up a feeling of history. Dix felt the room looked old and he said the place was 'creepy', but Jan liked the feeling of days-gone-by that the room evoked in him. He particularly liked the way the dark wooden beams contrasted against the plain white ceiling and walls. The actual room construction was prefabricated fibreglass, textured to look like wood and coloured to appear aged. There was nothing old in the dining hall. The room was large enough to accommodate about 100 diners, even though currently there were only 42 boys in attendance at the school.

After breakfast, precisely at noon, the boys made their way through the tangerine light of the cafeteria to the perfect bright yellow light of the outside field. It was another great day for field hockey. They jogged across the quad, past the Rod Laver tennis courts, to the Dhyan Chand hockey field where they would begin with the team selection. Because this was Wednesday, all the boys had dressed that morning in the appropriate uniform for hockey, including protective equipment.

The ample grounds of the Academy were laid out with several outdoor sporting facilities weaving in and out the more functional buildings. The tennis courts, basketball court, field hockey grounds and soccer pitch all appeared well maintained and manicured sufficiently to support professional level play. The grass was in fact synthetic, just like all of the other plants on the campus. There was a baseball diamond, but it was unused and sat dilapidated and uncared for. The soccer pitch, which Dr. O'Flanagan called 'Paradise', was right beside the student dormitory, and it was the only field that was lit at night (even though the boys never played after dark).

When the boys arrived at the hockey field, Coach Treinador was already there waiting for them. Treinador was a broad-shouldered man whose salt-and-pepper beard contrasted with his youthful physique. The coach selected the team captains for the game by throwing bibs at two of the boys. That day, he threw a red bib to Jan and a blue bib to Otto Penzler. Otto was a boy of Aryan heritage, with blond hair, blue eyes, and broad shoulders. His father was well-known to the doctors of the Academy as he was one of the wealthiest of the school's benefactors. Otto was one of the few boys that was physically on the same level as Jan. He was a fierce competitor and Jan knew right away that they would have a hard-fought game that day.

Otto was first to pick a player for his team. He had respect for Jan but didn't feel the same way about Dix. He knew that Dix would want to be on Jan's team. and he thought momentarily about selecting Dix just to split up the roommates. However, because Dix wasn't that good at field hockey, Otto picked his best friend Tam, as his first choice. Tam was a burley 16-year-old that looked like he followed a regular routine of 'sterobics', but his mass was pure natural muscle development. Tam loved to spend his spare time in the gym doing

The Gemini Project

weight-training and he was a specimen that the coaches and doctors were proud of ... next year's model of a Jan or an Otto.

Jan knew that a team starting with Otto and Tam would be tough to beat. There were four or five other players that were better than Dix at field hockey, but Jan picked Dix first, as per Dix's plan that morning. That meant that Otto picked next and was able to get three of the best field hockey players on his team before Jan was able to get his first real pick. Dix didn't realize the challenge that Jan had perceived, and he was especially happy when "fat-assed Jet" was chosen as the very last pick. Unfortunately for us however, thought Dix, he's on our team.

Despite the selection process, the two teams turned out almost evenly matched in their play. Jan's picks were based on creating a team rather than a group of the best players, so his side was balanced with no weak areas in its offence or defence. However, as typically was the case, the game was a lot of running around with very little physical contact. Coach Treinador made sure of that. Thus, the play relied more on offensive finesse rather than defensive skills and Jan's team selection reflected this.

"Nu nunner Nonno," Dix called over to Jan.

Jan's face let his roommate know that he didn't understand the instructions. Dix spat out his mouthguard.

"You cover Otto."

Jan and Dix were down by one goal with five minutes left to play when Dix scored the tying point. Dix was sure that his goal was due to his superior abilities. Everyone else on the team however saw that he had received an ideal cross field pass from Jan, which set up Dix perfectly for the shot. Dix was having a good day scoring. Jan was having a good day with assists.

Even despite Dix's best scoring effort, that afternoon Otto and Tam were too athletic to be slowed down by 60 minutes of running end-to-end down the field. They followed up Dix's goal with a passing play of their own to give them the lead. Then disaster struck.

Sometimes, the boys were split into different age categories for various sports. For field hockey however, all boys, ranging in age from 15 to 17, played in the same game. There was a significant difference in the stature of a 17-year-old boy compared to that of a 15-year-old boy. One of the slightest of the 15-year-olds on Otto's team was a ginger-haired boy called Elf. He was a pimply faced skinny pixie-like boy who had just started at the school earlier that year. Otto passed the ball to Elf expecting him to pass it back, however Elf saw an opportunity to shoot the ball through Dix's legs and run around him to receive his own pass. The move, known as a nutmeg, was executed perfectly. The speed of the manoeuvre led to Dix's confusion, and he lost his balance as he tried to spin around to stop Elf. On the way down, he realized that he had been made to look foolish by one of the Corpo kids, so Dix swung his stick, not at the ball, but at Elf's legs. The boys wore shinpads to protect the front of their legs, but a falling Dix had struck from the side and managed to break Elf's fibula.

Jan froze when he heard the sound. It felt like the cracking of the bone had reverberated across the field and throughout the campus. Coach Treinador was quick to blow three long blasts of his whistle and an assistant coach immediately ran toward the infirmary. All the boys gathered around Elf. There was no blood, but the sound of that crack hung in the air. Dix thought he had broken his hockey stick and was surprised when he stood up and found it intact. The assistant coach arrived with a stretcher and two nurses from the infirmary. One of the nurses told the boys to go get showered. The game was over.

There was very little talking on the way back to the showers. Jan started thinking about something his father had said to him when another boy broke a bone. Jan's father was Trevor Ericson, a well-respected doctor that came to visit Jan once a quarter. A tall striking blond-haired Scandinavian, his father seemed immensely popular with the other fathers. The staff at the Academy referred to Jan's father as 'Doctor Ericson', while the doctors called him 'Tre'.

Tre had originally enrolled Jan in the Gehirn Academy. As his father told it, fortunately when Jan turned 15, another youngster at Corpo broke his arm playing lacrosse and this allowed Jan to transfer from Gehirn to Corpo. Jan never understood why someone would want to leave Corpo, even if they had a broken arm, but his father often joked that this was Jan's 'lucky break'. While the misfortune led to Jan's opportunity to enter his new school, his father begrudged that it also eliminated lacrosse from the curriculum. Trevor Ericson paid a heavy premium to move Jan from Gehirn to Corpo, and he made sure to remind Jan to be grateful. Jan was sincerely grateful for his life at the school.

The Gemini Project

When they arrived at the showers, the boys finally started to talk and eventually joke. Dix gave a recap of the game, accepting that he was on the losing side even if the game ended abruptly, but he blamed the loss on the poor defensive play of Jet. Jet was a dark-haired, tawny-skinned boy of Southeast Asian descent. He was only about 15 pounds over his target weight, but Dix often said that he was too rotund to be very good at any sport except perhaps weightlifting. Dix told Jan that it was because Jet ate too much, but Jan felt that maybe Jet was just 'built that way'. Neither of them knew that the calorie intake of all the boys was being regulated daily.

All the boys showered again. The showering routine was mandatory even if they didn't break a sweat during the match. 'A clean body was a healthy body', Dr. Primero would remind the boys at their weekly 'sermon'. In the showers, Dix approached Jet with a wet towel.

Snap.

He whipped the towel at Jet catching his exposed rear end with the tip of the soaked weapon.

This was no fun towel snap … it was meant to hurt.

"Ow … what 'cha do that for?" Jet protested.

"That's for making us lose the game … fat-ass," Dix answered.

Jan was about to point out that Jet wasn't even on the field at the time the losing goal was scored, but Otto spoke first.

"He's not the reason you lost."

"What are you talking about Otto Penzler?" Dix responded purposefully using Otto's full name for emphasis, "No one asked you!"

"You lost because we scored more goals than you," Otto stated. "You were a forward, if you had scored more, you could have won."

Jan listened. Otto never struck Jan as particularly clever, but he heard something in Otto's voice. Jet wasn't even on Otto's team, yet Otto was defending him. Jan wondered if Otto was protecting Jet or attacking Dix.

"Who cares," Jan said trying to be conciliatory. "It's just a game."

Both Dix and Otto shot Jan a look.

"A game we should have won but didn't because of fat-ass here," Dix said pointing at Jet.

Jan had been coming to Dix's defence, but it was obvious that Dix didn't need or want him to do so. Dix's last comment hung in the air as Jet was rubbing the red patch on his posterior.

"I'll tell you what," Dix continued, "let's play with the same teams next week, and we'll play the full time, and the winner gets the loser's cut on steak night."

Jan expected to hear 'provided you guys take Jet on your team', but the condition never came.

"You're on," Otto said accepting the challenge, then playfully snapped a wet towel in the air in Dix's direction.

Cleanup was followed by lunch, which was always equally as healthy as breakfast. Today, it consisted of a bowl filled with ahi tuna, shredded carrots, diced cucumber and edamame, over the top of a rice base. After the food came a foamy shake that was served by the nurses. The boys got to rest a bit before the tennis matches, which began at 4:30 in the afternoon.

While some of the sporting events were organized to be competitive, the tennis matches tended to be a bit looser. There were no adults supervising tennis and Jan liked this. It was typical that one event during the day would be controlled, and another event would be left to the boys to self-manage. It was self-managed; but monitored. Since the boys ranged in age from 15 to 17, some were fitter than others solely because of their age. In the tennis matches, they played a tournament that consisted of one set of doubles. Usually the 17-year-old boys would each team up with a 15-year-old to even out the teams. That afternoon, the round robin was won by a team consisting of two 16-year-olds, one of whom was Tam. All the boys were amused with that outcome as it had been the first time in recent memory that neither Jan, Dix nor Otto had made it to the tennis finals.

Dinner followed tennis, which on Wednesdays was particularly worth savouring as the boys dined on bone-in ribeye steaks. The red meat diet wasn't good for Jan's hemochromatosis, but no one seemed to care. Jan noticed that Elf wasn't at the dining table. He liked Elf and had treated him like a little brother ever since he arrived. Elf was smart and funny and had even joined Jan for a couple of Dr. Osler's rants. Jan had thought that maybe he could teach Elf how to read, the way Dr. Osler had taught him during their unscheduled time.

Evenings on Wednesdays were also light. The boys had free time, which they usually filled by playing tag, or fooling around in their rooms. A few boys, like Tam, headed over to the gym for some extra weight training. Jan often went down to the main floor lounge in his residence.

The sizable lounge was one of the few decorated rooms on the campus. The room resembled an 18th century Victorian sitting room, complete with deep-coloured mahogany bookshelves. Here, you'd find ornaments and the only books on campus that were accessible to the boys. The books were as ornamental as anything else in the room. The sofas and chairs that filled the room were a deep maroon leather with brass metal studs highlighting their shape. Jan just liked sitting in the lounge, especially if Dr. Osler was sitting in one of the comfy wingback reading chairs. The doctor was on evening duty on Wednesdays and Sundays, and Jan would listen to him discuss aspects of his life beyond the school. It was during this downtime with Dr. Osler that Jan had eventually learned how to read. Jan had always flipped through the pages of the lounge's books looking at the pictures and eventually he asked Dr. Osler to explain how the words functioned. The doctor clearly liked Jan and he liked his willingness to learn, but what really impressed him was how much the boy had taught himself. Dr. Osler even thought that, given half the chance, Jan could make a decent doctor himself.

That particular evening, after field hockey and tennis, Otto, Dix and Jan were hanging out in the lounge reflecting on their day's performance, as Dr. Osler reviewed a few notes on his digivice.

"Otto, what does your father do for a living?" Jan asked.

"I don't know. Why? Who cares?"

"Well, when's your renaissance?"

"The third of November ... why?" Otto asked getting frustrated with having to answer questions. It wasn't so much that he didn't want to talk about this particular subject, as much as Otto wasn't used to someone asking two or three questions in a row.

"It's just that you'll be leaving here a few months after we do, and I just thought you'd know what you'll be doing," Jan answered.

"It will be the end of happy days for the three of you," Dr. Osler contributed as he looked up, glassy-eyed, from his digivice.

"What I'll be doing is working," Otto snipped, seeming to not even notice Dr. Osler's comment.

"And what I'll be doing is working," Dix added. "And what you'll be doing is working. And what none of us will be doing is playing ... anymore!"

"Yeah, but don't you think it could be fun at work?" Jan asked.

"You're crazy," Otto responded. "There is nothing fun about work ... that's why they call it work."

"I don't know," Jan continued. "My father seems to enjoy his work."

"Yeah," Dix added, "mine too ... but that doesn't mean he wouldn't rather be playing. Look at the doctors here ... do you think they'd rather be checking our temperatures or playing golf? Honestly Jan, I don't know how you are going to survive out there without me.'

"My father told me to enjoy playing while I could," Otto stated, "because he said after my renaissance my life would be over. It sounds to me like work will not be what you're thinking it is Jan."

"Oh," Jan spoke semi-introspectively, "my father said we'll be together after the renaissance and that sounds perfect to me."

"Otto's father meant that you should do less thinking and more playing Jan, now let's go get the checkerboard and play a game."

"Can we play chess instead?" Jan asked.

"I don't get that game," Dix responded. "It's too complicated."

"I'll play you," Otto said to Dix.

The two boys took the checkerboard off the shelf and started setting up for a game.

"I'll play you a game of chess," Dr. Osler called out from his corner chair.

"Really!" Jan blurted enthusiastically. "I'll go get the board."

They played chess for an hour and although the doctor won, there were a few tense moments when he thought Jan had him cornered. Dr. Osler tried to coach Jan a few times, but soon realized he didn't need coaching. Regardless, Dr. Osler liked to talk while he played. The doctor liked to talk in general, and usually dipped into the realm of philosophy.

"Don't surround yourself with yourself," Dr. Osler said. "Move on back two squares."

Jan ignored the kludge advice and asked Dr. Osler if he remembered when the boys used to play lacrosse.

"Oh yea," Dr. Osler replied. "We had to drop that sport after one game, when some kid broke his arm."

"What happened?" Jan asked.

"Well, there was a plan to start playing lacrosse, even though most fathers were against introducing the sport. One father, I think he was Canadian, really wanted to see his son play. Eventually, it was added to the curriculum and all the boys had to wear helmets, facemasks, shoulder pads and shin guards when they played. In the very first game, there was a particularly hard wallop across one boy's arm ... and that was it for the Canadian."

"But what happened to the boy?" Jan asked.

"Well, he was no longer Corpo material, I guess," Dr. Osler joked. The doctor saw the seriousness in Jan's face and added, "Shortly after recovering from his wound, he transferred to another school. As a side-effect of the injury, lacrosse was discontinued and replaced by a non-competitive, relatively safer game of tennis, where the coaches downplayed the competitive aspects and stressed the fun. There was the odd scraped knee after tennis matches, but there was never a broken bone."

"I think Elf broke a bone today," Dix called out from the checkerboard, taking no responsibility for the youngster's injury.

"What do you think will happen to Elf?" Jan asked.

"Well, if he broke a bone, then he's probably no longer Corpo material," Dr. Osler replied.

"So, if I break a bone, I'd get kicked out the school?" Jan asked a little frantically.

"No, no ... if YOU broke a bone, your father would have our collective necks."

And so it was, every Wednesday consisted of sleeping-in, getting up, having breakfast, playing field hockey, showering, having lunch, playing tennis, having steak dinner and then having two hours of free-time to play games and amuse yourself before lights-out. Even though there was no place in the formal agenda for the three Rs (and absolutely zero religious' studies), Jan had been educating himself by asking Dr. Osler questions.

Thursdays were more demanding, with an early rise and a full day of sports that included a swimming competition followed by an afternoon in the velodrome. Thursday was Jan's favourite day.

2. An Interview with the Doctor

As published in *Rolling Stone*, March 2034:

During a flight from New London back to Jardin, this reporter had the honour and the privilege of interviewing the distinguished, Dr. Bartel De Visie. Dr. De Visie, the creator of *The Gemini Project*, and the author of *The Book of Generations*, has provided me with some background that presents some insights as to how and why his treatise came to fruition. Here is the direct transcript of my conversation with Dr. De Visie:

Q: What were the driving issues that compelled you to develop The Gemini Project?

"Man has always struggled to determine the answer to two mysteries: the meaning of life and how to live forever. *The Book of Generations* provides an answer to the second question, which perhaps will allow man to continue to search for the answer to the first. Note, the question was never 'can' we live forever, it has always been 'how' can we live forever.

Throughout history, man's quest to remain young has reaped many benefits but has also failed to solve the focal enigma. The great Spanish explorer Hernando De Soto did not set out to trek halfway across the United States so he could map land from Florida to Texas. That was simply a byproduct of his real objective ... the search for the fountain of youth.

De Soto embarked on his ill-fated odyssey after arriving in North America and 'discovering' a race of aboriginals. His translator gave him the misguided belief that there was a great river that was the source of the youthful appearance of the natives. His search for this fountain of youth, took him across the American South, where he laid claim, for King and country, to thousands of square miles of land, until he finally discovered the Mississippi River. Drinking from the first 'Dixie cup', his hopes were dashed as the mighty river failed to deliver him a youthful appearance. Instead of discovering the river of life, De Soto died and was buried on the banks of the Mississippi."

Q: So, was de Soto wrong to search for the secret to aging?

"No, the bitter irony is that the answer had been right in front of him the whole time. He should have done less travelling and more observing. The people of the Seminole nation lived a lifestyle of pure physical activity. The men hunted, danced, and played sports. This was their way of life, so of course they would be extremely fit. The Seminole Indians ate well, too. In short, they cared for their bodies better than the European explorers who ate to excess and drank even more.

The Seminole religion worshipped the male body as a temple on earth for their Sun God. There never was a physical fountain for De Soto to uncover ... the fountain was simply a regime of life that the rum-drinking, womanizing, slave-trading De Soto could not see on his own misguided path. Still, he was one of the pioneers in the search and he dedicated himself to giving his life for the struggle. And when one man gives his life in the attempt to deliver everlasting life for another, we should worship this man as a hero.

Five hundred years after De Soto, after centuries of steady research, continued athletic activity and a never-ending snail's pace of medical advances, we had moved the average age of man from 34 years to 82 years. In the end, nine times out of ten, dying of old age generally means that something breaks down. The liver becomes infected, the lungs become diseased, or the heart just gives up. According to the World Health Organization, there are 8,000 diseases that can kill us. That means if you miraculously manage to avoid 7,999 of these, you will still wind-up pining for the Fjords. The real cancer on our lives, has been our inability to solve the plethora of medical issues that exist in every single organ in our body. Until we addressed this, there would always be some organ that could call us to our grave. We were doomed to be burdened by the fallibility of the weakest of our organs instead of realizing the salvation of the strongest organ. This was our fountain of youth!"

... continued on page 94

3. Doctor Osler

William Osler appeared to be the oldest of all the doctors on campus. From a distance one would say that he looked to be about 45 years old. In talking with him, he seemed to hold opinions and a depth of knowledge that betrayed his real age. His thick, dark mane, parted on the left, and his deep Southern European hues, contrasted sharply with his light blue eyes. The doctor could be described as ruggedly handsome, with his facial contrasts being acutely captivating.

Jan knew Dr. Osler better than anyone else and if Jan had to think about it, he would admit that he knew Dr. Osler better than he knew his own father. That being said, he really didn't know Dr. Osler that well.

While there was sometimes a softness to Dr. Osler, there was always an underlying edge. That edge didn't exist in the other doctors at the Academy. They seemed to just do their jobs and the boys barely discerned any differences in their personalities. Something wasn't quite right with Dr. Osler though and several of the boys perceived this. Perhaps that's what attracted Jan to him. Where other doctors would snap a conversation closed, Dr. Osler was willing to talk about almost anything. And there was no shortage of opinions, which he expressed even when they weren't called for. If the boys were talking, he would listen and then tell them exactly what he thought. If the boys weren't talking, Dr. Osler would talk about whatever he wanted, and he really didn't care if the boys listened or understood what he was going on about.

Jan had learned to read, thanks to a fish supper. When he was 16 years old, for one of the Fish Fry Fridays, the students were treated to a 'Traditional Fish and Chips' dinner. Dr. O'Flanagan returned from his weekly trip to New London with a shipment of Halibut, and the chefs set about firing up the fryer for the first time in years. In addition to the boys, the unusual feast was also attended by all of the doctors. The students sat at one end of a long table and the staff sat at the other.

The atmosphere was more festive than the typical dining experience at the Academy. Conversations were happening across the table and even intermingled between the boys and the doctors. The dividing line between the doctors and the boys was very rarely blurred, but that evening Otto sat right beside Dr. Asino. One of the most talked about items at the dinner was the unusual presentation of the fish, which was served in a paper cone. The greaseproof paper had been fashioned to look like a classic newspaper from the 1900s.

"Why is the fish wrapped in this paper?" Otto asked across the table to the other boys.

"It's newspaper," answered Dr. Osler, who sat diagonally across from Otto.

"What's newspaper? It looks more like old paper," Otto responded and laughed at his own attempt at humour.

"It is old," Dr. Asino replied cynically without even looking at the boy beside him.

"Old? It's ancient. A Fleet Street business model that failed to adapt," called out Dr. Primero from the centre of the doctors' seating. He always seemed to speak as if his words were a sermon and the definitive cornerstone to the conversation.

"Yea, but what's newspaper? Just something to wrap fish in?" Dix asked looking at Otto for an answer.

"A newspaper is something you use to start a fire," Dr. Asino stated, then purposefully turned the back of his head to the boys to start a new conversation with the other doctors.

The Gemini Project 23

After the unique meal, as everyone was leaving, Dr. Osler looked down the table and noticed Jan was examining the mock broadsheet. He had been the only boy to try to understand what was written on the fried fish wrapping. Up until that point, Dr. Osler hadn't even read the newspaper stories himself. The doctor unravelled his fish wrapping and smiled as he read the headlines: 'Hillary Clinton Adopts Baby Alien', 'Computer Virus Spreads to Humans' and 'Cows Lose Jobs as Milk Drinking Declines'. Someone had fun creating this he thought. He wondered if Jan had been able to decode any of the words.

Staring at the mock newspaper, Dr. Osler started to drown in emotions. Newspapers had played a significant role in his childhood. Seeing the headlines brought memories that had sat dormant for decades. As a child, he collected headlines. Young William had a big scrap book with a picture of the moon on the cover, but Dr. Osler couldn't remember who gave it to him. He did, however, remember his attachment to the faded pages. The last time he gave his headline collecting hobby any thought, was when he wrote about it in a 'mini-biography'. The writing requirement was assigned to him as part of a failed journey towards sobriety.

The assignment was part of Dr. Síceolaí's 'Roadwork to Abstinence' class and was fairly straightforward: write three pages about your life before your addiction. In your personal history include details such as a favourite toy or a childhood hobby, details about your relationship with your parents, and particulars on your education, work life, ambitions, first love, life ambitions, and significant life events, etc. Dr. Osler thought the exercise was blatantly obvious, and a little self-serving, but he had a fair amount of respect for Síceolaí's work, particularly when it came to his writings on neuropsychological testing computations, an area of mental function measurement that Síceolaí had practically invented.

Page 1

I used to write quite a lot, at first as a requirement of school, and then I published a few articles in medical journals to advance my career. But I really haven't written anything in years, and I don't think I have ever written in first person (at least not since grade school). I am not sure whether writing a mini-biography will help to change my 'evil ways', but I am willing to give the process a chance.

I was born in London, Ontario, or as I grew to call it: London-not-that-one-the-other-one. My parents were Stephen and Martha Osler. My father was a pressman for the *London Gazette*. He often told me that he had ink in his veins. I was probably about 10 years old before I stopped taking that comment literally. As a child, I would cut out headlines from the *Gazette* and glue them into my book in sequential order. The first headline I pasted into the scrapbook was on the birth of Prince George.

In 2016, my dad fell from the loading dock at the back of the printing facility. He suffered a severe brain trauma and went into a coma. That was the week that I stopped collecting newspaper headlines. The last banner I pasted into my scrapbook, the day before my dad's accident, was on Wildfires in Fort McMurray. For the next ten years of my life, I made weekly visits to St. Joseph's Hospital with my mother. I stared at my dad's expressionless face. He didn't stare back as his eyes were closed. On her daily visits my mother would talk to my dad, but I never did. I couldn't understand the point of talking to someone that was clearly not going to respond.

Despite lacking a father's influence, and living with an extremely distracted mother, I was a straight A student in high school. I was a loner with no one person that I would call a best friend, a fact that worsened with the COVID-19 Stay-at-Home order. Maybe I have my isolation and my lack of parental influence to thank for my strong performance in high school. At that point in my life, there was very little guidance, and I wasn't sure what I wanted to do as a profession, but I knew it would involve my favourite subject: Science. I remember my mother telling me that it was my dad's dream for me to be the first in my family to graduate university. With my dad in the hospital, I asked my mother if we could afford for me to attend university. I remember she started to cry.

When my mother told me that before his accident, my dad had saved enough to afford my university education, I had no words. She told me that he had always believed that I was intelligent, as she put it: 'he thought his little headline collector was a genius and he often said so'. To pay for post-secondary education, my dad had been saving since I was four years old. He banked everything he could, and he cut out anything that he thought the family didn't need. Thus, my dad drove an 18-year-old Toyota Corolla, and our family didn't go on any vacations. We rented rather than bought a home, and life's little luxuries (such as insurance policies) were dropped from the family budget. Fortunately, the unfortunate accident happened while my dad was at work, so he

The Gemini Project   25

was covered by the *London Gazette* employer accident insurance policy.

I didn't know about it at the time, but the insurance company offered my mom $100,000 for her husband's head trauma. That number would jump to $250,000 if my dad passed away, however, my mother couldn't claim both. The insurance company was forcing my mother to bet on whether her husband would live or die. She wanted her husband to live, but her fatalism prevented her from taking the lower amount. If her husband did pass, she would need to have enough money to live out the rest of her life. She put off the decision. Thanks to my father's frugalness and savings habit, my mom did not have to decide about the insurance policy, just to put her son through university.

So, with the public health system taking care of my dad, and my dad's savings taking care of me, I headed off to study biology at Western University. My under-graduate university selection was partly based on the scholarship they offered, which paid for half of my tuition, and partly because I could still live at home. I had to care for my mother. By that time, I knew she was an alcoholic, or at least I knew that she was hiding a drinking problem. I didn't know when the problem started, maybe it was a side-effect of my dad's accident, or maybe it was always there. After my first year of studies for a Bachelor of Science, I decided that I would make medicine my career. In my third year at Western, I was partnered with Katie Barlow, another third-year student who was studying to be a geneticist. Katie was a beautiful brunette girl who loved life. I knew that I was attracted to her from the moment I saw her in my Advanced Cell Biology class. When the professor posted the pairings for the major project, I couldn't believe my luck.

Our first meeting was also our first disagreement. We didn't see eye-to-eye on the topic for our research project. Katie wanted to delve into neurodegenerative diseases and their relationship to DNA, but I wanted to study neural signalling systems. This was exactly what the doctors said was failing in my dad's body. In the end, I let Katie choose the topic, not because I thought it was a good idea, but because I was smitten with her. I never explained to Katie why I was so interested in the body's signalling systems. For our fourth year in the honours program, we moved in together. Our apartment was small, but it was within walking distance to the university. I still made regular visits to the hospital, but I never took Katie with me. I also made sure that I met my mother for dinner once a week, and sometimes I would ask Katie to join us.

The final year of the program allowed me more freedom in selecting my studies. For my class on Independent Biology Study, I selected to author a paper on damaged cells, which allowed me to research traumatic brain injury ... the type that came after a violent blow to the head. My dad's catatonic state was the result of brain tissue that was bruised by a shattered piece of skull. My paper examining the long-term effects of bruising, torn tissue, bleeding, and other physical damage, was praised by my professor, who recommended that I consider a career in Neurology, a path that would lead me to Corpo Academy.

Sunday night at Corpo was Dr. Osler's time to reveal his beliefs to whichever boys wound up sitting in the student lounge. His agenda was never structured ... until that Sunday after the fish fry. The doctor asked the boys in the lounge if there was anything they would like to discuss, and Jan immediately asked him to explain how words worked. Maybe he was moved by watching Jan attempt to decipher the newspaper, or perhaps he was just overwhelmed by an urge to be nurturing, but he decided it was time for him to become a teacher.

To answer Jan's request, the doctor announced to the boys that if they wanted remedial reading lessons, he would hold sessions every Sunday evening. Until that point, The Corpo Academy had been an educational desert, however Dr. Osler's plan offered a change in routine for both the boys and himself. That first Sunday, 20 boys gathered around as he began to instruct the abecedarians. The number dwindled to a dozen for the second Sunday and by the third week only Jan and Jet attended. The decline in attendance didn't discourage the doctor however, who continued his sabbath day tutorage, often under the influence of Flash.

Outside of his unstructured teaching experiment, Dr. Osler spent the rest of his time in the student lounge giving unprovoked, spontaneous speeches. That summer, a few boys were in the lounge, discussing the day's tennis tournament. Otto made the mistake of saying that it was a great day to play tennis. The doctor overheard this and hijacked the conversation from his wingback chair.

"Sure. It was a great day. Every day is a great day. That's because you don't understand weather, far less climate. How could you? You've never been subjected to it. Climate change was never going to impact us the way we thought it would. Global warming is just a perfect example of how arrogant man had become. We argued for 50 years about it. Scientists amassed a mountain of material proof and

The Gemini Project

all it would take to restart the argument was one guy saying I don't believe it.

Why don't you believe it? Because if there was global warming, why is it still snowing in New York? I wanted to punch someone every time I heard that. They confused weather with climate. Don't you get it, that's not the way it works. In fact, because we were melting the polar icecaps, there was additional water in the system. This led to additional clouds that kept the cold front from dissipating, so when it was cold it was really friggin' cold. And when it snowed, it dumped on us big time. The atmosphere was warmer you moron, not New York city."

The boys stared at Dr. Osler, not letting him know that they had no idea what he was talking about.

"Global warming wasn't a 50-degree swing, it was a two-degree swing! That was enough to melt the poles. More melting, more water. More water, more weather. More weather, more fuck-ups. While some ass pointed to the lack of palm trees in Anchorage as proof that there was no global warming, there were more and more weather catastrophes ... more and more, every year."

"But what's a ..." Dix started.

"And that's just typical," Dr. Osler continued ignoring the boy. "We thought of what the weather meant to us and almost exclusively us."

"My island off the coast of North Carolina will be under water," Dr. Osler said in a high-pitched whiney voice.

"Arrogance!" he returned. "We never thought about what the shift would mean to other species. I mean, I guess someone thought about it, but not enough, damn it! We never thought about what climate change meant to insects and before we even acknowledged it, the bee population was already halved. Bees! You lose humans and the planet returns to a garden paradise, you lose bees and the world turns to a desert. Losing half the bees was enough to wipe out whole strains of plants. We were beyond the point of no return and some guy's complaining about the water levels at his summer home, while another guy is complaining about his shower or the level of water in his toilet tank. Shit. With all the resources that we had amassed, there was still nothing we could do to stop it, much less reverse it."

"Are there bees now?" Jan asked.

Dr. Osler smiled realizing that Jan was the only one who had followed his disjointed speech.

No matter the day of the week, Dr. Osler's appearance was usually slightly dishevelled, even more so on the nights of his greatest harangues. The other doctors knew that Osler tended the boys in his own style, but his peers never raised a concern. The boys had their own speculations as to why Dr. Osler was the way he was. Dix once told Jan that he heard his father say that 'Osler has a severe financial problem'. Jan doubted that because his father seemed to have respect for Dr. Osler. Jet said that his father told him Dr. Osler had a drug problem. Jet wasn't quite sure what that meant because the boys only took drugs when they were sick. The boys had caught glimpses of him as he imbibed, injected, and inhaled various pills and potions, but had either not understood what they were witnessing or assumed that there was a medical reason behind his actions.

The truth was, Dr. Osler did have a drug problem, as well as a financial problem. Even he was unsure if he suffered from an insatiable drug habit that had brought on a financial burden or a financial burden from which he used drugs to escape. Dr. Primero, the highest doctor at the Academy, would have had Dr. Osler removed if he could. However, Dr. Osler had too much experience in the renaissance practice to be replaced easily and it now looked likely that he would burn out or expire without any assistance. So, instead Primero just put up with Dr. Osler and tried to keep him under tight scrutiny.

Although Dr. Primero very rarely spoke to the boys individually, the Corpo Academy for Development was under his jurisdiction, and he communicated his direction through his reporting doctors. Through the little conversations the boys had with their fathers, they learned that Dr. Primero was once a very prominent doctor who became famous for his research, and he was now the head of their school. The fathers told this to their sons in a bragging fashion. In fact, Primero had been relegated to running a school for the extraordinarily rich, not because he loved education, but because he was ordered to. The doctors he supervised had pretty mundane duties, which seemed to consist mainly of constantly measuring the students' development and individual health. In all, there were eight doctors overlooking 42 boys at the Academy. The rest of the staff were also under Primero's authority, but the relationship between Primero and people like the coaches or the janitors, was unclear to the boys. Primero seemed to treat the others less like they were a different status and more like they were a different breed.

On Sundays, Dr. Primero required all the staff and student body to attend a one-hour lecture in the Main Hall. The building was in the centre of the quad area and was therefore in the centre of the campus. The hall consisted of one large room with rows of pews that faced a long table at the front of the room. Here, the High Doctor would give his dissertation to the attendees with no pause for questions or discussion. It was the only formal lecture the boys would receive all week. On occasion, Jan noticed that Dr. Osler dozed off during a few of Primero's Sunday sermons. The speech would ramble on about the value of hygiene, or the importance of healthy eating or how to avoid sports related injuries. Occasionally, after a particularly salient point, some of the other doctors might react with a small round of applause. Once, Dr. Osler said 'Amen' at the end of a long lecture, which evoked a few laughs from the other doctors. Other than that, unless there was a guest lecturer, no one else spoke at the sermons.

If there was a test on the content of the Sunday sermons, even Jan, who tried to pay attention, would have failed. He was attentive in the presence of elders but found it incredibly challenging to take in the Sunday morning discourse. On the odd occasion, a visiting doctor would give the speech, a sign the boys took to mean that the visitor held a high rank in the order of doctors. Jan couldn't tell how much higher, only that the visitor was able to make Primero listen to him, and it was clear that Primero begrudged this.

Other than Dr. Osler, the staff was very consistent in their clothing. All of the doctors wore white jumpsuits similar to the boys' bedtime uniforms. The two female nurses wore a flower-patterned long-sleeved jumpsuit, and the seven male nurses wore light blue jumpsuits. The coaches, trainers, and orderlies, all wore dark blue jumpsuits. Only the fathers, when they visited, seemed to vary their clothing.

Dr. Osler was a fashion exception. He often wore clothing unlike anyone else on the campus. His blue denim pants were typically topped with a t-shirt featuring a picture, some words, or both. There was a blue t-shirt featuring a large yellow 'happy face' with the words 'Don't Worry' above it, and 'Be Happy' below. This one was a favourite of the boys. There was a green t-shirt with a white striped flower and the word 'adidas' underneath it. There was a black tee with the picture of a pyramid that refracted white light entering from the left and a rainbow of light leaving on the right. Otto once asked the doctor what the picture was and he answered that it was 'a prism' (although if Jan had asked, he would have been provided a minimum one-hour dissertation on 'why Pink Floyd was so great').

Even visiting doctors, despite their perceived superior position, wore the same white suits as the Corpo doctors while on the school grounds. Jan often found a visiting doctor's discourse more interesting as it would involve some statement about life outside the Academy and did not sound like something that he had heard two hundred times before. The dissertation could contain a word or a phrase, which would spark his imagination and take him elsewhere.

At one Sunday morning sermon, a Dr. Síceolaí visited and talked about the difference between good and bad secrets. The doctor told the boys a story about the secret of the silver horse. Everything about this sermon awakened Jan's interest. He had heard Dr. Osler describe a horse race during one of his rants, but Jan had never seen an animal. Now he was hearing about a horse made of silver. Even the juxtaposition of good versus evil was a fresh concept to Jan. Until that morning, Jan had never thought that some stories could be told in a fictional manner. Dr. Osler's stories were sometimes wild, but Jan usually believed them to be based in truth.

In the middle of the sermon, a boy told a secret to his mother. Having never met his own mother, Jan listened intently as he tried to understand both the purpose of the story and the type of environment where a boy sees his mother and father every day. He noticed Dr. Primero rolling his eyes and scowling, as Síceolaí told the story. Jan had never even contemplated keeping a secret before that sermon, but one of the underlying messages was that it was okay to keep 'good' secrets.

After the sermon, Jan immediately went over to Dr. Síceolaí. He had very rarely even approached some of the staff doctors, let alone a visiting doctor.

"Excuse me, Dr. Síceolaí," Jan started.

"That's enough today, young man," Dr. Primero commanded. "Dr. Síceolaí has some things he needs to do before he leaves."

"Yes, but I was just going to ask …"

The Gemini Project 31

Primero's look stopped Jan from continuing. Dr. Osler saw the confrontation and came over to rescue the boy before he got himself in trouble.

"Jan, I wonder if you could help me with a small problem I have," Dr. Osler requested, in an attempt to sand down Dr. Primero's ire. "Oh, excuse me Dr. Primero, are you finished with Jan, I would like to borrow him for a moment?"

"Yes, please do," Primero responded. As Dr. Síceolaí left, Primero leaned over to Dr. Osler and with a semi-whisper said, "and see that you keep him away from any further contact with antiquated psychologists."

The comment was directed away from Síceolaí, but Jan overheard it. Jan knew that he lacked some basic comprehension to be able to piece together what had just happened, but he was sure that Dr. Osler was trying to help him.

As Dr. Osler directed Jan away from the visiting doctor, Jan asked "What's a sigh-call-ojist?"

"You're a good listener Jan. Too good, for your own good sometimes," Dr. Osler commented. "I'll tell you what, I'm going to teach you to fish, so I'm not going to answer you. Instead, I'll give you something and you can figure the answer out yourself. How does that sound?"

Jan was sure that Dr. Osler had just avoided the question and he would never get an answer. He did that sometimes. That evening however, the doctor arrived fully prepared to fulfill his promise to Jan.

Dr. Osler was trying to escape both his present and his past, but this hadn't prevented him from befriending Jan. He sincerely liked the boy. Jan was more balanced than the other students. Dr. Osler often thought that there was something different in Jan, something that didn't exist in his schoolmates. The doctor sometimes lied to himself saying he saw a little of his own personality in Jan, maybe something from before his own personal 'renaissance'.

This was untrue however as Dr. Osler and Jan were nothing alike. It was because they were nothing alike, that the relationship worked. One liked to talk, and one liked to listen. While the other boys were quite content to learn a lot about sports and very little about life, Jan had always engaged with the doctor on a different level than his schoolmates. Jan was a bag of curiosity, and he liked to ask questions. He liked to try to understand, so he would question Dr. Osler about why things were a certain way or whether they could be, or should be, different. That's what the doctor liked, a jump point and an audience all in one. Many times, Dr. Osler had to skate around the underlying reality of the discussion, but the doctor still enjoyed their time together. If the doctor had to think about it, Jan was probably his closest friend, or perhaps second to his drugs.

"Where does the King live?" Dix asked. He was one of three boys that were gathered around the doctor.

"What King are we talking about?" Dr. Osler asked from his familiar throne in the lounge.

"Jays," Dix replied.

"No, Janes," Otto corrected.

"James," Jan corrected the correction.

"King James? This is good. Where did you boys hear this cultural allusion?"

Dix looked at Otto and Jan for a translation.

"Where did you hear about the king?"

"We were learning to box, for about a week before it got cancelled, and the coach said we were learning to fight the way King Jays rules." Dix replied.

"I told you; the King of boxing is King Janes."

"James. And it was ... fight under King James' Rules."

"Ah ... King James, of course, the King of boxing. Well, he is king no more. I'm pleased to say that the societal structure known as kingdoms, or more accurately fiefdoms, is long gone."

All three boys looked at the doctor, each concluding in their own way that the answer was that King Jays or Janes or James, was no longer the King of boxing.

"Boys, boys, boys. It's not like when I was your age," Dr. Osler quipped, looking for one of the boys to take the bait.

"What's different?" Jan asked.

"Well, for one thing, we had to go to school five days a week."

"But I live at school." Jan responded.

"This isn't school ... this is what I called recess. When I was young, we had to read, study, do our maths homework ..."

"What's maths?" Jan asked.

Dr. Osler had been talking the way an 'old-timer' reminisces and then catches himself saying the same type of things that he remembered being said to him when he was young. The difference here was that there was no way to explain to Jan how much things had really changed.

"Mathematics is the study of numbers."

"You mean numbers like on the soccer uniforms?"

"Yea ... one, two, three ... you know, numbers."

"But why would anyone want to study numbers?" Jan asked, emphasizing the word 'study'.

"That is a great question and that is exactly what I used to say. In fact, sometimes I would skip maths and go smoke a ... er, play tennis," Dr. Osler responded, carefully catching himself.

When they first started to really talk to one another, Jan and the doctor talked a lot about sports. Where the other boys would be happy to get the rules, Jan wanted to understand the history of a sport. Jan was also more introspective than the other students. He wanted time to think about the rules and why they were a certain way. On several occasions, he asked Dr. Osler that question that none of the other boys asked: 'why?'. Not that the question was particularly profound when discussing the rules of a sport, but the underlying portent of any such question had impressed the doctor. It impressed him enough to make his visits with Jan one of the most bearable parts of his work routine. Besides, the question was just his jump point. If Jan asked a question about baseball, a banned sport, it wasn't long before Dr. Osler was headed down some nostalgic path and talking about the heyday of The Yankees.

In the main floor lounge, the bookcase held various trinkets and ornaments. On the top shelf, beside a small gold statue of a man swinging a tennis racket and between a pair of right-angled wooden brackets decorated with a shield of golf clubs, there were nine leather-bound books embossed with gold lettering. These were sports rule books written for children. Before he could read, Jan would flip the pages and look at the pictures and diagrams. He knew that letters told a story, but the boy had never been taught how to discern meaning from the symbols.

Once the reading lessons were down to a class of one, Dr. Osler and Jan spent the time reading the same nine rule books, over and over. The doctor became unsure if Jan could read or if he eventually just knew the text by rote, so he scribbled a few words down on a piece of paper and asked Jan to read them. Jan was literate. Dr. Osler and Jan continued to meet for the 'reading club', but since Jan had read all the books several times, sometimes they just sat and talked. It was during these times that Jan's enlightenment into the world beyond Corpo began.

The evening after Dr. Osler pulled Jan away from Dr. Síceolaí and Dr. Primero, Jan was in the lounge practicing his reading when Dr. Osler arrived at the dorm. He had promised to tell Jan what 'psychology' meant, but instead entered the room carrying a new book. Jan spotted it immediately. It was the thickest book he had ever seen. The book was the 1996 edition of the *Merriam Webster Dictionary* in paperback, which was 340 pages in length.

"Now I want you to keep this book in the lounge so everyone can use it," Dr. Osler said knowing that no other student would even notice it. "In here, you'll find the answer to your question about psychology."

Dr. Osler handed Jan the book.

"What is it?" Jan asked as he flipped through the pages.

The doctor chuckled to himself as he realized that Jan couldn't even use the dictionary to look up the meaning of the word 'dictionary'. It reminded him of an old joke, 'What do you use to find another word for Thesaurus?'.

Dr. Osler smiled as he watched Jan flip pages back and forth for almost five minutes. Finally, Jan looked up at the doctor. If Jan fathomed what opium, Flash or soma was, he would have been sure that one of these was the cause of Dr. Osler's watery eyes and wry smile.

"Well Jan," Dr. Osler finally said, "as much as I like having you kill time with me on Wednesday and Sunday evenings, I think it's time that you left the nest and learned to fly. So, I'm donating this book to the collection and with this book ... here, I've given you your wings."

"It's a dict-shun-ary," Jan sounded out. "I can see that from the front."

The Gemini Project

"That's right. And do you know what a dictionary is? It provides the meaning of words, so if you hear an unfamiliar word, you can look it up," Dr. Osler stated.

"It's really big ... but I don't think it has every word in here. It has some big words ... and some smaller ones," Jan said as he attentively continued to flip through the pages. "So, I don't know how it chooses what words to include."

Jan continued to explore several sequential pages, paused, then flipped to another section. He stopped on the entry for 'dictionary', a word he had learned to spell by the title of the book.

A book or electronic resource that lists the words of a language (typically in alphabetical order) and gives their meaning.

"You're amazing Jan! I thought you were just flipping pages, but I think you have figured out the book's topography," Dr. Osler mused without pausing to realize that Jan would need to use the book to look-up 'topography'. "So, there's nothing wrong with the book and it will probably keep you occupied for the rest of your life."

"Yes, but I must be missing something. I understand how it's sorted, in the same order that you taught me the alphabet, but when I went to the esses, I can't find 'sigh-call-ojist'."

Dr. Osler smiled. Jan was acquiring knowledge even faster than he had given him credit for.

"Try P-S-Y-C-H for starters. The English language is full of exceptions. You know what an exception is, right Jan? You are an exception at the Academy. It might take you a while to figure out how to spell things, but I have little doubt that you can do it. And don't be afraid to ask me for help if you get stuck. Next, I am going to try to find you a book on golf or tennis so you can read it with your dictionary, but in the meantime, you can study and learn some new words."

"How many different books are there?" Jan asked inquisitively.

"More than you or I could ever read," responded Dr. Osler.

Jan and Dr. Osler's relationship had evolved such that the doctor no longer cared if someone thought he gave Jan too much access to information. Dr. Osler valued one game of chess with Jan over anything that his position had to offer him. Never having raised a son of his own, Dr. Osler was also proud of what Jan had accomplished, of what he had become.

Jan never did put the book on the lounge shelf as instructed. Instead, he read it, in his room, faithfully every night. It was a 'good' secret. Sometimes, he would read in an orderly fashion, alphabetically through words, and sometimes he would just randomly open-up to pages and pick one word from that page. Often, a word would spark a thought or a question, and Jan would drift off trying to discern the meaning. There were so many words that he had never heard before, and Jan had to read the dictionary like he was connecting the dots.

The definition of one word contained other words that Jan didn't comprehend, so he'd have to look up those words too, which again might also point to a definition containing the unfamiliar. Sometimes he would be fifty words into a quagmire of letters before he read a full definition that he understood. Jan would then try to make his way back to the original word that he was trying to understand. Often, he didn't make it back. One of the first words in the dictionary, 'aardvark', required Jan to understand mammals, Africa, snout, claws, termites, and ants. Then each one of those words required greater study into the meanings of other words. It was a four-hour process before Jan was satisfied that he knew what an aardvark was:

> *Aardvark (ard-vark) n. A large burrowing nocturnal*
> *mammal of sub-Saharan Africa that has a long snout,*
> *extensible tongue, powerful claws, large ears, and*
> *heavy tail and feeds especially on termites and ants.*

Dr. Osler found discussions with Jan were becoming more entertaining, as the boy advanced not only his vocabulary but also began to express formulated opinions and ideas. Jan would often choose a word and then come to the lounge with that word as the jump point to start a discussion. Eventually, Jan and Dr. Osler weaved conversations starting from words like art, baseball, clowns, dilemma, elevators, faithfulness and even gallbladders. There were a few topics where Dr. Osler would shut the conversation down. The first one he ran into was when Jan asked about 'death'. Jan was not too forceful however and he was okay waiting to find out if everyone dies.

There were several words that had multiple definitions, and their usage confused Jan. Reading the definition for the word 'quarter', he

The Gemini Project 37

saw it was 1) one-fourth of something, 2) a coin, or 3) a place to live. In the example for 'a place to live', Jan read that 'no quarter' meant a battle would be a fight to the death. It took him a while to parse that an army that did not take prisoners, was offering no quarters for prisoners to reside in.

Jan was also very confused about the word 'renaissance'. What did the revival of art and literature in the 14th to 16th century have to do with his 18th birthday? He asked Dr. Osler but got completely shut down. There wasn't even a pretend promise that they'd discuss it in the future.

The more Jan learned, the less he spoke to Dix about anything consequential. Not that Dix ever discussed anything of real importance. When Dix saw Jan reading the reference book in their room, he commented that Jan cared more about rule books than winning. Jan wasn't listening to him as he had just opened the book and the entry had taken him elsewhere. It was a word whose definition Jan thought he understood, but after reading it, he just sat and contemplated for the remainder of the evening.

Mother (mu-ther) n. A woman who conceives, gives birth to, or raises and nurtures a child.

If only Dr. Osler was on duty that evening. Now Jan would have to wait three more days before he could discuss the word. Even though he thought he understood the meaning, he wondered about the person, not the concept. Jan wondered what his mother looked like. He wondered if she knew him as a baby. He wondered why she wasn't there now to raise and 'nurture' him. When Wednesday evening finally came around, Jan sat impatiently in the lounge, waiting for Dr. Osler to come in. Shortly before 7 p.m., Dr. Osler finally entered the room.

"Why don't I have a mother?" Jan blurted out before Dr. Osler was through the doorway.

"What are you talking about Jan?" Dr. Osler responded in a slow, deliberate tone. Appropriately, the doctor sported a Frank Zappa and the Mothers of Invention 'Freak Out!' t-shirt atop his customary blue jeans. "You were born weren't you? Of course you have a mother. I have a mother; you have a mother ... we all have mothers. That's still the way it works."

Dr. Osler looked around the room. He found Jan's emotions out of character and for a moment he wondered if Jan's meds were balanced, or maybe he had obtained access to soma or some Flash. It did tend to make you ramble on about the inane ...

Then Dr. Osler saw the dictionary sitting beside Jan. It was closed, but it clearly had been opened too many times and it looked like it was going to fall apart at the spine. Jan had fallen asleep on the book, and it almost naturally pushed open about the midway point. Dr. Osler bent over and placed the spine of the dictionary on his left palm. Half the pages fell one way and half another.

"Let's see what we have here ..." Dr. Osler said as he ran his finger down the open pages.

On the left side of his palm, page 172 started with 'ml'; an abbreviation for millilitre. On the right side of his palm, page 173 ended with 'mow'; a verb meaning to cut down. The doctor ran his finger down the pages and stopped at 'mother'.

"You know Jan," Dr. Osler started, "this book is old and out of date, but I've given it to you as a privilege ... a kind of trust. Hmmm ... a woman who conceives, gives birth to, or raises and nurtures a child. Do you think that you weren't conceived Jan?"

"No," Jan answered slowly, wishing that he had reread the word 'conceived'.

"Then perhaps you believe that you weren't born!"

"No, I don't," Jan said raising his voice in objection to Dr. Osler's mocking tone. "I just want to know why my mother hasn't raised me."

"This book that I lent you needs to be read in a certain way," Dr. Osler said trying to be less disparaging. "No one uses books like this anymore. We've come up with a better way. The same way we don't have mothers raise their children anymore, because we've come up with a better way."

The doctor flipped to the front of the book and read the first few pages.

"It's 120 years old. Look at this book more like a history class. We used to say in school ... those who don't learn history, are doomed to repeat the course ... so read it and learn. It's a view into what things used to be like. In some cases, things will have changed drastically, and in others, things will be the same as they ever were. We could just create all babies in test-tubes, but we chose not to move in that

The Gemini Project 39

direction, and I doubt we ever will. For now, know that you have a mother. I am confident that eventually you will understand everything, but we have to take it one step at a time."

Jan started to relax a little, but Dr. Osler could see that the youth was still unhappy with his answer.

"And," Dr. Osler continued feigning a tone of strictness, "unless you can read this book in a controlled manner and come to me calmly with all your questions... I will be forced to take the book back."

The menacing threat of sanctions hit home with Jan. His face changed from being irritated to being worried. He didn't want to lose the book. He realized that this 1996 paperback was the most valuable thing that he had ever possessed in his life.

"Jan, the last thing I would want is for Dr. Primero to find out that I gave you this book, far less that it has been infecting your mind. It could mean the end of what we both have here."

"And what is that?" Jan asked sincerely.

"Well, you're developing your mind, and I am helping you do that, and I'm ... I'm just barely hanging on here so you're helping me too. Now, as for the dictionary, do I have your word that you'll contain yourself and not be too demanding with things that you don't understand?"

The astute boy only had to think briefly. He had learned more in the past few weeks through reading the dictionary than he had learned his entire life at the Academy. Jan needed to convince the doctor that he could be trusted.

"Doctor Osler, I'm really, really sorry. I would do anything to understand more about things outside of the Academy. I'll try not to let my emotions get the better of me in the future. It's ... it's a psycholog-ical challenge that's all."

Dr. Osler smiled at the boy's attempt to demonstrate his knowledge. Jan was as eager to learn as ever, but he was witty too, and Dr. Osler liked that. Osler didn't mind teaching him further, but he needed to ensure that this little side project was under control.

"No big deal ... don't worry, it was a venial question Jan."

Jan looked puzzled.

"V-E-N-I-A-L, look it up later. Right now, give me another word that you read that sparked questions and I'll try to explain its context."

Jan hesitated.

"Look ... I promise we'll come back to the discussion about mothers again ... when the time is right. But for now, let's find some easier things to discuss."

"Okay ... tell me about skyscrapers," Jan requested.

"Skyscrapers. There's a word that I haven't heard in a long time. It used to be that, for some reason, buildings were being built higher and higher. The higher up in the building you were, the more important you must have been. It got to the point where it took you longer to get to the top of the building than it took to get to work in the morning," Dr. Osler said as he smiled at his own wit. "Then something happened to kill the skyscrapers for the captains of industry. Can you guess what that was Jan?"

"Some sort of accident?"

"Well, there were a few disasters, but it was a simple report that caused the real collapse of the skyscraper. A simple paper that was released on the evening news. We all thought that the higher you were in the building, the more important you were. However, it seemed that 90% of the most important business executives and world leaders lived and worked on the seventh floor. The reason was simple: buildings could catch fire and our firefighting equipment in the cities could only rescue people from the seventh floor and lower. After that report, people clambered to be on the lower floors ... a shorter elevator ride to your office showed how important you were. Like having the closest parking spot to the building. Egos are strange things. That report was the death warrant for skyscrapers. Then COVID-19 had people stay away from office buildings. That was followed by the Regulated Air Act which was passed to stop the spread of infectious diseases. So, it was only a matter of time before we went underground."

"People live and work under the ground in cities?"

"Exactly ... we still build big buildings, but they go down rather than up. Now, the lower you are, the more important you are. There are not many people who get to experience the outdoors, like at the Academy. But after your renaissance, you'll be saying goodbye to life on the surface."

Over the next two hours, Dr. Osler talked in detail with Jan about motorcycles, supermarkets, telephones, and satellites. Every word was described in a mixture of history and personal experiences. The doctor explained to Jan what a motorcycle was and how he would ride his to the hospital where he worked. However, he eventually crashed the bike when another driver flipped a cigarette out of his window. He told Jan how important a telephone was, and how each home had one, for about fifty years ... then they were suddenly obsolete. There was an old wall-style phone at the entrance of the dining hall, but it was just there for decoration. Jan imagined picking up the dining phone, dialling some numbers and making a call to talk with his father in New London. The doctor translated words into stories to give Jan a level of understanding as well as leave him with thoughts to process. Dr. Osler dropped some Flash, sat back, and continued to babble in his drug induced state.

Jan concluded that Dr. Osler probably knew something about everything. There wasn't a single topic that he could mention, without Dr. Osler being able to tell him more than what the dictionary stated. Jan welcomed the way Dr. Osler's commentary spawned all new thoughts in Jan's mind.

"Last word for the night, okay?"

Without hesitation, Jan spouted 'War'. He had been holding on to that one for fear Dr. Osler would put it in the same future-discussion-bucket as 'mother', 'renaissance' and 'death'.

"War. Now there's a word that we should never forget the meaning of. Ironically, you can trace the final wars back to an attack on skyscrapers. That war of religions that would eventually lead us here. It's a great word in a way, because to study the history of man is to study the history of war. Two thousand years ago, we lived in cities, and we would invade other cities to steal their food. A thousand years ago a group of city-states formed a country, which would invade other countries to steal their gold. A hundred years ago, the countries were run by multi-national corporations, which would finance the invasion of other countries to steal another corporation's oil. This all came to an end with the Incorporation Act."

The doctor paused. He wasn't sure whether Jan was following him or not. He also couldn't recall what subjects he had previously discussed with the boy. Generally, however, if Jan asked a question, it meant that he was still processing the information, if Jan didn't say anything then he was usually understanding what he was hearing.

"Incorporation Act?"

There it was.

"Yes. There have really only been two reasons that men fought and killed each other. If it wasn't in the name of religion, then it was greed ... to steal someone else's possessions. If a neighbour had something you wanted why not take it? In my day, it became obvious to everyone that as countries invaded other countries, it was really about getting access to raw materials and that usually meant fuel. Fuel drove the economy. So, when a country declared war, if you stripped it back, it was really an economic decision.

A few exceptionally large corporations grew to dominate their country, so when countries formed economic unions with other countries, they eventually amalgamated corporations such that the difference between the firm and the country became negligible. The Incorporation Act just finalized the process. With only five global corporations remaining, an end to greed-based war was almost in sight. New energies changed the economic reality, and each company needed the other company to survive. So, we moved underground, and the corporations were mandated to work together. Each city manufactured predetermined items that were shuttled to other cities. You see ... we found a better way."

Dr. Osler paused and then added, "Boy I sound like I've really been drinking the system's virtual Kool-Aid, don't I? I managed to tell that whole story without giving religion any credit. Sacrilege! Don't worry, I was never a big fan of the bible anyway."

"The bible?"

"Oh yes, it's the number one best-selling book of all-time. Now there's a work of fiction for you to read. However, its believers either took it as the 'gospel' truth or looked at the stories as parables. I mean, if you don't know how to explain how the universe began, because you don't actually understand it yourself, you just make up the events leading to Adam and Eve. That fable puts man at the centre of the universe, and I do mean man, not woman. I mean think about it, if there was no God, man would have definitely created one. There were over 4,200 religions on earth and almost 100 forms of Christianity alone. If the religion doesn't suit your actions, just create a new one that does," Dr. Osler rambled on.

Jan was waiting for Dr. Osler to pause for a breath, so he could interject with some questions. However, the doctor just seemed to gather momentum and Jan was having trouble remembering all the words he had questions about.

"You could create a religion to get a divorce, create a religion to marry more than one woman, create a religion to ban homosexuals ... hell, one guy wrote a book about space and created a religion out of it. Well, he actually created a sect, then a foundation, then the foundation went out of business, so he created his own religion out of his failed business. And he had followers even though his religion was supposed to be based on science, but no scientists seemed to be among the followers.

The war between science and religion was waged every time someone discovered something that wasn't self-evident. If religion said the earth was flat but man circumvented it, then religion had a battle until it learned to adapt. Religion said God put man on earth and the universe circled around it. Then scientists proved that the earth circled the sun, and that led to a hundred years of denial before science ... I'm sorry, before the truth ... finally won."

Dr. Osler was deep into his Soma state now. In his head, Jan kept an inventory of words for future conversations: multi-national, economic, amalgamated, Kool-Aid, sacrilege, gospel, divorce, homosexuals ... tonight's list was getting long. Sometimes providing the doctor with a word as a jump point, Jan would get a 20-second definition in response ... but other times, he would spawn an entire night's narrative with just a single word.

"You see, science doesn't get the luxury of faith. Science requires proof and even with proof in hand some people still have faith that their religion is right. A religion created by man with absolutely no proof, could outweigh science that was nothing but proof. Shit, I knew some guys that were flat-earthers. With a picture of the earth taken from outer space, these guys told me it was because I didn't have enough faith that I didn't understand that man was the centre of the universe. Science doesn't command that kind of faith ... it has to earn its followers.

Before De Visie, the answer to every question could be answered 'because God wanted it that way'. You wonder how a team won the Superbowl? It's because God wanted it that way. You wonder why your child died? It's part of God's plan, just have faith. You don't see any proof that God even exists? Then you don't have enough faith. If you don't have faith, then you were ostracized. But things have finally changed ... things are better now ..."

At that point, Dix entered the room.

"Why are things better now? Are you talking about Jan? I doubt he's getting better the way he's been playing lately. He always passes when he should fire one at the goal."

Jan didn't have time to ask Dr. Osler if he could read a bible. He was curious to understand how the number one book could be as bad as the doctor had described. He had his dictionary and there were still so many things to understand.

"And everything will be better now, right Jan?" Dr. Osler prodded.

Jan smiled as he tucked his paperback under his arm.

"Right."

Dr. Osler rose to leave.

"Now if one of you two is my partner in golf this Friday, I want you to know that I expect to win this week."

Dix assumed that Dr. Osler would have been pleased with either of them as a partner, but the doctor was thinking that he'd like to draw Jan again.

That evening, even though they hadn't finished the conversation about mothers, Jan finally got a decent night's sleep. He dreamed that he lived with his mother. His mental picture of his mother was fuzzy yet strikingly real. In his fantasy, his father was nowhere to be seen. As his mother approached him, Jan woke up with a clear picture of what his mother looked like. She was beautiful to Jan, and he was sure that his vision would be beautiful to anyone. As he drifted back to sleep, Jan wondered if his mental image was accurate.

Friday afternoons, after lunch and before the seafood dinner, the boys played golf. This was the only sport where they would be joined by the eight staff doctors and Dr. Primero. The nine oldest boys were selected to play, and the doctors were assigned their partner by a random draw that appeared to be for the amusement of the doctors. Jan was teamed up with Dr. Osler for the fifth time that year.

The course was a nine-hole executive par three at the far end of the Academy. There were enough challenges to make the course interesting. Even though the boys only played once per week, their natural abilities became obvious. Jan shot a great round with six holes under par and his partner, Dr. Osler, crowed at Dr. Primero about the victory of 'the dynamic duo'.

Back in the dorm, after the match, Dix complained about his partner. He had been paired up with Dr. O'Flanagan, who was slightly

The Gemini Project 45

overweight and sported an unfortunate moustache that made him look like a walrus.

"This club is banjaxed," Dix said, not understanding the phrase he was using, or the accent he was mimicking. He held his finger beneath his nose to resemble a moustache, then mimed breaking a club in half and throwing it away.

The boys laughed. The imitation was actually quite accurate.

"That should have gone straight, but the sun was in my eyes," Otto responded. All the boys laughed again, except for Dix. Otto was doing his best Dix impersonation, which was also quite accurate.

Earlier that week, Dr. Osler had found a new book that he was waiting to give to Jan and the victory provided the perfect backdrop. After shaking Jan's hand at the end of the round, he reached into his golf bag and pulled out '*How to Play Tennis: The Complete Guide to the Rules of Tennis and Tennis Scoring*'. Jan was excited by the gift and wanted to read and discuss the contents with Dr. Osler, but it wasn't the doctor's duty night, so he'd have to wait.

By Sunday, Dr. Osler started his rounds and had forgotten that his prodigy would be fired up about tennis rules, not the most interesting subject. As he approached Jan's room, he had a slight fear of having to broach taboo subjects again. The doctor knew that he still owed the boy a discussion about mothers. How do you explain why life is the way it is, to someone who had barely lived and had no external references. A watery-eyed Dr. Osler called into Jan's room and invited him to come to the lounge for a conversation.

As soon as Jan arrived in the student lounge, he started into a discussion.

"You know that book you gave me?"

"Yes, what was it called again?"

"*How to Play Tennis.*"

"Have you read it?" Dr. Osler fired, as he leaned back in the lounge chair and poured himself a drink from the decanter on the side table. He had forgotten that there was only water in the boys' decanters.

"I've made it through ten pages so far and I have so many questions."

"Questions on the rules of tennis? Like what? I mean, I'll try to answer but I'm not sure how much I can augment what the book says."

"It said that the modern rules were introduced in London in 1874 by Major Walter Wingfield."

"Oh ... I see ... so what did you want to know about, the old city of London or perhaps the army that the Major belonged to?"

"No. No, none of that," Jan responded hesitantly. "I mean, yeah I do want to understand that, but it's just that when they mentioned the new rules, they said that it ushered tennis into a brave new world."

"And?" Dr. Osler prompted.

"And the letters on the front of brave new world ... the B, N and W were all capitalized and there was a footnote."

"A footnote you say. And you want to know what a footnote is?"

"No, I understand that, but the footnote reads 'with apologies to Aldus Huxley'. What does that mean? I don't even understand the words. Neither word was in the dictionary."

"That one's easy. Aldus Huxley is a name. Huxley was a man, and he authored a book called *Brave New World*, so I'd say the author of the tennis book was apologizing for borrowing those three words."

"What's it about?"

"What's what about?" Dr. Osler responded only half listening to the boy. His usual interest in discussions with Jan did not hold to talking about tennis rules.

"*Brave New World*."

"Oh, that. It's a book that they made me read when I went to school. I don't remember much other than hating it."

"They 'made' you read?" Jan thought about the message that the doctor had delivered unintentionally. "Could I get a copy of *Brave New World*?"

"Oh, I wouldn't even know where to look for that type of book these days and I doubt you'd understand what Huxley is talking about. It's from a different time. Things aren't the same now and the book was barely relevant when I was your age."

"I don't want to seem ungrateful ..." Jan started slowly, "but I'm hoping that someday I'll get to read something more than a rule book."

"And what makes you think that Huxley's book isn't a rule book?"

"Nothing, I guess. It's just that it sounds like a book that would describe things that I'd like to know about. Maybe it's even fiction, like the bible."

"There's nothing in there for you Jan," Dr. Osler said to shut down the conversation. "It's a bagatelle. You've already got a lot more than any of the others would think is appropriate. Now, let's talk about something else. What else goes through that mind of yours?"

Jan realized that he had pushed too far all at once.

"Well Monday is father's day."

"Good. And are you looking forward to seeing your father."

"Yes."

"And what are you waiting to talk to him about?" Dr. Osler asked, half fearful that Jan might want to talk about something that might lead back to his special treatment of Jan.

"I want to ask him about my job in New London."

'Or maybe about my mother.'

4. Father's Day

The day before father's day, or 'father's day eve' as Dr. Osler called it, was a pretty heavy day for the boys. They had an all day, complete physical. It was a head-to-toe medical evaluation that was run by a team of doctors, nurses and orderlies that shuttled in from New London. The boys had to fast until they had finished their blood work and abdominal scans. The fasting was the part of the day that Dix hated most. When they were 15 years old, they were the last to have their blood work, but now that they were 17, they were first. After taking the blood samples, a nurse took the vials over to the Administration Building where it was spun to separate the cells from the platelets. For Jan, his blood would show a high ferratin level and higher than normal iron levels, consistent with his hemochromatosis. All of Jan's other blood results, including cholesterol, sodium, and glucose levels, were all in the normal or excellent range.

The fasting did not bother Jan. His least favorite part of the day was the urine test. He could never figure out how to pee on demand. As expected, his urinalysis would show an excellent quantity of electrolytes without any abnormal crystals or bacteria. In short, he had a well functioning liver.

Despite his size, Otto's least favourite part of the day was the immunizations. He just didn't like needles. He also didn't really appreciate the abdominal measurement process, which still relied on an ultrasound to measure the various organs. It wasn't the process of moving the transducer across his various organs that bothered him. He hated the gel applied to ease the movement of the transducer ... or more accurately, he hated the squishy feeling of the gel as it squashed across his stomach.

After the senior boys were finished the preliminary blood, urine, and organ mapping, they proceeded to more standard examinations including allergy testing, a vision test, a hearing test, a lung test, bone density measurement and a blood pressure test (at both the arm and the ankles). Jan's favorite test by far was heart monitoring, which still used a version of the electrocardiogram. One of the nurses placed ten electrodes on his chest and he was asked to run as hard as he could. Jan had phenomenal heart metrics, and the resident nurse was always impressed with how hard he could push with his heart and how short the repolarization period was. The complete process took the entire day and the end of the examination was signalled when the boys got a haircut at the final station.

The resulting 'report card' would be delivered to the fathers the next day. The report included feedback from all the tests, as well as a quarter-over-quarter and year-over-year comparison. If the fathers perceived any anomalies, they could schedule time to discuss the results with Dr. Primero, but there were very few unsatisfactory results.

Father's day came once every three months at the Academy. The last father's day before Jan's renaissance came on Monday, August 3rd. There was a significant amount of pomp and circumstances to father's day, so much so that even Dr. Osler wore the doctor's whites. The day started with the boys gathering in the new gymnasium to show-off their physique and physical dexterity for their admiring fathers. The fathers watched the show in the gym from the seats of the gallery. It had the feel of a grandstand from a 1950's gymnasium, but the comfort level was vastly improved through the supple, extra-wide cushioned seats. After the three-hour exhibition and show, the boys would either go back to their rooms or go for a walk with their fathers. This conversation time lasted only a half hour before the fathers disappeared into their shuttles for another quarter year.

During this brief talk, the boys would discuss life, their future, school, the outside world, and anything else that would fit into such a short length of time. Jan never felt like he had enough time with his father, whereas Dix ran out of things to say but still he really appreciated the time his father dedicated to him.

Jan and Dix both knew that their fathers were wealthy men, but Dix was absolutely sure that his father was the wealthiest of all the doctors. To Dix, the father's day event was all about the chance to showcase his athletic skills during the first three hours. His father really encouraged him to improve his performance each time he came to visit. On this father's day, Dix was determined to come in first in at least one event.

To Jan, the father's day event occupied only a small thought in the back of his mind, as he did not like showing off. However, more recently Jan's mind was overflowing with questions, and he began to overly anticipate the opportunity of spending the final half hour talking with his father. Trevor Ericson, on the other hand, enjoyed seeing his son succeed in the sporting events, but didn't look forward to spending time with him after the performance. This end-of-day conversation was a tradition that he could do without.

That Monday the shuttles started to arrive just after 9 a.m. The vehicles entered the grounds on an interlocking brick path that wound its way in through the faux forest directly in front of the Administration Building. The shuttles arrived at the campus barely emanating a sound. The arrival of the elders could have gone unnoticed if not for the insatiable banter between the fathers who probably spent more time conversing with each other before the event, than they spent talking with their sons afterward. All the men dressed differently, but the typical look was a turtleneck sweater and a traditional blazer. Jan imagined that this was how they dressed for work. Even though each individual father never seemed to wear the same outfit twice, their tidy garb gave the appearance of a bizarre military uniform.

After arriving, the shuttles were parked on the synthetic grass of one of the unused fields and the fathers stood with their comrades for upwards of an hour before heading off to see their sons' performances. It was the sound of the male laughter that alerted Jan to the beginning of the day's events. He got out of bed, showered, and dressed all within 15 minutes. The boys were not required to be at the gym until 11 a.m., but Jan headed down to the parking grass to look for his father. It was a full hour before the opening ceremonies.

Trevor Ericson stood beside his shuttle, talking about the best way to free up finances. As Jan circled through the various conversations in search of his father, he overheard two men talking about their sons' achievement in sports. He was unsure which boys' fathers these men were, but one anticipated another winning day and the other regretted another losing occasion. He heard the defeated father say that he just wasn't sure if this should be the one. Jan speculated that the man had two sons. Jan had never heard any other boy mention that he had a brother, but thanks to his dictionary he now knew that a brother shared the same father, and mother. As he wandered through the conversations and the shuttles, Jan wondered if he had a brother somewhere (he had yet to discover the word sister). Perhaps he would ask his father once he found him. The men continued talking without regard to Jan's presence.

Two other men were discussing an upcoming vacation to an island, which one of the fathers was planning. They were probably the least serious of the fathers as they were constantly making each other laugh.

"I've got one for you ... here's a joke you can tell your son at his renaissance ... Knock, knock," the younger of the two men said.

"Okay, I'll play along ... who's there?" the other father replied.

"Not you."

The two men broke out in another burst of laughter. Jan didn't understand why this was so funny, so he moved on through the maze of fathers.

A group of three men, one of whom Jan recognized as Dix's father, were discussing the viability of merging two entities. Jan was unsure if he said 'countries' or 'companies'. He stopped to listen as the conversation seemed to demand his attention. Of all the overlapping conversations, this was the one that Jan understood the least. If not for his recent discussions with Dr. Osler, he knew he wouldn't have understood the conversation at all. At one point, Jan wanted to interject something that Dr. Osler had said and point out that any one merger could shift a balance of power. He didn't. Jan retained his invisibility. He found himself listening to Dix's father's dissertation on 'viable alternatives', when one of the other men noted the new shuttle.

"So ... how do you love the new model X?" the man asked.

"It's great," Dix's father answered. "The auto drive is flawless. There is a two-centimetre sensory detection radius, six charging panels, a full 3-D GPS, and the best part ... a complete food and beverage preparation unit. It was either that or move from Level 48 to 49 ... and really, just how low can you go?"

The men laughed. Suddenly Jan felt a strong hand grab him from behind. He turned to see his father.

"Father!" Jan gasped.

"Fire," his father responded almost coldly. "What are you doing out here?"

His father had started calling him Firecracker when he was younger, then eventually shortened it down to just Fire. Jan didn't really like the nickname, so he didn't share it with any of the other boys. He knew he'd be dead if Dix ever heard the name as he'd be called 'Fire' from that point forward. However, he still responded to the name whenever his father called him 'Fire'.

"I came to find you," Jan replied.

It would be obvious to anyone that Jan was his father's son. Both shared striking blond hair, pale white skin with reddish cheeks and a defined physique. They shared the same Norwegian heritage. Only a few years earlier, it would have also been clear to anyone that Jan's physique would ultimately be more physically fit than his father's, once he had fully matured. Now, Jan's build had already surpassed his father's form in its prime condition.

Jan's father had rarely discussed his own past with his son. The only exception was when Trevor Ericson recalled his visit to the country formerly known as Norway. He went there as a young child to visit his dying grandfather who lived in a town called Oslo. Jan saw a tear building up in one of his father's eyes before he caught himself and ended the story abruptly. The thought of his grandfather's death evoked more emotion in Jan's father than any other event that Jan could recall. He never asked his father anything more about this, but Jan's interest in the concept of death began that day.

"Tre ... is this your boy?" a man asked. It was the same father that had been speaking to Dix's father about the Model X shuttle.

"Yes, this is Jan. Isn't he wonderful?" Dix's father answered before Jan's father could reply. As he made his statement, Dix's

The Gemini Project 53

father was looking at all of Jan's various physical features as though he was doing inventory. The other father noticed this and instead of wondering why Dix's father was looking at Jan in this manner, he started doing the same thing.

"Yes ... yes, he's in 'primo' condition," the man answered.

There was a brief laugh from Dix's father.

Jan had forgotten that his father's name was Tre. He rarely heard it, and he never used it. This thought was interrupted by his father's voice.

"Well, it's almost time for the games. Shouldn't you be getting ready?"

"There's not much to do. On the day of the father's day games, they don't let us in the gym before the ceremonies and they don't let us eat until after you leave ... and I'm already dressed and ready."

Uncomfortably, Tre looked around for something else to occupy Jan's time.

"Well ...," Jan's father started, "what was it that you wanted to discuss." He put his arm around his son and started to walk him away from the crowd. Dix's father could sense Tre's uneasiness in talking with his son. He wondered if the problem was with Jan or with Tre?

"Nothing really, I guess. I thought maybe you'd tell me about what I'll be doing when I move in with you in New London."

"Oh ... yeah ... that, that's easy. You'll be working," Tre answered in a less than comfortable tone.

"Working, yes that's great! Will I be working with you? Will it start right away? What will I be doing?"

"Why you'll be doing the exact same thing as me."

"So, I'll be a doctor?"

"No, no. I'm a doctor by training but there isn't as much need for medical staff these days. I do something much more important, I run the ordinateur business."

"I'm not sure what that is father."

"It's digivices, you know, holographones and computers. You'll be in the data processing business, just like me?"

"But I won't be doing the same thing as you father, I don't even know how to work a digivice."

"No, no, you'll be closer to me than you can imagine," Jan's father responded looking nervously back at the crowd. "We'll do everything together."

Dr. Primero approached the fathers and he caught a glimpse of Jan's father walking away from the shuttles. He sensed an uneasiness. Then he saw that the father was speaking with his son. Why was that boy even here? He immediately headed over to the pair.

"And what exactly is it that you do father?"

"I do synaptic research. We're trying to build an ordinateur device to simulate brain patterns and the like," he replied as he put an end to the conversation by extending his hand out past Jan to the approaching doctor.

"Ah, Dr. Primero. Good to see you again. I've just been speaking to Jan about what I do for a living and what he'll be doing after his renaissance. I've got a real curious young mind here doctor."

"I see. Yes, he is really blossoming this one," said Dr. Primero with an obvious disregard. He turned to the boy and stated, "Your father is a very smart and powerful man Jan ... you should be proud of him."

"But how will I be able to work alongside my father when I don't even know how to operate a digivice? Shouldn't someone be teaching me now?" Jan asked.

"Jan is developing outstandingly," Dr. Primero stated, totally ignoring the questions of the perplexed boy.

"Yes, yes. I can see that," his father added. "I look forward to the games today. Anything new on the schedule?"

Dr. Primero placed his arm around Jan's father's shoulder, turned his back toward Jan and proceeded to walk Tre back to the crowd. Jan stood there ostracized from the group of elders.

"Yes, yes ... we're going to change the format of the vault competition. This month we are going to try to allow the boys to ..." Dr. Primero's voice trailed off as they walked away from Jan.

The boy slowly followed the adults back to where the other fathers were talking. He overheard the group of men talking with Dix's father, who were still talking about the benefits of crediting for a new shuttle versus moving down a level. Jan found the conversation uninteresting and with a dejected look he turned to head back to the dorm. Jan's father saw him leaving the parking grass and relieved, he called out to his son insincerely.

"Thanks Jan, I'll talk to you some more after the games."

That was all Jan needed to hear. The abjection quickly dissipated, and he was back on top of the world. Jan was ready to compete, and he was sure that the better he did, the more inclined his father would be to spend time with him.

The fathers eventually made their way to the gymnasium and took their padded chairs on the north side of the gym. They would relax, drink 'fruit juices' served by the orderlies and watch the events, cheering for their own sons as the morning's proceedings advanced.

The opening ceremonies consisted of a short speech by Dr. Primero, which sounded to Jan like the exact same one from the previous father's day, then the boys were paraded to the front of the grandstand to the cheers of their admirers. The first event was the trampoline where Otto had placed first in the past four consecutive meets. Otto's skills on the trampoline were unrivalled and he finished on top again. Jan noticed that Otto's father stood up and clapped his hands at the conclusion of his son's performance, and again when Otto was given the red ribbon on the podium. After that event, Jan proved to be the most outstanding athlete in the remaining five of the six events. He finished first in three of them and second in another two.

The only event that Jan didn't make the podium for, was the uneven bars. He mounted the wooden bars with a lissome confidence and started the routine with a demonstration of technique, form, and composition. Halfway through the routine, his chalk didn't stick properly, and caused him to slip and fall off. The tumble looked worst than it was. As Jan transitioned from the top bar to the bottom one, he missed the grab. He was parallel to the ground at the time, and he headed straight down to the mats, face first. Only Jan's pride was hurt in the fall, as his hands were in the perfect position to absorb the impact of the accident. The gym fell silent until Jan started to get up. As he rose to one knee, he saw his father standing with one hand cupped over his mouth. As the boy recomposed himself, he caught the look of fear in his father's face. The fall had brought his father to his feet, a feat that his previous trips to the podium had failed to do. Jan wondered why it took his torso crashing to the mat before his father stood up that day.

Two male nurses made their way over to Jan. He raised his right hand to indicate that he was okay, and the audience immediately understood the signal. They started applauding for him as he continued to rise to his feet. His father, still standing, was also applauding. He hunched over to talk to a few of the other fathers who were patting him on the back and saying something to him. Jan caught his father flash a scornful glance towards Dr. Primero.

Dix finished first in the uneven bars. This wasn't typically his event, but that day, four of the top athletes had slipped off the bars and off the podium. It was the first first-place finish for Dix in any of the games. His father looked ecstatic with his son's performance.

After the award ceremonies for that final event, Dix's father took him down to the shuttle to show him his latest acquisition. Jan and his father walked over to his room. He finally had his father alone again. He expected that his father would be immensely proud of his medals.

Jan sat down on his bed and his father remained standing as the door to the room shut.

"What the hell happened out there?" his father asked in a tone that Jan had never heard before.

"What do you mean? I did the best I've ever done. The best I've seen anyone do at the games," Jan answered defensively.

"You know what I'm talking about ... the uneven bars."

Jan gaped back at his father. Could he really be upset because Jan lost one event? What about the ones he'd won?

"I don't want you getting injured," his father added as he gained composure. "Not now. Not when you are so close."

That's right. If Jan got injured now, it might prevent him from starting his new job in a month. Silence consumed the air as Jan's father tried to calm himself and Jan's mind went from his job, to his new home, then to his new city. His father wanted to make sure that he didn't get injured ... that nothing happened to prevent them from starting the next phase of their life together.

"I'm sorry father. I won't let it happen again."

"Well, there are no more father's days left for you to show-off at, so just make sure that you don't injure yourself trying something stupid, okay? If I hear that you're going at it too rough, I'll have you pulled out of here faster than a ..."

Jan's father's voice trailed off and he searched for a simile that his son could relate to. Jan wondered what 'pulled out of here' entailed. At this point of his life, he was looking forward to leaving school and starting work. They sat there in silence for a while as Jan's father regained his composure.

"Tell me about life in New London," Jan finally requested after the silence had dissipated into an awkwardness.

"What do you want to know?"

"I don't know. Are there people other than doctors there? Who makes the rules? Where do you go to fall in love?"

His father looked at him coldly.

"Fire, who's been filling your mind with such questions? You don't need to know that stuff until it's time," he said letting his voice return to its previous anger.

Jan knew that his father was upset with him, but he wasn't prepared to miss this final opportunity to gain a better understanding. After all, this would be their last meeting, before his renaissance.

"But father, I want to know. I want to know everything."

Tre Ericson wondered if his son wasn't sensing his discomfort or if he was consciously ignoring his displeasure with the direction of the conversation. He recomposed himself once again before answering.

"And you will know everything ... when you turn 18," Tre answered attempting to pacify his son.

"But I want to know now. I can't wait anymore," Jan shot back, mistakenly forgetting his place, and raising his voice in frustration.

Jan hadn't perceived the full level of fury that was hidden in his father's face but as he spoke, he could see that he had hit a nerve.

"And I can't wait any more either," Jan's father yelled.

Now Jan knew how angry he had made his father. The realization came just as the room door opened.

"That shuttle is so-o-o-o drastic," Dix said laughing as he entered the room.

The entrance of Dix and his father saved Jan from witnessing how enraged his own father actually was. The room fell silent again. He sat there comparing the two fathers. He used to think his father was fitter than Dix's but now he was unsure. His father's face had grown yellowish, almost bilious. Jan also noticed that Dix's father's turtleneck was made of a shinier material, and it looked softer somehow. He found himself wishing that he could feel the material.

"So, practicing extra time in the gym after gymnastics class has really paid off for the kid, wouldn't you say?" Dix directed his comment to Jan's father in an attempt to end the lull in the conversation.

Tre Ericson didn't respond as he wasn't sure who 'the kid' was. Was it a nickname for Jan or was Dix talking about himself? Dix's father was wondering if Jan's five podium appearances were also the result of extra gym time like Dix's one appearance. Jan didn't respond because he couldn't believe that Dix was complimenting himself for getting one medal.

"Yeah," Jan's father said finally, "… really paid off."

Tre had arrived at the realization that he really didn't need to answer Jan now that his roommate had returned, and this relaxed him substantially. The next time he would see Jan was at the renaissance celebration. This moment represented the end of all the awkward conversations with his son. He let a smile slip out and Jan caught it. Jan had several thoughts as to what could make his father smile at that point.

"So, Jan," Dix's father interjected, "Are you looking forward to your renaissance?"

"I live for it," Jan answered excitedly. "It's going to be the best day of my life."

"You got that right. You should speak to my son a bit more about it. He doesn't seem to be as excited."

"Aw that's not fair," Dix protested. "I didn't say that father … I just said that I didn't want my time at Corpo to end."

"Almost everything has to come to an end son," Dix's father responded. "It's the way …"

"Well, are there any sports in the city?" Dix asked trying to find something that he could like about his new life.

"There used to be," Jan's father answered getting back into conversation mode. "There used to be teams and leagues and the like. Every year we'd have great playoffs, and we'd celebrate the best teams. But life has changed. Coming here to watch the gymnastics once a quarter is the best sports entertainment we have."

"Yea, but you can't even bet on it," Dix's father added chuckling to himself.

"Does mother like sports?" Jan asked.

Silence. Jan had successfully shut down all conversation with one question, and he saw the anger return to his father's face. Dix's father was also caught off guard by the question. What did this kid know about mothers? Jan's father fought to remain calm. He had heard similar questions before. For the past three visits, there had been the inevitable question that he didn't want to answer. Tre just kept thinking 'one more month, one more month ...'.

"Son, you have so much to learn. One day soon you'll understand about your mother, your birth and even love," Jan's father stated, the words sounding suspiciously the same as every other time that Jan asked a question that concerned his mother.

Dix had never asked his father about his mother, so he didn't know that his father revelled in conversations about love. Dix's father couldn't resist adding his opinion to Jan's father's comments.

"Love will come to you one day ... in one form or another. And I am sure that you will father a child of your own who you can give the same privileges that your father's given you. Just be patient young Jan."

Jan had heard these words before too, but from his own father. For the first time, Jan wondered if he wasn't the only one being coached.

"Who cares?" Dix added his rhetorical punctuation to end the conversation.

Jan knew that his father really hadn't come close to answering his question, but he also knew that it was futile to try to extract anything more now that Dix was in the room. He also noticed that Dix's father said 'your father's given you', instead of 'your parents have given you'.

"One last question, then we need to leave," Dix's father said trying to move the conversation to a logical end point and ignore the melancholy air that had filled the room.

"Okay," said Dix. "What's your favourite sport?"

Frustrated, Jan realized that Dix had just used up the last question that they would get to ask their fathers before the renaissance ... and he used it to take a survey. He became extremely frustrated.

"Mine? That's easy," Dix's father started, "... basketball. Tre?"

Dix's father turned to Jan's father. Again, Jan heard his father's name and it sounded unusual to him.

"Lacrosse. I was looking forward to seeing it played here, but they eliminated if from the curriculum before I got to see one game."

Jan lost his frustration about the question when he heard something that he didn't know about his father. Dix's inane query had evoked a response that Jan could never have predicted. When did his father watch a Lacrosse game? Perhaps, maybe, his father even played lacrosse.

"Lacrosse, what's that?" Dix asked.

"It's a game with baskets on the end of a stick that you use to shoot a ball," Jan said.

"That's right," his father responded in mild amusement.

"How'd you know that?" Dix asked.

"They used to play it years ago," Jan answered, "but a boy got injured, so we lost the boy and the sport. When I found that out, I read up on the rules in one of the books in the lounge."

Jan's father looked at him in amazement.

"You can read?"

"Yes ... Dr. Osler taught me some stuff, but mostly I taught myself. In the lounge there are ..." he started before Dix clobbered his sentence.

"Yeah, he reads all the time. It's pretty handy 'cause there's some rule books in the lounge, but I mostly get the point of a sport by listening to the coach, so you don't really need the books. This guy likes to read the rules though and it's good 'cause sometimes he finds loopholes."

"Who got injured?" Dix's father asked turning to Tre.

"Gagnon's kid. Remember? He lost his place in the school," Jan's father responded deliberately.

"Oh yeah. Right," Dix's father said. "He got transferred to the Gehirn School, didn't he Tre?"

"That's right," Jan's father confirmed. "And after that, they banned lacrosse from the school, before there were any more injuries. Still, I love that sport and I'd love to see another lacrosse game. Now, we've got to be off, so you boys take care of yourselves, and we'll see you at the renaissance celebration."

Tre Ericson raised his digivice and said "Anjea, ready the shuttle for departure."

The two fathers rose and immediately started talking to each other as they left the room. Neither one waved, hugged or shook hands with the boys. They had just shut down the conversation and left the room.

It was an hour before lights-out, so Jan thought he'd head down to the lounge for a bit. He noticed the front door of the dorm was propped open, so he stepped outside to see if any shuttles were still on the campus. There was one still there ... his father's. Tre Ericson was standing in front of the shuttle, engaged in an animated conversation with Dr. Primero. Jan could see his father gesturing and pointing, first back towards the dormitory, then back towards the Admin building. It was unclear to Jan if his father was angry or simply trying to adamantly make a point. Then he saw his father reach into his jacket pocket and pull out a small box. From the box, he pulled out two brown cylindrical objects and gave one to Dr. Primero. They each put the object in their mouths but didn't eat them. Instead, they set the tip on fire and proceeded to inhale then blow out smoke. Jan retreated back inside the door and watched from the resolute darkness of the hallway.

As they puffed on their cigars, Jan's father told Dr. Primero that his son had become too inquisitive, a complaint that Dr. Primero had heard before. Jan's father pointed out that none of Jan's three other brothers had acted this way. Dr. Primero agreed, but he added that Jan was naturally a lot smarter than his brothers. Jan's father said that this wasn't necessarily a good thing, then he also told Dr. Primero that he didn't think that Dr. Osler was the right type of influence for his son. To placate Jan's father, Dr. Primero told him that they'd be monitoring Jan closely to watch his final development.

"You know, these things will kill you," Dr. Primero said as he puffed on the cigar that Jan's father had lit for him.

They both laughed.

"That's okay, I'm thinking of trading this body in anyway," Tre responded with a slight grin. "Besides, I haven't had a cigar in 25 years. Makes you wonder why we stopped smoking them doesn't it?"

"Yes. They're excellent. Where did you get them?" Primero asked.

"From Alain," Jan's father answered. "He's celebrating his son's performance today."

"That's right Dix did well, didn't he? But he pales in comparison to your son. Four's a fine physical specimen and for that, you should be proud of him. Everything has turned out well. There is nothing to worry about."

Jan thought about going outside and creeping closer. Close enough so he could hear the conversation. That's when Tre Ericson turned to look towards the dormitory. Jan backed further into the darkness. His father smiled then began to sing, slightly off key:

Ain't no sound but the sound of his feet,
Machine guns ready to go.

Then Primero added, "Besides … it's almost renaissance!"

The two men smiled at each other.

5. The Tunnel

Jan remembered playing lacrosse four or five years ago at his old school. Seeing his father's love of the game, Jan was anxious to play again. He thought that it would make a great present for his father if they could put on a lacrosse game as part of his renaissance celebration. The next day, he reviewed the rule book again in the lounge and decided that he could teach the game to the boys during one of the free times. The problem was he would need to find the equipment.

When he asked Coach Treinador if there was any lacrosse equipment on campus, the coach told him that they used to have some but that it was probably thrown out by now. When Jan pushed back a little, the coach just wanted rid of the boy, so he suggested that it could be in storage somewhere. Treinador said he didn't remember why they stopped the sport, and he directed Jan to go ask Mr. Verwalter to check the storage room.

Verwalter, the school's caretaker, was an elderly man that appeared grumpy to most of the boys most of the time, but Jan knew him to have a softer side. Jan found him cleaning up around the bins behind the dining hall and asked him about old sports equipment.

Verwalter wore clothing made of different material than the doctors, nurses, coaches, and students. He would often be seen with some sort of stain on his baggy grey shirts and pants, but the clothes would be mysteriously cleaned the following day.

The janitor told Jan that he remembered seeing the lacrosse sticks but couldn't exactly remember where.

"If Treinador said you should find them, then I suggest you look in the old gymnasium," Verwalter said.

Jan didn't correct the aging caretaker, letting him believe that the coach had sent him on this mission. That being the case, Verwalter was happy to point Jan where to look, but the caretaker wasn't going to have the time to go rummaging around to satisfy a coach's lack of planning.

The old gym was scheduled for flattening, and it had been that way for over half a decade. The building was the only eyesore on the campus. The doors and windows had been boarded up, so it wasn't possible to just unlock a door and enter the building. However, there was a utility tunnel that connected to the gym from the janitorial room in the basement of Renaissance Hall. The tunnel, Verwalter said, would lead straight over to the janitorial room of the old gym, and he doubted that it would be locked on either end.

"And I can get inside the old gym by taking the tunnel?" Jan asked.

"Absolutely," answered Verwalter. "But if anyone asks, it was Treinador that said you could go into the basement of Renaissance Hall and the old gym, not me. When we built the new gym, we didn't want to install another powerplant, so we just built the tunnel and routed the therma-cables from one building to the next. That's why we never demolished the old building ... we're still using its power for the new gym, the Admin building and for Renaissance Hall.

"One day we'll clean all that stuff up."

"Is it safe to take the tunnel?" Jan asked showing a fear of the unknown.

"No worries," answered Verwalter. "There's 20 inches of concrete in the tunnel walls so that thing could withstand a shuttle crashing into it if it had to. The therma-cables glow from the internal radiation, so you don't even need a glow-tube to make your way through. I used to go through the tunnels all the time when we first boarded up the old gym. I needed to get some flooring from the old gym, and I didn't

The Gemini Project

want to ask Primero to unboard the building, so I just went through the tunnel from Renaissance Hall. The tunnel leads conveniently from the gym to the janitorial room. I've probably been back to the gym for various things about a dozen times, and not all for me either, but I haven't been back for a year or so. I'll take you to the room and let you in, but after that, you're on your own."

"You're not going to take me to the old gym?" Jan asked anxiously.

"Stop your worrying. You're seventeen now. You're practically a man and it's time you start doing things for yourself. Besides, I'm going to my residence in about ten minutes and then I'm off on vacation. A well deserved one I might add, so I don't have time to hold your hand," Verwalter replied, obviously amusing himself as he contemplated his vacation in New London. "There's only one door in the Janitorial room, so just take that to the gym. All the doors down there are unlocked. You'll figure it out. If not, go back and get Treinador to help you."

Verwalter walked Jan over to Renaissance Hall, down a flight of concrete stairs at the back, then he unlocked the janitorial room by placing his hand on the lighted pad beside the door.

He held the door open for Jan and said, "The entrance is right over there but its lights-out in just under an hour so you better hurry yourself. Oh, and don't blame me if you're not quick enough, 'cause I don't even know you're here."

Jan was pretty sure that Coach Treinador would not have allowed him to go on a hunt for lacrosse equipment if he realized what a great endeavour it was turning out to be.

Verwalter watched as Jan passed him and entered the janitorial room. Jan was one of the few boys that knew him by name. The caretaker had watched him mature over the last three years and was impressed enough with the boy to feel confident that he'd find the equipment.

"Just close this door when you leave and it will lock behind you," Verwalter called as he smiled and ascended the concrete stairs.

'That boy would be a great athlete one day ... if he lived to develop to his full potential,' the caretaker thought. He stopped smiling.

Beneath the reception of the Renaissance Hall in the janitorial room, Jan found himself alone in a strange room. With all his time spent living life at the Academy, this was the first time he had descended the stairs to the basement. It dawned on him that his lack of curiosity about his surroundings, was also shared by all the other boys. Now however, Jan felt like he was venturing on a great expedition ... going where no boy has gone before. His imagination overpowered his lack of confidence as he walked through the janitorial room, past the equipment that the caretaker brought out to clean the floors each night.

On the far side of the room, Jan saw the door. It was partially blocked by a cabinet, a mop, and a pail. He pushed the cabinet aside, moved the cleaning supplies and pushed a bar to open the door. As the glow from the tunnel entered the janitorial room, Jan could feel his chest pounding. He had felt his heart racing after a strenuous athletic activity or just before a swim meet, but never had he felt his chest well up just because he saw a light. There was an almost indiscernible hum from the tunnel. Jan entered and had to walk down another four stairs to reach the tunnel floor. Now he could see down the length of the tunnel, but the soft blue glow on the grey painted walls made it difficult to see to the other end. He was unsure of how far it was from Renaissance Hall to the old gym, so he was picturing the grounds above to calculate how long it should take him to get through the tunnel.

He started to walk slowly away from the safety of the janitorial room. This was the most adventurous thing that Jan had done in his life. As he stepped slowly into the tunnel, the light around him began to change. The yellow tones from the janitorial room were being devoured by the deep blue glow of the therma-cables. There was a sudden thumping noise as the door boomed closed. Only the blue light remained. Jan felt nervous and perhaps a little afraid of the semi-darkness, another new feeling for him. He looked back at the janitorial room door and contemplated returning to familiarity. He focused forward and his eyes peered down the shaft. Jan took a deep breath, then walked at a more regular pace. As he proceeded through the eery tunnel, he felt a chill in the air and sensed a dampness.

The flat grey tunnel walls continued down either side of him as he proceeded. His eyes were adjusting to the dim light, and he could see a little further down the tunnel. There was something mounted on the wall ahead on the right-hand side. He continued past some sort of valve system with gauges attached, and then he saw a side door marked 'Steam Room'. He would have welcomed the end of his journey, so he tried the door handle, even though he was sure that he had not yet made it to the old gym. It was a turn type handle, but it didn't even turn part way round before stopping. The door was locked. Perhaps Verwalter's recollection of unlocked doors wasn't accurate.

There seemed to be wind growing in the tunnel. The back of his neck, now wet with sweat or dampness from the tunnel walls, sensed modest temperature changes. He continued to head down the tunnel. After another thirty seconds of walking, he became overwhelmed with a sense of panic, and he wished he were already at the old gym. He quickened his pace until a jog turned into a flat-out sprint. Maybe it would have been better if he hadn't engaged on this quest. The adventure had quickly lost its romantic appeal. He saw some wires labelled 'Li-Fi' and another set of valves, followed by another side door labeled 'Lib', then before he could even think about slowing down his pace, he saw the definitive end of the menacing tunnel coming into focus.

Four stairs at the end of the tunnel leading up to a metallic door mirrored the appearance of the tunnel's starting point. His worries abated, and Jan felt foolish for having let his mind get the best of him. What was it that he had been afraid of down here any way?

Now thinking about lacrosse again, Jan imagined how it would feel to emerge with the equipment. He mimicked the actions of shooting a ball with the lacrosse stick as he ascended the stairs to the old gym. The handle on the door was a vertical contraption that required you to grab it and push down on a trigger with your thumb. Jan had only seen this type of doorhandle a few times in his life. At first Jan just pulled on the handle. The latch didn't release, so Jan tried to push down on the trigger with his thumb, but the trigger didn't move. After about 60 seconds of pushing, pulling, and squirming with his thumb, fingers and both palms of his hands, Jan pulled vehemently on the door until he finally had to give in to the fact that this door was locked after all.

The deflated boy wondered if he still had time to run back and ask Verwalter how to open the door. He stood back and examined the entrance to the old gym. There was no light pad or key card reader, but he could see a place to insert a key … the kind of metal key that the caretaker carried on a metallic ring on his belt. He turned dejectedly and headed back toward the entrance to the tunnel. He realized there was nothing scary about the tunnel at all and his mind filled up with the disappointment that he would not be able to play lacrosse tomorrow.

When he made his way back to the entrance door, he ascended the four stairs and panicked when he saw that there was also a handle with a trigger on that door. Jan tried to push down on the trigger with his thumb, but this trigger was also motionless. This door was locked too. Jan turned his back to the vexing metal door and out of frustration he kicked it with his heel. His mind started to wander again as he kicked the door repeatedly. Jan started yelling. As he cried out for help, he wondered if he would be reprimanded for being caught down there. He wasn't really on a mission for Treinador, as he had let Verwalter believe. He was almost sure that he was doing nothing wrong, but the situation just didn't seem to be permitted.

Two minutes of calling out and then Jan sat on the top stair. He wasn't going to be heard this far from the sports grounds. No one would come there searching for him, because other than Verwalter, no one knew he would be there. He gazed back to the other end of the tunnel. His eyes could see much further now. He could clearly make out the first set of valves and the locked door to the Steam Room. As he sat pondering his options, he imagined that he could see right to the far end of the tunnel. From one metal prison door to the other.

Under the therma-cable glow, he sat for five minutes wondering if there was anything he could do. The only way he would be heard calling from the tunnel, was if someone came down to the janitorial room …. and that wasn't going to happen while the caretaker was on vacation. Again, he looked at the other end of the tunnel, then he realized that he couldn't really see the full length of the shaft because he couldn't see the second set of valves. Suddenly, it occurred to him that he had passed a second set of steam valves beside a second door, and he hadn't actually tried that other door. Maybe it was an unlocked door that led out of the tunnel. He got up and headed briskly back into the blue milieu. As he ran, he tried to think … even if the door were open, what building would it lead to?

The tunnel had become familiar territory as Jan headed towards the old gym. Approaching the second door, he noticed that his last chance to find an exit was marked 'Lib' and not 'Steam Room'. He closed his eyes as he tried the handle.

The Gemini Project 69

As the handle turned, Jan expected it to stop like the Steam Room door had, but it didn't. This door was unlocked. The door opened to the inside so Jan pushed but it would only move a few inches before it seemed to get stuck. Great. Jan pushed harder and he felt the door open slightly, then it pushed back against him. He could tell that it wasn't locked or jammed. There was something wedged up against the door. He pushed but could not get the door to open. He got down on his back and put his feet up against the door. He drove his legs into the door as though he was using the leg press machine in the weight room, and he could hear a clattering noise on the other side. The door still wasn't going to open, so Jan pushed harder and this time he heard a hefty clatter followed by a crashing thud. The door opened just wide enough for Jan to squeeze himself into the room.

No lights came on. They were obviously not automatic, so Jan looked around for an old-style light switch like the one in the dining room. With the blue glow of the tunnel's therma-cables squeezing only partially through the half-open door, he couldn't find a switch. As he felt his way into the darkness of the room, Jan saw that the noise had been caused by books falling off a shelf and then the bookshelf itself finally falling over. The shelf had been placed in front of the door. Jan picked the books up and place them in a pile. He then lifted the bookcase back upright and slid it to the side so that he could fully open the door. The blue light spread across the room and Jan could see numerous rows of shelves laid out like dominos and filled with books. He started to make his way around the room when he heard the faint blast of a horn. It was the lights-out horn. He needed to get back to the dorm within the next half hour.

At the far side of the room, Jan could see two glass doors. Jan crossed slowly through the thin light over to the entrance. There was no lock on these doors and even though their wooden frames surrounded large panes of transparent glass, the dirt on the doors still seemed to limit light from passing. Jan peered through the glass and could just barely distinguish a set of stairs on the other side. The stairs led up to whichever building he was under. He knew that he had to ascend the stairs and try to find an open exit.

Jan wanted to shut the door to the tunnel but closing it would leave him completely blind. He needed to get back to the dormitory soon. He went back and grabbed some books then propped a few of them in front of the glass doors such that the stairway would get as much light as possible. He then headed up the stairs to what he assumed would be ground level. At the top of the stairs was another metallic door. This one had a long metal bar across it. Jan's heart sped up again as he pressed the horizontal bar. When the bar clicked to allow the door to open, instead of slowing down, he felt his heart speed up again. He would now find out where he was, and whether he would be able to find an exit. He cracked the stairway door and keeked out into the hall.

Jan was coming up from the basement of the Administration Building. The door that led down to the old library sat in a ward that had been dormant for a number of years. Locked from the outside, in the middle of an unused hall, there was very little interest paid to the grey metal door.

As he opened the door and stuck his head out into a dimly lit hallway, Jan could see a sign at eye-level saying 'LIBRARY' in big bold letters. Slowly and quietly, he entered the hall and tried the door handle from the other side. It was the same trigger-style locking mechanism as down in the tunnel. It was permanently locked just like the others. Without a key, these were one-way doors. He decided he might need this door open, so he ran back down to the library, grabbed a book, and placed it between the door and the jamb.

Halfway down the hall on the right was a window with soft white light spilling out into the hallway. Looking left, it was darker with only a red glow at the end of the hall. Jan needed to choose between the white light and the red glow. He focused on the red light and realized that the light was made up of the letters for 'FIRE'. It was as though his father was calling him. Jan headed left.

As he moved down the hall, Jan could make out muffled voices coming from somewhere nearby. He had just noticed that there was another window down this end of the hall, when white light suddenly flooded into the hallway. The window had blinds made up of horizontal panels and although the blinds were closed, enough illumination passed through the cracks to light up the empty hallway. As he approached the window, he saw that he could see through the cracks of the panels. He ducked down and crouched below the bottom of the window, then waddled his way past.

Near the end of the window, he brought his eyes up to glimpse through the blinds. He recognized a hall and he realized that he was in the Administration Building. Across the hall, underneath the glow of fluorescent lighting, Jan could see Nurse Banaltram moving from one room to another with a clipboard in her hand. She was slightly younger than Nurse Rossignol, but somehow came across as more matronly. Jan had heard Dr. O'Flanagan refer to Nurse Banaltram as an 'old battleaxe'. The five-foot two-inch shrew seemed to stop and stare back at the window exactly where Jan was standing. After a brief pause, she continued her routine.

He worked his way down the hall to the red light that bore his father's nickname for him. He examined the door. Yet another bar-type door that could be pushed open from one side. He pushed the bar. The door opened and Jan could see that it led to the outside. It was already starting to get dark, but thanks to the night lights from the soccer field, Jan could see the surroundings. He recognized the golden cane palm shrubs. The silk leaves ran down each side of the Administration Building.

Jan was about to leave when he paused to consider the evidence of the trail that he had left marked behind him. He no longer needed an escape route, so he decided to go back down the hall and remove the book that held the library door open. He quietly crept back past the window, down the hall and pulled the book out of the hall door letting it shut. As the door snapped closed, he realized that he should have pushed the book in behind it. He had accidentally acquired a souvenir of his explorations. He smiled. He was glad to be saddled with the book.

Again, he slipped back down the hall, waddled past the window, and this time he exited out the FIRE door. He ran through the shrubbery, then across the soccer field towards the dormitory. Once at the dorm he crept quietly in and then headed up the stairs to his room. It was Dr. Asino's duty night, and he was already doing his final rounds. Asino was strict and Jan thought he had little to no personality. Jan heard the doctor's voice and he quickly headed into the washroom area. There was no one in there, so Jan jumped fully clothed into the shower, pulled the curtain shut and turned on the shower.

Seconds later, the doctor opened the washroom door slightly and called out "Jan, is that you? Time for bed. Meds are in two minutes young man."

"Just finishing," Jan called back as he took off his wet clothes.

"Be quick about it."

The washroom door closed.

Jan threw his jumpsuit out of the shower into the wash bin. He stood there naked, holding his treasure from the tunnel library. While not the thickest book he had ever seen, it was the largest. It was a square shape, which was also unusual to Jan, and it was probably close to 12 inches by 12 inches. The book started to get wet. Jan held it high above the spraying water and stared at the cover. The appearance of a stone castle built beside a moor, backed by rolling green hills was extremely unfamiliar to Jan. He wondered if this was New London. The colour picture ran across the entire cover. He bent his body to keep the book as dry as he could and as his eyes moved to take in the title, he heard someone approaching. Jan quickly tossed the book into the clothes bin and pulled his shower curtain shut again.

Dr. Asino entered the room and came straight over to the shower then pulled the curtain open.

"I mean it this time, Ericson. Get out of the shower and get to bed. I've got better things to do and if you are not in bed in one minute, I'll have Nurse Rossignol come deal with you."

After threatening Jan with a sedative bearing nurse, Asino marched out of the room and headed down the hall again. Jan quickly came out of the shower and grabbed two towels. He dried himself with the first and wrapped it around his torso. He then bundled the book in the second towel before heading down the hall.

"What did you do all night?" Dix asked as Jan entered the room.

"Just looked for some lacrosse equipment."

"You're a fool you know. There's no way they are going to allow us to play that. Now tomorrow, we need to squeeze in some tennis practice before the game. I want to get back on a winning streak again."

Jan took his evening meds. The cocktail of vitamins, anti-Viagra and muscle relaxants, were just part of the Corpo routine. After Dix went to sleep, Jan unwrapped and re-read the title of the book: *An Illustrated History of Scotland* by Chris Trabraham. What a strange name for a book. Jan was excited about finding a history book but to fully understand the title, he would have to look up Scotland in the dictionary. He would also have to figure out what to do with his bounty. He couldn't turn the book in without a lot of explaining and he couldn't return it to the library even though that might be the best thing.

The lights slowly turned to a deep blue hue and reading became a challenge.

Jan grabbed the dictionary and turned to 'Scotland'. Nothing. He knew a library was a place to store books because he had often heard the doctors refer to the lounge as the library. He looked up the definition anyway. It was in fact a place that contained books, periodicals, and other material for reading. As Jan read further, he learned that people borrowed books from the library and then returned them.

His eyes became heavy as he tried to make out words in the ever-dimming light. Perhaps he was doing nothing wrong as it looked like he was only doing what the library was intended to be used for. Regardless, Jan didn't want to get caught with the *Illustrated History*, so what to do with this book tomorrow? He put the book under his pillow, and he slept on it.

6. Visiting the Library

When Jan awoke the first thought he had was that it was less than one month to his renaissance. He then realized that it was Wednesday, so he glanced over at the clock. 7:00 a.m. ... he had to remain in bed for another four hours.

He had a pain in his neck, and he tried to remember what sport he had done the day before for his muscles to feel so stiff. Then his consciousness flooded back to life with thoughts about his previous day's discovery. He realized that the treasure under his pillow was the source of his sore neck. For a fleeting moment, he feared that he'd dreamt his exploits, but he quickly confirmed reality as he felt the rigidity below his pillow. He grabbed a glow-tube, pulled the sheets up and cracked open *An Illustrated History*. The colourful book was filled with photographs of historic buildings, locations and scenery. There were a few pictures with Scots standing proudly in front of a valley or a monument, and Jan laughed at these when he saw the men were wearing plaid skirts, It was funny because it looked like the same style that nurse Banaltram once wore to dinner ... when a Dr. Devissy came to give a speech. Jan remembered listening to 'A Healthy Future Starts With You'.

The Gemini Project

As he ploughed through the text, Jan soon understood that Scotland was a country. Although the paragraphs under the photographs were brief, for the next three hours Jan read bite-sized nuggets about Scotland, Scottish Kings, clans, and highlanders. He used the dictionary as though it was written as the companion guide to the history text. Jan revelled in the tale of William Wallace. He wondered about the Scots' fixation with the game they called football, which looked exactly like soccer. After gazing at a richly coloured picture of a bottle filled with amber liquid, he wished he could try Scotland's national drink whisky (or "the 'water of life"). The limited number of words worked out well, as Jan didn't get too bogged down with the dictionary. He spent as much time staring at the pictures as he spent reading the stories. The coffee table edition was perfect for Jan to both grasp meaning but also spark his imagination.

As soon as he heard Dix start to stir shortly after ten, Jan quickly shoved the book back below the pillow and thought about what to do with his acquisition. It now surpassed the dictionary as Jan's greatest possession. He wondered if he should bring Dix into his newly found secret world, or if he should leave him in a blissful abyss? Surely Dix would want to be let in on Jan's discovery. Jan decided he'd take the day to think about it.

Before lunch on Wednesdays was the field hockey game. That day, Dix and Otto were selected as the team captains, and they took turns choosing their teams. As usual, Dix chose Jan first. Also, as usual, Jet was selected last. Jet's size and his rotund physique made his selection undesirable, but it was actually his complacency that made him a burden to any team. That day he would be Otto's burden.

The game was played on a field of synthetic grass, using sticks that were flat on one side and round on the other. The objective was to knock a solid, plastic ball past a goalkeeper into a cage to earn a point.

Despite the Jet handicap, the teams were evenly matched and after 30 minutes of play, the game was tied seven goals each. In the first half, Otto had Jet as his goalie and his size, not his agility, had saved many goals. At halftime, Jet asked Otto if he could get a chance to play forward. Dix overheard the conversation, and he came to Otto's defence, pointing out that Jet was a fairly good goalkeeper. Otto didn't like Dix siding with him, so Jet was moved to forward for the second half. With only 11 players allowed on the field at the same time and 21 players on each team, Jet now became one of the players that had to rotate on and off the field. He came on briefly a few times during the half but was sent off again at the next stoppage in play.

The game was tied 10 points each, when Dix noticed that Jet wasn't getting his fair share of playing time.

"Hey Otto, you have to play Jet, he's on your team and you have to play him," Dix protested.

"I have played him," Otto answered, "he never sat out one minute in the first half, so he is due a rest."

"Yeah, but his rest is over."

"Fine then," Otto conceded, "I'll play him, but you've got to sit out now. You've been on for the entire second half."

"Fine. I could use a break anyway," Dix accepted.

With only two minutes left in the game, Jet found himself receiving a pass while he stood right in front of the net. He may have had his eyes closed as he swung at the passing ball, but he connected sending the ball straight to the back of the goal. That made the score 11 to 10 for Otto's team.

"No goal, no goal," Dix protested from the sidelines.

"What are you talking about?" responded Tam.

"He was over the striking circle. You have to be outside the 16-yard line or it's no goal."

Dix marched over towards Coach Treinador who was almost fast asleep across the second row of a five-row metal grandstand. Jan ran after Dix.

"Let it go Dix," Jan implored.

"No, it's not fair. That fat shit was inside the line," he said to Jan before raising his voice and calling out "Coach Treinador, Coach Treinador."

"Dix, it's Jet's first goal this year. Let him have it and we'll score before the end of the game," Jan pleaded.

"No, it's not right," Dix repeated as he marched towards the awakening coach.

"It's just a game," Jan asserted.

Dix stopped abruptly. He turned towards Jan.

"What?" Dix asked indignantly. "What was that you said?"

The Gemini Project

Jan looked at Dix's eyes. He had never seen anger like he saw at that moment, and he realized that it was directed at him, not Jet.

"What's the problem boys?" Coach Treinador asked.

"Jet scored a goal, but he was inside the 16-yard line," Dix snapped.

"No goal then," the coach called back as if his words were some sort of final ruling on the truth. He put his head back down on his metal throne.

The teams faced off again and Otto scored the winning goal for his team 20 seconds later.

At lunch Jan said to Dix that he should have left Jet's goal alone, their team had lost anyway. Dix said that Jan, of all people, should understand that rules are made to be followed, not to be broken. Jan saw Jet walk by with the same vapid smile that he usually had, and Jan realized that it didn't matter to Jet if he scored, but it did matter to Dix if the goal was legal or not.

After lunch, Jan came up with a plan to fake a stomach cramp. He was relieved from the afternoon tennis matches and told to go report to Nurse Rossignol. Rossignol was an elderly woman in her late 60s that Jan thought had more lines on her face than any person he had ever seen. He didn't like her appearance. Her age was betrayed by her silver hair tucked up in a bun and a face that was marked with laugh lines around her mouth and eyes. Rossignol had been a stunning, French beauty in her youth but now she begrudged her age and the lack of attention she commanded at Corpo.

In the Administration Building, Jan found himself ushered into one of the small rooms. Before entering, he looked down the hall and saw the window that he had peered into the previous evening. In the examination room, he sat in the lone chair, waiting for the nurse, and rallying his acting skills. Rossignol entered the room and directed Jan to climb up on to a stretcher. Jan rolled up his field hockey shirt on command and Rossignol pressed a few times on Jan's stomach. She told him he'd survive and then told him to go to his room to lie down for the afternoon. She also gave him a small cup of deep maroon liquid to drink.

Leaving the building, Jan walked past Renaissance Hall and he looked down the steps to the janitorial room door. It was still slightly ajar. Verwalter hadn't closed the door after letting Jan in, and because

Jan hadn't exited that way, he hadn't pulled the door shut behind him. Jan could get back into the janitorial room and back into the tunnel.

Realizing that he now had options, Jan returned to his room and lay on the bed. Although the idea of lying down for the afternoon would have never appealed to him in the past, Jan needed to think. He needed to process his discovery of the library and decide what to do with *An Illustrated History*. There was no way that he could tell Dix about the book. Dix would not be keen on bending the rules and was too focused on winning. There was a chance that Dix could turn Jan in, just to get the credit as the one who caught the perpetrator.

Even keeping the book in his room began to weigh on Jan. He was afraid that someone would come in unannounced and catch him with the text. And besides, Dix was always fooling around in the room, and he would often grab a pillow to hit Jan with. He would have to move the book. Thanks to the maroon liquid, Jan didn't get any more time to read *An Illustrated History* and instead he drifted off with the thought of making a return visit to the library.

Dix came in the room bragging about his victory in the tennis round-robin. He was speaking loudly as he opened the door. Jan woke with a start.

"You really were sick?" Dix asked seeing the look on Jan's face. "You've slept the afternoon away so get yourself out of bed, it's time for dinner."

With that, Dix went down the hall to shower before dinner. Jan had concluded that he had to return the book, before he got caught with it. Since he hadn't left the tunnel by the same way that he went in, he hadn't pulled the janitorial room door shut, like he was instructed to do. That meant he could return to the library that evening, drop off the book and put everything back the way he found it.

Jan had slept for four hours that afternoon. His plan was to hopefully wake up some time in the night or early in the morning, then sneak back to the janitorial room and head to the library to replace the book. After lights-out however, he lay there awake thinking about *An Illustrated History*, and about all the things that he now knew that he didn't know when he woke up that morning. He couldn't sleep, so after half an hour he called out "Dix, you awake?"

Silence was his answer. That was good enough. Jan used a glow-tube to re-read a few passages under the covers. Two hours quickly passed, and Jan had still not gone to sleep. He decided that it was time, so he crawled out of bed and started to leave his room with the book in hand. At the last second, he also grabbed his dictionary. He carefully walked down the hall and headed down the wooden spiral staircase to the first floor. As he looked across the soccer field, he could see that the Administration Building looked particularly busy that evening. For a fleeting moment he thought that his escapades were too dangerous, then he realized that if he propped the metal tunnel door open, there would be no need to exit through the Administration Building.

With that thought, he skirted around the corner to Renaissance Hall. The hall was usually only used during a student's renaissance. Since Jan and Dix were the next two boys to have their renaissances, there couldn't be a better building for Jan's clandestine activities. He descended the stairs at the back and entered into the janitorial room. Before entering the tunnel, he grabbed a mop and placed it between the metal door and the jamb, to prop the door ajar, then he descended into the blue veil of the therma-cable glow. His eyes adjusted rapidly, as he traversed through the tunnel quickly without even a thought of his previous night's apprehensions. This time he was carrying a large canvas bag, filled with glow-tubes. He pulled one of the lights from the bag, lit it, and entered the library.

The first task was to reassemble the library back to the way he found it. With the functional room no longer in darkness, he looked around and took in the rows of shelves and books. When Jan had forced the library door open, one of the 'history' bookcases fell like a domino and was leaning against the neighbouring 'reference books' shelf. He managed to push the shelving back upright without blocking the door and without knocking over too many books. Jan then picked up the stray books from the floor and put them back on the shelves. One of the larger books from the reference section was a dictionary. This one was three times the size of the book that Dr. Osler had given him. He briefly flipped through the text, then returned to the pressing job of tidying up.

The shelf that had blocked the door was part of the history section. He picked up a couple of dozen books and placed them more or less back in their proper position. He crossed the room, picked up the books that were propping open the glass doors, and allowed the library staircase to disappear back into the darkness. As he placed the final books back on the shelf, he was captivated by the smallest book he had seen.

The writing on the spine and on the cover was nothing like Jan had ever seen before. It was composed of an alphabet of scribbles:

孫子兵法

Jan opened the text and read the title on the first page: *Sun Tzu on The Art of War, The Oldest Military Treatise in the World, Translated from the Chinese by Lionel Giles, M.A. (1910)*. Jan had no idea what this sentence meant, but he continually sounded it out ... the oldest military treatise in the world. This book was indeed a find! The treatise was short, and Jan squatted down to flip through the pages using the dictionary as a translator. After a few minutes, he understood that the book was about waging war in a time when generals stood behind large troops of men and directed them in combat against other armies of large troops of men, all fighting to their death. Jan was trying to understand why men waged war, but he was soon fascinated by the strategy decisions that the generals had to make. He realized that most decisions of when to be aggressive and when to be passive were the same type that he wrestled with (both in sports tactics but also in life). As he restacked the books on the shelf, he looked at the cover of *The Art of War* by Sun Tzu and knew that this was a book that he would eventually come back to read.

Jan's interest had been too heightened for him to leave now. If *An Illustrated History of Scotland* and *The Art of War* were both contained in this room, what else could be on these shelves? Before leaving, Jan decided that he'd walk around and get an understanding of what all the books were about. There were books concerning energy production processes, one on the modern western philosophy of Spain & Portugal, another on the philosophy of Christianity and still another on international migration and colonization. He was overwhelmed with what he didn't know. He held a book and wondered how long he would need to study it to understand what the book on social welfare problems was even about. Why didn't he need to know about dialectology and historical linguistics, yet someone had authored an entire book on it? No, two books! No, ten different books on the same subject and he didn't even understand what the subject was!

Wandering around the library, Jan held the glow-tube up so that he could read the book titles and cross reference them with the dictionary. He now understood that the different rows represented different areas of interests. One row was filled with psychology books ... Jan knew what that meant. The psychology shared the shelves with philosophy books, while another row had both sciences and mathematics. He began to comprehend that the ten rows of fiction books were stories that had been invented. He was less interested in these, and his real desire was to understand what the rest of the world was really like. The two rows of the aisle labelled 'literature' contained books that were studying the books on the fiction shelves, so Jan also held little interest in these rows.

Several hours had passed as he wandered back up and down the aisles. He had continually told himself that he would leave right after reading one more book flap, but by this point he had just about completed his mental map of the library layout. The inside flap of the cover had become his quick way to understand what books were about. He became good at judging the books by their covers.

Just after the books on theatre, Jan found the sports section. He noticed the cover of a book that he had seen before, *Field Hockey: Start Right and Play Well* by Bill Gutman. This was one of the largest books that they had in the lounge, and it was one of Jan's favourites. Jan had turned through its pages at least 50 times. He almost didn't pick it up because he had read the rules and strategies so many times before, that he could repeat many sections from memory. One last glance at the book drew him to flip it open. Perhaps it was because the hardcover appeared slightly thicker than the version that he was familiar with. The book almost naturally opened to page 42, roughly the middle. Opposite page 42 was a page without a number. It was the start of a different section. This section was unlike the other pages, in format, content and paper texture. The pages in this section were printed on a high gloss paper. Jan saw that this section, about eight pages in length, was filled completely with colour photographs.

As he turned the pages in the picture section, Jan wondered why one of the few books that he had ever seen in the school, would be missing the most vibrant pages. The pictures were brilliant as the teams were obviously in fierce competition when the photos were taken. As he looked at the fourth picture, he realized that the competitor's in this match all had long hair. Then it dawned on him that these were women playing the match.

Jan had never seen young women before, far less physically fit competitive young women. It had never occurred to him that they existed. He studied the photos silently comparing Nurse Rossignol to one of the girls. He continued to turn the pages realizing that most of the pictures were young women. The sport seemed to be less of a boys' sport somehow, but Jan had played it all his life. He reached the end of the section, and the next page on the left-hand side of the book returned to regular paper and also returned the numbering system at 43. He gazed at the last picture across from page 43. One young lady, with blonde hair in a ponytail, was dressed in white shorts with a red and black vertically striped shirt. She was jumping over top of another young lady, who was similarly dressed but with a blue and green top. He stared at the blonde girl who was clearly a good athlete and, in Jan's mind, was definitely going to complete her jump over the opposition, be first to the ball and would score for her team.

Impulsively, Jan tore the last of the picture pages out of the book. He then slammed the book shut and put it back on the shelf. A feeling of panic came over him and he decided it was time to leave. He put down the field hockey book and saw a book on lacrosse on the next shelf. He thought about taking the book to read the rules but decided against it. He had to start heading back to the dorm.

He turned towards the tunnel and was about to head back, when he took one final glance at the books on the aisle beside him. This was the history aisle. The aisle where he had grabbed the books to prop the doors open on that first night. This is where *The Illustrated History of Scotland* came from. He knew he had to leave, but he felt overwhelmed with a determination to understand more about history. Every time Dr. Osler gave Jan the definition of a word, he always related it to some sort of story that happened in the past. Jan had come to realize that he could never truly understand who he was unless he understood where he came from, and Jan did not understand where he came from.

He couldn't leave yet. He looked at the titles and then leafed through some of the history books. Some of the texts didn't have concise descriptions of the content on the flap, so he had to quickly audit the pages to gain an understanding. As he flipped through the pages of a small book with a large title, *The Art of Democracy: A Concise History of Popular Culture in the United States* by Jim Cullen, Jan decided that he couldn't really understand what this book

The Gemini Project 83

was about just by flipping pages. It needed to be read, digested, and maybe discussed, before it would be understood. Jan placed the picture of the page-43-girl in the middle of the pages of his new book. He then snapped the book closed, put it in his back pocket and headed back to the dormitory. He shut down his glow-tube, leaving the bag of lights behind him, and headed through the now familiar tunnel. His new exit route was a little longer than if he had exited through the Administration Building, but it was less likely that he would be spotted exiting the same way he came in. When he got to the door to the janitorial room, Jan took a rag and laid it along the door jamb to ensure that the exit door wouldn't close on its own. He was already planning his next visit to the library. It was 4 a.m. before Jan was back in his room and settled down to sleep.

Thursday morning was the swim meet.

The day came early for Jan. Sleeping right through until the morning wakeup horn, he didn't have any time to look through his new book before heading to the pool. Jan's favourite sports were all water sports. He particularly excelled at freestyle swimming. That morning however, he was out of kilter. Dr. Primero was watching and quickly realized that for the first time in months, Jan was going to lose the weekly swimming competition. Worse than that, he didn't even finish in the top five.

Dr. Primero mentioned it to Dr. Osler, who simply smiled and said, "The more things change, the more they stay the same."

Primero turned to Osler and said, "Shut up Bill."

Then he added. "And put on a damn doctor's uniform!"

The deep purple t-shirt that Dr. Osler wore had a crown with the words 'Keep Calm and Carry On Operating' written in white block letters below it.

"I can't ... I'm no Babbitt."

"You look like a brain-washed Heb."

"That's my style man, you wouldn't ask me to change my style, would you?"

Dr. Primero scowled and looked back at the pool. After the swim meet, Jan tried to get out of the afternoon basketball game so he could read, but neither Dix nor Coach Treinador would let him go back to his room.

Thursday evenings were quite light and after dinner Jan was sure that he'd be able to get some time reading (while Dix was playing games). He went to bed and pulled up the sheets and had just cracked the spine of *The Art of Democracy*, when someone came through the door to his room. Jan frantically closed the book before pulling the sheets down to see Dr. Osler. This was Thursday night, wasn't it? Dr. Osler was usually only there on Wednesdays and Sundays.

"Hey champ, are you feeling okay?" Dr. Osler asked.

"Yeah ... yeah, I was just a little off today."

"What are you in bed with a glow-tube for?" Dr. Osler asked indicating the luminous glow from under the sheets.

"Oh ... I was just going to shine it on Dix's face when he came back to the room," Jan covered. He decided he would not let Dr. Osler in on his discovery for fear of the library being closed off to him.

"Oh yeah, I guess he deserves the spotlight after coming in second in the swim meet today," Dr. Osler joked.

"Yeah, I'll beat him again next week though," Jan said as he uncovered himself and shut off the glow-tube, coyly keeping the book under the sheets.

"And I hear you were sick yesterday too, what gives?"

"I don't know, I guess I've just got a lot of stuff on my mind."

"I thought it was your stomach. You've got stuff on your mind? Kid, you don't even know what that means."

'But I'm learning', thought Jan.

"What are you doing here tonight? You don't usually work on Thursdays?" Jan asked trying to control the subject of their conversation.

"That's right, but Dr. Asino has to go to a conference tomorrow, so they asked me if I would do some extra time. I told them only if I got to spend time with you. Do you want to go down to the lounge, and I'll review that tennis book with you?"

Of course, Jan didn't want to go. He wanted time to read on his own. However, he went, partly to avoid suspicion and partly because he knew that Dr. Osler got just as much, if not more, out of their sessions. They went downstairs and Dr. Osler forgot all about his offer to review the tennis book. Instead, they talked most of the evening.

The Gemini Project 85

Later, Jan came back to his room to find Dix already in bed.

"You're keeping a lot of late nights these days," Dix stated not realizing his contrast in terms.

Jan wondered if Dix had woken to find his roommate's bed empty the night before.

"Yeah, I was down in the lounge talking to Doctor Osler," Jan responded as he felt around under his sheets for his book.

"I know ... I saw you down there," Dix said sitting up. A cruel smile spread across his face. "Looking for something?"

The book wasn't there. Dix must have taken it.

"Where is it?"

"Why whatever are you talking about?" Dix asked, pretending to be unaware of Jan's missing item.

"You know what I'm talking about. It's mine. Give it back!"

No reaction from Dix.

"What do you want Dix?" Jan asked, worried that Dix would question him as to where he found the book.

"Okay, here's what I want. I want you to let me win at golf tomorrow."

"I can't do that."

"Look, I've never won at golf, and I don't want to leave here being the only guy who's never won."

"You don't understand, I can't do that. There's no way that I can control my play, my partner's play, your play and your partner's play!" Jan anguished.

"Fine, you'll get your book back when I win at either golf, tennis or one of the swim meet events. Otherwise, I'm keeping it."

Jan realized that Dix's ransom of the book wasn't as bad as he had feared. Jan doubted that Dix would even be able to assemble any meaning from the title *The Art of Democracy: A Concise History of Popular Culture in the United States*. It was also clear that Dix had not even opened the book. If he had, he would have found the page-43-girl and they would be having a very different conversation.

Dix lost at golf the next day. Jan thought about going back to the library that night and checking out another book, but he decided it was challenging enough having one book in circulation.

On Saturday, the boys ran the obstacle course. Jan tripped on purpose and got himself eliminated early. He headed back to the room and searched through Dix's things looking for the book. He didn't find it. By the time Dr. Osler came around on Sunday evening, Jan had gone four days without reading, so he reminded the doctor about the tennis book.

They flipped the pages together and Jan listened to Dr. Osler both read and tell more stories. At one point, the book highlighted the best tennis match of all time. It stated that the match was undoubtedly the 2015 U.S. Open between the senior Andrew Roddick and the young sensation Wo Chang. Every set went at least 15 games, and the final game, set and match point was a four-minute volley.

"I remember watching that match with my dad. That was the year before he ..." Dr Osler said as his words trailed off.

Jan noticed the doctor's eyes were beginning to well up.

"He loved tennis. He taught me when I was a boy. I always imagined teaching tennis to my own son ..." Dr. Osler said as he trailed off again.

Jan had concluded several months ago that many of Dr. Osler's stories were 'tall tales' and he was fairly sure that the doctor hadn't watched a tennis match 100 years ago. Jan wasn't always able to tell what was real, and what was made up in Dr. Osler's ramblings, but they were always entertaining, regardless.

As his eyes drifted across that page, Jan once again saw the reference to Aldous Huxley's *Brave New World*. Dr. Osler recognized the change in Jan's face, and he looked to the footnote to see what Jan was reading.

"That's what we needed then and that's what we need again Jan. We need someone to lead us in the creation of a brave new world. We need someone who is brave enough to explore new territories. Someone who is not afraid to fail. Are you that someone?"

"I might be," Jan answered hesitantly.

Dr. Osler smiled, thought a bit, and then replied "No, no Jan, I'm afraid you're not that person. Neither am I for that matter. We are both destined to be just cogs in the grand machine. We'll live out our days on this planet answering to Big Brother and then when we die, it won't be long before we are forgotten."

The Gemini Project

Jan gave little thought to the 'Big Brother' comment and instead thought about his destiny. Jan resolved to visit the library again that night. He decided that he would be an explorer once again. As he listened to Dr. Osler babbling in the background, he was already starting to plan his escapades.

At bedtime, Jan lay there waiting for Dix to go to sleep. He thought that maybe he'd been too quick to discount the fiction section. It dawned on him that *Brave New World* was probably a work of fiction. Perhaps the fictional stories were as good as Dr. Osler's tales and if there was a basis of truth in them, then Jan would be entertained and educated at the same time. Once he was sure that Dix was asleep, Jan headed out, realizing that he didn't need the book the Dix had hidden. He was on his way to find a better one.

In the library, Jan found a row called 'Paperback Novels'. He reviewed the plot on the back cover of several of the novels. There was one about a Scottish detective in Edinburgh, and another about a man who can read people's thoughts, and yet another about a man with a clinging wife and a son who works for a newspaper, *The Daily Mail*. He moved on to the 'Fiction and Classics' section. He had been there less than five minutes when he found what he had been looking for. On the middle shelf, in the section marked 'Classics', sat *Brave New World*. Jan didn't bother to read the flap. He immediately opened to the first page and read the first paragraph. With every word, Jan's mind took him into the past and into the future. As he read, he found it challenging to know what was fact, and what was fiction. He spent 15 minutes working his way through the first page and when he finished it, he started again.

When Aldous Huxley wrote 'only thirty-four storeys' to describe a building in the first sentence of his book, he was trying to evoke a sense of awe in his fictional society. In the 1930's, thirty-four storeys would have been extremely tall, and the reader would have to imagine looking up at a building of such height. Even though this was almost 200 years later, Jan had only ever seen the two-storey buildings of the Academy, so ironically Huxley's words had the desired effect on Jan. He imagined with trepidation looking up at a 34-storeyed structure.

'Skyscrapers', he thought.

The book depicted the Central London Hatcher and Con Centre. The dates in the book were unfamiliar to Jan. He now knew however, that London was a real place, and as he read further Jan determined that the story took place in the past. Perhaps the events of the book happened around the same time that they were perfecting the rules of tennis.

Jan didn't contemplate reading another book. He moved through the doors of the library and sat on the stairs to read *Brave New World* by the light of the glow-tube. There was so much that excited Jan's mind. The people in Huxley's book had achieved happiness through the control of reproduction and genetic engineering, as well as the assistance of the pleasure drug Soma. Jan thought about Dr. Osler's 'rumoured' Flash addiction and how he often referred to it as Soma. He continued reading and was absorbed by strange objects such as a 'Feelie', a type of movie that stimulated the brain through sight and touch. Then as the characters developed, he found himself empathising with Bernard who felt that something was missing from his life. Jan appreciated that the absence of individuality and the existence of mass sterility were issues that had obviously been overcome. But as he read the words of the World Controller trying to explain to Bernard and the Savage why contentment is more important than freedom or truth, Jan wondered if there were parts of this society that still existed in his world.

On the last few pages, there was a review of the book, where the author compared the pre-war Huxley manuscript to the post-war Orwell book *1984*. Jan wondered if the war fixed some of the problems that he saw existing in the society in the book. He searched for the book *1984*, but he couldn't find it. Frustrated, Jan knew it was time to return to the dorm. It was almost daybreak. This time Jan didn't take a book with him, for fear that Dix would find it. Besides, even with hemochromatosis, he was feeling tired. He knew he would be sleeping, not reading, for the rest of the day.

Jan didn't partake in any of that day's activities. The nurse that gave him a pass came in to see him several times, only to find him sleeping. She reported the case to Dr. Primero, who instructed Dr. Osler to go have another look at Jan.

"We can't afford to lose that boy at this point in the game," Primero stated.

Dr. Osler came into Jan's room just as Jan woke up.

"It seems like I'm always asking you how you are feeling Jan. What's going on?"

The Gemini Project 89

"It's nothing. I'll be fine," Jan grumbled. He was quite moody because of his lack of sleep and he was acting like a typical 17-year-old teenager, something not customary for Jan.

"Look, I can tell that something is bothering you and you aren't running a fever. Are you worried about your renaissance again?"

"No. I don't care about that."

"Then what is it? Is there something I could give you to make you feel better?"

"I'd like you to get me a book," Jan stated.

"Sure champ, I'll try. What sport are we talking about?" Dr. Osler enquired.

"No sport. *1984*."

"1984?" the doctor asked raising an eyebrow.

"*1984* by George Orwell."

"Where did you hear about this? I'm not sure I could give it to you even if I found it. I'm going to have to review these rule books before I give them to you from now on," Dr. Osler stated, thinking about his 'Big Brother' comment on the previous day.

He had tried to make an innocuous statement to dismiss Jan's request, but he could see that Jan was still waiting for a real response.

"Look, Jan ... *1984* is a piece of fiction, there is no point in you reading fiction. Let's just stick to the sports stuff."

"Fiction?" Jan posed, pretending not to know the word.

"Yea, you know ... make-believe ... stuff made up for the purpose of entertaining the readers."

"Then wouldn't it entertain me?"

"Sure, I guess ... but that's not the point. It's about stuff that you wouldn't understand."

"I think I'd surprise you," Jan said revealing a little too much to Dr. Osler.

The doctor already knew that there was a deeper understanding in Jan than most people realized, but requesting a book that he should have no knowledge of, displayed a new level of comprehension.

"Yes, I don't doubt that you would champ. Alright, look, the book is about a society that burns books. Everyone's lives are controlled by the all-knowing Big Brother that spies on people. A guy called Winston tries to get away to a group known as the Brotherhood, but in the end, the Thought Police capture him. There, is that what you wanted to know?"

Jan wondered how many pages it took Orwell to say the same thing. He also wondered if he asked for a synopsis on *Brave New World*, if he'd get a 15-second version of that as well. Dr. Osler saw Jan's disapproving look.

"Look, I'm not getting you the book, so that's that. Now I'm going to tell Dr. Primero that you're fine and you'll be participating in everything tomorrow, so stop moping and get yourself out of bed in the morning."

With that, Dr. Osler left the room and when he muttered the words 'spoiled brat' under his breath, Jan pulled the dictionary from the drawer in the side table and read what Osler was referring to. Jan was seeing a side to Osler that he didn't like.

After lights-out, Jan went back to the library. He made it a nightly routine for the next five nights, sometimes staying for only two or three hours, sometimes spending more than half the night reading. He didn't risk taking any more books out of the library though. His performance in the daily sporting activities was noticeably poorer. Coaches, trainers, and doctors all pointed out the rapid decline, but Jan didn't care. He caught a quick nap and wound up sleeping past his tee-time on the Friday, and Dr. Primero was particularly upset as they had been paired up.

Saturday was the easiest day to get caught up with sleep, because when you were eliminated from the obstacle course, you headed back to your room. The last person at each station was automatically eliminated, so Jan just made sure he trailed Jet to the first set of ropes. Jan stood at the bottom of the rope ladder for what felt like a perpetuity. At one point, he considered pushing Jet over the obstacle. Finally, he finished last and was eliminated. He headed back to his room for a nap.

That evening, he went back to the fiction section again. He flipped through books to get an understanding of what they were about, and then delved into the ones that interested him. One book, *The Fixed Period* by Anthony Trollope, puzzled him, even though he used the dictionary to decode the text. Set in the year 1980, in the country of Britannula, the citizens were forced to retire at the age of 67 at which time they would prepare for euthanasia.

Jan became upset when he read the definition of euthanasia:

The painless killing of a patient suffering from an incurable and painful disease or in an irreversible coma.

To the people of Britannula, age was a disease that was cured by the killing of its citizens. Why would it be acceptable for people to be killed in this way? Jan slammed the book closed and threw it to the library floor. It left him with an uneasy feeling, almost a nausea. The flap on the back of the book said that it was published in 1881 and was a satirical view of the future. Jan hadn't read the back flap.

Jan moved to another section of the library. He was interested in finding a book on science but found himself in the 'Biography' section. He found a book on *Fifty Famous Scientists* by Mungo Walker. The scientists were presented in temporal order, so Jan first struggled to read about Archimedes and Hipparchus. The chapter on Marie Curie was easier to read but was still difficult to understand. He flipped ahead to scan chapters on Albert Einstein, Stephen Hawking, Tim Berners-Lee, and Bartel De Visie, then decided his time would be better spent elsewhere.

He moved to the back of the library, where he discovered a shelf that he hadn't paid attention to before. The 'Periodicals and Magazines' shelf was filled with unbound and bound texts that were usually accompanied by plenty of pictures. Jan gravitated to one magazine that seemed to have the most amazing covers: *Rolling Stone*.

He looked at the September 1980 edition and saw a large picture of Billy Joel who was posing in a boxing stance. On the cover of the Rolling Stone, he read: 'Billy Joel is Angry', 'Van Halen Hits the Top', and 'Jimmy Connors Grows Up'. He started reading about Billy Joel ... 'In a gutsy interview with Rolling Stone, the *Glass House* superstar throws a few stones of his own'. Jan lost interest as he didn't understand what an album release was. Next, he moved to the story of Van Halen, but he couldn't discern the meaning of the words 'Heavy Metal Lust' or why someone released 'Women and Children First'.

However, he did understand most of the story about Jimmy Connors, a story of a tennis player who had 'antics' on and off the court. Apparently, Connors was one of the great players, but he was also known for his bad temper. Jan thought it reasonable when

Connors concluded that his career was over at the age of 27. The article reminded Jan of Dr. Osler's statement that he had watched the greatest tennis tournament in 2015. He decided to close the 1980 magazine and try to find details of the 2015 match.

He flipped through the magazines until he found the April 2015 edition of *Rolling Stone*. On the cover was a close-up picture of David Bowie. Jan was fascinated by Bowie's piercing eyes, his funky hair style and the stubble on his chin. The main stories were 'Black Sabbath Reunite', 'Al Gore's Grim Warning'. 'On the Road with Muse' and detailed coverage on 'David Bowie's Surprise Return'. The Al Gore story was the only one that Jan understood easily. It read like one of Dr. Osler's climate rants. Jan was missing too much context to understand the other stories. He looked up 'group' in the dictionary but somehow the definition wasn't explaining what 'the group announces a new tour' meant, and there were two stories that revolved around this fact.

Next, he moved to the March 2034 edition. The main stories were 'An Interview with The Doctor', 'Black Sabbath Reunite, Again', 'The Rolling Stones Upcoming Tour' and 'The Cello Makes a Rock-n-Roll Comeback'. The cover featured a picture of a doctor that Jan didn't know, but behind him stood a young doctor that Jan thought looked like Dr. Primero. The face was so familiar that Jan decided that it had to be either Primero or perhaps his younger brother. But who was the doctor in the foreground and why would Dr. Primero even be in the picture? The picture wasn't taken at the Corpo Academy.

He turned to page 18 as instructed on the cover, then began to read *An Interview with the Doctor*. There was an introductory section where a Dr. De Visie discussed the explorer Ponce de Leon. The articles said that De Visie was the creator of *The Gemini Project*, and the author of *The Book of Generations*. Jan had no understanding of the project or the book. He continued to read the article, but he was more interested in pushing through for an explanation as to why Dr. Primero or his brother would be on the cover. There were a few more pictures of just Dr. De Visie, then the article said, "continued on page 94". Jan was getting frustrated having to use his dictionary only to find out that the article was full of fluff.

He flipped to the article's continuation. In the latter half of the magazine there were fewer pictures and a lot more words. Jan decided

The Gemini Project

to read a few more paragraphs to see if there was anything interesting, and then move on if it didn't pick up. He was about to read a paragraph on the Gemini Project. Dr. Osler had told Jan that life is usually a journey, but there are always precise moments when that journey takes a change in direction. Jan was at one of those points. Once he had finished reading the *Rolling Stone* article, his life would become consumed by the underlying message.

7. An Interview with the Doctor, con't

... continued from page 20.

"The brain is man's most powerful organ. It is the organ that holds the capacity to resolve the medical challenges that reside in all the other organs. The miracle of our firing synapses was the precursor for the first hyper-computer and the model for true artificial intelligence. By in large, the brain is virtually infallible. While there may be cases of dementia or other brain related diseases, resolving these should be the primary focus of our medical research. Extend the life expectancy of the brain and you can extend the life expectancy of the organ that holds our collective knowledge, our memories, and our hope for the future. There is little point in spending time and effort on the other organs, given the importance of the brain. On Jardin Island, we removed a human brain from a dying body and stimulated it on 'life support', and that original experiment has resulted in the survival of an individual's brain for over twenty years now. That is twenty years beyond the death of its original body.

This was the start of the Gemini Project, where the challenge then became how to find a new vehicle to support the brain once the body no longer thrived. The unfortunate opportunity arose when a fatal head injury left a fellow islander in a coma. His body was still strong but he had suffered severe anoxic brain injury. At the same time, one of our staff was in his last days battling a cancer that was eating away at his lower body. That's when we made the bold move and attempted to salvage the best remaining organs of both men. We performed the first successful human brain transplant out of the necessity presented to us by two dying men. At first, the operation appeared successful, and our cancer patient even revived long enough to discover that he was no longer a middle-aged balding man. He had become a twenty-three-year-old, well conditioned youth. After a few hours however, he lost consciousness, and he was unable to enjoy his newfound life. The body rejected the foreign organ, taunting us with the knowledge that the brain could survive in another organism, but with little insight as to why the transplanted organ did not take root."

Q: What were your next steps?

"For the next five years, we concentrated our research on why one body rejects another man's organs and came to some pretty non-dramatic conclusions that may appear obvious in hindsight. Before you can perform a transplant, there is a multitude of prerequisites to consider. You have to ensure that the host and the donor are free from certain infectious diseases, and you have to determine the health of the host system with respect to other non-transplanted organs. That means for something as simple as a liver transplant you are performing an x-ray to determine how the lungs and chest are functioning, an electrocardiogram to determine how the heart is functioning, an ultrasound with Doppler examination to determine the openness of the bile ducts and major vessels, a CAT scan to provide a computerized image showing the size and shape of the patient's liver and a total-body bone scan in the case where the host patient has a liver tumour, to ensure that it has not spread to his bones. That's all in addition to the pulmonary function test, the hepatic angiograph, the technetium scan, the upper and lower gastrointestinal series, and the renal function studies that are all required for the liver transplant. In short, even the simplest organ transplant is relatively complicated.

With all of these tests, the human anatomy is such that it still expects certain fundamental physiological structures to be present in every organ that the body contains, or it will reject the organ. Thus, for one body to accept an organ from another body you also have to match blood chemistries, blood type, tissue type, immune systems and DNA forms. That is why it is likely that one brother can donate a liver to another brother without it being rejected, provided of course that he has the same blood-type, etc. In simple terms, you can't put an engine from a 2024 Chevy into a 2015 Toyota."

Q: Did this change your approach?

"Of course. We needed to put that 2024 Chevy engine into the chassis of another 2024 Chevy, which in human terms meant that our research then shifted on how to best increase the matchability of the physical organs. Since we detached at the spinal cord, the host held a rejection factor, but the spinal cord still had to match the cerebellum and the lobes of the cerebrum; in essence the body had to match the brain.

Then in the summer of 2013, a tragedy once again provided us with an opportunity. Twin brothers, ironically both medical students from Italy, were involved in a boating accident, one brother damaging his head on a rock, while the other severely damaged his legs on the boat's propeller. Albeit for different reasons, both brothers were on life support systems with little hope in the prognosis. With the family's consent, we performed a revolutionary transplant procedure to see if the brain would permanently accept new spinal cord roots.

Within a week, the newly formed brother, consisting of the two halves of the dying brothers, was able to walk, eat, feel, and think. The body of young Corpo Rocco Primero was the perfect host for the brain of his twin brother Cervello Angelo Primero. The extraordinary factor was that, because they were maternal twins, stemming from the fertilization of a single ova by a single sperm, Cervello's physical body was so similar to that of his brother's that he was conscious for days before he realized that he was no longer living in his own body. If not for a childhood injury to his lower calf, he may have never realized his transformation. So, I declared that Cervello Angelo was alive, and that Corpo Rocco had passed on.

As a condition of our funding however, the success of this operation wasn't made public at the time. In order to repay our benefactors, we would need more than one success before we went public. The challenge with going public is that your competitor gains the knowledge of the possible, so we needed to make sure we could replicate this success before we lost our first mover advantage.

We were not so lucky however with our next attempt. The subsequent operation between twins failed, even though the tests indicated that there was a high probability of a match. Both brothers had the same blood type, etc., but as fraternal twins, they were the product of the fertilization of two distinct ova by two different sperm. There was nothing to say that these two brothers were even conceived during the same act of coitus. It became clear that the matching tests needed to hone-in on more sophisticated factors other than the ones we were testing for at that time."

Q: How long did it take to find the solution?

"It was a full decade later before we had our next break-through. The brain is an amazing thing. It never ceases to amaze me at how creative it can be or how it holds the natural ability to repair itself.

One of my favourite stories on neuroplasticity is the story of Barbara Arrowsmith-Young. As a child she was diagnosed as being dim-witted, so they put her in a class for slow learners. But she wasn't slow, she was brilliant. Her brain just didn't function correctly. The neuron clusters that processed relationships were failing. So, you could tell her this is the mother, this is the daughter, then ask 'what is their relationship?', and she wouldn't be able to answer you. However, she realized that if she read and re-read assignments, she could memorize the answers even though her brain couldn't derive the answer. So, she read every assignment ten times, memorized answers, got out of the slow class, worked her way through high school and university, then became a doctor in a research lab, where .... get ready for it ... she researched her own cognitive malfunctions and created a neuroplasticity program to cure her own disease.

Why is that story relevant? Well, we had been advancing our research slowly when a young graduate doctor approached me with an idea stemming from the application of our most recent theory. Our tests were such that we believed that only a maternal twin was guaranteed to provide an acceptable host, and not everyone has a maternal twin to supply spare parts. At the time, we were working on the theory that a same-sex child, with certain like-characteristics, could provide an acceptable host. The young doctor that helped us succeed to the next level was also the first successful survivor of The Gemini Project, Dr. Cervello Primero. Of all people, more than anyone, he understood the value of life beyond one's own body's expiration date. With no fanfare, he came into my office and stated that he wanted us to test his eight-year-old son for suitability as a host for his brain. The rest, as they say, is history."

And the rest really *is* history. Dr. De Visie's now famous manuscript, *The Book of Generations*, became the basis for The Gemini System and life as we know it. There are numerous diseases that have been wiped out thanks to Dr. De Visie and even the hope of world peace stemmed from Dr. De Visie's toils. Dr. De Visie has not only made it possible to 'live forever', but he has made it desirable to do so.

8. Generations

Dr. Osler entered Jan's room to see if the boy was feeling any better. Since Jan had participated in all of that day's activities, he was sure that Jan was over his bout of melancholy and perhaps the two could have another meaningless but entertaining conversation. Jan was there by himself, sitting on the edge of his bed with his head draped down, cupped between his hands.

"Are you heading down to the lounge now?" Dr. Osler asked.

"*The Book of Generations*," Jan blurted out.

Osler's face changed. He had been accused of many things before, including in a newspaper article that highlighted his disregard for an ex-girlfriend's life, however he had never been this close to a capital crime. He did not like it.

"Who have you been speaking with?" Osler snapped.

"No one. I want you to tell me about *The Book of Generations*," demanded Jan.

They were attempting to stare each other down, not unlike the tactics they sometimes used in a game of chess. Osler's adamant voice had laid down a Sicilian Defence to Jan's opening demands, but the boy's aggressive response had countered with a Smith-Morra Gambit. Osler looked around the room as if he expected to see someone or something that could explain Jan's newfound knowledge. He reflected for a moment, and a prick of guilt entered his mind. Had he been the one to blurt something out to Jan, while in the midst of a drug-induced conversation?

"Look, I don't know what you've heard or who you've been talking to, but don't think for one minute that you can make demands of me. Trust me, this is for your own good, as well as mine."

"I'll repeat ... I've spoken to no one. But you might be interested to know that I believe that my whole life is a lie. My life is based on a work of fiction ... some sort of deception and everyone around me has been lying to me ... for my entire life ... and that includes you. So, I will make demands. I demand to know the truth. And if you don't tell me to my satisfaction, I'll tell Gemini Project graduate number one, Dr. Primero, what I know, and I'll tell him that it was you who clued me in. Now ... *The Book of Generations*."

The boy had sacrificed his pawn, placed his bishop on the attack and the doctor was searching for a suitable place to post his queen. There was an air of confidence in Jan that Osler had never seen before, outside of sports. He didn't like it. It was based in anger, and it reminded him of Dr. Primero. Osler looked at the youngster for a change, instead of gazing through him. He could sense the determination and he knew it would be pointless trying to placate him. But Osler also knew that if he said anything further, it would be committing a crime. Fuck it, what difference would it make if the kid understood his ephemeral existence? The end was inevitable and if any boy deserved the truth, this was the one.

Knowing that he needed to give Osler time to think about his options, Jan didn't say anything further.

"Fine," Osler finally stated, "it doesn't really matter to me. I'm dying here anyway. I've had enough of this whole thing. I'll tell you what you want to know, but don't tell me afterwards that you wish I hadn't told you. So, let's start with what you know."

Jan had been careful not to indicate what he knew and how he knew it.

"No, you tell me about the book. You tell me about how The Gemini Project led to the book which led to all this. You tell me about how Dr. De Visie created this nightmare."

To Osler, it almost sounded like Jan already knew everything and was just looking for confirmation. Could he have reasoned it out for himself? No, that was inconceivable. However the student had come to ask this question, Osler was impressed. Jan's growing distrust of the doctor was also clear. He was convinced that Osler was stalling, but Osler was actually just trying to figure out where to begin ... how to recount this story to someone who had lived through so little in their lifetime. Someone who lived a life so far from reality that, up until this point, they didn't even know that they were living a life based on total falsehoods. But the boy knew now. Osler thought that he shouldn't talk about things that were legally defined as unmentionable, but he decided that this didn't bother him. What bothered him was that he could barely bring himself to think about the acts that would have been proscribed when he attended med school.

"Okay," Osler said raising his voice in frustration, "just give me a minute here."

With that cue, Osler reached into the inside pocket of his jacket, pulled out a small electronic device and held it to his eyes. A brief flash reflected off the doctor's face and when he lowered his hands, Jan could see that the flash had been accompanied by a light-blue liquid, which was running down Osler's cheeks. Jan noticed that Osler's eyes had changed, they had dilated. He thickened his gaze.

"There," Osler started, "now I'm ready for you."

Osler stared at Jan waiting for a cue.

"Well?" Jan eventually snapped, letting his frustrations show.

"Well ..." Osler said laughing to himself, "here's one for you ... so the doctor was selling brains and asked $5,000 for a man's brain and $100 for a woman's brain. 'Wait', objected the woman. Why is a woman's brain worth so much less? It's because the man's brain was in better condition ... because it hadn't been used. You get it?"

Osler's newly induced state was frustrating to Jan and the boy countered with a harsh stare that trapped Osler's attention.

"Anyway, I used to start my speeches with that one, and it always brought a laugh ... nothing? Fine," relented Osler, "but you have to give me a starting point so we're not wasting each other's time. I have no idea what you know, what you think you know and what you don't know."

"Okay," Jan agreed, "Dr. Bartel De Visie lived on Jardin Island. It was there that he conducted the Gemini experiments and wrote *The Book of Generations* ..."

"Right," Osler began slowly. "Damned Jardin Island ... a privately-owned nation state and for all intents and purposes it was independent of any other country. De Visie had been hired by a wealthy industrialist at the turn of the century. There was a fair amount of panic around Y2K and the end of the world, so people were getting ready for the apocalypse, some more than others. Anyway, De Visie was to continue his work on trying to escape the hand of death. Stop me if you've heard this, or if I am going too fast for you or if you don't understand this stuff."

"Just talk," Jan fired back, letting his rage remain at the surface.

"Right. De Visie had studied under the Russian surgeon Dr. Vladimir Demikhov," Osler continued. "Now there was a number. Old Vladimir was the first doctor to transplant an auxiliary heart into the chest of a warm-blooded animal. He pioneered much of modern surgery, and he was the first to perform successful heart and lung transplants on dogs in 1946 ... that's over 170 years ago. He probably would have been one of the most renowned surgeons and everyone would know his name, but then Vlad turned out to be one really sick puppy. He grafted the upper body of a dog onto another dog, creating a two-headed mutant. He had no medical reason to create the beast, he did it just to say that he could. Although the animal died within the month, it did live for a period of time and that was all that mattered to Vlad.

Here's where the hand-off happens ... in 1980, Vlad hired a young nip-and-tuck doctor from Holland to translate his work in 'transplantology' into Dutch for him. The young doctor was extremely interested in the two-headed dog and wondered why Vlad had stopped experimenting. Soon, Vlad and his protégé were back in the lab trying to figure out how to make the dog live longer, but also how to function with two brains. Surely with the medical advances of the last quarter century, the two men could produce a better Frankenstein. I know, I know ... Frankenstein is the doctor not the monster, but don't blame me ... blame the movie 'Bride of Frankenstein' ... that's where the confusion started."

"Dr. Demikhov!" Jan prodded to get Osler back on track.

The Gemini Project 103

"Yea, yea. When old Vlad retired in 1986, he left all his lab notes to a young doctor De Visie, but not without leading him down the transplantology rabbit hole. De Visie got serious about performing a brain transplant in a mammal, but then Vlad kicked the bucket before De Visie reached the pinnacle of his success.

On Jardin Island, armed with a crazy amount of funding, De Visie was able to continue Vlad's work. But it wasn't just the money, he also had fewer constraints so there was nothing to stop him going wherever his scalpel took him. He soon discovered he was able to keep a human brain alive after the body had given in. He concluded that a well-cared-for brain could last as long as four or five hundred years, providing you avoided a few degenerative diseases. If you could keep the brain alive, the next step was to attach it to a willing host. Thanks to a fortunate accident, he finally conducted the first successful brain transplant, and proved that one human vessel could be used to house another. Once cephalic transplantation in man became a technical reality, the task was then understanding what made a good host vessel. The best candidate for hosting a male brain was first thought to be a maternal twin, but it turned out to be a male offspring …"

Osler's voice trailed off again as he pondered the next piece of his tale. Jan was used to the doctor's banter taking a turn as he recounted a story, but this time he needed to ensure that Osler kept on point.

"Yes," Jan goaded him on, even though he was unsure of exactly where the story was headed, "and that's when Dr. Primero, Dr. Cervello Angelo Primero, offered his son as a host."

Osler could see that Jan had somehow done his homework and that he understood the doctor's narration up to this point. The doctor deduced that somehow Jan must have got access outside of the school's boundary wall. But how? Digivices were keyed to the owner's biometric protocols, so no student could use it even if they found one. Some of what Jan said could be deduced, but the basic premise required some underlying knowledge of the facts. Could the story be derived somehow by reading words in a dictionary? Osler had stopped telling his story as his mind wondered down the path of trying to understand Jan's newfound knowledge.

Then Jan blurted out, "You tell me where, when and why men stopped dying at the expense of their own children."

The bluntness of this last statement was a revelation for Jan even as he said it. He may have acquired some information about *Generations*, but he was processing the ethical dilemma that had been burdening Osler.

"Right," Osler snapped as his mind went back to storytelling mode. "Where was I? De Visie and Primero ... okay, so together they raised Primero's first-born son to be the ideal host for Primero's change of mind. Then on the kid's 18th birthday, poor little Uno said goodbye to the world as he knew it and went under the knife. When he awoke, Dr. Primero was an eighteen-year-old body with the mind of a fifty-year old man. That mind was now living in its third host.

You would think that Primero would have been satisfied with this, but it was less than a month before he was already talking with De Visie on how soon he should pack up his cerebral tent and make the move to Uno's younger brother. De Visie however had moved on to bigger and better things. The success of the transplants went public, although the story was spun as a miracle to solve a medical necessity. This transplant cast a world-wide spotlight on De Visie and when the spotlight shines on you, sometimes you cast a large shadow.

De Visie's discoveries were too late to save the fatherless wealthy billionaire who had financed the project up to that point, but there were plenty of similar megalomaniacs waiting in the wings to take his place. They all started courting him, but De Visie held off. After the billionaire passed away, De Visie was on the verge of losing his island and he needed to come up with a way to further fund his experiments. And by this time De Visie was already in his 70s, so he also needed to find a host for his visionary brain. However, his youngest child was a daughter, and his son was already 35 years old and still lived in Holland. De Visie invited his son to the island for an all expenses paid visit with his now famous father and soon after the son arrived, his father passed away. Before you could say 'generations', the son was operating the family business as though he already knew how to do it."

Osler dropped another Flash, let his eyes roll further back and continued his speech with even more animation, almost as though he forgot that he was speaking to Jan.

"That to me was the harshest regeneration. It wasn't bumping off a person that you barely knew ... someone that had been cultivated for a specific purpose ... it was your adult son that you encouraged to come over for a visit because he loved you. Everyone knew that it was just the same Dr. De Visie in a new chassis, but it would be years before he admitted that he took his own son's body as a host.

Anyway, it was this De Visie, Bartel De Visie junior, that wrote *The Book of Generations*. That was a decade after his own rehosting and by then De Visie was the richest man in the world. De Visie was now an 89-year-old brain in a 45-year-old body, confessing that he was really the father, not the son. I'm not sure he knew how people were going to take his book. *Generations* is a combination autobiography and surgical procedures manual, which also attempted to tackle the associated moral dilemma. The book documents the fundamentals of the transplant, but it reads more like a religious treatise than a medical procedural manual. However, De Visie didn't write for the masses. He wrote to portray a way of life and justify why that way would be better for mankind. You knew that he believed he could lead us to his new utopia, and I bought into the philosophy. I became part of his medical team that let the rich of the world buy into the fact that they could live forever, not IN the eyes of their children but THROUGH the eyes of their children. Fuck it … many of them raised their kids dispassionately anyway, through nannies and private schools and the like, so the leap wasn't as far as you might think. I made it. Kids were raised to be vessels for their father's brains, and that was that."

As Jan listened, he was anticipating the story's endpoint. The punchline to another one of Osler's jokes that wouldn't evoke his laughter. But the final sentence confirmed the fear that had been growing within him … boys were raised to be vessels for their father's brains, and that was that. Jan was being cultivated for his father to assume his body. He was unsure if the exchange happened at the school or after the boys headed into the city, but either way the renaissance was a death, not a rebirth after all. That meant that if nothing changed, he had only a few weeks to live.

'Renaissance Hall … renaissance, re-birth … just not mine … I get it. I get it now,' Jan thought to himself.

"Okay, keep up with me now. I skipped over how the medicine turned into money," Osler continued. "With the backing of the wealthy, De Visie was able to penetrate political regimes and the economic world faster than anyone could have imagined. A few well-placed hosts and you could dominate an industry. You wouldn't understand how well an 18-year-old kid, who really had the maturity, savvy, and experience of a 50-year-old businessman, could do when he 'entered' the labour-force. Especially when you enter with the type of connections that could get you anywhere, anything or anyone. De Visie and his band of select immortals were able to further perfect his medical research, but along the way De Visie also amassed a considerable amount of wealth for himself. He invested heavily in technology and with advancements in artificial intelligence, De Visie knew the value of big data. AI imitates the brain's processing but with access to virtually infinite data, an AI solution was a better solution."

Osler had lost Jan, who was sitting on the edge of the bed saying nothing ... but once again, Osler was no longer even paying attention to his audience. He was saying things aloud that he only barely formulated previously.

"De Visie was actually a lot more intuitive than I gave him credit for. While others were working on nanobots to repair the body, De Visie skipped this step in the road to immortality by rendering it needless. While the rest of us thought that technology would lead to robots doing mundane tasks, he knew that big data would replace opinions, not replace tasks. He knew that doctors would be replaced before nurses. I mean I really didn't see that coming, but the traditional doctor was just an educated person making a prognosis based on the information he had access to. An AI doctor could take the symptoms and take more data into consideration, to come up with a better analysis. Then in the end, in the short term at least, you still needed the nurse to give you that needle.

With De Visie's ability to grow a network and the network node's ability to grow themselves into positions of power, the good doctor soon controlled most of the world's traditional political and economic structures. With that powerbase, he proceeded to build a world that was mature and continued to improve, but in a controlled fashion. By the time *The Book of Generations* was published, the world had already become the world according to De Visie. I know I said that the good doctor didn't invest in drug companies, but that was when they were in their evil carnation. Eventually, his consortium held the controlling interest in all the major drug manufacturers. After that, all it took was one bad airborne virus, where De Visie says 'Let it Ride', and the creation of a vaccine was magically delayed, and the population was under control. You put that together with the failure to acknowledge the climate crisis, and you have a planet surface that no longer supports our lifeform. That's when I joined De Visie's team ... that's when I HAD to join De Visie's team."

There was a lot of information for Jan to process. More than he needed to hear. He was still stuck on wrapping his mind around his inevitable death. However, he did realize that he was also just informed about a philosophical societal shift that led to the growth of a new empire, all built on the deaths of young boys. An empire where his death was just part of the basis for how society continued.

"Wait, you're not saying that you believe that this is a good thing, are you?" Jan asked, again displaying his obvious anger.

"Jan, you wouldn't understand. You don't know, what you don't know. You were born 18 years ago. I was born in 2004. I'm 112-years-old and I have seen the best and the worst of mankind. The worst was a century ago. The world that I was raised in consisted of poverty and hunger, with one-third of us living in conditions that were unfit for animals. The advanced nations didn't want the underdeveloped nations to pollute, because they had already pillaged the natural resources to gain an advantage. War was inevitable. Before we launched the Gemini System, crop blights and dust storms threatened humanity's very survival. Corn became the last viable crop. The world had evolved into a post-truth society where younger generations were taught false intelligence that used to be considered conspiracy theories, such as the idea that the Apollo moon missions were faked. De Visie brought an end to that. He architected a new hope for mankind. All because he solved the mystery of the brain.

Did you know that people used to believe that memory loss was a natural part of aging ... what a ridiculous thought. It was part of a disease that was brought on when you were older. By focusing research on the brain and dropping nugatory research on other organs, De Visie revolutionized medicine. Not long before I entered medical school, we used to shock people with suspect brains, did you know that? Electroconvulsive therapy they called it ... but it was outright torture.

We gave people antidepressants that didn't even come close to addressing the cause of mental disorders, and instead just masked them. That's how we treated the brain. De Visie declared war on the goddamned insurance companies. He did a lot of investing in corporations and even lobbyists, but he never put a dime into insurance companies, and he only invested in drug manufacturers to enact change. It was De Visie that banned Zoloft and instead he used the research money to look for the root cause, not to drug away the effects of something like post partum depression, but to cure it. Man, when I was a kid, Ritalin was the first street drug that I got addicted to. It was De Visie who proved that there was no such thing as a real chemical imbalance. He is the reason that my mind didn't waste away sometime last century.

It was De Visie who put an end to Alzheimer's disease, and he did that within the first year of opening the De Soto Research Institute. There's a good example of a disease that we once thought was hereditary, but it turned out to be nothing of the sort. A simple combination of storing food in tin cans and the release of androgen into the body ... who would have thought? De Visie, that's who! No one else put together that the disease didn't exist before we stored food in cans. No one else put together that women never contracted the disease until after menopause ... that's when testosterone overwhelms their chemical balance.

I tell you, you wouldn't understand Jan, but the reality was that no one really cared enough to fund the research because it was a degenerative disease that afflicted the elderly, who were probably going to die of something else once their bodies gave in anyway. You see, research was dictated by drug companies. Solving a disease that only afflicted the elderly didn't give you many years to get a return. Providing a drug like Ritalin to kids and getting them hooked on it, gave you a lifetime of sales. But thanks to De Visie, once you take away the problem of the body failing, you suddenly realize that solving the Alzheimer enigma grows pretty important."

Osler stopped and looked at Jan who was still processing the information as best he could. The doctor began to get introspective, caring even less about his audience.

"The fact that the memory faded but emotions remained in Alzheimer patients makes it all look pretty obvious in hindsight."

He paused again. Jan waited, trying not to show that he was getting overloaded with information.

"Dr. Asino, now there's a jackass for you. He was one degree of separation away from Vlad and the two-headed dog. De Visie admired his work in neuroplasticity, so he gave him a wide berth to figure out how we could cram more into our brains. You see it was easy to learn a second language when you were five, but it was damn near impossible when you were fifty. With all these aging brains, we needed to be able to store more and recall more. Asino cut open the head of a newborn chimpanzee and mapped the firing of the synapses as he prodded each of the chimp's fingers. He then smashed one of those fingers rendering it useless and confirmed that the associated synapses were no longer firing. He sewed up the chimp's head, then six months later opened it up again. Lo and behold the unused synapses were now firing when he prodded the other fingers. Through this type of brute force, Asino's experiments were not only able to prove that the brain wasn't hardwired, but he was able to derive a way to rewire unused synapses. Asino probably went through a couple of hundred chimps on the way, but De Visie valued the results, not the methods. And the result was a way to remap unused portions of grey matter, so that it could be put to better use. If you wanted to learn Spanish and you had a fifty-year-old brain, no worries, we just used the part of your brain that questioned authority and society's standards.

De Visie had dozens of similar separate tracts that were exclusively working on exploring the brain, its functions and its diseases. Soon we were discovering the homogeneity of aging within the cortex and the dramatic differences in aging between cortex and cerebellum. We were realizing through molecular and cell biology that we could diminish brain cell erosion. We were uncovering that every time humans blink, the part of the brain that deals with vision briefly shuts down, so we could actually learn how to put the brain to sleep for nanoseconds to extend its life expectancy even further. We were relaxing our constraints on stem cell research and therapy, so we tested on animals to learn how best to treat diseases of the human brain."

"But it's just not right," Jan protested, sounding like he was objecting to stem cell research, but he was still stuck on the principle of brain transplantation. "You killed people for your own purposes. You were purposefully killing off man's future and retaining its past."

"Don't you think that we, especially those of us in the medical field had to deal with that?" Osler responded, finally looking at his audience again. "But the advancements came on too quickly. On one hand mankind needed to reinvent itself, while on the other hand mankind wasn't ready socially, philosophically, or theologically for what De Visie presented us. Who knew that the intrinsic individuality, personality, emotional structure, intelligence, and memory would all continue to function after a transplant? With the realization that you could transplant consciousness, it was clear that the rest of the body only existed to support the brain. Therefore, the brain, not the body, is the casing for what we call the spirit or the soul of a man. This caused a religious upheaval. One that De Visie would also win."

"What do you mean soul?" Jan asked.

"I guest you haven't come across the concept of a man's soul. That has never been explained to you, has it?" Osler asked rhetorically, slowing down his pace. "I guess you haven't read that word in the dictionary yet. But you understand the word spirit ... because you demonstrated it every week in your sport, Jan. Well, the soul was a concept that was preached in the predecessor to *The Book of Generations* ... remember *The Bible*? I used to belong to a religion called Roman Catholics and we believed everything that it said in *The Bible*. But then ... I mean 'May the Body of Christ be With You', kind of lost its meaning."

Osler's speech continued to slow down.

"But De Visie offered a more tangible form of immortality, and he showed us that the soul could also be immortal. All you had to do was make a few sacrifices every so often. Man was always making sacrifices for one religion or another. But now, instead of a goat, it was your son."

Jan could see that he was starting to lose his orator, who had become increasingly reclusive. For the first time, Osler also sat down on the edge of Jan's bed. He took out the electronic device again and held it to his eyes. Flash. Blue Liquid. No Pain.

"The words of *The Bible* soon started to fail us. 'There is a spirit in man: and the inspiration of the Almighty giveth them understanding' ... that's from the chapter called Job. I don't know why, but that verse still sticks with me. De Visie was about to pick up that spirit and move it. He could move it. He could relocate the soul to a new housing. To many, he wasn't just PLAYING God. So, with the death of modern religion, a new religion was born and De Visie grew in spiritual strength the same way he grew in economic strength. It's hard to pass on your beliefs when your parishioners are dying but the members of the competitive religion continually live on, for generations and generations. Scientology proved that you could invent a religion and get some heavyweight people behind it in short order. With *Generations*, either you got on board, or you died … that's a pretty powerful motivator. And De Visie decided who he would let get on board."

Osler lay down on the bed and continued to talk about his Catholic religion complaining that he was a fool for 'paying false homage to the Roman Papal fallacy'. Jan could no longer follow the conversation. Eventually the doctor's words dissolved into what sounded like gibberish and then Osler finally passed out. Too much Flash had been dropped for one evening.

Jan didn't even pay attention to the crashed doctor on his bed. He was stuck on wondering what he could do to fight off his hosting future, when Dix entered the room about ten minutes later.

"You know, sometimes I listen to those guys talk and I can't even remember what they just said. It's like I'm hypnotized or something."

Dix looked down at the bed.

"What's wrong with the doc?" Dix asked.

"Overtired, I guess. He's been working extra shifts you know. I tried to wake him but he's just out of it."

"Let me try," Dix said as he approached Jan's bed.

"No, wait …" Jan called out as Dix started to shake Osler.

"You know what I'm talking about," Osler said almost instinctively sitting up in bed.

"He's not sleeping. What are you talking about, Dr. Osler?" Dix asked as Osler stumbled to his feet to continue his oration.

"There wa-sh a time," Osler slurred slowly, "when man didn't need doctors to stay healthy. We used doctors only if we were sick, but we lived a life of challenging work and natural exercise. Then we moved into offices, and we all got fat."

Dix started to laugh at the thought of people getting fat. He sat on the bed and prodded the doctor to continue.

"We got fat working hard. Working hard for your money … work's hard for the money … why you ask? You get a good job with good pay and you're okay. So, you save your money, you save up just to see a show. A show with lasers. And there on the stage the doctor says 'Relax, I need some information first … just the basic facts. Can you show me where it hurts?'"

"How long has he been going on like this?" Dix asked.

Dix had heard Dr. Osler babble before but had never heard him talk this way. He had never seen someone who was completely out of it, not even that time Jet tripped during basketball and smashed his head on the pole that holds up the basket.

Osler stood up and paced across the floor, gesturing with his hands. Jan got a good look at the doctor's eyes and saw that they were almost completely dilated.

"No, no ... not everyone went to the show. Some stayed back and worked and some of those refused to get fat. Some even exercised and stayed healthy. But, for every one person that exercised, we had nine more that were out looking for the quick fix. We had abdominoplasty, bariatric body contouring, blepharoplasty, Botox injections, augmentation mammoplasty, liposuction collagen fillers and even stomach staples for those who just couldn't control themselves. Yes, we were just too damned lazy. Oh, but we went one better than that didn't we. We couldn't be happy living in our disposable society, unless we created disposable bodies. Now you don't need to care for yourself because there's a new 'yourself' just around the corner! Sometimes you need a good revolution ... all it takes is one of us."

And with those final words, Osler turned and headed out of the room.

"What the H E double L?" Dix said.

"He's just talking in his sleep," Jan stated.

"Malarkey ... he's juiced!"

"Dix," Jan started solemnly, "just leave this one alone. Dr. Osler is the best doctor we've got here, and we don't want to get him in trouble."

"But he's baked more than a potato," Dix said, quoting something he'd heard his father say. "We should report him! I might get extra credits for this one. He is really juiced."

"D-iiiii-x!" Jan implored, but Dix just laughed and went to get changed for lights out.

The next day Jan was summoned to Dr. Primero's office. He knew he wouldn't be able to look at Primero the same. He knew that he would be looking into the eyes of Primero's great, great, grandson. As he was escorted in by Nurse Rossignol, Jan briefly wondered if there was any relationship between Primero and Rossignol ... not now, but at some point, in one of Primero's many pasts. He could sense something, first from the nurse and then he thought he caught something in Primero's face as she left. As Jan waited to be 'spoken to', he examined Primero's face. Jan wondered why it had never occurred to him before that Primero was so young. He looked just as young as his picture on the cover of the April 2034 edition of *Rolling Stone*.

"Jan," Primero snapped, catching Jan off guard. "I need you to help me with something."

Primero was demanding, not asking for 'help'. Jan used to wonder if Primero liked children. He no longer wondered. The doctor really didn't speak that much 'with' the boys, and he only occasionally spoke 'to' the boys. But Jan knew immediately ... this was different.

"Mr. Gémeaux here has made some pretty severe accusations," the doctor continued.

Primero had made a hand motion towards Dix. Jan looked over to see his roommate sitting in the corner of the room.

'Dix was being referred to as Gémeaux by Dr. Primero,' Jan's mind processed. '... but this is Dr. Cervello Angelo Primero, the first man to volunteer his own son for a renaissance operation.'

Jan tried to contain his anger.

"What? Are you, dense boy? Got nothing but muscle upstairs, I guess. Mr. Gémeaux here ... Dixon ... Alain's boy."

"Y-y-yes sir," Jan stuttered in a combination of nervousness and ire.

"Young Dix here said that Dr. Osler was 'juiced' in your room, is that true or not?"

"What do you mean 'juiced'?"

"Come on boy, I don't have time for this. Young Master Dix here said, and I quote 'he was higher than a baked potato'. Does that sound familiar to you now? Was Dr. Osler acting at all unusual in your room last night?"

"No sir ..." Jan started.

"Now look boy, before you answer, I already know that Osler is a Flash-addict, and I could hook him up if I cared enough, I just want to know if he was stoned in your room or not?"

"N-no sir," Jan continued, "we were just talking about history, and he was doing an imitation of a guy he called Hitler."

"Hitler? What the hell did he tell you about Hitler?"

"Nothing sir, just that there once was a crazy man who tried to burn all the sports books in the world, and that a fast runner in the Olympics embarrassed him. When I asked how crazy he was, Dr. Osler started raising his voice and gesturing with one hand. He said he was pretending to speak in another language. He was just trying to amuse me because he knew that I haven't been feeling too well."

"Is that right?" Primero asked. "Mr. Gémeaux, you said that you didn't understand all the words that Dr. Osler was saying?"

"Yea, but I didn't hear him talking about any limb-picks. No … I thought he made them up because he was juiced!" Dix responded.

"It's Olympics boy … juiced indeed. Gémeaux, I don't have any more time for your shit. Now, you boys get out of my sight. I have enough to do without babysitting both the boys and their doctor. Osler … talking about Hitler … you boys just stick to asking sports questions, okay?"

He didn't wait for a response, and just looked down at his digivice. The boys left the office and walked down the stairs. As they exited out of the Administration Building, Dix was unsure if Jan was angry or not. Once they had crossed the soccer field, Jan turned towards Dix and punched him, throwing his full weight behind the blow. Dix fell to the ground. His nose started bleeding.

"You stupid, stupid, stupid little boy," Jan screamed. "I told you not to get Dr. Osler in trouble. I need him."

"I'm sorry," Dix said as he cowered away. "I didn't mean for anything bad to happen. I just wanted to …"

Dix stopped speaking, seeing a different side to Jan. He wasn't his conciliatory, complacent self. Dix grew afraid of him. He knew that if they had a fight, Jan could beat him easily. Under normal circumstances Jan wouldn't engage in a brawl because his heart wouldn't be in it, but this was a different person. There was a fire burning inside him, and he was unusually angry.

"Shut up. And give me my book back," Jan barked and then he continued his march back to the dormitory.

They got back to their room and Dix sheepishly pulled *The Art of Democracy: A Concise History of Popular Culture in the United*

States by Jim Cullen, out from underneath his mattress. Jan abruptly grabbed the book. He would return it to the library after Dix was asleep.

That night, Jan searched the library for the *Book of Generations*, but was unable to find it. He barely read the spines of any other books while he searched. These visits to the library were now feeling like an effort and Jan was weighed down by the thought of his impending renaissance. He needed to talk with Osler about what to do next. Tomorrow was Tuesday, Dr. Osler's day off. Jan would have to wait until Wednesday evening to see the doctor again.

9. A Plan to Survive

Jan ran on autopilot the next day. He moved up and down the pitch at Paradise during the soccer game, but he rarely touched the ball. He couldn't stop thinking about what to do next. He concluded that he would need to get away from the Academy, but he had no idea where he would go. The only life he had known was at Corpo. But he now understood that his entire life had been based on untruths and falsehoods ... his story was fiction. While he had been waiting for his renaissance so he could live with his father in New London, every adult had known that there was a different plan. Even Osler, someone he thought was his mentor, his teacher, his friend, even Osler had let him believe in the fallacy.

At the end of the day, Jan sat alone in the lounge, wondering if there was a way out of the Academy. The only people that entered and exited the schools, did so via shuttles. Jan had never been inside a shuttle.

As he contemplated his options, Osler entered the room.

"Guess what? You've got me working Tuesday nights now. It seems that everyone thinks you are suffering from some sort of

The Gemini Project 117

teenage depression, so I've been assigned to babysit you. I don't know if that's because I'm so great at motivating you or because I have to pay some sort of Primero penance."

Jan sat in silence. He hadn't prepared his mind for a visit with Osler. Even though Osler's presence was a good thing, Jan still had to figure out how to get what he needed from the doctor.

"Oh. don't get me wrong ... they have no intention of curing you at this point. They just want to get you through to your renaissance," Osler continued. He could see what looked like tear tracks on Jan's cheeks. "And thanks for covering for me with Primero. Hitler was more inspired than you realize, and I guess he does sound like someone on a Flash rage."

"I didn't do it for you," Jan replied quietly.

"Still, you did it," Osler responded wondering why Jan was speaking so softly. He looked around the lounge again and could see they were alone.

"I want you to get me out of here," Jan said.

At first, Osler thought he meant the lounge, but then he realized the youth wanted to leave Corpo.

"I can't. It's not possible."

"Not only is it possible ... you'll do it."

Osler looked at Jan, realizing the boy was trying to exert some sort of control. He wasn't afraid of him, and Jan sensed that. The boy wasn't a threat. Osler sat down in his usual wingback. A few drops of potassium chloride in Jan's morning shots could bring a quick end to this conversation. There were so many ways that Osler could get rid of Jan and the school would just have to endure a little backlash from Jan's father.

"Stop trying to threaten me Jan," Osler said, without even an attempt to lower his volume. "It doesn't look good on you, and it won't work."

"I'm not threatening, I just ..."

"You just ... have to accept that I am not your enemy. I am a piece in the chess game, the same as you. We're both pawns at this point."

"So, does that mean that I have to be sacrificed? Will you help me or not?" Jan asked.

"I don't know how to help you, but I promise that if there's anything that I can do ..."

Osler's voice trailed off as Tam and Otto entered the lounge.

"Good evening boys. How was the game today?"

"We won," Tam replied. "Again. Four-nothing.'

The two boys sat on the couch on either side of Jan.

"And this guy," Otto said throwing his arms around Jan, "he was probably the worst player on the pitch."

"Well, that's because he was probably anticipating an evening of stimulating conversation with his favourite doctor," Osler said smiling at Jan.

All three boys stared back at the doctor who sat in his customary wingback chair.

"Well, what shall we talk about tonight? I can tell you about the Romans, or about my days in med school, or maybe you'd like to hear about the country of Spain!"

Tam and Otto groaned loud enough for Osler to hear.

None of the boys said anything. The only thing Jan wanted to talk about was how he could stay alive past his renaissance.

"Come on now," Osler prompted, "there must be something on your minds."

"How did we get here?" Jan asked.

There it was. The boy was asking 'how' but he really wanted to know 'why'. Jan never seemed to disappoint him. The doctor assumed that the boy was giving him permission to continue a diatribe on why society ended up the way it did. Something he could say in front of the other boys and only Jan would follow along. Okay Jan, you want to understand how bad life was when I was your age and you can see if the ends justify the mean, then get ready. Get ready for some unadulterated William Osler history and philosophy. See if you can handle this.

Osler started with the four basic societal doctrines. Predictably Tam and Otto got bored in less than two minutes and they retreated to the floor for a game of checkers. After five minutes, Osler finally paused to see if Jan was fully up to speed.

"Are you following me? Or do I need to go over some more of the history again or delve into the part that technology investments played?"

"You're not answering my question. I mean, how did *we* get *here*, me and my father," Jan asked with an undertone of anger.

"Oh," Osler muttered softly so the other two boys didn't overhear, "you and your father ... that's a bit harder to explain."

He couldn't explain it, but the doctor began to smile. As he gathered his thoughts, he took amusement in knowing the punchline to one of the greatest historical jokes: what had pulled down the great states of the twentieth century? Healthcare caused the bankruptcy of publicly funded systems, private systems and the goddamned insurance companies.

The paradox that it had been vast improvements in healthcare that destroyed the status quo really amused the doctor. He sat back in the reading chair and smirked as he thought about the irony that it wasn't a global pandemic that destroyed the systems, but it was instead the success of the medical advances used to fight the pandemic. In just under a decade, the average lifespan increased from 72 to over 82 years old. Thanks to improved antibiotics, DNA editors, gene therapy, stem cell research, and mRNA advancements, there was a momentous leap in medicine, which meant people just weren't dying soon enough. He wondered if he should explain to the boy that as more people lived longer, the cost of healthcare tripled, and the great states and the insurance companies became crippled. Dr. Osler amused himself with his rhyming thoughts, then muttered that countries were spending more money to defend themselves against external threats, only to fall to the most obvious internal threat: the cost of living. Ironically, a tragic loss from a war might have been the only solution to save the existing systems. A large death toll from war would have reduced the long-term healthcare costs. Unfortunately, the war came too late.

People were living longer, but this didn't mean they were healthier. Where previously a bout of pneumonia could kill an 80-year-old patient, now pre-emptive vaccines and stronger antibiotics kept them alive to become a further toll on the system. By living longer, the patient had more time to contract more diseases, and if a patient lived long enough, they would eventually develop cancer. Instead of having one 90-year-old patient in the waiting room, there were ten of them. More surgeries were scheduled, more homecare was required, and more prescriptions were filled, especially for pain relief.

The great Dr. De Visie reported that with just an additional ten years added to the average lifespan, dementia had quadrupled. The disease had a much longer time to feast on the human mind. He coined the term multi-generational dementia, to describe where an elder child was dealing with a parent's dementia, only to develop the same symptoms themselves before the parent had passed.

Countries with publicly funded systems were the first to go. The public still expected to retire by age 65, but rather than live another five or ten years, they were suddenly living another 15 years, and eventually another 25. The disproportionate cost of this extra life became insurmountable. The collapse of the national health system in Great Britain was a bellwether for other countries with similar systems. Then, with almost two billion people in India, the government rapidly failed, and the country devolved into regional governance. Canada and Australia tried to prop up their systems by implementing a 'new and improved' two-tiered healthcare system. Initially, this worked for the rich, but failed as the general population fell into a state of sickness. A scarcity of resources soon meant that diseases, which were once infecting 5 percent of the population, were now infecting 100 percent.

Other countries, which relied on privately funded healthcare, fared no better. The numbers were just not in favour of such a radical change in lifespan. After a successful thirty-year career at the same company, a retired individual depended on the company's insurance provider to pay for future healthcare. But when that insurance company declared bankruptcy, the individual was left with no healthcare options other than to pay as you play. Again, initially the rich were protected from the lack of affordable care, but soon resources and diseases trumped even money.

This was now of course all ancient history, but thinking about how quickly the world devolved, made Dr. Osler pleased that he wound up where he did. However, now he had to explain why a failed healthcare regime led to a society where this boy's father would kill him, the same way his father had killed the boy's older brother.

"You know your father is a doctor, right?"

Osler paused in exasperation, while Jan waited intently for the doctor to gather his thoughts.

"There's just so much you don't know yet ..."

"I know that if I do nothing, I die. What if I kill my father, would I be allowed to live?"

Jan spoke quietly but didn't seem to really care if the other two boys overheard him. Otto and Tam continued their game without even glancing back at the conversation.

"I guess that's one idea, but killing your father is not the answer. You need to find a place to hide, and probably not that long, then your father won't be an issue. He's not a particularly healthy man, and without you I doubt he'd live out to see another year. But figuring out where you can go undetected and then getting you there, well there's the challenge."

With his newly formed knowledge, Jan took a slight perverse pleasure in knowing that his father would die if Jan could find a way to survive.

"We've got a little time before your renaissance," Osler continued. "I will do whatever I can to get you out of here. I'll come up with an escape plan."

Even as he said it, William Osler knew he had an aversion to planning. In his journal for Dr. Síceolaí's 'Roadwork to Abstinence', Osler had stated that he thought it was too much planning that cost him his relationship with Katie.

Page 2

At the end of our first year living together, Katie and I both graduated with a Bachelor of Science. That's when it became clear that we didn't agree on what our next chapter would be. We had never discussed it before, and I just assumed that she would continue her studies in the same university that I would study medicine. I had my life-plan mapped out and I thought Katie understood it, but I guess at that age we didn't communicate very well. I knew what type of med school I wanted to attend, what type of work I would do after graduation, and how long I would hold off before starting a family. Most of what I had planned, was the opposite of what Katie wanted. I wanted to apply to universities in the United States, but Katie had no desire to head to 'the land of the somewhat free'. She disliked the country and all it stood for. However, I knew it was essential for my medical career.

Despite Katie's protests, I applied to and was accepted into the medical programs at University of California, University of Michigan, and Johns Hopkins University. Even though it didn't offer scholarships to foreign students, I selected JHU. It was highly respected, and it was within a one-day drive back to London-not-that-one-the-other-one. I believed that I could make everything work. I planned on making bi-weekly visits back to see my mother and Katie (who was starting a graduate program at Western). I still didn't consider a visit to the hospital as a visit to see my dad.

The challenge with Johns Hopkins was being able to afford the cost of tuition for an international student. I told my mother that I had applied for a loan to pay for the tuition, and that's when she told me about the insurance policy dilemma. I admired her for carrying that burden by herself for so long and I knew that she would prefer to have my dad back over a $250K 'windfall'. My mother said that whatever way the insurance landed, she would be able to pay off half of my student loan. This made the weight of the debt almost bearable.

I moved to Baltimore to start med school studies, still holding on to my unrealistic belief that I could maintain my relationship with Katie. Things became quickly strained, partly because of the distance, and partly because we still held different plans for life. She wanted to start a family and I told her that I really didn't have the time for kids. I guess, deep down I knew that I had clearly put my career ahead of our life together, but somehow, I had convinced myself that she would come around. In the first month, I made two trips from Baltimore back to London-not-that-one-the-other-one. My visits with my mother were fine, but my time with Katie really felt like visiting an ex-girlfriend after being dumped. I'm sure she felt the same way. Around that time, she told me that she would not wait ten years to start a family. On the second trip, we departed with a hug rather than a kiss. Classes kept me busy, and if I wanted to succeed, I had to work hard. I failed to make a trip home during the second month at JHU.

When I finally made another visit back for Thanksgiving weekend, I decided I would surprise my mother rather than head straight to Katie's place. I arrived at the house late on Friday night and found my mother sitting in the living room, wearing only her panties, singing to a CD of Adele's greatest hits. She had tears rolling down her cheeks, a bottle of Pinot Gris in her hand and two other empty bottles on the coffee table. She said it burned as she cried. I worked to sober her up and then I put my mother to bed. I sent a text to Katie letting her know that 'something had come up', and that I'd see her the next day.

On Saturday I visited Katie, but she had to work in the evening, so I didn't stay the night. On Sunday, I visited again, and the conversation was extremely clumsy. After discussing our current school workload, our courses, and our various professors, we ran out of things to say. There was no talk of anything that involved a future together. It was clear to me that she wanted me to leave. I awkwardly explained that my mother needed me, which was true, but I purposely neglected to explain how I had been nursing her through her inebriation. Katie took this as a brush-off, and she shook my hand at the door. I thought she needed to be more understanding, but I know I could have been more open with her. She was signalling that our relationship was over, and although I accepted this, deep inside I thought that I could win her back once I became a doctor and she understood why I chose the path that I did.

Near the end of my first year at JHU, Katie unexpectedly called me. She hadn't talked to me in three months. She told me that she had seen my mother drunk and distraught in the Valumart. Katie drove my mother home to sober her up but thought that I should be aware of how badly my mother was struggling. I called home but my mother was too embarrassed to talk. I booked a flight and was back home in under six hours. My mother was now sober and completely coherent.

She explained that after more than a decade of visits, she had accepted the reality that it was time for my dad to move on. The statement didn't shock or disgust me. For me, my dad passed away when I was 12 years old. I remember explaining to my mom that there was such a thing as being in a catatonic state but still receiving all input to the brain ... still understanding everything that was going on around you. But that wasn't my dad's condition. The fMRI scan saw no neural responses to any external activity. There was nothing that was going to bring my dad back to the world of the living. My mother had discussed the matter with the hospital and the doctors agreed that life-support could be removed. She asked me if I would make the arrangements on her behalf.

From my childhood home, the house that my parents had rented for three decades, I planned my dad's death. I contacted the hospital, the funeral home, and the insurance company. Everything seemed to be arranged for a compassionate farewell until the insurance company called back. A not-so-compassionate person on the other end of the phone informed me, using far too many legal phrases, that if it was the family's decision to remove life-support, then my dad's death would not qualify for the $250K payment. I had to explain to my mother that she would be better off if she waited for my father to pass, but that I agreed it was more compassionate to let him go now. She was furious that 'the goddamned insurance company was now making her keep her husband in a catatonic state if she wanted to get a larger payout'. Their involvement in her life decisions were enough to overwhelm her and I suggested that perhaps it was time to get the lawyers involved. This was going to be a longer process than I had anticipated.

I returned to Baltimore for the rest of the school term. My only two visits home were at Christmas and once during the summer break. My hard work at school was rewarded as I received the gold star for first year academic excellence thanks to my two favourite courses: Clinical Foundations of Medicine, and Foundations of Public Health. By the time I was in third year, and doing my practicum at Johns Hopkins Hospital, I was considered a shoo-in for the neurology internship. It was the night before my Metabolism exam when I received word of my dad's passing. I attended the funeral the following week and that would be the last time that I saw either Katie or my mother.

The night after Osler had promised an escape plan, Jan lay in bed frustrated. He was unsure if he could trust Osler, or whether the doctor was just trying to placate him until the renaissance. It was late and he was tired, but he still couldn't get to sleep. Maybe Jan could speak to his father and get him to agree to something. His adrenaline was flowing more than at the start of a swim meet. If he fell asleep, he was afraid that he'd never wake up. He started to doze off at one point, but he thought he heard his father's voice and he pulled himself awake. If Osler couldn't come up with an escape plan, then Jan had to. But he lacked the knowledge to try to save himself.

He sat up. He needed to develop his own plan. He needed to go back to the library and check out some more books. This visit would be different, however. This time finding the right books could mean the difference between life and death.

Jan took the now familiar path across the school grounds and through the tunnel to the library. He spent the first hour looking for *The Book of Generations* again. He looked under science and then under religion. At one point he thought he had found it, but he had found a biography on De Visie. He threw the book to the floor and sat down leaning his back on the shelf. He began to weep. He was

The Gemini Project 125

overly tired. He wasn't sure what it was that he needed to read, but his time with Osler had left him with more unanswered questions than he had started with. After a brief time expunging his desperation through tears, Jan regathered his composure and decided not to waste his time in the library feeling sorry for himself. He would search through the texts and find the right books to help him escape.

Jan moved up and down the aisles taking in more words than any previous night. He read both fiction and non-fiction. Eventually, he gravitated to his favourite section; the one where he had found *Brave New World*. It was there, in the section titled 'Classics' that he decided to spend the remainder of the night. The books were sorted alphabetically by the author's last name, so Jan started browsing through the books in that order. He no longer wondered how so many things could be considered a classic.

As he flipped through the pages of one of the books, the words on the page called out to him. 'It was the best of times, it was the worst of times …'. It reminded him of something that Dr. Osler had said. The doctor had read this book! A few weeks prior, Jan would have said that he was living in the best years of his life, but his recently acquired knowledge had shattered this belief. *A Tale of Two Cities* by Charles Dickens started with this one line that captured Jan's full attention. He read on. It was 1775 and Mr. Lorry was in London. That city again. Jan wondered if it was renamed to New London, or if New London was named after the original? Lorry went to Paris to help Lucie free her mentally enfeebled father who was imprisoned. Jan decided that he needed to take this one with him, so he shoved the paperback into his right rear back pocket and moved down the shelf. He was beyond caring about whether Dix would find the book or wondering what possible punishment could be given to him. It looked like he would never see New London after all.

When he reached the S's, he picked up *Catcher in the Rye* by J.D. Salinger. He read the paperback's description on the inside of the back sleeve:

> *Salinger's constant wry observations about what he encounters, from teachers to phonies (the two of course are not mutually exclusive) capture the essence of the eternal teenage experience of alienation.*

Phoney teachers ... that was all Jan needed to decide that he would take this one back with him too. He planted the small red book into his left rear back pocket.

Next, Jan picked up a book with a familiar title and it sent a chill throughout his body as he read. He had randomly opened to the page where a doctor was performing a brain transplant. Jan knew that he had to read this one as well, so he put Mary Shelley's *Frankenstein* in his front right pocket, having to squeeze it in as it was a little larger than the others. 'Frankenstein is the doctor, not the monster,' he said to himself. For the first time in days, Jan smiled. He was beginning to wonder if it wouldn't be easier just to move his room into the library.

Enough fiction, Jan crossed the library and went back to the periodicals. He sat down in front of the shelf and pulled a bunch of magazines down then started flipping through pages. He found it difficult to relate to most of the short stories and eventually Jan dozed off. Like a driver drifting off on a late-night drive, Jan woke himself with an abrupt start. He had no idea how long he had been asleep for, but he realized that he needed to make his way back to the dorm right away. Even though he still had one empty pocket, he started to head back.

The Book of Generations was a large, leather-bound text that rested in its place as the last book on the bottom shelf of the history aisle. As Jan crossed the doorway to leave, *Generations* caught his attention partly because of its immaculate condition and superior quality, but also the sheer magnitude of the book. Jan was surprised that he hadn't noticed it before. The shadow from the open door had been obscuring the book's location.

He pulled the book off the shelf and opened it up slowly, with a sort of reverence. He began to read. Before he was halfway through the introduction, he heard the wakeup horn sounding. It was morning. *Generations* was too large for him to take back. He needed to read as fast as he could. His fingers ran down the words. There were a few pages at the start with reviews from various experts including one that called the book 'the first owner's manual for the brain'.

He carefully read through the Introduction, which started with a quote:

> *"The strange computational material in our skulls is the perceptual machinery by which we navigate the world."*
> *- - David Eagleman*
>
> *In recent years, neurology has been moving fast, so stepping back to evaluate where we are is important if we want to ensure that we have set out plans to head in the right direction. Our future depends on it.*
>
> *In addition to being responsible for how we perceive the world, the brain is responsible for the decisions we make and even the imagination that we forge. It is therefore fitting that we can now imagine a world where this wonderous organ can continue to be passed from generation to generation.*
>
> *This text is different from my other neural science books and even the academic articles that I have written. This book attempts to provide a direction for the human, and by doing so, provide a direction for mankind.*

Jan was barely taking in any meaning as his mind grappled with the pressure to get back to the dorm. The first chapter was on 'Where Man, As a Species, Is Headed'. This chapter on the future of humanity sounded like one of Dr. Osler's rants. Chapter two was entitled 'An Alternative Approach'. Chapter three addressed something called 'New Neuron Generation'. This chapter addressed the loss of neurons as a part of aging, but stressed that these long, stringy cells passed on electrical signals but did not directly contain our intelligence. The 'thought' process was provided by synaptic entanglement. Jan struggled to understand the concepts but continued to scan through the text. The next chapter, 'Passing On Knowledge', was on surgical procedure. Jan didn't even pretend to understand this part, so he quickly flipped through the pages. Finally, he found the chapter he needed to complete the picture: The Renaissance.

> *The transplant shall happen during the process known as a man's renaissance. At that time, the body will be reborn, and the mind will continue to live on.*

Jan fully understood. He understood the plan for his future, and he now understood the timing. His life would end on the day of his renaissance. Time was not his friend. He needed to get back to the dorm quickly, and with only two weeks left to live, he needed to find a way to change his future.

While he was overwhelmed by this thought, Jan knew that he couldn't afford to stay in the library any longer. He felt the immense pressure from the threat of being discovered absent that morning. If Osler did come up with an escape plan, Jan did not want to mess it up by raising suspicions. He needed to leave and leave now. The size of the book made it impossible to take *Generations* with him. He would have to come back to read more another night.

As he thought about heading back through the murky tunnel, he decided that the route would take too long, so he headed back upstairs to the Administration Building instead. This way was faster, but riskier. It required him to make his way through a building, then cross a lot of open spaces, and it was probably daylight already. His mind bounced back and forth between small details and overarching threats. His first thought was about how he would explain to his roommate that he got up early to shower, and then his brain switched to the school's plan to cut his head open on his 18th birthday. Passing on knowledge.

As he crept through the doorway into the Administration Building, he could see the yellow light shining in from the windows down the hall. He knew the second wakeup horn would be sounding very soon. He passed the corridor where he had seen Nurse Banaltram on his first visit. He should have crawled right past the window to the Fire Exit door, but in his tired, adventurous, furious state, he couldn't resist taking a quick glance through the window. Standing there, down the hall, was his father.

Jan was completely stunned. He couldn't understand why his father would be there when it wasn't father's day. Then Jan took in the figure that his father was speaking with. It was Osler. Perhaps the doctor was informing his father about Jan's recent quest for knowledge. Or maybe they were discussing his upcoming procedure. Jan lowered his head below the window and pressed his ear against the wall. He could hear the beat of a conversation, but everything was muffled.

'Mmfph … mmfph … Fire.'

He's talking about me, Jan thought.

'Mmfph … Renaissance … mumble, mumble.'

The Gemini Project 129

Silence.

The conversation seemed to have ended, so Jan stood up and looked back through the window. Dr. Osler was gone. His father, however, was walking straight over to the window. He stopped inches in front of the glass and was peering through the blinds. His face was less than a foot away from his son's. Nervously, Jan stared right back. He was sure that his father was looking right at him, but from the inside the overhead lights glared and reflected off the glass. Tre was looking at a mirror.

Tre Ericson smiled then began to sing, slightly off key:
> *Such an effort ... If he only knew of my plan*
> *In just seven days ... I can make you a ma-a-a-an.*

Tre turned and headed out of the room, then out of the building. Jan didn't remember making his way across the yard and back to his room. He didn't remember convincing Dix that he had been an early riser. In his overtired state, his mind was flooded with the thought of his father's unscheduled visit and his own impending death.

Halfway through the day, Jan decided to play sick once again and catch up on his sleep. He was sent back to his room and Dr. Chirug came in to check up on him. The doctor entered into the chart that the adolescent suffered from a lack of sleep due to growing pains and that a little less strenuous muscular activity was recommended. Perfect. That evening, after dinner, Jan awoke realizing that it was Wednesday evening and Osler should be in the lounge. Jan went down and approached the doctor who was sitting enjoying a quick Soma break.

"Jan, I was just sitting here, waiting to talk to you," Osler started.

"Did you have a nice conversation?"

"What?" Osler responded sincerely, still getting used to hearing the aggression in Jan's voice. The enlightened Jan seemed to have lost a lot of the lovable characteristics of the Jan from even a week ago.

"With my father ... did you have a nice conversation?"

Osler said nothing. He was trying to process how Jan knew so much. How the hell did he know about a conversation that took place in another building at 11 a.m.? Where was this kid getting his information?

"Well, did you?"

"Sure. We were discussing your renaissance."

"It's not my renaissance ... it's his! It's the last moments of my life ... then, 'the mind will continue to live on'."

It seemed like every time Osler spoke with Jan, the boy had gained an even greater understanding of the truth. Jan now appeared to have specific knowledge of the contents of *Generations*. He seemed to know exactly what the renaissance was.

"Don't worry, I don't plan to be here for the party anyway," Jan added. "Now, I think you owe me something Dr. Osler. I want my escape plan."

"Oh," Osler said in a forced whisper turning into a suppressed animosity. "You think I can come up with an escape plan in one day, do you? The entire social, economic, political system is built around the renaissance, and you think it's easy to just skip one? In the end, you're all alike. You privileged birthlings are all the same. So demanding. Do you realize the liberties that you have been given? Weaker birthlings are not given the honour of attending the Corpo school system. Instead, they are sent to a school where they study, do homework, and live a relatively normal, albeit demanding existence, until they enter the labour-force. That's the life of the Hebs, they work until they die because we don't grant them any real medical assistance. That's a real escape plan."

Jan noticed that Osler's eyes were dilated, yet again. He wasn't sure if he was dealing with a fully juiced Osler. Jan liked it better when the doctor was at least in a semi-coherent state ... when Osler was lucid. He wondered if he was going to get what he needed, or if he would have to wait another day. However, even in his relaxed state the doctor could see that Jan wasn't in the mood for anything short of direct conversation about leaving the Academy. Osler regained his focus.

"You and your father have more similarities that I realized. You are both unjustifiably demanding."

"What do you mean? Why were you meeting with my father? It's not a father's day."

"Having a father visit on an off day is not altogether that unusual. We probably get ten to twenty visits each quarter by one father or another. They come individually, usually arriving at night or in the early morning. A shuttle sweeps in with very little noise, they park on the grass outside the Admin building, and they are gone before any of you boys realize it."

"Why do they come if they are not here to see their sons?"

"They come for various reasons. Father's day is just a show, but sometimes they want to really delve into how their protégé is doing. They want to understand if their host has any physical deficiencies, and I stress the word 'physical' because they really don't care about your mental state. Dix's father was here last month to discuss the pluses and minuses about putting him on a diet. Tam's father just wanted to go over his offspring's blood work ... in detail. I had to sit down with Tam senior for over two hours. Damned hematologists."

"And my father?"

"Well, your father has presented us with a new wrinkle," Osler said as he assessed Jan's state of mind, "but I think you're already too upset for me to share this with you. So, if it's okay, I think I'll leave it for another day."

"Tell me. Please tell me now," Jan pleaded, somewhere in between an ask and a demand. He was trying to contain his emotions, and Jan realized that Osler's mind was sufficiently limpid today, and he might not be the same on another day.

"Well ... there is a lot to take in and I haven't formulated how to explain this to you, but you asked for it ... it seems that your father is redlining with his liver. Your father is a drinker, a heavy drinker. He loves his Scotch, maybe a little too much ... although I don't know why they still call it Scotch when it comes from a lab. Anyway, as per usual, your father is committing suicide by lifestyle choices. Medically, two years ago he moved from hepatitis to fibrosis, and he was advised to cut down on the booze. At that stage, the damage was reversible. But your father being who he is, or who he thinks he is, and on seeing how well you were turning out ... well, he didn't change his ways at all. Last year, he moved to cirrhosis, which is an irreversible hardening of the liver tissue and ..."

"What's a liver?" Jan interrupted.

Osler looked at him. Sometimes he forgot that Jan was intelligent, but it was intelligence without knowledge. There was a strange mixture in the boy, too much information about one subject, followed by zero information in another. Had he not been interrupted. Osler probably would have babbled on for another five minutes about the diagnosis and treatment regimes for the liver.

"The liver is an organ that sits right here," he motioned to an area above his stomach with his right hand. Jan mimicked the motion and pressed on his own liver.

"And in the world of organs, this one is probably third in importance, just behind the heart and of course the brain. But your very existence has provided your father with a blank cheque to abuse his liver, until last week when he thinks he suffered a mild liver failure. Ironically, in the good old days we would have assessed you to see if you would make a viable candidate for a liver transplant."

"So, my father would take my liver?"

"Yes, but you'd survive, and your father would live on. And I'd bet if I asked you to donate part of your liver to your father, there would have been no hesitation on your part. As it sits right now, your father has been told that there is a 50/50 chance that he won't make it to the renaissance after all."

"You mean he might die?" Jan asked.

"That's what he believes."

"And if he dies," Jan surrendering to a hopeful smile, "does that mean that I survive the renaissance?"

"That's not an option. Your father has his own plan to survive."

"He's going to take my liver?" Jan objected.

"No. That would only buy him a few more years. He wants the whole car, not just the muffler. He's offered me 100,000 credits to advance his renaissance."

"You can't," Jan protested, realizing that this would give him less time to live. Less time to work out a plan. "You couldn't do that could you?"

"Not by the book ... not legally."

"So, you wouldn't do it, would you?"

"Well, I haven't said 'yes', yet, but I'm thinking this might be to our advantage."

Jan's distrust of the doctor had grown even stronger. How could advancing the date be of any help at all to him.

"I don't have a plan for your scheduled renaissance," Osler continued, "and I'm not sure that I'll be able to come up with one. But throw in some unscheduled activity that gives us a disrupter and there might be some great opportunities to capitalize on.

What your father is suggesting isn't legal, so this introduces some clandestine activities on his part. He wants to do the renaissance secretly, so he gets his new host early."

Osler paused to gauge Jan's reaction. There was no obvious emotion on Jan's face. The boy still didn't know how this could help him, and he wanted to hear more from the doctor before he reacted.

"By now you realize that the renaissance isn't a party. It's a surgical procedure and it doesn't come with pomp and circumstances. Usually, only the father, the son, and the holy doctor attend, along with a little support from an anesthesiologist, a nurse and maybe an orderly or two. So, your father wants me to bribe a team to assist in an early transplant. He would then go home in his new host and stay hidden. He'd then secretly come back on the night of the scheduled renaissance, enter the hall where this time there would be no operation. Then, as planned, the next day he could emerge in his new form. Since the renaissance usually takes place at night, he believes he can arrive under cover of darkness, and no one will be the wiser."

"How would this help me?" Jan asked.

"I'm not sure yet, but the fact that your father is operating outside of the rules might provide an opportunity for us to also operate outside of the rules. But I don't know exactly what we'd do yet, so I might have to call an audible."

Jan looked quizzically at Osler.

"I guess you never played football, did you?" Osler asked rhetorically. "I just mean the plan might develop on the fly ... develop as we go through the procedure. You know ... we'll have to follow the Scout's motto ..."

"Be prepared," Jan completed the thought, then added, "... Scouting for Boys."

It became clear to Osler, yet again, that he had no idea what Jan knew, far less how he knew it. Still, he was always pleasantly surprised when the boy displayed some bizarre piece of trivial knowledge. Osler wouldn't have suspected that during the previous week Jan had read the scouting motto on the front page of the 1908 edition of *Scouting for Boys* by Robert Baden-Powell.

The scouting statement put an end to the conversation. Jan wondered if the doctor had paused waiting for some words of thanks or appreciation, but so far, the only plan that was offered was to 'plan to make a plan'. Jan stared at him, still waiting to hear how this could be of any help. To Jan, it sounded like his life had just been shortened.

"It's not just a matter of keeping you alive," the doctor eventually said, "we'll need people to believe that you are dead. Unless you complete your renaissance, they'll track you down. You can't just run away. You can't simply disappear."

Again, a pause for a reaction that didn't come.

"What do I need to do?" Jan asked a little tersely.

"You have to trust me. Do you trust me, Jan?"

Jan stared at Osler. He didn't trust him. How could he trust anyone anymore? However, Jan also knew that any hesitation in his answer could reveal his lack of conviction.

"Yes, I trust you. But I am also very worried and very upset."

"Good. Good on both accounts. I can't give you details right now, because I don't know them myself yet … but I do need you to trust me and when the time comes, do as I say. If we can give you your life back, I'll get you setup in New London. Once there, maybe you can live a happy life," Osler said, then added with a chuckle, "unless you become an Outsider."

"What's an Outsider?"

"According to fable, the Outsiders live outside the system. They believe in what they call the Real Renaissance. They are dreamers who think they can live on the surface of the dead planet and somehow they won't die from extreme temperatures, disease, or any one of a dozen inhospitable factors."

Osler was enjoying starting to recount yet another story, but as he spoke, he became very conscious of the smile on Jan's face. He changed his tune and his tone.

"There is a myth that they live in some happy community on the planet's surface, but trust me, this is just a myth. There is no El Dorado; there is no Xanadu; there is no city filled with a bunch of sterile Outsiders walking around smiling. There is just a bunch of fools who decided to head for the planet's surface, then once they leave the System, they die. What else could be expected with underdeveloped immune systems?

I've never understood why someone would choose to die or why they'd want to leave the system, but that's what they do. They say

The Gemini Project 135

'goodbye' to a life where they are guaranteed work and a relatively good existence ... why would you want to give that up?

But enough of folklore ... for you, we need to get you to New London, and we need to find you work. Then you can live a full life. The first step is to get you out of here and somehow convince everyone that you are dead?"

Dix and Otto entered the room.

"Listen to this," Otto belted out. "Dix has a brilliant idea."

"I'm all ears," replied the doctor dryly.

"Well," Dix started slowly, "you guys like to play chess and we like to play checkers ... soooo ... we challenge you to a game where we line up our checkers pieces on our side, and you line up your chess pieces on your side. If you win, we'll admit that chess is the better game, but when we win, you'll have to declare checkers is the best game. Brilliant idea or what!?"

"It's an idea to die for," Jan responded cynically. "And you thought of this brilliant idea all on your own?"

"Never mind him," Dix said to Otto. "He's been like this for the past few weeks."

Osler just laughed and stood up.

"Well boys, it's time for me to hit the hay, so you figure out a plan for this new game, and maybe we'll play on Sunday evening."

He left the room, leaving Jan wondering what the next steps were. If Dix was observant, he would have seen the slight smile of hope on Jan's face quickly fade to dejection. After the doctor left, Jan watched Dix and Otto as they set up for a game of chess-eckers. A quarrel broke out about the rules of the new game. Jan couldn't take any more, so he headed up to his dorm and the two boys didn't even notice him leave.

Jan lay on his bed. He wanted to stay awake so he could make another trip to the library. He found himself wondering about his father. For years, he'd just assumed that his father loved him, now he viewed this love to be the same way that Dix loved steak nights. Dix walked in and Jan realized that soon he might be seeing the last of Dix. Jan should probably say something, but what?

He briefly gave some thought to filling Dix in, but he settled on the bleak realization that Dix wasn't really a friend. He was just someone that Jan went to school with. He couldn't define what attributes Dix needed for Jan to call him a friend, but he knew that Dix didn't have them. A month ago, if he thought about it, Jan would have said that Dr. Osler was his friend too. Now he realized that Osler was probably also just selfish and opportunistic. He thought about the characters in *Lord of the Flies* by William Gerald Golding. Jan was sure that Osler had found himself on this island at the Academy, and he was out for the betterment and survival of only one person. Dix and Osler ... Jan's closest allies at the Academy ... one was thoughtless, the other was furtive. He decided that he would no longer trust Dix or Osler.

"Tomorrow, if I'm selected as captain, I'm going to choose Otto first. You don't mind do you Jan? You're not that great of a catch right now, if you know what I mean, and I'd really like to win."

Jan almost longed for the time when he was able to live in such ignorant bliss. He rolled over and looked at Dix who was getting ready for bed.

"That's alright. I might not play tomorrow anyway."

Before Dix could say anything more, Nurse Rossignol entered their room pushing a small cart.

"Okay boys, time for evening meds."

She handed Dix and Jan a small paper cup with various coloured pills in it, then handed them each a glass of water. Jan was already in his sleep gear, so he lay there watching Dix get ready, wishing his roommate would hurry up and fall asleep so that he could leave for the library. Jan soon drifted off himself. He would not wake up to go to the library. Nurse Rossignol had included a dose of Z drugs in his meds.

10. The Betrayal

It was Wednesday, August 18th, about two hours after lights-out, and Osler returned to the dormitory with Nurse Rossignol and two orderlies. The orderlies pushed a gurney over to Jan's bed and proceeded to move the boy. As they left the dormitory, Osler looked across the soccer pitch, thinking that the brightly lit field was a bit of a waste of energy. The floodlights shone down from midfield, as well as from each corner, illuminating the field stronger than daylight.

The orderlies pushed Jan into the theatre of Renaissance Hall. Nurse Rossignol was quick to direct the gurney to its position and adjust the lighting. Jan's trolley was positioned under the spotlights directly parallel to another gurney. Jan's father, dressed in a hospital robe, was sitting up on the other gurney watching the proceedings.

"Now there's a good little corpo ..." Trevor Ericson muttered under his breath, but Osler overheard the cynical comment.

The sound of his father's voice penetrated Jan's dreamworld. He couldn't feel his arms or legs, but he was slipping into consciousness. He turned and looked at his father.

"Father?" he muttered in a hoarse tone.

"What the hell?" Tre called out, looking around the room.

"Don't be startled," Osler stated. "He's not quite out of it. He's just semi-conscious from the sedatives right now, but Nurse Rossignol has been promoted to an anesthesiologist tonight. She'll have him under in no time."

"What ... a nurse administering the anesthetic?" Tre said, displaying a privileged ire.

"Well, the options would be to involve another doctor, which would require a greater payment, but it would also require another person keeping this matter private," Osler replied. "Besides, you gave me less than two hours notice that you were on your way. So, the holographone will guide her through the process and the system is setup to maintain brain blood flood, as well as monitor blood pressure and oxygen levels. For me, the anesthesiologist job has been made redundant."

Jan was more conscious than Osler realized. The first thing he became aware of was the doctor's dress. No t-shirt and jeans ... he wore the white jumpsuit that the other doctors wore. The doctor accessorized his outfit with a surgical cap, latex gloves, and a mask. Very non-Osler attire. Jan fought to move his arms and legs, but nothing was happening. He was still staring at his father trying to figure out where he was.

"Be - Tre - Y'All," Jan said hoarsely.

"What?" Tre called out, looking at Osler for a translation.

"Bee-Tray-Awl,' Jan said again emphasizing each syllable, not realizing that it sounded as though he was referring to his father.

Osler shrugged at Tre and proceeded to prep the anesthesia.

Jan was searching through the 1996 edition of the *Merriam Webster Dictionary* in his head. This was the word that overpowered his thoughts:

> *Betrayal (bi-'trā -ə) n. The violation of a person's trust or confidence, of a moral standard, etc.*

Betrayal. He had been betrayed. A betrayal by his father was expected at this point, but Jan had hoped that his bond with Osler somehow still meant something more. He was finally able to clench his fists, but his arms were too heavy to lift. Osler fastened a mask around Jan and adjusted it.

The Gemini Project 139

"Stay with me Jan," Osler said softly into the boy's ear. "We can get through this."

"Betrayal!" Jan's father said with a guileful laugh. His grin showed his admiration of Jan's courage, but also his lack of love for his son.

"I wish I could bottle some of Fire's tenacity and take it with me," Tre said, then he turned to Jan and added smugly "… it's not a betrayal … it's just part of the rules. You are just Sarah and I'm Johnny Bananas."

Jan stopped trying to squirm or talk.

"He'll be completely under and ready in five minutes, so it's time to get you prepped, unless you want to change your mind."

"No, let's get on with this … sorry Mr. Bryson, but we do not have to pass our existence within one warm wobble of flesh … we have options now," Tre retorted with a half smile.

"Okay," Osler responded, "It sounds like he's ready … Nurse Rossignol, prep the patient."

Osler approached Jan from behind. As the boy began to go under, the doctor shaved his head. Jan stared back and was sure that he saw sorrow in the doctor's eyes.

The boy's brain was still firing as he listened to it whisper its final thoughts. How could he have been so stupid? How could he have trusted anyone who had lied to him all his life. He tried again to muster up some muscle movement. His mind was no longer communicating with his body.

Jan accepted it. This was the start of his renaissance. His father had won.

"Okay Dr. Ericson," Dr. Osler said to his patient, "It's your turn. I'm going to put you under now too. You count backwards and I'll tell you the one about the doctor and his dying patient …"

"What?" Tre said as he started to drift off.

"He's about to start his routine," Nurse Rossignol warned drolly from the back of the surgical theatre, "Right Shakespeare?"

"Oh, Shakespeare isn't here tonight. There will be no talk of 'what a piece of work man is'," Dr. Osler said to his nurse, then turned to his patient and added, "I know I look like a doctor … but my real first choice of occupation was a philosopher, and my second was a stand-up comedian … not really that much difference between the two occupations ... there aren't jobs for either. So, you're in luck today you get the comedian. After the operation, don't forget to tip your waiter ... I mean nurse!"

Dr. Osler nodded towards the nurse who feigned a disapproving grin. She has heard all of his routines a dozen times before.

"So ... the doctor called up his patient and said I've got bad news and worse news.

'Give me the bad news,' responded the patient.

'According to your results, you've only seven days to live'.

'If that's the bad news, what's the worse news?' asked the patient.

'Well, it seems I got these results back at the beginning of last week!' replied the doctor."

Nurse Rossignol groaned and muttered under her breath 'time for some new material'.

Dr. Osler looked at her and smiled, as their second patient slipped into a dream state.

For Jan, time passed both slowly and quickly at once. Everything was surreal. A virtual perpetuity of thoughts raced through Jan's mind as he tried to remember everything that had ever happened in his life. His memory starts from when he entered Gehirn. Perhaps he could hold on to some thought or find some meaning for his existence, other than to create a housing for his father's memories. Maybe he could push his thoughts out to his body, and they would re-enter his father's mind after the operation. Jan was sure he could look through his closed eyelids and see the bright lights of the operating theatre shining down on his body. Next, he believed that his head turned, and he looked over only to have the white iridescent walls blind him. He sensed he was looking down on his father's body as he floated above the other gurney. His father was motionless. Jan saw Osler walking back and forth between the father and son. He tried to call out, but no sound came out of his mouth.

"Isn't technology wonderful?" Dr. Osler said to his operating room nurse. "We don't even have to raise a knife to make an incision thanks to lasers and we also don't have to stitch up thanks to lasers. I remember studying surgical procedure and in the first class they had us peel a grapefruit, then we had to sew it back together."

"And I've seen you sew ..." Nurse Rossingnol roasted uncharacteristically.

The Gemini Project 141

"Exactly, and the lasers have also come a long way with respect to scar tissue and healing. When I was in med school, we had to … use … a … scalpel … to …"

Jan was no longer floating above the operating tables. He fell completely under and never heard the end of Dr. Osler's recollection.

Once they were into the heart of the procedure, Dr. Osler's character seemed to change. He was neither a philosopher nor a comedian. He was a neuroanatomist. Removing Tre Ericson's brain was relatively easy, as it was not in its original casing. For more than 75 years, the added step of adapting the brain stem to attach it to a bayonet electrical connector, meant that there was a 'quick removal' for the next operation. This step was performed robotically and made it easier to reconnect to the small narrow spinal cord. Even with the added bayonet, the brain only weighed 1,600 grams. Assisted by two robotic arms, the doctor carefully removed Tre's grey matter, leaving the pituitary glands in the body. He then held the delicate and vulnerable organ in his palms. Nurse Rossignol was waiting for a joke, but none came.

"There is nothing more complex, more amazing, in the entire world, than the spongy mass I hold in my hands," Dr. Osler said. "I love how soft it is. People expect it to be more solid, like a muscle, but it reminds me more of Jello pudding in its consistency."

"Next you'll be asking me to get some spoons," Nurse Rossignol attempted to joke, but then quickly realized that the doctor was no longer a comedian. She was familiar with this version of Dr. Osler as well … once he has put his audience to sleep, he was no longer performing. It was time for her to work in silence. After over 500 transplants, Dr. Osler was still in awe of the human brain.

"Everything you know about life on this planet, is fed to you by this jiggly mass, which has never actually seen, smelt or touched anything. It lives inside your head in silence, and in darkness, it operates on a stream of electrical pulses. Of course, protons of light have no colour, sound waves have no sound, and olfactory molecules have no odour … so our brains just decide what our senses are telling us … it makes up our own unique truth."

He turned to his nurse holding Tre's brain upside down in his left palm and he pointed to the front center of the pink and grey object.

"Right here … the optic nerves are very obvious, as are the olfactory nerves. With this electrical input, the brain will tell you what a warm breeze feels like, or the kiss of a lover, or the heat of an open flame touching your skin ... but it has never felt any of that. It just receives the electrical flow from its various receptors and creates the world as you know it. It creates our thriving, three-dimensional world for us and then gives us the ability to survive in that world.

For us humanoids, the brain also decided to use some of these electric pulses to delve into more creative areas like art, music, or philosophy. Think about it ... pun intended ... you don't need to play a musical instrument to survive on this planet, yet the brain has enough spare firing capacity to allow Mozart to compose Eine Kleine Nachtmusik, or Pink Floyd to write Dark Side of the Moon. Why does the brain spend time on such trivialities?

That's just one of the many things that the brain won't tell you. In a way ... the brain is in charge, not you ... that is of course, if there is a 'you' outside of your brain. I don't believe there is. De Visie convinced me of that. Yet there is so much we still don't know about the brain. We don't even understand why the right side of the body is controlled by the left hemisphere, and vice versa. We can move the master controls from one vessel to another, but that doesn't mean we understand everything about how those controls work. You see the shapes here of the cerebral cortex ..."

Osler ran his finger across the two hemispheres.

"... here, across the surface of the brain ... the bumps are called gyri and the grooves are sulci. It turns out that no two brains have the same pattern of bumps and grooves, so your brain is distinctive, like a fingerprint or an iris scan. No one knows why the floor plan for the brain is different for each of us, or even whether there is a benefit to one layout over another."

Dr. Osler moved and spoke slowly. He held a reverence that reminded Nurse Rossignol of the time she visited the Pearl Harbor War Memorial. Once she entered the museum, no one spoke ... they just read the names of the dead in silence. She understood now ... Osler was in pure work mode. He turned and placed Tre's brain in a small vat of clear liquid.

"The brain is usually encased in membranes, cushioned by the cerebrospinal fluid, all of which is further encased within the skull," Dr. Osler continued, fighting with his brain not to think about his dad. "Very few people actually get to see the brain outside of its packaging."

Because of the lack of solid supporting tissue, even preserved in its fixation solution, the brain can't be left to sit on the floor of what Dr. Osler refers to as the 'brain bucket'. It can't be allowed to settle on the bottom and distort out of shape, so Dr. Osler looped a cord through one of the arteries and suspended the brain in the liquid. This simple process replicated one of the purposes of the cerebral spinal fluid ... to allow the brain to float inside our heads. Dr. Osler moved over to Jan's body and pointed back to the vat of grey matter.

"This is a 'Handle With Care' procedure, because unlike other organs, if you damage a small piece of the brain, it can change your personality ... it can change who you are! That is not Trevor Ericson's brain. That is Trevor Ericson," Dr. Osler said, letting his eyes flow towards his nurse. "The Gemini Project proved that your brain isn't a part of you ... it is you. Everything else is that makes up your body is just windows, plumbing, electrical wiring, and framing.

And the brain does everything it does with great efficiency. Your brain will consume 400 calories in a day ... that's about the same as a pain au chocolat at the French Café. It's able to create your entire sensory world, and it only requires the energy equivalent of a French pastry. And the more productive your brain is, the less energy it has to consume before it goes into standby mode. That's why there was nothing wrong with helmet laws for motorcycles but there was something inherently wrong with a sport that pitted two men crashing against each other's head on a football field."

Dr. Osler stopped talking. His mind slid briefly down to the thought of his dad's head, crashing down on the bed of a pickup truck. He thought of the irony after his father's traumatic passing, that he would go on to cradle so many brains in the palm of his hands.

Page 3

In my third year at Johns Hopkins University, my mother called me. She was drunk, again. I was getting used to these calls, but there was a flavour of urgency and anger to this one.

She had been fighting with the insurance company over the past few months but didn't want to tell me. It turned out that my dad had been making some extra money at his job with the *Gazette*. After the daily paper had been printed, he would take the plates off the printing press and dump them in the bin out by the loading dock. One day, he was approached by a man, who didn't work for the newspaper, and offered $2 per plate. For a 40-page newspaper that amounted to $80 a day. All my dad had to do was take the plates to the bin at the end of the shift, and instead of throwing them out, he would lay them down in the bed of a waiting pickup truck. The plates were then melted down for their silver content. My dad didn't know how much money the silver thieves were getting out of the deal, but as the plates were garbage anyway, he saw no harm in adding to the university savings account that he started for me. So, each week he received about $400 in cash for plate recycling. This is what paid for my undergrad education.

On the day of his accident, my dad was carrying plates to the back dock, when he slipped, fell off the dock and hit his head on the side of the waiting pickup truck. The ambulance took my dad to St. Joseph's hospital, but the police questioned the individual with the pickup truck that had a pool of blood in its bed. The man didn't work for the paper and had no good reason to be there, so it didn't take long before someone realized that he was there to pick up the plates. The man was charged with theft, but my dad had been spared for compassionate reasons.

My mother's insurance claim through the *Gazette* policy was denied for two reasons: 1) my dad was in the act of committing a crime, and 2) my dad was carrying the plates for his own purposes, and thus he was not covered under the work policy. I listened to my mother's slurred words and was fairly sure they could be decoded as 'the goddamned insurance company knew this all along, but they couldn't deny my claim until I submitted one'.

It was close to the Christmas break, and I probably should have caught a flight home immediately, but I decided that my mother's problem could wait until after my final exams. It sounds cold, but I really didn't know what I could say to her to justify her husband's white-lie theft, or how I would be able to help her out financially, especially if I failed to write my exams. The small stipend that was paid to me, went to paying rent for my apartment across from the hospital. My own financial agenda was to pay off my debt once I finished school, but I also accepted that now I would have to support my penniless mother. She was lucky that the newspaper was not coming after her for the profits from the plate theft.

Before I finished my exams, I received another tragic call. It seemed that if a call came in from London-not-that-one-the-other-one, it was generally bad news. This time it was from the Ontario Provincial Police. The officer was fine with his approach to me, but there is really no good way to inform someone that their mother had died in a car crash. I asked for the details and was told that my mother had crashed head-on with another vehicle, killing both drivers. The officer gingerly let me know that it was my mother's fault and when I pushed for more details, he told me that my mother was impaired at the time of the accident. I briefly thought

The Gemini Project

that maybe the world would be better with one less alcoholic, then guilt quickly set in as I remembered that another person had died in the collision.

This time, I applied to the school for a compassionate exemption from my exams and was granted a grace period before I would have to write. My relationship with Katie had been non-existent over the past two years, so I didn't call her to let her know about my mother. She didn't need the burden of a former boyfriend's dead mother added to whatever else she had going on in her life. However, I did consider that maybe we could meet up while I was back in town ... and maybe we could arrive at that meeting of the minds that I imagined was in our future ... that is, if she wasn't already planning a family with someone else. It sounded to me like a slightly more morbid plot from one of the lifestyle movies that Katie used to watch. I imagined her with a new boyfriend who worked for an international forest company. I would return home for a funeral, and Katie would have to decide between me, who was ruggedly handsome, and her new beau who was handsomely rugged. I smiled and decided I would probably tell Katie about my movie plot.

At my mother's funeral, a reporter approached me to see if I had any remorse for my mother's drunk actions. My first reaction was to punch the guy, and my second was to walk away, but by then I thought that the insurance companies were as much to blame as the Seagram's Seven Crown. This was my opportunity to explain how my mother had been misled by a corrupt financial institution. I answered the reporter's question but part-way through I lost my train of thought when I realized that the reporter was probably from the *Gazette*. As I stumbled over my words, the reporter cut me off to ask: 'But what do you have to say to Katie Barlow's family ... to her mother and father who have just lost their only daughter?'

William Osler had lost his mother and Katie in the same accident. This was the start of his drug addiction. Osler's access to drugs at the hospital was far too easy, especially for a superstar student that no one suspected would require pain relief.

As Jan's father woke up, his head throbbed. His brain's plasticity had been struggling to keep things firing where they should be firing, so his visual cortex sent him into a dream state. He dreamed that he was on the other side of the operating table, and it was his brain that was being replaced and not his son's. Distressed, he pulled himself back into reality, and he remembered the purpose for being in an operating theatre. He called out demanding ... "Nurse! Nurse, bring me a mirror!"

"Relax Trevor. You look great."

Nurse Rossignol was sufficiently comfortable in her place, that she didn't feel the need to refer to Jan's father as 'doctor'. Tre looked towards the other gurney, only to see that it wasn't there. Then he realized that he needed to look in the other direction. There on the righthand gurney was his old body, just where he left it.

"So, everything went according to plan?"

"Yes, you're good for another 25 years, or maybe 10 to 15 depending on your habits," Osler answered obviously amusing himself.

Jan's father felt enough strength to roll his head and look around the room. Across from the two gurneys was a trolley with a mirror. Nurse Rossignol had anticipated the request and was already heading to the trolley. She passed it to Tre, and he gawked into the reflection. He saw Jan. As his strength returned, he soon became very conscious of the power in his arms. He wondered why he had to look in a mirror when all he had to do was look down at his body. Something inside him needed to see his new face properly. Nurse Rossignol saw Jan's father leaning too far over the side of the gurney, trying to take in his new physique.

"Come on Trevor, you know you've got to take it easy for a while."

A few hours of mandatory recovery felt like a life sentence when you were itching to try out your new torso. Within a half hour of waking up, he felt strong enough and suddenly he wanted to go outside to kick a soccer ball. He knew that this frame held superior physical strength to the one he was used to, even in its prime. Over the next hour he was gradually improving, and he regained sensations that he had all but forgotten. A grown man and he couldn't help being as giddy as a schoolboy. Tre Ericson started to chuckle as he got an erection. He called out to Osler to tell him about the sensation. Both men laughed.

Tre was wheeled into a recovery room where he rested for the remainder of the morning. When Osler came back to check up on him, he told Tre that he could be released early, as early as that afternoon.

The Gemini Project 147

Later that day, Nurse Rossingnol returned with some extra bulky clothes, and she dressed the patient up with some bandages, a hat, a scarf, a hoodie, and an oversized coat. They put Jan's favourite running shoes on his feet.

The doctor, the nurse and an orderly then sat the patient into a wheelchair and proceeded to push him towards the exit of Renaissance Hall. As they walked down the hall, they passed the surgery theatre where Tre had been granted his new physique. Next, they came to a second recovery room that had the words 'Contagious – Doctor Only' marked on the door. Jan's father chuckled when he read this. Finally, he was wheeled out of the hall and over to the parked shuttle.

Once at Tre's shuttle, the patient stood up from the wheelchair and entered in bouncing. Osler smiled at the scene, and waved good-bye to his patient. The doctor turned and headed back to Renaissance Hall, telling Nurse Rossignol to leave the cleanup to him. She knew that this meant he would probably salvage some other body parts for sale on the dark market. The doctor might be able to sell the organs in return for certain favours, which loosely translated to his drug habit.

Osler enters the second recovery room. The room is double sealed requiring the doctor to pass through two entry doors before piercing the cold of stage two. A gurney lays there with a cadaver completely covered in white linen. Osler uncovers the carcass and looks at the old body of Jan's father. The body should have been lifeless and missing a cranium, but the doctor had done some remedial work after dismissing the staff. The skull has been shaved then sealed back together. Suddenly the head moves slightly, and the eyes open up wide.

"Doctor Osler?" the cadaver calls out.

"Relax kid, you are going to be fine. You're in our primary recovery room," Osler replies.

"What's going on? I don't feel right."

The gruff voice comes from the body of Jan's father, but the brain that is controlling it is Jan's.

"You'll be a little drowsy for a few more hours. I couldn't give you the riser until I got rid of your father."

"What happened?" Jan asks groggily in an aged voice.

"I called an audible," Osler answers as he takes Jan's pulse then his blood pressure. "I probably should have thought of this before. When I remove a child's brain from his skull, I might as well toss the cerebrum into the organ can in the corner. The only thing it will be used for is a paper weight or maybe some stem cell testing. But with yours, every effort was made to minimize damage to the surface. The Klingler preservation method was utilized, with some minor adaptations, and the organ was suspended, by means of a ligature placed around the basilar artery, in a vessel containing 10% formaldehyde solution."

There is no pause.

"Dr. Klinger originally used this technique to prepare for dissections of both fibre tracts and the nuclei. It keeps the brain in a suspended state with little deterioration for longer than you'd imagine. I then stored the fluid and your brain at minus ten degrees Celsius, while I dealt with your idiot father. Once I finished his operation, and the rest of the staff left, I took your brain out of the formaldehyde so that I could insert it into your father's body. And you'll never guess what I used to ready the brain for insertion ... cold running water, as simple as that. And I did all that without the aid of a single person."

Jan's eyes are darting around the room and although he feels like he has regained focus, he notices that the items closest to him are blurry. There is no animosity on Jan's face, only a dumbfounded stare indicating that he hasn't comprehended most of the doctor's soliloquy.

"Can you repeat all that, Doctor Osler? I wasn't following you," Jan requests politely.

Osler lifts up a mirror and passes it to Jan. Jan holds out his arm and lifts the mirror to his face. The reflection is his father's. It is the face of a man that Jan had once loved but has grown to hate. He drops the mirror to the floor.

"What's going on? What have you done?" Jan calls out raising his voice and trying to sit up.

"Calm down. I've kept you alive," Osler snaps back. "And if you make much more noise, it might only be for one more day. Did you have another available host that you think would have accepted your DNA that you would have preferred me to use?"

Jan, now fully conscious, comprehends that not only did he have his father's body, but his father is in HIS body. Osler has switched both bodies.

"You ... no ... not good," Jan says, then he starts to cry like a child.

Osler is moved as he realizes that this weeping, 53-year-old man really has the emotional maturity of a 17-year-old boy.

"Look kid, I'm sorry," Osler says as he approaches Jan and puts his arms around him. "It was all I could do. No one will miss your father's body and I needed to find you a host."

Jan is gaining control of himself, but he struggles to accept his new exterior.

"What am I supposed to do now?"

"I haven't got it all worked out yet," Osler answers. "I've been working on a thousand things at once, but now we need to get you to New London. There you can live and die, as you wish. That's what you wanted isn't it? Of course, one challenge is that you actually have very little skills, so you might not get a lot of credit for your work. In the meantime, you will stay here until your renaissance date.

Oh, ... and I told your father a white lie. When he came to me for a second opinion, I agreed with his doctor's report. I agreed he would be lucky to make it to the renaissance date. He does have a bad liver, but not as bad as his doctor said. With a little TLC, you can probably get another two or three years out of this body. The AID report that I showed him, I'm sorry, the artificial intelligence diagnosis, was doctored by this doctor," Osler said quite pleased with his pun and his deception.

The doctor pauses for the admiration that would come when Jan realizes the genius behind the plan and its perfect execution.

"You did want to live, didn't you?" he asks when the appreciation fails to materialize.

"No, not like this. I wanted to be me."

"That wasn't an option. There was no other way," Osler says with a mixture of anger and remorse. "You are still you, mostly. This wasn't the perfect plan, but it was the only plan I could come up with to keep you alive. Your father abused his body, just like he's done three times before ... with your older brothers. When he came in for an 'off-the-books' opinion, this plan should have been obvious, but when your father offered his old organs for harvest as part of the payment, everything just seemed to fall into place. Harvested organs can be sold, and your father knew that I could make this happen.

Now your father has been renaissanced and gone back to his place in New London. In the meantime, I've marked you down to be under my care with a nasty viral bout. Renaissance Hall is the only building with an isolation ward, so you'll remain here, and no one will be looking for the young version of Jan. Your father will have to make sure that no one sees him for the next few weeks and then he'll return here where we'll perform a fake renaissance. The next day, he will emerge like a phoenix as Fire Ericson.

Everyone will be convinced that the operation was a success, and I will pay off a couple of orderlies to carry off a box of medical waste, which will contain a few roasts from the kitchen instead of your dad's old body. He'll go home in his new body that he adopted weeks earlier. Then, since no one will be looking for you, hopefully you'll be off to a new job ... provided I can find you one of course. You can stay at my place on Level 34 in New London. I can give you access and say you're my caretaker or something."

Jan strains to look down at the wrinkles on his body. He struggles to understand how to operate his new exterior, it doesn't seem to respond properly. He is young but he is old at the same time. Jan finds it difficult to define who he is. The old definition, where he was young, he was an athlete, he was a son, he was a student, he was Dix's roommate ... no longer fits him. He wouldn't have the time to adjust to the aging process and in his recovery, he'd find it hard to adjust to his inability to control his basic bodily functions. His wrists will hurt when he squeezes a juice glass. His stomach will dictate when his bowels move. He wouldn't be able to read anything up close. He will be constantly tired. He is different, yet in his mind, he knows somehow everything was the same as it ever was.

"Listen," Osler says with modest empathy, "I can't promise you that I know how you'll survive, but I know that I've been able to let you live past your 18th birthday and that's something, right?"

Osler can see that Jan isn't in the mood for one of his dissertations.

"Look Jan, you need to wrap your mind around this, as it were. I was able to get you into your father's body, but now a lot will be up to you ... but anything I can do to help ..."

"You've never done this before, have you?"

The Gemini Project 151

"No, of course not. It would mean my life if I got caught. I did it because I think of you as a friend, and I haven't said that about anybody in almost a hundred years."

Jan's face grows softer as the thought of being alive pushes past the horror of being stuck in his father's wasted body. It isn't the perfect solution, but he can't think of a better alternative.

"Do you know what happiness is, Jan?"

"Sure, it's when something makes you laugh or smile," Jan answers.

"Yes, that's part of it. But happiness is being content. Being content with your life ... and contentment is continuing to desire what you already have. You will have to learn to be content with your new body ... learn to be happy if you want to survive. You will also need to fit into the system. Meet new friends. If you act different to the others, you are bound to be lonely.[1] You will have to adapt."

Jan thinks about what has happened. The initial shock is beginning to wear off and he gradually accepts that he is better off being alive in his father's body than being dead in his own. He realizes that Dr. Osler was taking some huge risks in performing the operation.

"I guess you didn't have any choice ..." Jan says quietly. "I will adapt ... Doctor Osler ... thank you for being my friend and for saving my life, but I think I'm going to need some time to really understand what's happened ... before I can be content."

"That's perfectly understandable. I guess all bad things come to those who wait!" Dr. Osler says in a weak attempt to amuse Jan. "You take your time. I wouldn't expect you to regain your emotional composure faster than your physiological composure. We still have a lot of details to work out."

"What do you mean?"

"Well, to be honest, this half-assed plan came together pretty quickly, and I don't really have the next part worked out. I just haven't had the time to think about what happens next. I need to figure out how to get you into the labour-force in the city. I need to work on your long-term accommodations. Hell, I need to divine a way to get you off the school grounds."

"Wouldn't I just take a shuttle to New London?"

---

[1] With apologies to Aldus Huxley.

"Shuttles are smarter than that. They know who they are taking and where they are going. We have to get you out of here without leaving any breadcrumbs."

"I think my brain hurts," Jan says rubbing his temples.

"No, that won't be the case. I performed plenty of brain surgeries, even before The Gemini Project. The brain doesn't have pain receptors, so it literally has no feelings ... even if a person was awake during surgery, they would not feel pain in the brain."

"No, I mean my brain hurts from thinking about what has happened," Jan responds.

"I see. Let me leave you to your thoughts. There are no renaissances scheduled before yours, so no one should come in here. This is an isolation room and as a precaution, I have marked the room as 'Doctor Only'. But you still shouldn't make too much noise just in case someone has a reason to enter the building."

Dr. Osler taps the block walls to show Jan that the room is relatively soundproof.

"I'll be back to check on you as soon as I'm able."

With that, Dr. Osler leaves Jan to contemplate his new physique.

After a half hour of lying there looking at the ceiling and processing that he has now become his father, Jan gets up and impatiently walks around the room. He doesn't know how much rest is normally required after an operation, but he wonders how he would even know that he has recovered, given how weak his father's body feels. He looks in the mirror and examines the scars around his shaven head. A slight ache emanates from below the cranium, and although there is some bruising where the laser has sealed his skin, he can't see any obvious reason for the pain he feels.

As he examines his head, Jan realizes again that it is his father's face in the mirror. He is already getting used to seeing his new old body. He is still frustrated by the littlest things, such as being unable to bend over or unable to read the chart that is at the bottom of his bed, but there is something natural about his form. It is almost as though he has aged overnight in his own body.

There are no windows in the room, so Jan can't sneak a look out at the school grounds. He wonders what time of day it is and thinks about what the other boys are doing. Jan feels like he is imprisoned in his father's body, which is also locked up in the Corpo Academy. He makes a split-second decision to leave.

The problem of how to get out of the campus and get to New London, shouldn't be the doctor's concern. If Dr. Osler didn't have a plan, then maybe Jan can help. He goes to the other recovery room and finds his father's clothes neatly laid out in the closet. He walks to the kitchen area and grabs a couple of apple juice boxes from the fridge. Finally, he quietly heads out of the room, and out of the building.

11. Road Trip

It is dark as Jan heads down the stairs of Renaissance Hall. His balance is out of kilter. He has grown old over night without the luxury of adapting to the change. Without having the time to age, he hasn't had the time for his vision to slowly decrease, or his muscles to slowly weaken, or his reaction time to gradually slow down. With half the hair cells in his ear's cupula, he stumbles down the steps. Over the next few hours, he will discover he suffers from a weaker heart, lower lung capacity and thinner bone structures. His brain's plasticity is working overtime to understand what he no longer has.

Jan looks right and left, planning to head over to the shuttle grass, but he notices the stairs leading down to the janitorial room on his righthand side. 'Be prepared' Jan thinks. One final trip to the library might be a wise move, so he heads down the stairs and through the library tunnel.

Jan starts by heading to the geography section. He has flipped through the pages in this section before but has never found anything to hold his interest. This time, he purposefully forces himself to work through some of the texts. There were graphics, pictures, diagrams, and of course maps. At first, Jan doesn't understand the purpose of a map, but after he flips through *Maphead* and *Ten Maps That Tell You Everything You Need to Know*, he begins to think that he won't be able to make the journey without a map. Looking for his next book, he notices a long flat box on the bottom shelf. He pulls the container out to find it filled with individual city maps. Eventually, he finds one entitled *London 1886: A Map of the City and the Surrounding Area*. This is exactly what he was looking for. His confidence surrounding his journey has just received a boost.

Jan decides to spend a couple of hours flipping through the pages of a few history books trying to consume the information that he might need to survive. His time is limited not only by the approach of morning, but also because he plans to read more of *The Book of Generations*. He briefly considers bringing *Generations* with him, but the book is too heavy. The thought of taking one last book seems to give him some satisfaction, so before he leaves, he decides to grab a novel for the journey. He picks *Treasure Island* by Robert Louis Stevenson, not just because he likes the way the words flowed together but also because it is a pocketsize edition. His dictionary is in his dorm and the library dictionary is too heavy to make the trip. He knows he might struggle with the Stevenson text, but this will be his treasure for the journey. He tosses the book, the map, and his juice boxes into the bag with the glow-tubes, then leaves the library for the final time.

In khaki pants, a long-sleeved golf shirt and loafers, Jan exits the library the way he came in. This time he removes the towel and allows the janitorial door to lock shut. There is a sense of finality as the door clangs closed. It is still night, but the lights of the soccer pitch allow Jan to plan an escape route. If shuttles came in from the path through the artificial trees, there must be an exit there. He heads to the shuttle park and then follows the path, past where he would wait for the fathers to enter the schoolgrounds. Because the boys have such structured schedules, their days are pretty much planned, leaving very little time for exploring. Their minds were also not encouraged to think beyond the health and fitness regime. Still, Jan wonders why he had never taken a walk passed the treeline that surrounds the campus. Beyond the trees, the shuttle's interlocking brick path split into several artificial grass paths, so Jan has to pick one. He chooses the right-most path. It winds through the forest but then comes to an abrupt end. Jan stares at a solid line of trees in front of him. He is unaware that the wooden structures are formed from fiberglass. There are about 50 different designs for the trees, and then the pattern repeats. Since none of the boys know any better, no one ever questioned why there are never any leaves to be raked.

He enters the darkness of the forest and for five minutes he walks in what he thought was a straight line. Eventually, he comes to the edge of the treeline. As he exits, he finds himself looking at the soccer pitch. He has somehow walked in a circle and is mildly amused at how easily he has been turned around in the dark. He isn't amused by how difficult he is finding it to adjust to his 'new' body and his already aching legs. He turns 180 degrees, lights a glow-tube and heads through the forest again. He holds the light down low, so it won't be seen by one of the staff members of the school. Eventually, he comes to another treeline and this time he exits the forest into a narrow laneway of artificial grass.

At the other side of the synthetic meadow, he enters a second set of trees where he is happy to find that it is slightly less dense. Crossing through this forest, the light changes. It becomes intense and less consistent. Above, there is a dark sky, but he can make out silvery clouds swirling. Jan feels the temperature noticeably warmer as he works his way through the forest. The heat makes him uncomfortable. He wonders if this is a result of his new frame or if it is just warmer in this part of the school grounds. In either case, it is an unfamiliar feeling to him.

Fifteen minutes later, the forest comes to an abrupt stop. Ahead, there appears to be a wall coloured with a dark green gradient tone that bleeds directly into the night sky. He had been very good at clearing the walls on the Saturday obstacle course, but he is having second thoughts on how well his father's body will cope with climbing. As Jan approaches, he can see the wall formed endlessly to his left and right, but he can not discern where the top of the wall is and where the night sky begins. He reaches out to touch the wall and feels a light emitting fabric that stretches in all directions as he pushes on it. He looks up to see the night sky bending as he presses the material. The wall and the sky were all one fabric.

The school grounds in fact are contained in a large spherical arena. The structure is based on the design of the Las Vegas Sphere built in the early 2000s. However, the school grounds hold more that 1,900 acres of ground space. The 256K resolution wraparound LED fabric

The Gemini Project

that forms the walls and sky, are enclosed in a temperature-controlled environment that displays the appearance of both day and night using 4D effects. As he pushes on the fabric it becomes clear to Jan just how much effort has gone into the deception that had been his life.

Jan pushes at the fabric again, this time harder, but it is too strong to give way. He takes a few steps back and runs towards the wall, throwing his body into the fabric. The thick material flexes outward, and then snaps back tossing Jan's father's frame to the ground. He feels the pain rip through his right shoulder as he lands. He sits up, massages his right side with his left hand as he stares at the barrier. He isn't sure, but he thinks that his old body, his own body, would have been able to rip through the screen.

After settling his thoughts, Jan stands up, then using a glow-tube he walks around the exterior of the structure. There is a ten-foot gap between the treeline and the fabric wall. The dome encloses the schoolgrounds in a large circle. However, the same way the length of the earth's circumference could fool sailors into believing the earth was flat, the outline of the massive complex leads Jan to believe that he has walked in a straight line. The colouring of the wall and the sky is very consistent, so Jan's travels soon become monotonous. Looking back over his shoulder, the view is the exact same as looking forward. Then the light in the sky begins to slowly change. Morning is coming. He begins to jog, but after a minute he knows that his father's body isn't up for anything more than a quick paced march. Jan is unsure if any of the staff venture out this far in the school grounds, but something makes him feel more exposed in the daylight. He needs to find out if there is an exit somewhere along this wall.

Slowly he becomes aware of a hum in the distance. As he moves towards the sound, he soon hears a deep throbbing below a whirling noise. He finally reaches a change in the path, where the trees have been laid out to accommodate space for six metal boxes eight-foot square in size. Jan bends down to read a metal plate on the side of one of the units. It is still semi-dark, so he has to hold up his glow-tube to read the plate. Underneath 'Johnson Controls' are a lot of letters followed by numbers. Even with the light, Jan has to squint to read the plate. There is nothing to indicate to him that these are the air conditioner units that service the environment for the entire complex.

Jan walks around the A/C units trying to understand what the boxes are. Each unit has a thick cable running out of the back, through a metal grommet, and out past the material wall. At the final unit, he notices that there is a small amount of light passing on the outside of the grommet. Jan goes into the forest and breaks a fair-sized branch off the artificial tree. He starts to ram the fiberglass at the side of the grommet. The material begins to tear, and Jan can see more light working its way through. A few more stabs and Jan drops to his knees then rips the fabric by hand. As the wall comes apart, Jan can see a series of wires that hold the LEDs together on the back of the fabric. By pulling on the wires, the material separates easier, and soon there is enough space for Jan to squeeze through the barrier. He drops his glow-tube and pushes his way to the other side.

Outside the sphere it is already daylight. It is also hotter than anything Jan has ever felt inside the dome. This is intensified by unfamiliar humidity. There is long uncut grass and he can smell the blades as they move in the wind. He heads across the meadow of greenery where he notices small yellow flowers sprouting up above the shin-high blades. There is also a sweet smell coming up from the flowers that remind Jan of something from his childhood, but he can't quite place it. The splendour saturates Jan with a feeling of contentment. At the far end of the meadow, the ground turns brown, and plants become sparse. Jan looks back at the material that had imprisoned him, and he can see the projection of the sky that appears on the inside of the structure. Above that is another sky. This one is blue with a scattered cloud pattern in a form that Jan has never seen before. He briefly wonders if this is the real sky, or just another type of deception. He walks away from the sphere, and across the dusty ground. The heat quickly becomes unbearable. Jan thinks about being 'prepared' and realizes that he should have brought some food and water with him. As he walks, he occasionally back over his shoulder at the dome. He can see the enormity of the structure. The projection of the sky is gradually turning to the azure blue that Jan is used to. 'Morning', he thought. The boys will soon be getting up, showering, and heading to breakfast.

A steady buzz starts and constantly changes in pitch, timbre, and volume. It seems to follow Jan. He thinks that it may be the sound of a shuttle and he wonders if there is anyone from the school following him. He is moving as fast as his elderly body will carry him. Still unsure of what the buzzing is, he begins to sweat. The heat is hot, and the ground is dry, and the air is full of sound. He pushes on.

Eventually he comes to a road that at first appears to blend with the earth. It stretches diagonally in front of him and might be part of the path that leads to the school grounds. The slightly uneven pavement is a mixture of black and dark grey. Its surface is extremely hard but is cracked every couple of feet. If Jan follows the road there is a chance that he could be spotted, but he feels quite alone and unguided on the unpaved ground. The road seems like a better option as it is clearly manmade for a purpose, so following it should eventually lead to civilization. Since the terrain is sparse and only slightly undulating, Jan decides that he would have enough time to react if anything approached. The decision to take the road comes relatively easy, but now Jan needs to decide left or right. He peers down the road in each direction, focusing and squinting his eyes to see as far as he can. To the left, the road is straight, and Jan can make out the trail for about ten football fields before it dissipates into a watery haze. This route might take him back to the school. To the right, the road begins to wind, and the eventual direction is less clear. Jan is unsure as to where this route might take him. He heads right.

Walking along the road, he can feel heat emanating from the surface and broiling its way through his loafers. He tries walking barefoot, but this idea only lasts two steps before Jan is clamouring to put his shoes back on. Occasionally, there are signs on the side of the road with black arrows painted on a deep yellow background. About half the signs that he sees, have fallen to the side of the road. Jan deduces the purpose of the signs, as he realizes that the arrows indicate which direction the road is about to bend. Still, what is the purpose of the signs, considering the shuttle technology?

Shuttles are self driving vehicles surrounded with cameras and sensors. Together with a mapping system, the shuttles use the sensors to trace their path and adjust speed as they approach objects (or other shuttles). The shuttle motor runs with a quiet whoosh, so Jan constantly checks over his shoulder. He notes the white line that runs down the centre of the roadway, sometimes solid, sometimes dashed, and sometimes both. This road is old, and Jan is sure that it is from another era. He wishes that he had taken a few more books from the library. Then he thinks about how heavy the canvas bag is starting to feel. One book, one map, two juice boxes and a half a dozen glow-tubes is already a lot for his father's body to haul around.

Once the thought has entered his consciousness, the weight of the bag seems to be growing. Jan hikes it up and loops his arm through the handle, carrying the bag over his shoulders. It feels lighter now that his torso absorbs the weight rather than his arms. Rounding a corner, a large rectangular green sign comes into view. The first line reads 'New London 25', followed by 'De Soto 312'. Jan assumes that these are distance markers. He also deduces that De Soto is a city like New London, and he considers the historical significance of the figure that this city has been named after. Most of the stories about De Soto, revolve around the land that he discovered. Jan has trouble thinking of De Soto in high regard as he really didn't discover anything ... there were already bands of people living in the areas that De Soto 'discovered'. Maybe De Soto is just discovering places for himself and that's why the books referenced him as one of the great explorers. By the same logic, Jan too is now an explorer, and he has the signposts to guide him towards his discovery of New London. His thoughts bring a smile to his face and a lighter gait as he proceeds down the road.

Jan looks at the unfamiliar environment that surrounds him. He has lived on the school grounds all his life, and CAD didn't offer any field trips. Eventually, ahead Jan spots a tower at the side of the road. Nearing it, he sees that it is surrounded by a small fence and a patch of yellow grass. The grass of the school sports fields never turned yellow. Once he reaches the structure, Jan circles around the large metal tower and looks up. He can see that the tower directs orange light back towards the school. Jan thinks about climbing the structure but decides that his body isn't up to it, and he needs to move on.

Past the tower, it becomes significantly warmer still. Jan begins to sweat. He has never perspired by just simply walking. He is cautious as he continues along the side of the road, ready to dive into the small ditch if a shuttle approaches. No shuttle ever appears, so eventually Jan decides that it is safe enough to walk down the centre of the pavement. The further he walks, the more the silvery clouds change to darker shades of gray. A relatively light wind starts to pick up and he is pleased that it helps to cool him down. For most of his journey, the road remains a consistent width. It is just about wide enough for a shuttle to fit on and has dashed lines painted down the centre. An hour into the journey, some yellow fields now line both sides of the road. Eventually, the roadway widens. There is enough room now for two shuttles, but the centre line is painted solid and there are dashed lines running down each side.

Jan passes several road signs, but none that tell him how far he has left in his journey. When he spots a sign in the distance, he gets excited, partly because it is just something different than the same straight road. Most of the signs are smaller and say things like "Buckle Up, It's the Law', so Jan gets enthusiastic when he sees a larger sign, faced down on the side of the road. The two wooden poles that held it up are broken and the sign is covered in sand. Jan flips it over and reads 'Next Services 72 miles'. His early disappointment in not finding a city marker is soon replaced by the realization that this can help him with his understanding of distances. If he finds another similar sign, further down the road, with a different number, then he'd know how far he has walked.

The sky continues to darken, both from the growing obsidian clouds and the setting sun. As the horizon blackens, Jan can see a faint glow ahead. Suddenly, he feels some wetness hit him on the shoulders. He spins around expecting to see someone throwing water at him. There is no one there. He hears a rumble, followed by a deep 'boom'. Water begins pouring down on him. Jan has never experienced rain before, far less a thunderstorm. There is a flash of light, followed by another rumble, and the rain pelts down harder. Black clouds slowly float by overhead. Jan hasn't moved since the start of the rain. He instinctively hunches up his shoulders and feels a shiver runs down his spine. He has gone from too hot, to too cold in a matter of minutes. He wonders if he should continue down the road, then he gets an idea.

He runs back to the Next Services sign, picks it up off the ground, then crawls underneath it. It keeps him mostly dry, but water rolls off the road and over his drenched loafers. He stays there for a quarter of an hour before the rain finally dissipates. Crawling out from under the sign, he uncomfortably continues his trek, racing against the oncoming darkness. He comes to another upright sign that indicates that New London is now 19. With this measurement, Jan knows that his pace will not take him to New London before nightfall.

Looking down the road, Jan sees a shadow moving in the distance. He pauses, watches, and waits. Then he discerns the sound of a shuttle whisking towards him, and he quickly retreats, ducking down in the tall grass. The shuttle sound seems to approach and then it recedes far in the distance, without ever passing Jan. He peers out of the grass but can't see any sign of the vehicle. The day has rapidly turned to dusk, and Jan feels his body needs rest. He isn't used to the feeling of tired muscles without having exercised, so he decides the field will make a safe resting spot. He flattens down some blades of grass about 50 feet from the road and lays down.

As the night devours the sunlight, Jan does his best to settle in, but he is very aware of his wet clothes. He thinks about taking them off to dry, but the chill of the night air convinces him otherwise. He can see a radiant-glow miles behind him and he realizes that this is probably the sphere that holds the schoolgrounds. It is the familiar azure blue of day at Corpo Academy. The school seems so small to him now. For some reason, night within the school arrives at a different time to night outside the school. As Jan thinks about this, he wonders what Dr. Osler will think when he arrives at the isolation room and finds it empty.

Under the light of an extremely bright moon, Jan cracks open *Treasure Island* and begins to read. He works his way through the first chapter and, even without his dictionary, understands most of what he reads. He learns about the innkeeper's son Jim Hawkins, and a sword fight between Black Dog and Billy Bones. He is as amused by the character names as the story. By the end of the first chapter, his eyes feel heavy. He stops reading and sips his first juice box. He is very aware of the unfamiliar noises that surround him. Hissing, buzzing, snapping. The louder sounds echo slightly, repeating twice or even three times. Despite this, Jan has no trouble getting to sleep, however he wakes up in the middle of the night, shivering in a bitter chilly wind. This is yet another temperature … he is not very amused by his list of new sensations. He arranges some shrubbery to form his bivouac for the rest of the night. 'Scouting for boys,' he thinks as he pulls some tall grass down on top of him to form a blanket. It keeps him warm for a while but eventually he rolls over in his sleep and loses his grass blanket.

Again, he wakes up. There is a shooting pain. His leg muscles have cramped and he has to hold his leg about six inches off the ground. He can't put it down and he can't lift it up. Anguish lies in either movement. Holding his leg straight, the pain is excruciating. It is still dark. There seems to be even more noises engulfing him. He can't contain the urge to go to the washroom. Finally, his leg relaxes and

The Gemini Project

he is able to move it. He lights a glow-tube to fend off the strange discordance, but the noises only seem to get closer with the glow of the light. He gingerly stands up and heads to a bush. It is awkward peeing using another man's apparatus and Jan thinks he will have trouble adapting to the frequency of the impulses from his father's body. After he finishes the call of nature, he decides he will not be able to get back to sleep a third time. He has become too conscious of the unfamiliar surroundings. He packs his book back into his canvas bag and starts down the road, glow-tube in hand. It is still dark.

Progress through the darkness is slow. Eventually Jan senses the glow of the rising dawn behind him. Walking in the aurora of the morning, the appearance of upright light posts brings on an unfamiliar feeling of melancholy. The lights are not functioning, but he recognizes the style as similar to the ones that surrounded the tennis court before they were replaced by the therma-cable system. As the night sky slowly gives way to morning, Jan's anxieties concerning the strange noises also begin to rescind. Rubbing his face, he feels the tingle of yet another new sensation: the stubble of a man's beard growing in.

As he walks, Jan can feel the torturous muscle cramp that woke him. He notices a large black bird flying above. He has never seen a bird before, so he stops to look up and admire it. The bird seems to be flying in circles around him. He doesn't recognize the creature from his page flipping of *The Animal Kingdom*. He looks down and notices that the surface of the road, with the white lines, is remarkably similar to the tennis courts. He wonders if the roadway was ever used for some sort of sport. If it was, it must have been a few years ago because the condition is such that small plants have forced their way through and are growing in the cracks in the road.

Another sign, this time it reads 'New London 15; Youngstown 3'. This is new information. Before reaching New London, he will arrive at Youngstown, and it should be visible on the horizon very soon. Jan quickens his pace. The barren land around him is flat. The beige landscape stretches in all directions with much the same appearance. If not for the road, he doubts he would be able to walk in a straight line across this terrain.

Jan glances up and now there are three birds encircling him. They are either larger than he had originally perceived, lower, or both. Jan can see something cutting across the road and across the landscape.

When he reaches the anomaly, he is confronted with two parallel metal rails, sitting on wooden crossbeams, that stretch out to the horizon on both sides. Jan wonders if it makes sense to follow the iron tracks to get to New London. He might have even given the idea a more serious consideration, except that if he did follow the tracks, he would have to choose to head left or right. The thought of heading in the wrong direction and coming across a sign that read 'New London 40', convinces him to stick to the blacktop. Jan proceeds to follow the road, and the birds continue to follow Jan.

Ahead, in the distance, the road seems to flicker in waves again. Jan thinks that maybe he is looking at water. His feet start to ache, and he puts it down to the loafers. He longs for his favourite sneakers, and he wonders why his father wore such uncomfortable shoes. As he walks further, he can feel his legs cramping up. He bends down several times to massage them but realizes that the process of even bending down is a slightly painful one. Once he has completed this road trip, Jan's father's body is going to need some regular toning to avoid these cramps. The sun has risen, and the heat comes with it. It is already at the unbearable level.

Peering off to the horizon, it looks like the road disappears and then reappears. The disappearing road is the first valley that Jan has come across in the mostly flat terrain. He spots a river flowing perpendicular to the road. When he reaches the part where the road heads downhill, he is able to make out buildings at the bottom of the hill. Other than the structures in the two schools that he attended; these are the only other buildings that Jan has ever seen. His heartrate quickens and for a few minutes he breaks into a jog. As he runs, he looks up and notices that there are now seven birds hovering above him. Every so often, one of the birds seems to swoop down closer to Jan. Out of breath and slowing down, he can now make out a sign. The white letters 'Youngstown, Population 16,000' are written in clean block print on a blue background. A yellow line is spray painted across the numbers and '100' is written underneath it. The signpost is surrounded by a puddle of muddy water.

12. The Birth and Death of Youngstown

The DNA of the communities along Route 116, were all pretty similar. It was typically the geography that led to the selection of the spot where a society would gather. Once a village was established, some grew into towns, and others evolved into cities. Youngstown was no exception.

10,000 years ago, a river began to flow at the site where Youngstown would be established. The flow of water was the result of melting glaciers that had covered the land for more than 100,000 years. When the water hit a small mound on the earth's surface, if could have flowed left or right, and worked its way around the embankment. However, the topography was such that the melted ice pooled in front of the mound, gradually gaining in volume, and eating its way through the impasse. The artery cleaved its way through the land, creating what would become known as the Grand River. Over the years, the Grand eroded more of the mound's earth, creating a valley through the centre of the hill.

The protection offered by the valley, together with the flowing supply of water, made the area perfect for a settlement as the Europeans pushed westward. For over fifty years it was only used as a good sheltering spot, before the continuance of a longer journey. The settlement had one false start when four pioneers passed out drunk by the side of the river. Two families, each hauling everything they owned, saw the prospector's campfire and decided that they would also stop beside the river for one night's rest. At that moment in time, the settlement had 17 people camped beside the river. Sitting around the fire, Jedediah Smith said to his brother that the valley offered everything they needed and maybe this should be the end of their travels. When they awoke, the four frontiersmen had sobered up and headed out. The families, seeing no other people in sight, decided to pack up and continue their journey west as well, leaving the riverbanks without inhabitants.

The next spark of life came when James Young arrived on his drive heading west. His small Scottish family consisted of himself, his wife Maggie, and his son James. When the senior James first saw the river, he wondered what was wrong with it. Perhaps it dried up in the fall or overflowed in the spring. There had to be some reason why no one had settled at such an idyllic location. They chose to stay there a few days and consider their options. Youngstown population: three. Based solely on the lack of anyone else inhabiting the riverbanks, Young came close to moving on. However, before he had firmly made up his mind, another family entered the valley to stay for a night.

Alwin Ernst was a carpenter, and he was travelling west with all his family and tools. When James Young told Alwin that he was a miller looking for a place to establish a mill, the two men smiled knowingly at each other. In the next four months, they set about chopping trees, planing logs, and constructing the first permanent building in Youngstown. Other travellers and frontiersmen continued to arrive at the river. Some passed through and others decided to end their journey at the village with a mill. By the time James and Alwin conscripted six other men to assist in the installation of the water turbine, there were 60 inhabitants living on the east side of the river. The people of Youngstown strategically decided not to construct a bridge, leaving the travellers to make their own way across the river. This usually meant that most travellers would spend at least one night in the village, which provided a 'pioneer tourism' boost to the economy.

The Gemini Project 167

Over the next few decades, the village continued to flourish into a town, and soon the mill was no longer the biggest employer. When James Young passed away, there was talk of erecting a statue in his honour, but nothing came to fruition and the next generation would forget the first name of the man who founded the town. The talk of a town founded construction project did result in a stone bridge finally being built across the Grand. The town was still booming when it took its first economic blow. In selecting the route for the westbound railroad, National Rail decided to build the tracks around the town and cross the river on a new bridge. This meant there would be no stop in Youngstown and worried residents started to look elsewhere for their livelihood.

The town would probably have continued to spiral in decline, had it not been for Compass Minerals. Compass was interested in lands that had been squished down by glaciers and they performed some initial test drills on the hills surrounding Youngstown. When Compass bought tracts of land and mining rights to other properties, the revitalization of the town was clearly on the horizon. The sexiness of gold or diamond deposits was not what Compass offered. They mined for deposits of potassium sulfate; a compound used to produce potash used in fertilizers. The discovery didn't result in hoards of prospectors swamping into the town, but it did provide consistent employment well into the 20th century. James Young's great-great-grandson, Jim Young Sr., was employed as the shaft 3 site supervisor at Compass Minerals.

Thanks to the revenue of Compass Minerals, Youngstown was selected as a location for one of the new Walmart superstores. Well, not exactly in Youngstown, but within a three-mile drive, in the direction of Wullerton. While the town's mayor took a lot of credit for attracting the 179,000 sq. ft. retail store, the reality was that it killed the downtown businesses. Why go to Stoney's Hardware when you can pick up that adjustable wrench in the same place you can replenish your toilet paper and pick up some new socks? By the time Jim Young Jr. was born, about a third of the stores in the downtown were down and out. His father passed away when he was nine years old.

Jim Young Jr.'s mother wanted him to work at Compass, just as his father had. Every time she reminded Jim that his father had worked in the mine, he'd silently add '... right up until the day he died'. Fortunately for Jim, but unfortunately for the town, the mining operation folded before he finished high school. His high school years in Youngstown were highlighted by the closing of the mine and the disruption of the stay-at-home order in response to COVID-19. The virus had infected his education with his SAT score reflecting the gaps in his studies. Jim's ambition was to work for one of the large mobile gaming companies on the west coast, but instead he resolved to remain in Youngstown. He managed to get accepted into an online college, where he studied information technology.

Much to the delight of the remaining downtown store owners, the virus also took its toll on Walmart. Not wanting to expose themselves, the elderly population of the town made the jump to ordering items from Amazon. It would have taken nothing short of a pandemic to get the people of Youngstown to stop making their weekly three-mile trip to the superstore. This didn't help the downtown, but it gave the small businesses some perverse pleasure watching the retail giant struggle with diminishing foot traffic, something they had lived with for twenty years. The small stores of Youngstown would reinvent themselves as niche, selling products that people wouldn't order online. When the change in shopping habits eventually led to the closing of the superstore, several of the original downtown shops still remained, including the Valumart grocery store where Jim managed to get a part-time job.

Jim performed well on his online exams, but when he graduated there were still no gaming companies knocking at the door to employ him. They didn't hire from the online campuses. However, his high marks did land him an offer from De Visie Teradata. The offer was to work in their data mining division …. at least it was a job in IT and it might eventually be a path to gaming. Jim's mother couldn't help but be amused when he told her about his new job, and she pointed out the irony that he was going to do mining after all. It was at that point that the refrain 'worked doing data mining … right up until the day he died' infiltrated his thoughts. Deep down, he knew he would never be able to make the transition to gaming.

Jim continued to live in Youngstown. Working from home, he navigated his way through the corporate ladder from programmer, to analyst, and eventually to management. Most people of his generation tended to move from company to company, but as Jim's mother aged, his desire to stay with Teradata led to the perception that he was loyal to the company. De Visie Teradata had no desire to buy real estate and the company relied on a remote workforce technology as a centrepiece to its corporate culture.

In 2038, the same year as his mother passed, Jim was promoted to Director of Forecasting. His direct supervisor often referred to him as the company's Chief Prognostication Officer. To celebrate his promotion, Jim bought himself a new electric car; a BYD Model Z. The first major project under Jim's supervision was to use a DNA data base and data mine to identify potential hires who had relationships that were not listed on their bio's. In some cases, the candidate was not even aware of the relationship that was stored in Teradata's DNA database. The team was given a list of very specific positions to research and Jim was never told what happened with the resulting study.

In 2039, DVT was still expanding across geopolitical borders and part of Jim's department's responsibilities was to recommend where to hire and where to avoid. The team used national predictors, UN data and custom research that included GDP, education levels, poverty levels, geopolitical stability and even a happiness index, all of which was assigned to each applicant based on their location. The objective was to ensure that investments in regional training would not be wasted by economic or political disruptors.

In early January 2040, Iran, Syria, and Palestine, declared war on Israel by launching simultaneous drone attacks that pierced the Iron Dome. Within a week, the United States showed its support for Israel by putting troops on the ground in Iran.

This was the start of what might have been called World War III, if it weren't for the contemporaneous outbreak of an acute respiratory pandemic. The airborne transmission of ARP-40 was determined to have a basic reproduction number of 8, meaning each person who was infected, would likely infect 8 other people with an incubation period of one day. By comparison, COVID-19 had a BPR between 2 and 4, with a six-day average incubation period.

ARP-40 did not expose itself with flu-like symptoms that could be ignored. It attacked both the respiratory system and the digestive system, often initially making its appearance known through an onslaught of diarrhea. Jim was on a video call with his direct reports when he first experienced how rapid the incubation attacked the system. The 20-person meeting opened with an overview of objective planning provided by one of his assistant directors. An hour into the meeting, that director abruptly stood up and left the room. The entire team heard the low-level sounds of a diarrhea attack in the background until someone finally muted the AD's microphone. It was then that the human resources person decided to mention the symptoms of a new disease called ARP-40 and the possibility of another global pandemic.

Jim, sitting in the confines of his house, wearing a 'There is No Planet B' t-shirt, was quick to point out to his team that pandemics seemed to be on a 100-year cycle. Even if this was something that was going to spread quickly, thanks to their childhood, everyone on the call could rely on their '2020 hindsight'. His attempt at humour only brought a false laugh track as most participants pondered what they had done wrong to have to live through two pandemics. Jim continued to make light of the situation, using the term 'Panda-war' to describe the juxtaposition of a pandemic arriving at the outbreak of a global war. The seriousness of the situation hit when the virus moved to the assistant director's lungs, and she passed away within a week. Within the first month, seven members of Jim's team had passed. It was clear that for survivors of the previous pandemic, stay-at-home meant stay-at-home-ish. Jim was a poor shopper and a worse chef. As a result, he only did groceries once a month and largely bought canned goods. He was serendipitously set up to shelter at home.

With a population that grew up under the shadows of COVID-19, you would think that there were lots of lessons learned. However, slow reactions, duplicitous communications, and complicit denials seemed to be the initial response. There was no inventory of respirators or stock of PPE, and the current government could only point to this as a failure of the previous government. People quickly started to hoard supplies and global shortages were once again led by a lack of toilet paper. Unlike COVID-19, ARP-40 held no discrimination and had no preferences. It attacked the young and old equally. The R-factor, the lack of protection, and the veracity of the disease soon started killing off as many hospital staff as patients. As a result, many doctors decided to stay at home with everybody else. There were no pots and pans being banged to welcome hospital staff as they came home from their shift. The future relied on the rapid development of a vaccine. Most experts predicted that De Visie Laboratories would be first to the market with a DNA-clone vaccine.

Disease and war were soon the cause of a global famine. Although humanity had feigned interest in correcting its global warming course, the political influence of the petroleum companies had successfully ensured continued reliance on the oil formed from the remains of dead dinosaurs.. As predicted but ignored, the increase in global temperatures meant that icecaps melted and water levels increased accordingly. The resulting loss of low-lying farmland, together with an almost Malthusian population growth, was leading to a global food shortage that would have been at a critical state by 2050. The supply chain disruption, caused by the Panda-war, made for an instant crisis. Food became a luxury item and the only way to ensure you had enough to eat was to grow it yourself.

The larger cities were the first to fall victim to the perfect storm of manmade disasters. At first the streets were empty thanks to the success of the stay-at-home order. However, when you ran out of food, eventually you had to go outside to find some. Grocery store shelves were quickly emptied and there were no truckloads of fresh produce making their way across the country. There were no shipments of anything going anywhere. In the first few weeks of the pandemic, people would cross to the other side of the road as they approached someone. When they stopped crossing, it meant that they wanted to know if you had anything of value ... including food. If someone was carrying a bag, it was unlikely that they were going to make it home. Both offense and defense looked for safety in numbers. No one walked alone. Soon, gangs of 20 to 50 people, all of whom wore masks (even the anti-maskers), started roaming the streets in search of supplies. It became clear that there was no police force that would curtail the crowds. It didn't take long before wealthy suburbs were overrun by mobs in search of subsistence. The homeowner's only defence was firearms and the only way to let the mobs know you were armed, was to let off a round or two.

Jim sat in his mother's living room, smoking weed and watching his ordinateur screen. Like most rural residents, he watched the decline of New York City and San Fransisco on CNNX. As the failure of the social contract spread to the smaller cities, the interweb became the only way to witness the events. The mainstream media could not operate without staff, but there was plenty being transmitted either by someone in the mob trying to capture a successful looting, or a homeowner trying to warn off people from coming into his firing range. Eventually, the digital communications became sporadic and finally fell dark.

Youngstown didn't have the opportunity to plummet into decline like NYC. Just before the airlines stopped flying, a group of older citizens had made a trip to Florida for two weeks of sun and casino visits. They returned home the day before the pandemic was declared, then immediately headed out to replenish their groceries and supplies. The group had returned infected and the town's death rate over the next week was greater than half the population.

Jim inherently knew that vaccine development couldn't possibly be advanced quick enough to save the majority of the population. His hopes were pinned on experimental or non-approved vaccines. What he didn't know was that the major drug manufacturers, owned by De Visie Enterprises, were making absolutely no attempt to produce a solution.

For Jim, Plan B was New London. Two years prior, the construction arm of De Visie Enterprises, DVC, had broken ground on the development of a new type of living environment. The new 'city' was to be built underground with a climate controlled, air filtered, green eco-system, that would have enough food production to make it completely self-sufficient. All the director level positions at DVT had their names entered into a lottery to be granted living quarters in the new facility. Coincidently, the site for the development was just 60 miles down the road from Youngstown. Jim took a drive over to the construction site and the area was completely fenced off. When you are building down, it was impossible for looky-loos to see the progress.

The day of the corporate leadership lottery, Jim was going stir-crazy waiting for the 2 pm announcement. He had been in the house for three weeks solid. He decided it was time to take an inventory. Out back, in his mother's garden, the cannabis seemed to be growing well. Inside, in the pantry, he was down to his last case of Heinz Beans and Campbell's SpaghettiOs. His biggest concern was his lack of potable water. He was okay showering in the town water, but it hadn't passed through his lips in years.

The global water shortage coincided with the acid rain's poisoning of well water in rural areas, resulting in a high price for bottled water.

If he wasn't selected in the lottery, he would need more food and water in less than a week. He knew that the stores would likely be completely empty, and that's when he had an extremely morbid thought: if people died in their homes, maybe he would find food or water in the houses of the dead. He pushed the thought aside and elected to first shop the more traditional route. At 11 am, he took the two-mile drive into town to see if there was any activity. It was the first time he had left his property since the start of lockdown.

Jim was pleased with his purchase of a battery powered vehicle, especially when he saw that the gas bar appeared to be permanently closed. In fact, Gales Gas Bar had run empty three-weeks earlier and was the first business to completely shut down. Driving down Main Street, he couldn't see any signs of life. There was nothing open and no one on the street. The only light he saw came surprisingly from inside the Valumart grocery store, his first employer. He pulled into the parking lot.

Exiting his car, Jim could hear the buzz of the cicadas, which seemed to be doubling each year. Peering through the grocery windows, he saw that the shelves had been scavenged weeks earlier. Like Jim, the grocery store had switched to solar power and the lights would remain on for several years. With his back to the road, he failed to see the three men that approached him until it was too late.

His first inclination that he was in danger came when he caught the reflection of a shovel in the grocery store window. The impact on his skull spun him around and he faced his assailants. His brain didn't register that he knew the men from The Stagecoach Restaurant. One was a server, one was a cook and the third was the restaurant owner. The men watched as Jim's body fell over, face forward, and blood cascaded through his hair onto the sidewalk in front of the grocery store. The threesome had attacked Jim for his car. Their Plan B was to scavenge Wullerton, a small town 37 miles north of Youngstown. The men were extremely disappointed to discover that there was no key fob required for the Model Z and that access to the vehicle was granted through a biometrics protocol. After 20 minutes of arguing how they could get the car to run, they picked up Jim's body and threw it in the trash bin behind the grocery store.

There was no lottery for living space in New London, neither for the tented construction workers, nor the management team of De Visie Enterprise. The decision of who would be invited to live in New

London, was determined by pure necessity and design. As the Director of Forecasting and an expert in data mining, Jim was one of the lucky employees selected to join the team in the new facility. He failed to respond to the invitation.

By the end of that month, a mutation in the virus resulted in a 2500 increase in the R-factor. The new virus, ARP-2500, spread rapidly, killing almost everything in its path. Within two weeks of its identification, there was barely any perceivable human civilization on the planet's surface. Youngstown population: zero.

13. On the Road Again

The street that leads into the town becomes wetter and wetter as small rivulets work their way between the buildings. There are dilapidated houses on either side of the road ... most are still standing but are on their last legs. Jan stops to peer into a large bay window of an isolated home with a collapsed fieldstone fireplace. In the grey wood-sided house, he sees a living room with a sofa and a wing back chair. The chair reminds him of the lounge at the school. Both the chair and the sofa are aimed at a wall with a large screen on it. Jan wonders why the seats would be pointed to a wall rather than towards each other, or better yet out to the front yard. He can't see any movement, so he heads to the front door. He tries the handle. It's locked. He heads back to the street and further in towards the downtown. By the time Jan makes it to the first commercial building, he is wading through six inches of water that flows across the road, perpendicular to the route that Jan is walking. His father's loafers are soaked through again. The water isn't going to stop Jan from entering the town.

There are about twenty commercial buildings on each side of the main road, all one or two storeys. Definitely no skyscrapers. Jan pauses and looks at the first two buildings, one to his left and one to his right. There is no movement, no lights, and no sounds. To his right is 'Simpson's Pharmacy' and to the left is 'Gales Gas Bar'. Jan heads to the gas bar first. There is a small building with four sides of smashed out windows. There are also metal boxes connected to hoses. Jan approaches the building and looks in. He sees one empty chair with torn black material exposing mouldy foam. He moves around and examines the metal boxes, trying to understand the numbers displayed in the glass. The hoses are locked and, judging by the rust, they have clearly not been used for years. Jan tries to free the hoses but fails. He can't understand their function, so he gives up and moves across the street to the next building.

Although it is dark inside, the daylight allows him to see in the pharmacy window. There are rows of shelves about one-third full of various boxes and containers. He can see items in the cosmetic, stationery and seasonal aisles. There is a counter at the back with a 'Prescriptions' sign above it, but the top-half of the counter is closed behind a metal gate. He heads to the front door and is not surprised to find it locked. Jan thinks about breaking one of the windows to get some more supplies, but he is not sure he sees anything he needs. He decides to check some of the other buildings before starting to destroy things. He could always return to the pharmacy.

Jan continues wading through the water to the next building, 'The Stagecoach Restaurant'. There are a few windows, smaller than those of the pharmacy. He pulls on the door and this time it opens. He enters to find a counter on one side and tables on the other side of the room. To Jan, one side of the room looks like a workshop while the other looks like a study area. He pauses as he thinks he hears a noise from inside. He strains his eyes to see the back of the restaurant. Splash. There is definitely sound coming from the door behind the counter.

"Hello," Jan calls out.

No response. He had expected that by now he would have seen at least one person outside the school grounds, but so far there has been nobody. The myth of the Outsider society flashes in his thoughts.

"Is there anyone there?"

He follows a runnel leading from the dining room to the counter. On the counter, he finds a small box with white powder. He is unsure of its purpose and, thanks to his father's weak eyes, in the partial darkness he has trouble reading the blurry writing. He knows his father used glasses to read, but unfortunately Jan doesn't have any on him. Maybe this is a protein powder that he should take with him. He pours some powder out, licks his finger, dips it in then taste the white substance. The bitter tang makes him spit it out immediately, but he has trouble getting rid of the taste of the rat poison.

Jan wades further into the restaurant, past the counter towards the kitchen area. When he gets to the half door, he calls out again. There is just enough light for Jan to see into the room without pushing the door open. He can make out the oven, stoves and cutting boards. He realizes what the room is used for, and he now understands that he is in an eating area.

Splash.

There isn't enough light for Jan to see the source of the splash. He is sure that there is definitely something in the room, but it isn't large. He pulls out a glow-tube and lights up the room. On the far side of the kitchen there are three 50-pound sacks stacked about three feet high, with only the bottom sack sitting in the water. The sacks, labelled 'Flour', start to move. Jan waves the glow-tube from left to right, then suddenly the entire kitchen comes alive. Rats seem to scurry out from every corner, clamoring up and down the stainless-steel countertops.

From deep in the sacks of flour, in a burst of frantic motion, out comes another two dozen rats. Several are knocked off the counter and they screech when they hit the water. The splashing waves and countertop stampede all seem to be quickly making their way towards Jan. He turns, drops the glow-tube in the water and runs to the door, sloshing his way back through the dining area. He pushes the front door open, and it slams behind him. Once outside, he keeps running and heads further into the town before finally slowing down and taking a look back to make sure the rats are not following him. He looks up ... the birds are also no longer there.

Moving slowly through the centre of town, he takes in more building signs. A hardware store, a barber, a small grocery store and another restaurant. All appear to be empty. Away from the rat restaurant, there is no movement and no sound other than Jan's wading motion. Jan calls out just in case, but he isn't inclined to go into another building. In front of the grocery store, there is parking for about two dozen cars. Jan looks over at the only car in the parking lot, a BYD Model Z. The car reminds him of the golf carts that the doctors rode in, but with slightly larger rubber wheels. He gets a shiver looking at it and decides to stay clear of the store, its parking lot, and the eerie car. He continues trudging his way down the main street.

The water seems to be moving across the street faster now and Jan feels raindrops falling on his head again. He has yet to get used to the sensation of the water randomly falling from the sky. He looks up and sees a constant stream coming down. It is warmer and lighter than the day before and is almost welcoming. Like a four-year-old running in the rain, Jan tries to dart in between the raindrops. He decides that he likes rain after all.

At the cross street beside the river, he sees the signs 'Main Street' and 'Riverside Drive'. The rain starts to beat down intensely as Jan reaches a bridge at the far end of town. The bridge crosses a river rushing past the far side of Youngstown.

The rise of the bridge takes Jan's feet out of the water, but since he is soaked by the rain, he barely notices. From the bridge, he can see the water flowing from his right to his left. The river has overflowed its banks and flooded through the streets of the town. The other side of the bridge dips back down, and the river swallows the road again. Jan stops at the top of the bridge and looks down at the rushing waters. There are pieces of patio furniture being pulled rapidly downstream. At the other side of the bridge, Jan has to wade back into the water. Stepping off the far side of the bridge, he puts his feet into four inches of water. Ahead, the road climbs its way back out of the river, where it heads back up a hill.

Jan begins to trudge his way towards the hill and the water is halfway up his calf by his second step. On the third step, the water is up to Jan's knees, and he can feel the force starting to push him downstream. He leans his body upstream to balance the force of the water, holding his bag of treasures above his head. On the next step, the pavement has been cut away by the overflowing river and, forgetting his body's lack of muscle conditioning, Jan loses his balance. He falls backwards and the torrent of water surrounds him, pulling him downstream. He bobs up and down, gasping for air. His hands are flailing as he searches for something to stop his downstream momentum. His bag, that was across his torso, is now around his neck and choking him. He has travelled a hundred feet when he gets a mouth full of river water that seems to go straight into his lungs.

Disoriented, his body crashes into something beneath the waterline, and he hears a crack as his torso pushes up against a stump.

Fortunately, the crack came from a branch and not from one of his bones. He hangs on to a branch stemming out from the stump, while he tries to assess his situation. Jan is a phenomenal swimmer, but how will his father's body do in this current? He looks at both banks and determines he is equidistant from either side. He doesn't think he can make it to dry land with the force of the current. It is at this point that Jan discovers his father's mild case of rheumatoid arthritis. His fingers stiffen up as his joints begin to swell. He attempts to straighten his hand to improve his grip, but the harder he tries, the greater the pain. Jan feels his grasp slip. His fingers finally respond, so he desperately grabs for another branch. The mud makes it is impossible to get a strong enough hold on anything to hang on. He soon finds himself travelling back downstream, arms returning to the familiar flailing motion.

Another fifty yards, another mouth full of water and Jan feels his body crash into the trunk of a tree that has fallen into the river. Jan suffers from this one as his abdomen wraps awkwardly around the tree trunk. His bag rips and he watches the contents sail away. His eyes follow the trunk to the shore where he sees that the widening of the river has weakened the roots, causing the tree to fall over. If he can hang on, he could pull himself across the tree trunk to the shore. He begins to pull but can feel the ache in his left side. Jan knows his chest will be bruised at best. He continues to wrench himself along the tree and is able to gather up his bag as he moves. When the water is shallow enough, it becomes easier to heave his body across the tree trunk, and eventually on to the riverbank.

Once on shore, he lies facing the sky, listening to the torrential waters as he tries to catch his breath. After a couple of minutes, Jan sits up and inspects the torn canvas bag. His one remaining juice box, *Treasure Island* and all the glow-tubes are gone. The only thing left is a wet map of the *City of London 1886*. He is relieved because at least he still has the item that should be of greatest help to him once he reaches the city. He looks upstream towards Youngstown. He is at least 300 yards away. A hill sits in front of him, and he is no longer near the road. He massages his tender left side and pulls his exhausted body up the side of the hill, grabbing on to the occasional bush and thick yellow grass to aide his climb. At the top of the hill, the grass is replaced by rocks and boulders.

Jan's eyesight isn't the 20/15 vision that was assessed during his 'father's day eve' medical exam. He squints to see what is ahead of him. He travels on a diagonal path, taking the hypotenuse towards the road. Being wet from the river experience, he hardly notices that it is still raining until the rain stops. He watches the grey clouds float past him towards the school and wonders if it had ever been raining outside while the inside projected clear blue skies. Another lie.

Jan feels a muscle at the inside top of his leg as it tightens up. He gets a reminder of the pain with every step. He slows down his gait and walks with a straight leg to lessen the pain. Taking a diagonal route, with the groin pull it takes him a half hour to reach the road. The pain has finally subsided and he can continue his route towards New London. It is already midafternoon, and the sun has dried out Jan's wet clothes. Everything feels stiff. On the side of the road, he senses a slithering motion across the rocks, but whenever he turns his head, he doesn't see anything. At one point he hears a hiss, so he decides to pick up a few stones for protection. Be prepared.

He reaches a bend in the road, signified by a sign with an arrow on it. Jan fails to realize that there is a bobcat slinking through the dried shrubbery behind the sign. The cat steps slowly out on to the road about 20 feet in front of him before he notices. The boy stops. Other than seeing rats and turkey vultures, this is his first close encounter with an animal, and he looks directly into the bobcat's eyes. Had he seen a wild animal before, he might have acted differently. He isn't afraid of the beast so as he stares, the cat snarls. This is Jan's first inclination that the animal might want to hurt him.

When meeting a bobcat, it might be scared off by acting large, but it will always chase if its prey runs. Jan is unaware of this and he just stares right back into the cat's eyes. At this point, there are several other ways to make the cat attack. Play dead, and it will pounce. Act too large, and the cat will attack because it feels threatened. Stare directly at it, and it will see this as either threatening or a sign of weakness, either way it will charge. In short, there are a number of actions that Jan can take, all of which will lead to the same outcome.

Jan continues to look directly at the cat, waiting for it to move off the road. If Jan had known to look at the bobcat's stomach, he would have seen that it is empty. He would have seen that it is feeding time.

The animal starts slowly towards Jan baring its teeth. Now Jan is sure that this isn't a friendly approach. He reaches into his pocket and feels the stones that he has picked up earlier. They would be totally inadequate for a beast this size. The bobcat lets out a growl and the soundwave pulses through Jan's body.

Suddenly, the cat lunges. Jan's face is the first to register the sting of the claws which brings blood dripping from his cheek. His arms instinctively come up and he is somewhat successful at fending off the large paws. As the cat passes over him, he is staring at the massive fangs at the back of the top row of teeth. A snarl, then a snap! Everything about the animal seems larger. For the second time that day, Jan realizes how little strength he has as he tries to shove the bobcat away.

He is stumbling backward as his attacker quickly regroups. The animal begins to circle, as his prey moves to keep facing towards it. Jan is no longer just staring back. He now knows what the outcome of a staring contest will be. His eyes are darting, trying to take in his surroundings. There is a stray branch in the shrubbery behind the bobcat. He joins the circle dance and starts to rotate along with the cat ... each animal once again locking their eyes on the other. Jan is getting closer to the branch. The cat stops and starts circling back in the other direction. This prevents Jan from making his way to the wooden limb.

The cat lunges again and this time it manages to sink its teeth into the arm that Jan raises into a defensive position. Pain dominates his every thought. He imagines that this is what death feels like. In agony, he instinctively punches the cat in the nose. The animal maintains his grip and Jan punches it again. This time he hits the cat in the eye. It lets go.

Jan immediately runs at the beast pushing it back and uses his momentum to follow through to the other side of the road, stopping only when he reaches the piece of wood. As he picks up his weapon, the one-eyed feline reaches out to Jan with one paw, snarling. Jan sees the blood dripping from his arm. The bite has done more damage than he had realized but his adrenaline is fighting against the pain. Again, the predator lunges but Jan winds up following through with his best tennis forehand, and he hears the wood crack as it breaks across his attacker's chest. The damage is done, to both his wooden weapon and his attacker. The cat falls on its side and Jan realizes that the branch has disintegrated. From the Tuesday wrestling sessions, Jan instinctively knows that the best time to go on the offense is when your opponent is down. He throws his body onto the cat and immediately regrets this decision.

His new form came with none of his former strength and his new body doesn't hold any of the cells required for his muscle memory to function properly. Jan is also feeling the damage to his arm and face. The animal squirms as the two wrestle. Jan thinks that any second the cat will wriggle free. He forces his leg muscles up towards the cat's head and presses on the bobcat's throat, carefully avoiding its mouth. The cat squirms and Jan knows that if he lets it go, he will be an easy prey. He squeezes his legs with all his father's might and continues to hold his grip on the animal's throat. Eventually he senses the cat slow down its movement, then stop breathing. The boy has now not only experienced death, but he has also caused it.

Jan slowly stands up and once on his feet he is overcome by the urge to start running. Bolting down the road, he quickly glances back at the carcass to make sure that the cat isn't getting back up. He is losing blood badly from his arm wound and he can feel a depletion of energy. He slows down as a light-headed feeling overcomes him. He puts the map in his back pocket, rips the light canvas bag and bandages it around his arm. In seconds, the blood starts to seep through, so Jan doubles up on the canvas bandage.

He is still faint as he realizes that he hasn't eaten anything in the past two days. As he walks slowly, he watches the surroundings for something to eat. There is nothing available at the side of the road and once again, darkness is beginning to set in. Ahead, Jan notices the road slips through a tunnel. There is another road running perpendicular above the one he has been following.

He approaches the overpass and climbs up a moderately sloped embankment. About 20 feet up, he reaches the other roadway. Instead of being the familiar black pavement, the crossroad is made up of a blue rubber. Jan can see the surrounding land is dusty and brown to the right but is alive and green to the left. Now he has a real decision to make. He can either continue following the current blacktop, or he can change to the new blue road. If he follows the new road, he will also have to decide whether he heads left or right. He is scanning the horizon of each of his choices, when he realizes that something is approaching. Even though he is looking in its direction, he hears the familiar whoosh before he can see its shape.

A shuttle is approaching from the verdant side of the blue road. He slides back down the hill. It is unlikely that anyone would be looking out of their shuttle while travelling down such a mundane path, but Jan plays it safe. After two minutes, the shuttle speeds by, pushing a rush of air over the side of the road and down the embankment to envelop Jan. The indigo glow of the shuttle's sensors fades into the darkness as it speeds away. Jan's heart pumps faster. He is fairly sure that no one would have seen him as he scurried down the slope at the side of the blue rubber road.

Jan doesn't know it, but this is a delivery shuttle that is unmanned and it has been programmed through the guidance system to travel from De Soto-07-042B to New London-34-119E. The vehicle's speed of 200 miles per hour creates very little sonic disruption thanks to the air propulsion and efficient aerodynamic design. The air that rushes over the embankment, and over Jan, was the air pressure that's generated by the transport cluster. This mechanism is powered by zero-emission, hydrogen exchange fuel cells. Having never been inside a shuttle, Jan has no appreciation for the recent advancements in vehicle technology. He lies still on the side of the embankment even though he knows the vehicle had passed. He feels weak. He pulls up some of the grass with his right arm and starts to chew on it. It isn't a meal, but it is something ... at least it helps to quell the pang in his father's stomach.

After a light grass snack, Jan walks back up the embankment to the blue road. He stands in the darkness pondering his next steps. Without warning, he catches himself as his legs begin to buckle. In addition to his hunger and his injury, Jan feels an overwhelming tiredness. He has been operating on extraordinarily little sleep and has been walking for almost two days solid. His father's weak muscles are aching, and Jan feels the pain. He decides it is time to rest, so he retreats below the underpass and finds a slab of level concrete to use as his temporary bunk.

As he sits down on the concrete, he feels the cold come up through his body. He curls his back and drops his head between his legs. He thinks about his journey so far: about the bobcat, about the rats, about the raging waters. His eyes start to well up and the boy, for the first time in his life, feels sorry for himself. The new emotions overwhelm his 17-year-old mind and Jan begins to cry. The sobbing becomes uncontrollable. Jan can taste the saltiness as his father's tears roll down from his eyes to his lips. He feels ill prepared for this journey.

Attempting to regain some composure, he wonders how his map might help guide him. He wipes his tears and pulls the water-soaked map of London from his back pocket. He carefully unfolds the damp paper and begins to examine the streets. The map hadn't made sense to him in the library, but he assumed that once he made it to New London, it will be extremely useful. In the top right corner is a drawing of a lady in dark robes labelled 'Queen Victoria'. The queen has some similarities to Nurse Rossignol, but she is clearly far more regal. Jan wonders why the map would have a picture of a woman featured so prominently, as though she is held in high regard.

He traces his finger following the river that runs through the centre of the city. On the riverbank are wharfs labelled with the supplies that are shipped from that area. He sees timber, cement, refuse and manure. He moves from the river to the streets and begins to trace along a road labelled 'Fleet Street'. He reaches a square representing a building that reads 'Printworks'. Next to that is a pub and next to that are urinals. Jan really regrets not having a dictionary. Eventually he comes to University College, where a wall surrounds dozens of buildings, including one labelled 'Library'. This is it. This will be his objective: When he gets to New London, he will find Fleet Street and then make his way to the library.

With this comforting thought in mind, he lies down on the concrete for a quick nap and drifts off faster than he could have imagined. As he sleeps, another shuttle passes unnoticed on the overpass above him. The sun sinks slowly as if it hesitant to leave the sky, and eventually Jan is engulfed in the tunnel's darkness. Unbeknownst to him, a scorpion crawls across his body and three vultures come scavenging through the underpass. Jan sleeps deeply through the night. When the early morning sun rises, it fails to penetrate the shadows of the underpass. His father's body needs far more rest than Jan's regular ride.

Eventually, the sun rises sufficiently to stream into the underpass tunnel. A butterfly enters and flutters its way towards Jan. It lands on his hair and folds its wings straight up. The motion wakes Jan. The butterfly passes in front of his nose and heads back out of the tunnel. There is the sound of another shuttle. Jan briefly ponders if he has been awoken by the sunlight, the butterfly or the approaching shuttle. He scurries out to the embankment to watch the shuttle pass. As it nears then whisks past him, Jan notices how high the sun is and realizes that it is probably close to mid-morning. He wonders if his sleeping problem has been resolved as he has probably just slept past the two long blasts of the school's wakeup horn. Another shuttle passes, going in the opposite direction. The blue road is relatively busy.

It is clear to Jan that if he wants to travel covertly, he had better stick to the safety of the old road. Besides, there is something comforting about reading the distance markings on the signs.

Walking away from the tunnel, Jan can hear another shuttle approaching on the blue road, so he runs back to the underpass. He looks down the black covered road and sees a bend about 200 yards away. The road winds around some bushes and a sparse forest. Jan massages his injured left arm and when the sound of the passing shuttle subsides, he sprints down the road towards the bend like a wide receiver running for a Hail Mary pass. Even in his old body, he is running flat out at a speed that might have made Coach Treinador proud. He reaches the bend and doesn't give up his momentum until he is around the corner and behind the small group of trees, out of sight of the shuttle road.

As he continues down the older road, he is glad that he hadn't travelled last night. Jan can see wear and dilapidation in the road that wouldn't have been as perceivable under the cover of night. He stumbles as his toe hits a crack in the pavement. The decay at the edges would surely have tripped Jan if he had attempted his journey in the darkness. It is challenging enough traversing the pavement during daylight.

The forest beside the road has different types of trees compared to the ones at the Academy. The trees are just as green but are denser and more triangular in shape. Soon he is walking past a field of tall grass and purple flowers. The flowers look magnificent to him as the sun intensifies the brightness and colouration. Before this week, the only time Jan had ever seen flowers was on the tables of the dining hall when there was a special dinner for a visiting doctor that Jan can't recall the name of.

The buzzing sounds from the previous day are replaced by a different variation of noise from the forest. Jan looks up to the sky.

He hoped to see the birds flying overhead again, but there are none to be found. He remembers the book on animals that he had flipped through. At one point he had considered asking Dr. Osler if there was a zoo in New London, but never got around to it. His mind shifts as he once again hears almost imperceptible movements in the sparse forest beside him. He is sure there is a sound, and it seems to be keeping pace with his movements.

Another green sign, 'New London 12, De Soto 299'. This sign also has some less structured paint work on it. The fluorescent orange writing with dripping letters looked as though it says: 'BRAIN DRAIN'. 12 more somethings to go. Jan knows he has travelled at least half the distance to his objective, and he feels good about his progress. He imagines that if it were night, he'd be able to see the glow of the city across the sky. He is also acutely aware that he is very hungry. Breakfast is probably already over at the Academy. This is the longest that Jan has ever gone without eating. At his current pace, it might be night again before he is able to make it to New London.

By mid-afternoon Jan knows that he will be in trouble if he doesn't find something to eat that day. He is beginning to feel ill, and he needs to get to the city ... sleeping on the side of the road again isn't an option. The imposing sun is once again bearing down on him. His old muscles are stiff from his new exercise regime. Jan wonders if there really are people that live outside the system, as Dr. Osler had said. Why is there no one on this road? His thoughts are put on hold as he notices a change in the road ahead. It ends abruptly. The broken road turns into a gravel road, which shortly thereafter is consumed by grasses. A field lay where Jan expected the road to be. As he peered across the almost barren landscape, Jan can see a field of brown earth and sparse ugly green plants. There is no sign of the road restarting. Without this to guide him, he has no idea of the direction to travel to make it to New London. He wonders if he should rest until the sun sets so he can look for the glow, but his grass dinner from the night before is causing too great a pain inside his stomach. He needs to use his remaining energy to at least try to make it to the city.

Looking around, Jan is faced with a field in front of him, the road behind him, a small mud marsh to the right of him and light shrubbery to the left. Even though the field is the continuation of the path, it seems clear that it doesn't go anywhere. He decides the best choice is

The Gemini Project

to head through the bushes on the right. If he is lucky, he will be able to find another road or link up to a blue road. At first, the shrubs are easy enough to traverse but sharp nettles stab through Jan's pant legs. The shooting pain makes him stop a couple of times to pull out the embedded barbs.

Jan rubs his legs until the pain of the nettles subsides. There is an unctuous smell coming up from the ground. This is followed by a noise that reminds Jan of the opening of a bottle of sparkling water. The unalarming hiss gradually turns into a more foreboding growl. The sound seems to be coming from one of the bushes. Jan approaches slowly. He pulls back the branches of the bush and exposes the deep blue eyes and the gnashing teeth of a wild animal. The four-legged creature widens its mouth and intensifies its growl. Jan has grown accustomed to the feeling of fear. Even though it is smaller, this creature is still equally as frightening as the wildcat he had met the day before. There is no pretense. It is clear to Jan that the animal wants to harm him.

He backs up slowly, letting the thorns scrape across his legs. He hopes that the creature will let the showdown end, but the animal offers no quarter. He locks on to the eyes creeping out of the bush towards him. Jan is in no condition to engage in another fight. With barely a thought as to what the strategy will be, Jan turns and runs. He senses that the animal is running too but he can't risk losing any speed to look behind him. Then Jan sees another animal approaching him diagonally. The creatures have short brown fur and pointed ears. A long tongue hangs out the side of the second animal's mouth as this beast too bares its teeth and growls. Suddenly the new creature lets out a long howl. Jan gets to a point where he realizes that even though he is keeping pace, the animal behind him is going to force him into the path of the other attacker.

Jan stops, picks up a rock and throws it back towards the first animal. He misses, but he momentarily breaks its stride. He picks up another rock and throws a fastball at the other advancing creature approaching diagonally towards him. He hits the second beast square in the head, and it lets out a yelp as it topples over. Jan turns and heads in the same direction as his perfect pitch. He hurdles over the heap of the fallen creature. In the process, he is able to catch a glimpse behind him. He can see that there are now four or five creatures emerging from the bushes to join in the chase. He has used up his sprint speed.

He feels himself beginning to slow down, but he doesn't sense that the animals are beginning to wane. Again, he hears a howl released by one of his pursuers and the sound has its desired effect.

Ahead, there is an embankment that either leads up a small hill or supports a road. Jan is quite sure that at least one of the relentless pack will catch him as he reaches the top of the embankment. He shoots up the side of the hill, crosses over a blue rubber road and stumbles down the other side. He braces himself for a pounce from one of the creatures but nothing comes. He gets up hurriedly and continues running. He is pushing himself as hard as he can. He feels his heart thrusting in his chest from both fear and physical exertion. Exhausted, Jan slows down when he realizes that he can no longer sense his pursuers. Maintaining a jog, he finally glances over his shoulder to confirm that the chase is indeed over. The beasts have abruptly stopped following him. They are nowhere in sight.

Once he lets his heart rate drop, Jan pulls down his pants and tears out the barbed thorns that have hooked their way into his legs during the chase. There are at least fifty cuts and gashes. He isn't taking very good care of his new body. Jan pulls more thorns from his pants, gets dressed and walks slowly back towards the shuttle road. He needs to be able to follow that road. Carefully he climbs the embankment and peers left and right. He is half expecting to see the animals on the pavement, but they are still nowhere to be seen. Jan pauses. He feels his back pocket and he realizes that in the chase, he has lost his map. He needs that map.

As he steps on to the road's blue surface, Jan still can't see where his stalkers are hiding. His eyes focus on a flapping sound, and he sees a large piece of paper trying to escape a thorny bush, about 100 yards back through the thicket. The map of London! This might be the only way for Jan to get to the library. Maybe he can make a run for it if he is sure the creatures are gone. He keeps his eyes locked on the fluttering paper and slowly moves to the centre of the road. The map is waving in the wind and the thorns are tearing through Queen Victoria. Jan hears the low growl again. He pushes himself up onto his toes and looks down the embankment to see fourteen eyes staring back at him. Jan freezes waiting for the pack to make the first move this time.

The chase doesn't resume. Staring into their eyes, Jan wonders if they are waiting for him to come for the map. Hiding down the side of the embankment is a clever manoeuvre to catch Jan if he returns for his belongings. The creatures move back and forth along the side of the road. Occasionally one of them heads partway up the embankment, and Jan gets ready to restart his retreat. However, the creature turns with a jerk and heads back down the hill. Jan deduces that they won't step onto the blue surface, even though it is clear that they want to. How long will the threat of the blue road keep the animals at bay? Sporadically one of the creatures locks its stare on Jan and howls at him. There is no way to get the map unless the beasts leave.

It is a waiting game. As the standoff continues, Jan wipes the sweat from his brow and feels dried blood crumbling from his face. He then massages his pulsing temples and feels where his skin has been laser sealed after the transplant. He knows he is unfamiliar with his new body, but he now understands he is also unfamiliar with his new face, especially in the condition it is in. Running his hand across his chin to the back of his head, he thinks that the stubble of his beard and his incoming hair are probably at the same level of growth.

He decides that he will have to give up on the map. He has to get moving before one of the creatures becomes brave enough to chase him again. Since this road is parallel to the old route, Jan concludes that he will probably reach the city if he travels in the same direction he was previously heading. He breaks his stance and begins to slowly edge his way down the blue highway. As he moves, the beasts prowl beside him. They have a combination of white, grey, and black fur, each one with a slightly different appearance. The lead creature has piercing blue eyes, not unlike Jan's. Jan quickens his movement to a jog and the creatures keep pace. He is running away from the map of London. Jan continues his trek with his pursuers following along, at first growling and eventually panting with their long tongues hanging down toward the earth. He gets his breath back again and is able to quicken his pace even more. The pack picks up its speed as well and remain alongside Jan. He focuses on the lead beast and the creature looks right back. Jan is unsure if the alpha is stalking him or befriending him.

The sounds of Jan's awkward trotting and the creatures panting, soon give way to a faint whoosh from a shuttle approaching from behind. Instinctively, he almost dives down the embankment on the left, which would have placed him on the same side as the animals, but he catches himself and ducks down the right embankment. He hears the animals scatter too. The shuttle passes and Jan walks back up to the road. The creatures slowly creep back to the side of the embankment. Jan needs to avoid the shuttle, but he can see that the beasts are also conditioned to stay clear. He wonders if it is the road or the shuttle that keeps the creatures at bay. If it is the latter, eventually they might venture on to the road.

Picking up his pace again, Jan is pleased to see the animals sticking to their pattern of staying clear of the road. After about an hour of jogging and dodging three more shuttles, he is becoming frustrated that there are no signs marking the remaining distance. He also wonders why he can't see any lights on the horizon. Jan figures that he has to be close enough to have some indication of the city by now. Finally, on the lefthand side in the distance, he is sure that he can make out rows of buildings separated by perfectly square streets. However, as he approaches, Jan realizes that all he had seen is the beginning of another forest. The trees are planted in perfect rows, ten feet apart from each other. The realization that he has been misled by trees, further compounds his frustration. His exhaustion and gnawing hunger are winning the psychological battle. There isn't that much daylight left.

As Jan gets closer to the organized forest, he sees that there is one large building near the trees at the side of the roadway. It is a strange looking structure with no windows. The building is clearly dilapidated. It consists of crumbling stone on the bottom that runs up about a quarter of the structure, with the remainder of the walls made from the same wood that was used to construct the roof. The wood has been painted red on the sides and green on the roof, but over half the paint has faded and peeled off. Jan looks at the straight lines formed by the trees and they remind him of the bookshelves in the library. Each tree has bright red apples growing on it, and there are also many browner ones on the ground surrounding the trunks of the trees. Jan knows what an apple is, but he has never even considered where they come from.

As he leaves the road to investigate further, he looks back to see if he has to worry about the beasts. Only one creature has followed him this far. It is lying down at the start of the treeline, panting, and watching Jan explore the surroundings. It seems to be hesitant to enter the orchard.

At the trees, Jan first picks up a brown apple and bites into it. It is soft and mushy, so Jan spits it out. He reaches up and pulls a redder apple from the tree. As he bites into the Red Gala, he feels the juices run over his tongue and down his throat. He is hyper aware of the sensation. This is great food ... even better than the apples that they serve at the Academy. Jan looks at the apple as he chews and sees a long thin creature squirming its way back into the fruit. He has bitten the creature in half. The taste is satisfying, so Jan finishes the apple and then grabs another. Before biting into the second apple, he wonders if the animal would like the taste. He returns to the safety of the road, walks back to the start of the orchard, then rolls an apple down to the beast. Before the apple hits the bottom of the road, the rest of the pack come running from a thicket of bushes. The animals pounce on the apple, with the winning creature running back into the bushes, pursued by two other creatures. The alpha did not join the fight for the apple.

Jan goes back to the trees, rolls up his shirt to form a loose bag and grabs as many red apples as he can carry. This time, instead of rolling them, he throws the apples one at a time. The beasts chase after the apple and the fastest creature grabs its prize and races off. While the pack chases the fruit, Jan tosses an apple to the alpha, who has remained at the bottom of the embankment. The pack returns, but none of the creatures seem to want to enter the orchard. Jan throws another apple and this time the blue-eyed creature, the one that first approached him in the bushes, joins the fun. He repeats the game over and over. The alpha is winning the most apple races. It is also the most efficient at devouring its prey and returning for more. When Jan has only seven apples left, he throws them out, one after another, in rapid succession, sending the creatures in different directions, each with a prize. Jan returns to the apple trees and picks another apple; this one is for himself. He heads over to the dilapidated building.

As he eats his apple, he examines the building. There are two large doors on the front, perhaps the largest doors that Jan has ever seen, but there are no windows on any side. He pulls on one door, but it will not budge. When he pulls on the second door, the entrance gives way as the hinges come off the wall. The wooden slat door crashes to the ground. Jan jumps back momentarily, then cautiously returns to peer inside. There is plenty of light streaming in from the many holes in the walls. The light beams bolt down to the ground from various angles and almost look like they are holding up the structure. From the outside, the building appears as if it could be two or three storeys tall, but inside it is all just one room. The floor is covered in yellow dried grass. Jan enters slowly and sees machinery against the walls, which he thinks look like some of the contraptions in the janitorial room in the basement of Renaissance Hall. He walks around the room and examines the machines. One is marked 'Cider Press'. Another is labelled 'Progressive Apple Wedger'.

The most interesting apparatus has four large rubber wheels supporting a green vehicle that is labelled 'John Deere'. Up top, there is a seat. Jan knows immediately that this is a form of transportation, like a large one-man golf cart. He climbs up the side and sits down on the green metal seat. It turns out to be surprisingly more comfortable than it looks. He bounces up and down on the seat, holding on to a large wheel mounted to a pedestal that rises from the floor. He feels the hefty metal springs of the seat pushing back on his buttocks. The smile that creeps into Jan's expression, as he continues the bouncing motion, is similar to the one that appeared just before every father's day.

He continues his exploration of the vehicle. The device has several hand and foot levers. As he looks back and forth, Jan tries to guess what each device controls. He notices two gauges, one marked Oil and the other marked only with the letters 'E' and 'F' at opposite sides of the gage. The second gauge is pointing towards the 'F', and a set of keys is dangling from the dashboard. Jan tries to pull the keys out, but they seemed permanently affixed to the vehicle. As he attempts to apply some pressure, he wiggles the keys from side to side. Suddenly, as he moves the keys to the right, the vehicle starts thumping from behind. It pushes out a puff of black smoke and then thrusts forward jerking Jan, almost throwing him off. After composing himself, he turns the keys left, then right again and the same single thump pushes the vehicle forward again, but this time Jan is prepared and easily keeps himself on the seat.

He decides to try some of the levers. After moving the hand lever and turning the key, he finds himself riding out in a forward thrusting motion again. On his next attempt, Jan steps on the two foot levers. This time, when he turns the key, the single thump is followed by another and another, until there is a constant loud chugging noise. Jan is convinced that he has performed the right actions up to this point, but now wonders what the next steps should be. Should he turn the large wheel, or move the hand levers, or do something else with the foot pedals? The pressure of holding the foot pedals down is making his leg cramp and without thinking, Jan releases his downward force.

The vehicle jerks forward and rips out the wires that run from the battery to the back wall. It starts to jerkily move around the building. Jan loses his balance momentarily but then regains his equilibrium by pulling on the horizontal wheel. While this allows Jan to pull himself back up, it also has the side effect of turning the vehicle to the left and throwing Jan to the right. The machine chugs around the floor of the building in a counterclockwise circle. Jan turns the wheel again and this changes the vehicle's direction … now it is going straight. While it isn't travelling at a rapid speed, it is still fast enough to cross the barn floor in less than four seconds. This gives Jan just enough time to think about how to operate the direction of the vehicle before the right front tire crashes over the Progressive Apple Wedger. The tractor avoids the machinery and is crossing the grass floor towards the barn wall.

Realizing that the vehicle is going to crash into the wall, Jan jumps off and tumbles on to the yellow grass as though he is trying to recover from a failed dismount on the parallel bars. The tractor hits the stone wall, which crumbles surprisingly easily. The boards above the wall then come collapsing down and crack as the tractor climbs over the rubble of stone and wood. Jan sits crab legged, watching the vehicle exit the building towards the orchard. He springs up, runs through the barn door and around to the side of the building, arriving just in time to watch the tractor plough into a row of apple trees. The first tree comes tumbling down, but its remnants along with the strong rooting of the second and third tree, bring the vehicle to a halt. As the large rear wheels spin around to fight the trees, there is a loud bang followed by another big puff of black smoke. The tractor stops chugging.

The only sound that remains is a hissing from the front of the vehicle, which is gradually dissipating into silence. When the sound of the steam dies, Jan realizes that there is a hissing also coming from behind him. He quickly runs behind the barn and listens to the noises emanating from the blue road. Another more mechanical sound begins to crescendo. As the resonance grows louder, Jan feels the earth start to tremble and he touches the ground with his fingertips.

There is a loud boom followed by silence. Then Jan believes that he hears the sound of a shuttle warm-up and leave. He crawls from behind the barn to the embankment, where he can see a shuttle departing in the direction of Corpo Academy. He stares down the road in each direction but sees nothing else unusual. The pack has backed away from the road and the orchard. They slink back to the embankment, panting. Jan wonders if the noise of the tractor had prevented him from hearing the shuttle approaching, but he also wonders what the great rumble was that had preceded the departing shuttle's hiss.

Returning to the side of the building, he looks at the wheeled contraption that now rests gently on the remains of the apple tree. He is sure that this was a mode of transportation from the past and he imagines that these types of vehicles must have travelled down black roads like the one he was following the previous evening. With only room for one passenger, Jan deduced that the roads would have been extremely crowded with John Deeres.

His thought is gradually interrupted by the sound of another approaching shuttle. He heads up toward the road and lies down on the embankment. The shuttle slows down and stops about 100 yards down the road. Jan ducks down further, afraid that he has somehow been spotted. He hears the high-pitched hissing sound start up again and then he sees white clouds burst from the roadway in front of the shuttle. The roadway splits across its entire length, then a rectangular shape lifts to reveal a downward tunnel. On the side of the tunnel hatch, written in block letters, is 'NEW LONDON'. The shuttle enters the tunnel, and the hissing begins again. This is followed by a loud boom as the roadway closes back up. The pack scatters at the sound.

The steam clears, everything falls silent. The road looks the same as before, with no signs of the tunnel entrance. Jan runs up the embankment to inspect the hidden entrance. He can see the line in the road where the tunnel appeared and he tries to pull on the metal strips, but the access mechanism won't budge. This is the entrance to the city. Jan has arrived. Now all he has to do is get through the entranceway somehow. With no obvious way of exposing the tunnel, Jan decides that he'll have to follow a shuttle in. He takes a position down the embankment and waits for the gate to open. Instinctively, he lays low in a military-type position at the top of the trench. The window of time to enter isn't very long, so Jan will have to remain as close as possible to the opening.

Lying there for five minutes, trying to remain perfectly still, he hears a panting sound. He turns around slowly and sees that one of the beasts is about ten inches away from his face. It's blue-eyes, the creature that he had first encountered. The creature is panting, and its eyes become fixed on Jan's. It moves slowly, stretching its paws out in front as it tentatively comes even closer towards him. Realizing that the canine isn't scared, Jan also relaxes his stance. He sees that instead of baring its teeth, the creature is wagging its tail. Abruptly, the dog darts away from Jan. The sudden motion makes Jan think that it might be on the attack again, so he instinctively rolls over. Seconds later, Jan hears an approaching shuttle.

He decides that he will watch the procedure one more time, this time from close up, before attempting to find his way down the tunnel. The shuttle stops within inches of the metal strips and the hissing starts immediately. The white clouds of smoke spill over the edge of the embankment and Jan can feel the wet air burning at his face. He braces through it and watches as the gateway rises like a triangle from his new vantage point. The shuttle enters and the tunnel swallows it up. The final boom comes as the drawbridge closes, sending a burst of air rushing over Jan. The motion is followed again by silence. Being this near to the entrance, the closing noise is much louder. Jan figures he has about twenty seconds to get into the tunnel before it closes on him. That seems do-able, even using his father's legs.

Jan doesn't have to wait long before the tunnel begins to open again. He looks down the road and there is nothing approaching. The entranceway is wide open. Jan considers making a run for it but decides he will wait until he sees the shuttle coming down the road. There is still no shuttle approaching. He hears a hollow sound, then a shuttle surprises him by coming out of the tunnel. Jan realizes that this is an exit, as well as an entrance, so he decides to make his move. He stands up from the side of the embankment and runs towards the open tunnel.

Four, five, six ... he is counting to twenty in his head. He hears the dogs howling behind him, his own little cheering section. Eight, nine, ten ... he is twenty feet away from the opening. The howling becomes louder. Without warning, there is a hissing noise and Jan senses that the tunnel is going to close in less than the 20 seconds. Before he can stop himself, he has one foot over the metal strip that marks the beginning of the tunnel. Hiss. He isn't going to make it, so he pulls back just as the roadway closes up in front of him with a thud. The force created by the closing, knocks Jan four feet back and he winds up on his rear, back in the crab position. He feels foolish as he sits there. Of course, when a shuttle is entering, the gateway has to remain open long enough for the vehicle to get clear inside, but when a shuttle is leaving, the door can close as soon as the vehicle departs.

Jan looks at the canines.

"You guys were warning me? Pretty smart ... I guess we're even for the apples now."

He picks himself up and settles back into his military position on the side of the embankment. He waits for a good half hour, but still another shuttle hasn't approached. Jan notices that the sun is setting, so he decides to go over to the orchard to pick a few more apples in case he needs sustenance in the city. He is too late in coming up with the idea. The dogs scatter as the swoosh of a shuttle approaches in the distance, from the direction of the Academy. The roadway opens up again, like a mouth ready to swallow the shuttle. Once the shuttle starts to enter, Jan heads up from the embankment and runs to the tunnel. Eight ... nine ... ten. Just before entering, he looks over to see blue-eyes sitting at the edge of the road, panting and wagging its tail. For a moment, he thinks that his new friend might follow him. Jan makes it into the tunnel.

Inside, the downward sloping roadway is comprised of the same blue rubber material as the main road. Jan feels the slight springiness as he runs down the ramp. He hears the gateway hiss and then slam shut. He has an impulse to duck, but the closing happens so suddenly that he is caught by surprise. He finds himself in complete darkness. He hears the fading sound of the shuttle that had preceded him, as it whisks off down the entrance tunnel.

In the murky darkness, Jan wishes he had a glow-tube. He also wishes that he had taken a better look at the direction of the roadway before the light was swallowed up. He edges his way slowly through the dark and thinks briefly about waiting for another shuttle to enter. He could use the light to guide him, but there would also be a better chance of him getting caught if he is standing still. He is convinced that he probably won't be much better off with a few seconds of light, and it will be safer if he proceeds into the darkness.

Sliding one foot forward through the shadows, Jan then drags the other one along to pull his feet back together. His progress is slow. He hears sounds off in the distance, but he can't distinguish the direction or content of the noise. The reverberation seems to be all around him and at an unusually low level. The sound is a vague rumbling that could either be caused by some far-off machine or a distant soccer game. The boy has no way to discern the difference, except by continuing to edge closer.

After travelling about 50 yards, his foot hits the wall. He places his hands against the side and uses the wall as a guide. The entire journey has been downhill so far, but Jan is convinced that he has gone reasonably straight. So why did he run into the wall? He feels the wall begin to take a curvature shape. He is going down a spiral and he follows it trying to calculate how many times he completes a circle. Once, twice, three times ... by what feels like the tenth turn, Jan is beginning to feel ill. Age has stiffened the fine gelatinous layer in his father's ear ventricles, and this makes it easier for Jan to get dizzy as he winds down the shuttle tube. The noise grows faintly louder with each turn and now he can hear it is a combination of both people and machines. It is 25 turns down before Jan starts to see a dim light entering the corkscrew roadway. The light gets brighter relatively quickly, and Jan quickens his pace as he sees the end of the curving spiral walls.

Jan no longer needs to hug the side of the coiled roadway, and he can now discern the blue colour of the road. There is a flat spot in front of him. Suddenly, there is a loud horn blast that reminds Jan of the Corpo wakeup horn. The outside wall opens up and Jan can hear an approaching shuttle. The shuttle enters the spiral then starts slowly heading up towards the surface. Heading up toward Jan! He starts to run back up the spiral, but his father's legs struggle to cope with the incline. The vertigo hasn't stopped yet and Jan falls to the center of the road. He senses that the shuttle behind him is starting to pick up speed. He decides to escape by rolling to the side wall. Before he can move, the shuttle's air-filled bumpers push on the back of his knees. He is face-first on the road and pinned there by the bumper. The shuttle is about to drive over him.

14. New London

Jan can feel the intense pressure of the air pushing hard on his body. The force of the air from the shuttle's hover drive mechanism has pinned him solidly into the blue rubber. His legs are completely squashed below the spongy surface and his torso is about two-thirds under. Still faced down, he begins to struggle for air. The shuttle floats ten inches above him, and he has no choice but to hold his breath until the vehicle passes.

When its sensors pick up the uneven surface below, the shuttle comes to an abrupt halt, lifting itself two feet higher into the air. Jan fills his lungs as his body decompresses from the rubber. He is still gasping when he hears the shuttle's side door start to open. Rising to his knees, Jan crawls backwards through the rushing air and out the rear of the shuttle. He can see the tunnel's entrance gate is still open. He stands up and dashes towards the beginning of the corkscrew before the shuttle's passenger door is completely open. As he approaches the gateway, he crosses through a green mist that sprays down from the tunnel ceiling, up from the floor and across from the entrance sides. The liquid completely covers him and soaks through his clothes. As it washes over his face, Jan tastes the bitter fluid, then he winces from the sting in his eyes. Forcing his eyes open, the light floods Jan's vision and he blindly pushes through the gateway. He has entered the shuttle hangar.

As his pupils contract to limit the light intake, he begins to focus on his surroundings. Inside, the blue rubber road runs in a large circle around a central column. Left and right, are rows of shuttles, which encircle the entire area. As his eyes readjust to the light and regain their focus, Jan can see at least 100 shuttles on each side of him, with several empty bays. The walls behind the shuttles are 50 feet high, reaching up to a ceiling that reminds Jan of being in the library tunnel. Pipes and tubes run the length of the hangar. All the walls are a deep grey. There are also people walking in front of, behind and between the shuttles. No one seems to have paid any attention to his arrival.

The gateway behind him starts to close, and Jan is compelled to move. Dripping wet, he heads to the right and behind the shuttles. There are several windows and doors lining the wall that runs encloses the area. It reminds Jan a little of being on the streets of Youngstown. He stops to shake some of the green liquid from his clothes. He spots a man dressed in dark blue overalls. Jan continues his stride, feigning confidence as he approaches. The man is on his knees adjusting a large spring underneath a shuttle. Jan walks right by, and the oblivious man pays no attention to him. Shortly afterward, another man, wearing the same clothing, comes out of the lane between two shuttles and catches Jan off guard. Their eyes meet briefly but the man continues to walk around to the other side of one of the shuttles, saying nothing to Jan.

Eventually, Jan comes to a long window where he can see an extremely functional room with several people in white shirts busying themselves over screens and digivices. One of the white shirt team looks up and sees Jan walking by. He bolts up from his chair and runs ahead of Jan to an exit door. He comes out to the street and turns towards Jan.

"I'm sorry," the whiteshirt says, "did you need something?"

Jan looks panicked. He doesn't have an answer. What is he doing there? Jan is sure that the man is looking at his condition with an air of suspicion.

"Excuse me," Jan begins, trying to read the whiteshirt's pose. He considers asking for directions to the library, but quickly dismisses that tactic.

"I mean, I'm sorry sir, we weren't expecting you. Your shuttle's not ready, but we can prep it in about five minutes if that's okay."

'My shuttle? He must think I need to be transported somewhere.'

Before Jan can say anything further, whiteshirt barks into a metal device built into his collar.

"Tony, can you ready Dr. Ericson's shuttle, he's ready to leave."

'He thinks I'm my father!'

"Roger that," whiteshirt's collar barks back. "It can be ready in less than three minutes."

"No. You don't understand. I don't need to go anywhere."

"Tony, hold off on that prep," whiteshirt calls into his collar, then stares at Jan.

"So, is there anything else we can do for you?" whiteshirt says, only half trying to hide his hint of sarcasm.

"No, I'm fine," Jan says, then he nervously sidesteps the man and continues along the sidewalk.

Whiteshirt watches Jan walk away, then he turns and goes back into his office. Jan can hear the conversation before the door closes … 'Emdees, they act like they rule the world,' says whiteshirt. 'That's because they do rule the world,' says another whiteshirt laughing.

Doing a confident Dr. Ericson swagger, Jan walks away from the whiteshirts … but can feel eyes on him. He ducks down between two shuttles. Once at the front of the vehicles, he thinks he will look to see if he recognizes his father's shuttle. He wanders out to the centre of the blue road, then he hears another horn blast and sees an amber light flashing at the tunnel entrance. The gateway opens and soon Jan hears the familiar whoosh as a shuttle enters the hangar from the spiral tunnel. Jan quickly scurries to the walkway that surrounds the column in the centre of the area. He circles the column, which stretches all the way up into the ceiling. There is a curved, large dark grey metal door on either side of the column. He is still walking around the pillar, when one of the doors opens by sliding into the wall. Two men dressed in brown shirts come out of a small room, and immediately head across the street towards the long window.

The doors close like curtains and blend once again into the grey wall of the pillar. Jan is examining the door when he hears a rumble from within the column. It reminds him of the rumble that the river made. A minute later, the door opens again and this time another man, wearing blue overalls, exits the small room. The doors begin to close again, and Jan impulsively jumps through them. Inside the small room, the walls are all metal, with a series of numbered buttons to the right of the door. At the bottom, just below the numbers and a larger button labelled 'Shuttle Hangar', are buttons labelled 'Door Open', 'Door Closed' and 'Emergency Stop'. The last button is coloured red. At the bottom of the buttons was a small door labelled 'For Firefighters'.

As Jan examines the buttons, the floor starts to rumble, and he gets the sensation that the room is moving downward. He wrestles with the sinking feeling as the doors open again and a man wearing green overalls enters.

"What level?" the man asks.

"I'm not sure yet," Jan answers.

The man shakes his head, mutters something that Jan doesn't understand, then presses the number five. The number lights up and the room begins to move again.

When the room stops and the doors open, Jan sees the number five painted in white at the side of the entrance way. The man, who is standing in front of the door, immediately exits. Jan looks past him and notices how different the surroundings are, compared to the shuttle level. As the doors begin to close again, Jan jumps out of what he now knows is an elevator. In doing so, he stubs his toe on the doorway and spills out onto the sidewalk.

"Are you alright, sir," a voice calls out from beside Jan.

He looks up and sees an older man ... older than Jan but probably even older than his father. The obeisance of this elder man, referring to him as 'sir', puzzles Jan.

"Excuse me?" Jan asks standing up, and also stalling for time.

"Are you alright sir," the man repeats.

Jan is surprised by how tall the man is. He is taller than anyone at the Academy, so he is the tallest man that Jan has ever seen. The man addressing him is six inches taller than Jan.

"Why do you call me 'sir'?"

"I'm sorry, sir. I can't say that I know your name. Perhaps I know you and just don't recognize you ... sir."

If the man doesn't know Jan, what was it about his appearance that would lead the man to such deference. His clothes are still wet from the green shower at the shuttle entrance. Jan is suddenly afraid that he is going to give himself away, so he decides that he isn't yet prepared to engage in any further discussion. He backs away from the man slightly.

"Thank you ... never mind," Jan says as he walks around the man, pretending to know where he's going.

He takes in the new atmosphere. This level consists of one wide expanse that encircles the elevator. On this level however, there is no blue road, just a large interlocking brick sidewalk, like the shuttle entrance at the Academy. The size of this level is about the same as the one he has just come from, but it isn't as utilitarian as the previous level. Behind Jan, the overly polite man is entering the elevator. The environment on this level is more pleasing as the surrounding walls are constructed to resemble individual buildings. Each building in the circle appears to be separate from the one beside it, but Jan can see that they are touching each other. At the top of each structure there is a roofline, but above the roof is the grey wall continuing up about 50 feet.

'So, this is New London. Time to find Fleet Street and make my way to the library.'

Jan wishes he still had his map. From his memory, most of the roads ran in lines, not in circles. He takes in more of his new surroundings. The pristine air is filled with an olive light, but Jan can't see any visible light source. He looks around the open area. The various flat-faced buildings encircle the main column and are a few hundred feet away. They are all the same height, with windows for three floors. On each side of the elevator is a large garden, with trees, bushes, and flowers. Once again, Jan notices people closer to the buildings. Someone is approaching the elevator, so Jan avoids them by heading towards one of the gardens.

Walking through the path that weaves between the shrubbery, he is able to take a closer look at the people from a distance. There are definitely more individuals wandering around on this level than on the shuttle level. Jan observes the actions of the men moving along the sidewalk. They all seem to be going to different places and are walking with a sense of purpose. He approaches the first building façade and turns left to walk around the large circle. There are signs on the front of each building. He reads the placards as he walks past: 'Barber', 'Florist', 'Furniture'. The front of the Furniture building has

The Gemini Project 203

a large window, so Jan approaches closer and peers inside. It is a large area with rows of chairs, tables, and beds. He doesn't see any need to enter this area, so he continues exploring the street.

The temperature on this level is perfect, much like at Corpo, but somehow Jan feels warm. He touches his forehead, and it causes a slight burning feeling. His father's body seems to have different sensations than what he is used to. He continues to walk around the street, as he watches people coming in and out of the buildings. The street is more alive than any place he has been to, but then again, he hasn't really been anywhere. There is a vitality to the noise, as sounds grow and subside at various intervals.

Off in the distance, he hears a more rhythmic version of the noise. The closer he gets, the more he realizes that this is a constant set of various tones being pushed out of one particular facade. There is a woman's pleasing voice, speaking melodically above the rhythm:

Quand il me prends dans ses bras
Il me parle tout bas
Je vois la vie en rose

Stopping in front of the shop, his mind is consumed by the dulcet tones. Other than the occasional humming by the staff at Corpo, this is the first time Jan has ever heard real music. He looks up at the ornate 'French Café' sign, then down at the people sitting at small tables sipping drinks and eating various pastries. Two men wearing the shuttle overalls walk past him to enter the café. Jan immediately follows them in. He doesn't perceive the eyes that are diverting away from his dishevelled appearance. The delectable smell of the freshly baked breads and cakes make Jan realize again just how hungry he is. He continues to listen to Édith Piaf as he tails the two men past a glass display.

Jan has never needed to pay for anything before, and his only point of reference for being served food is in Corpo's dining hall. He listens as the man directly in front of him places his order.

"I'll have a pain au chocolat and a java please, Justin," the shuttle worker requests.

The man moves down the line and Jan is now in front of Justin.

"Yes, sir ... how can I help you?" Justin says in a dulcet tone that reflects the mood and music of the café.

Jan doesn't know exactly what the blue overalled man had said, but he looks over and sees the shuttle worker is being served an inviting puff pastry.

"I'll have the same thing."

"Pain au chocolat and a coffee, sir?" Justin asks respectfully.

"Sure."

Jan wonders why he is getting a coffee when the other man had ordered a java. He moves down the counter, still replicating the motions of the man in front of him. At the end of the counter, there is another young man who places Jan's plated pastry and a cup of brown liquid onto a small tray.

"That will be two credits."

Looking quizzically at the server, Jan is considering whether he should let him know that he doesn't understand. While he stares, he is also looking at the iris recognition scanner mounted behind the server, which captures the unique arrangement of spots, wedges and spokes that made up each customer's iris. He catches a glimpse of a red light that is momentarily blinding, before it quickly retreats back to a less piercing green.

"Thank you very much Dr. Ericson," the second man says as he passes the tray to Jan.

Like many of the people who preceded Jan, he picks up his tray, heads outside and he takes a chair by one of the small tables.

As Jan listens to the sound of the street, he bites into his pain au chocolate. The slightly warm chocolate oozes out of the pastry and into his mouth.

'This might be the best thing that I have ever tasted in my life. Why don't they serve this at Corpo?'

He realizes that on his three-day walk to New London, the only thing he has put into his stomach is one juice box, a little grass, some apples and half a worm. This is vastly less than his usual regimented consumption. With that thought, he takes a sip of his drink and immediately spits it out onto the sidewalk. One of the café workers who has been clearing tables comes running over.

"Is there anything wrong, sir?"

"No, no," Jan says, trying to gently dismiss the man.

'This might be the worst thing that I have ever tasted in my life. I'm glad they didn't serve this at Corpo.'

He briefly wishes that they had given him java instead of coffee, but the thought is interrupted by the start of a new song. The music begins with a steady rhythmic beat and then the same woman's voice sings:

Non, rien de rien
Non, je ne regrette rien
Ni le bien, qu'on m'a fait
Ne le mal, tout ça m'est bien égal!

He wishes he could understand all the strange words surrounding him. 'Pain au chocolat', 'Java', 'Je ne regrette rien'. If only he had his dictionary. He continues to enjoy his pastry as Édith Piaf sings in French: "No, I don't regret anything; Neither the good things people have done to me; Nor the bad things, it's all the same to me!"

Jan looks at the men around him, who are generally alone or sitting with one other person. He sees a blue overalled man with a coffee, or maybe a java, sitting talking to a whiteshirt man with a glass of milk.

'That's what I'm going to go in and get ... a glass of milk.'

There is no reason for Jan to think that food needs to be paid for. None of the boys back at Corpo have ever paid for food. He still has no idea that his father paid for his meal thanks to the iris scanner. Other men pass the café without stopping and Jan wonders if they have ever tasted pain au chocolat. At that moment, he is overwhelmed by a thought. The thought that this is one of the happiest days of his life. He can't think of any other day that could match the feeling of sitting at the café, eating his pastry, and watching the workers walk by. It is a simple pleasure, but one that Jan can get used to.

He observes people as they come into the café, and watches what they order. There are so many items that Jan wants to try, mostly things to eat. He definitely isn't interested in trying coffee again, even in the small cups that some men are ordering. He watches as the server passes the various trays of food and after the tenth customer, he realizes that people are having their eyes scanned. Then he thinks about the number of times Dr. Osler complained about running out of credits.

'This is how they pay! I wonder how many credits, of my father's, I have access to with these eyes.'

Still, he has to find his way to the library, and he is still uncomfortable speaking to any of the other people to ask directions. He has lost track of the days. Without a regular routine, he has to think if it is golf day or soccer day. He knows that one day a week, Dr. Osler is off, and he spends that time in New London, probably getting juiced. Osler is the one person that can help him. Then he remembers Dr. Osler saying that he lives on level 34. All Jan has to do is make his way there and see if Osler is home.

He heads back to the elevator in the centre of the level and waits for the doors to open. He stands there for five minutes with nothing happening. He looks around to take in more of his surroundings while he waits. In front of him is a sign that says 'Plaza Mayor'. Somehow, in his clumsy elevator exit, he had walked right past the sign without noticing it. A passerby dressed in very dirty brown overalls, notices Jan standing there, staring.

"You have to press the button, sir," the man says sarcastically as he approaches two buttons on the wall in front of Jan. "You going up or down?"

"Up, to 34," Jan responds confidently.

"So down then?" the worker asks rhetorically, then he mischievously presses both buttons. The up arrow and down arrow immediately light up.

The man then continues on his way and Jan hears him say something under his breath that sounded like 'funky moron'. Without his dictionary, he is unsure if this is a good thing or a bad thing. Jan hears the familiar whirl and soon the doors open up. There is no one else on the elevator, so Jan enters and, just like he had observed the person before him, he presses the button for the level number where he wants to go. Nothing happens. Jan presses 34 again, but still there is no movement. He notices that the light did not come on like it had for the previous passenger. He stares at the number. He thinks, maybe he is supposed to press the three, then the four ... so he presses the three. Before he can press the four, the three lights up and immediately the apparatus begins to move. It is a very short ride from five to three, so before Jan can process what is happening, the doors open up. Jan sees the number three painted on the side of the elevator entrance.

He exits. There are two gardens that look identical to those in Plaza Mayor, but this level has an entirely different feel. The light is slightly

The Gemini Project 207

dimmer and there is a metallic smell that consumes the air. The street sign for this level reads 'Logan's Run'. Jan starts to move around the mall walkway. Although there are still building facades, they are all painted the same ashy colour and Jan thinks there is very little personality to the buildings. Again, he reads the signs as he walks by, and all the buildings seem less inviting: 'Hardware', 'Electrical Repair', 'Uniforms'.

The front of the Uniforms building also has a larger window, so Jan approaches and peers inside. There is a considerable area filled with racks of clothes. Each rack has one colour and style of clothing. He spots the blue overalls from the shuttle level and the green overalls worn by the man who shared the elevator with him. He contemplates going inside the building to look through the racks to see if he can find something that his father would wear but decides instead to continue exploring the street.

Further on, he notices a facade with a sign that reads 'Lost and Found'. It only makes sense to him that he will be able to find directions inside, so he enters the building. There is a reception area with a large counter and a receptionist sitting behind it. Behind the man, is a wall with a door that leads to the rest of the building. The receptionist looks up and assesses Jan suspiciously.

"Can I help you sir?" the receptionist asks.

"Yes, I'd like to get to Fleet Street."

"Fleet Street?" the man repeats back as a question.

"Yes, Fleet Street."

"I'm not quite sure what that is."

"I think it's where the library is?"

"The library, sir?" the receptionist repeats back again as a question.

"Yes, the library," Jan snaps back, unable to contain his frustration. By this point, he is also overwhelmed by tiredness. He has spent three days on the road, and he woke early that day after sleeping beneath an underpass, before walking 12 miles, only to be chased by dogs through a thicket of thorns. He needs to find the library. He needs information. He needs to find out how to work an elevator so he can get to Dr. Osler's place.

He stares at the dumbfounded receptionist for a moment and then storms out. The receptionist isn't insulted, but he is still suspicious.

Jan walks aimlessly around that level, with his arm in a makeshift bandage and dried blood on the side of his face.

Behind Jan, unbeknownst to him, two gendarmes in brown shirts have started watching him. They are headed his way, thanks to a heads-up from the overly cautious receptionist. Obliviously continuing his examination of the level, Jan notices a familiar face kneeling in front of the garden. He immediately approaches a young man.

"Elf," he calls out, "Elf, it's me."

The young man looks up at him surprised. He drops his gardening tools and stands up. Jan notices that Elf looks stronger, has less pimples on his face and now has longer hair.

"Dr. Ericson?" Elf responds, surprised that Jan's father would know his name.

"Elf, it's me."

Before Jan can explain, Elf notices the approaching gendarmes.

"I'm not sure, Dr. Ericson, but I think those gendarmes are headed our way."

"Gendarmes?" Jan asks having never heard the word before.

"Yes. Maybe it's about the blood on your face. Did something bad happen to you?"

Jan realizes that he has several signs of his journey to New London, not the least of which is the homemade bandage on his left arm. He doesn't understand who is approaching, but he senses danger in Elf's voice. He will have to think of something fast. He gives his face a quick dry scrub and readies himself to perform his best father imitation.

"Gentlemen," one of the approaching gendarme states.

'A shuttle accident, that's what I'll say.'

Jan is relieved that Elf had given him advanced warning. He spins around to face the two officers, keeping his left side facing Elf.

"Yes," Jan states authoritatively.

"Oh ... Dr. Ericson, I didn't see it was you ... sir."

'There is that word again ... sir. This is good. The gendarmes recognized my father and clearly have deference towards him.'

"There was a report of a possible Outsider stumbling in from the surface to the shuttle level, and then the Lost and Found receptionist reported a visit from someone in golf clothes that might be high on Flash."

"And what does any of that have to do with us?" Jan retorts feigning confidence.

"Nothing sir. We ah ... we just wanted to warn you, sir."

"Okay, I'm warned," Jan says as he turns back around to face Elf, keeping his injured arm out of sight. He sounded like his father when his father talked down to people.

The gendarmes continued their patrol.

"Elf, it's me."

"Yes Dr. Ericson. I recognize you from father's day, sir."

"No, Elf, it's me, Jan."

"What do you ..."

Elf looks at him unable to discern why Jan's father is saying that he is his son. Jan realizes the problem.

"Elf, remember when I taught you to do a tennis backhand? Or when you and I had a playoff for the golf championship?"

Elf just stares back, unsure of what to say.

"Okay, the day you broke your leg at Corpo," Jan said, "it was Dix that swung the field hockey stick at the back of your leg."

Elf still stares back quizzically.

"And he did it on purpose because you made a good move on him, making him look foolish. He was always a bit of an asshole Elf, but in the end, you'll be the one laughing."

"Because he's going to be renaissanced?" Elf concluded.

"Because he's going to be renaissanced! It sounds like you know the truth about the renaissance, so you should understand ... inside this body, it's me ... Jan."

"But if you're Jan," Elf tries to reason, "what happened to Jan's father?"

"He took my body," Jan answers containing his anger. "And that's why I'm here. I'm going to find him."

"Why? When I was told about the renaissance, I was actually relieved to be here. I would have been dead in two years if I hadn't broken my leg."

Elf is wearing green overalls. He has become part of the New London labour-force.

"I could probably get you a job in the gardening department and you could just take care of the shrubbery, like me. It pays 500 credits per week. I got a position, and I can't even read. Life is good for me. It's safe here, no one's going to cut your head open to make their own lives better."

Jan nodded.

"And it's not really that bad knowing that one day you will die."

"It's not bad for you, because you've got your body. I've got my father's body, and it is probably going to give up in a matter of years. I want to see my father and I want to school him on why this is all wrong."

"Are you sure you want to do that? Maybe you should just leave it. It could go really bad for you if you attempt to make demands, especially with your father. You can work with me ... take an easier path."

"A path that is too short for me," Jan said, thinking that Elf has matured significantly since he last saw him.

"Okay, it's your life ... what can I do to help?"

"I need to get to the library so I can figure some things out."

"The library?"

"Why does everybody act that way? Has nobody ever heard of a library?" Jan asks with a laugh that disguises his frustration.

"I've never heard of it, but I can ask my supervisor," Elf says. "He knows everything ... kind of like Dr. Osler. You should meet him anyway. He gets it. He's the one that filled me in on how the renaissance really worked. It made me think of you, and Otto, and Dix. I wished I could come back for one more field hockey game and break all of your legs."

"That is such a touching thought Elf," Jan laughs. "Thanks for that."

Jan and Elf are walking slowly around the mall. Elf has a distinct limp, probably from the damage that Dix wrought, along with the lack of adequate physiotherapy. He leads Jan to the spot where a large garden is planted.

"I did this," Elf says pointing to the newly planted shrubbery. "I did this on ten levels and I pollinated these flowers this morning."

Jan smiles at him. Elf then walks his friend back to the facades and stands in front of a relatively generic building.

"This is where I work. Do you want to come in and meet my supervisor? He's the smartest person that I've ever met."

"Sure," Jan nods, "but I'm not revealing who I am until I decide that I need to."

The pair pass through a metal door into a large square room with rows of plants on tables. Jan is not used to the aroma of real plants. There are so many plants, he can't tell if there is anyone else in the room.

"Mr. Tuinman?" Elf calls out.

An elderly man comes out from a row of Magnolia trees. He has thick white hair and is wearing the green overalls of the gardening team. Slightly hunched back, he walks over to the 'boys'.

"Elf," Tuinman says, "are you finished already?"

"No Mr. Tuinman, I wanted to introduce you to my friend Jan."

"Oh, yes?" Tuinman replies suspiciously, as he looks at Jan's overall appearance.

"Jan Ericson," Jan says extending his hand the way his father would.

The gardener doesn't shake Jan's hand. Instead, he eyes him up and down. He notes the dried blood on Jan's face, the homemade bandage, and the dirty golf apparel.

"Jan Ericson," Jan repeats. "It's Norwegian."

There is a silence as Elf looks in deference to his manager. Elf isn't even sure that 'nor-wee-Jan' is a word, but the manager begins to smile slightly. Jan doesn't perceive any malevolence in the smile, in fact it makes him feel safe.

"So, this is your friend, is he?"

"Mr. Tuinman, Jan is a Emdee," Elf responds stressing the position of his guest to explain Jan's clothes. Jan doesn't quite understand the reason but wishes Elf hadn't said anything.

"Okay," the gardener says with a slight laugh, "this might be your friend, but this is no Emdee. This is someone that wants something. He appears to be in disguise. He doesn't have the walk, the voice, or the attitude of an Emdee. An Emdee would shake my hand, but he would never extend his first. Yes ... what we have here is someone pretending to be an Emdee."

Jan and Elf stare back at Tuinman.

"So, Mr. non-Emdee Norwegian Jan Ericson, what brings you to gardening HQ?"

Elf is right, Mr. Tuinman might be one of the smartest people Jan has ever met, as well. He seems to process in a logical manner, asking questions, rather than just accepting statements as facts. However, Jan is still not ready to reveal himself to the gardener.

"Well," Jan says as he retracts his handshake and again tries to mimic his father's superior attitude. "I'm here to go to the library and then I would like to visit a friend on Level 34."

"Level 34 ... Really? What's his name?"

Tuinman is tough. Jan senses the obvious distrust in the gardener's attitude but he needs his help. He has to try to win Tuinman over.

"Dr. William Osler, sir," Jan answers, mistakenly showing respect.

"'Sir' ... very funny ... and Osler lives here?"

"He's actually from the Corpo Academy for Development," Jan answers, purposefully.

"Ah, one of the renaissance factories." the gardener responds with a sigh that slowly turns angry. "He must be a great guy. He likes playing games with little boy's minds ... and I think YOU might be playing with me. Do you like to play games?"

Jan did like to play games. That's all he'd ever done.

"Well, I ... I think so," Jan answers letting his trepidation show through.

"I think you should leave."

"No, wait," Elf interjects, looking towards Jan to see if he will tell Tuinman his true identity. "I know him. Please, give him one minute."

"You want my help, Mr. Ericson? Answer a question for me, and this time answer honestly ... how did you get to New London?" Tuinman asks, speaking in a stricter and even more demanding tone.

Jan contemplates telling a story about taking a shuttle from Corpo Academy, but he realizes that Tuinman is testing him.

"I walked here," Jan says softly, looking over at Elf.

The Gemini Project   213

Elf gives him an approving nod.

"Good, a little bit of truth goes a long way. In addition to the blood on your face, you haven't shaved in three or four days, and you've got a sunburn that looks like it's also a few days old, so you've been on the surface. I think you're an Outsider," the gardener accused, "and if you are an Outsider, then I could be charged for even talking to you. So, do I have anything to worry about?"

"No, I'm not an Outsider. I'm not even sure what an Outsider is."

The gardener looks at Jan intently, taking in his words and appearance.

"I call bullshit, Mr. Jan Ericson. Maybe you should come back to see me when you are ready to tell me the truth. And until then, you might want to shave, wash your face, and buy a hat so you don't raise suspicions. As for level 34, Elf can't take you there, he's only authorized down to level 19. I can go below that level, but to get there, I need to go to level 19, where I would catch the service elevator to the lower levels. If I get off at level 34, I am greeted by the floor's service manager who gives me a pill. Then, the next thing I know I am getting the service elevator back up to level 3. So, there is no way that I can take you there. So, if Dr. Osler has authorized you with guest access to level 34, just take the elevator. If he hasn't authorized you, then there is no way for you to get there."

"But I pressed 34 and the button didn't light up."

"Then you have your answer," Tuinman states definitively, "you are not authorized and there is no way for you to get there. Elf, on your way out, take our guest over to the sink so he can at least wash his face."

The gardener dismisses his guest, then turns away to prune some roses. He has names for all his roses, and right now he is working on Desmond and Francois, two beautiful red rose bushes. Elf looks at Jan and shrugs.

"Why don't you tell him," Elf whispers.

"Maybe later," Jan mouths back.

The pair briefly watch the trimming process, then head to the sink. Jan looks into the mirror and is surprised at how haggard he appears. He has never seen his father look this bad. The combination of dried blood and sweat on his face made him an obvious foreigner. His face is redder than his father normally looks, and skin is starting to peel off. His pants are torn through, and he is grazed on his legs from the thorns. He washes the blood off his face and then gently removes the three-day old bandage from his arm. The gash is scabbing up, but it starts to lightly bleed again as he peels back the canvas. Jan puts his arm into the large basin and washes away the fresh blood. He then dampens his arm with one of the many green cloths from the counter at the side of the sink and nods to Elf.

"Nice work, 'Doctor'," Elf says, and the boys smile at each other.

They head towards the door and have just exited the building when Tuinman calls out.

"You did look into the eye scanner, didn't you?"

Elf keeps the door open so Jan can answer.

"Ummm ..." is all Jan can reply.

Tuinman approaches the exit.

"You really aren't from around here, are you? Once you press a restricted level, you have to have your eye scanned to ensure that you are authorized. Elf, why don't you take our Norwegian foreigner to the elevator and show him how to use it."

Tuinman returns back to work on Desmond and Francois.

Elf smiles at Jan and says, "Come this way."

They walk to the elevator.

"Do you think you'll be authorized?" Elf asks.

"Well, my father would be authorized, and now I'm seeing things through his eyes."

"But wouldn't your father change the authorization after the renaissance?" Elf asks.

"No. It wasn't his official renaissance. It would raise suspicion if he dropped access for himself before his renaissance date. So, I guess he probably gave guest access to me ... I mean, my body and eyes, the young me ... so he could get access to his home. Until my renaissance date, I should still have full access to anything he had access to."

"That makes sense. Then, maybe you could use some credits to buy me a shuttle," Elf jokes.

The two boys enter the elevator and Jan presses 34. Elf points to a flat dark glass panel above the buttons. It is a less obvious iris scanner.

The Gemini Project 215

When Jan looks at it, the number 34 immediately lights up. Elf presses five.

"You're not coming with me?" Jan asks.

"I need to get back to work, and besides, I'm not authorized. If you need me, and you figure out how to give me a guest pass, then you know where I am. And Mr. Tuinman really is one of the good guys, once you get to know him."

"I know," Jan responds. He is not as confident as Elf about that but sees little point in disagreeing.

The elevator doors open on level five, and Elf exits smiling back at Jan.

"Good luck."

The door closes and the elevator heads to level 34. When the door opens again, there is a young man, in a black suit, sitting at a desk directly in front of the elevator. The man looks up as soon as Jan steps off.

"Dr. Ericson," the young man says, slightly alarmed.

Jan lets his own slight surprise show on his face.

"Dr. Osler said that you might be visiting him. Are you okay sir?" the young man says motioning towards the wound on Jan's arm, which looks fresher than it is.

"Yes, thank you," Jan answers. "There was an accident … with my shuttle, but yes … thank you."

He knew that standby excuse would come in handy eventually.

"Can you direct me to Dr. Osler's place?"

"Of course, sir. He lives at number 742 … circle around on the right and its about halfway down."

"Thank you," Jan replies and immediately begins to walk away, with a confident indifference that his father would use.

There is a street sign with a name on it, but to Jan's disappointment it didn't say 'Fleet Street'. The sign reads 'Evergreen Terrace'. 'That sounds like a nice place to live,' Jan thinks as he continues towards his destination. Level 34 is very green. In front of each building façade, there is a lawn, as pristine as the soccer pitch. There are trees laid out sporadically on each lawn. The facades still run down each side of the large walkway, but they are set out to look like individual houses. This level is also taller, so the house facades don't take up the full height of the back wall. Above him, is a familiar blue hue. It is the same colour that is displayed in Corpo. Jan takes comfort in the sky's appearance.

Arriving at the door, Jan wonders if he should enter, or if he should knock. What if Dr. Osler isn't there? The blacksuit at the elevator reception probably could have told Jan if he should expect Dr. Osler at home, but Jan prefers to act like he knows what is going on. He is feeling exhausted as he approaches the door. He knocks like he would as if he was called to Dr. Primero's office. No response. He knocks again. No response. He decides to try the handle and is quickly panicked with the thought of 'what if it doesn't open?'

As he reaches for the handle, he notices an iris recognition scanner at the side of the door. He looks into it and hears a whirling noise of the door unlocking. He turns the handle and enters 742 Evergreen Terrace.

"Welcome," a soft woman's voice calls out.

"Doctor?" Jan queries as he enters a large hallway.

There is no response.

"Hello, are you there?" Jan calls out again before entering further into the residence.

"Always, Dr. Ericson," the voice answers.

"You know who I am?" Jan says, peering through the home to discern where the voice is emanating from.

"I recognize your voice print, as well as your iris scan. Dr. Osler told me to expect you."

Jan slowly works his way through the foyer and into a hallway. As he enters the room, the lights come on and the woman's voice seems to follow him. Jan realizes that the voice is being projected, just like the music at the café.

"Please let me know if I can be of assistance."

"Is Dr. Osler home?"

"Dr. Osler is still at the Corpo Academy for Development. He has a shuttle scheduled to bring him to New London next Tuesday. Shall I contact him and let him know of your arrival?"

"No, thank you. Not yet," Jan says working his way through to a kitchen area, a large room consisting mostly of polished stainless steel and multi-coloured marble. The voice continues to follow Jan to each room.

"Can you tell me where the library is?"

"The library? A library is a building or room containing collections of books, periodicals, and other media, for use or borrowing by the public or members of an institution. The last public library in The United States of America closed on November 5, 2046. Did you want to know the address of the last public library?"

"No, that's fine. Are you saying that there are no libraries in New London?"

"There have never been any libraries in New London, however I can read a book to you, if you'd like."

It sounds to Jan like the voice itself is claiming to be a library and he wonders what information the voice has access to.

"Can you read the first lines in *A Tale of Two Cities* to me?" Jan asks, trying to create a test for the voice.

"Certainly. It was the best of times, it was the worst of times, it was the age of wisdom, it was the age of foolishness, it was the epoch of belief, it was the epoch of incredulity, it was the season of Light, it was the season of Darkness, it was the spring of hope, it was the winter of despair... Shall I continue?"

The words were dictated with a type of empathy that seemed to show an understanding of the text.

"No, that was great," Jan answers unable to conceal his sincere excitement. "Can you tell me about Fleet Street?"

"Fleet Street is a street in the former city of London, England. It ran from Temple Bar to Ludgate Circus and was an important route since Roman times. The street became known for printing and publishing at the start of the 16th century and by the 20th century, most British national newspapers operated here. Shall I continue?"

"No, that's fine," Jan says as he enters a room with a long table, surrounded by a dozen chairs.

'This is Dr. Osler's dining room.'

He no longer needs a map. He no longer needs to find Fleet Street. He no longer needs a library. It seems that all knowledge is in Dr. Osler's residence. All he has to do is ask a question. He walks into a living room with a sofa on one wall, and a worn wingback chair in the corner beside a side-table. The wingback ... of course. This is where Dr. Osler probably does his Flash when he's at home. There are pictures on the wall. A photograph of Dr. Osler with a few other doctors standing outside a gothic church. Another photograph shows young boys outside playing in shorts. Jan thinks one of the boys is probably Dr. Osler as a child. A third photograph is a headshot of an elderly woman, much older than even Nurse Rossignol. Jan realizes that he has stopped talking to the voice.

"Hello?" Jan calls out.

"Hello, how can I be of assistance?"

"Do I just call out when I need to talk to you?"

"Certainly, I'm always listening. You can also just say my name. I'm Anjea."

"Thanks Anjea. I need to rest. Can you direct me to the dormitory?"

"The bedrooms are on the second floor. Dr. Osler's room is at the top of the stairs and the two guest rooms are at the end of the hall."

He heads upstairs. In one of the guest bedrooms, he slips off the loafers and lies down on the bed.

"Anjea?" Jan asks hoping that the voice has followed him upstairs, "can you turn off the lights?"

Without answering him, Anjea dims the lights and Jan switches off his father's body.

Exhausted, he sleeps fully clothed for 14 hours, barely stirring. He dreams about going to the library back at Corpo, except he is accompanied on his journey by a young woman. It is one of the field hockey players from *Field Hockey: Start Right and Play Well* by Bill Gutman (the library version that includes the pictures, not the Corpo lounge version). Jan talks to the young girl, and her voice has a French accent. Jan doesn't even know what a French accent sounds like, but in his dream, he has given the girl the voice of a young Édith Piaf. She asks where he wants to go and Jan is trying to think of an answer, when he wakes up. His first thought is that somewhere he has the picture of the page-43-girl that he 'borrowed' from the library. Then he realizes that he doesn't know where he is. It's still dark in the room, but he can make out his surroundings, his unfamiliar surroundings. He rolls from his back to his side and feels the pain of the bobcat bite. He's in Dr. Osler's New London Flat.

"Anjea, lights on please."

The Gemini Project 219

The room lights up and Jan sits up on the side of the bed. He fell asleep in the same clothes that he's had on since leaving the Academy, and they have a definite smell to them. HE has a definite smell to him. He sees that there is a washroom connected to his dorm, so he heads in and is pleased to find a shower. He takes his first shower in his new body. He is still not used to finding all of his father's body parts connected to where he expects to see his own. After the shower, Jan wraps a towel around himself, and walks through the other rooms. In Dr. Osler's room there is a large closet with the doctor's familiar clothes. Since Osler is about the same size as his father, Jan decides that the doctor wouldn't mind if he borrows an outfit. He chooses one of Dr. Osler's most conservative attires: dress pants and a turtleneck sweater. After getting dressed, he heads for the kitchen, where he finds some yogurt and muesli for breakfast.

"I wish I had some fresh fruit," Jan says out loud.

"I can order you some fresh fruit. What would you like?"

"No, that's okay Anjea ... I forgot you were listening."

As Jan ate his cereal, he remembers the chocolate pastry from the day before and decides he will head back to the café for seconds.

He puts on a tweed jacket and leaves the residence. He feels and acts more like his father as he heads for the elevator. On board, he presses the button for level five. Before arriving at his destination, the elevator stops at level 25. A woman enters. Everything changes.

Jan's acting ability falls to the wayside. Other than Nurse Rossignol, Nurse Banaltram and the picture of the page-43-girl, Jan has never seen another woman before. He shakes from a combination of bewilderment and excitement. The woman presses the button for level 21, and soon becomes very aware that Jan is staring at her. She is used to this type of behaviour from Emdees. The elevator stops and the woman steps off. Jan follows her.

With all the facades replicating similar flat-faced buildings, Level 21 looks more uniform than the other levels Jan has visited. There is a street sign with the generic name 'Riverside Drive'. This place is nothing like its namesake in Youngstown. Jan doesn't see anyone else on the street. The woman heads left, and Jan follows. She circles back towards the elevator, and Jan continues to follow. She cuts through the garden, and when Jan follows again, he is confronted by the young woman.

"Are you following me for any reason?"

Her voice is slightly irate, but it is still soft and pleasing to Jan. The familiar tone reminds him of the singing voice at the café or maybe ...

"Anjea?" Jan asks.

"Excuse me?"

"Anjea, is that you?" he repeats in a half whisper.

"Sir?"

The woman looks at Jan trying to understand why he is acting in such an unusual manner. Jan is taking in her scent. Not only has he never seen anything like her before, but he has also never smelled anything like her. Yet, she had just walked onto the elevator as though her presence was commonplace. She is standing in front of him. Still staring in disbelief, Jan looks at her in silence.

"Sir, is anything wrong?"

Jan says nothing. He is detached from the conversation as he wonders about her very existence. Are there more women inside the buildings on this level? As he takes in more of her appearance, he thinks about how similar yet how different she is from him ... not his current form, but the young version of Jan.

"Sir?"

She is now beginning to worry. Her auburn hair reaches down to the pale blue, knee length skirt that she is wearing. Jan has taken in every feature of her face and is now examining her physique. She appears to be about half the age of Nurse Rossignol. She is extremely fit, and Jan wonders if she plays field hockey.

"Sir? Is there something wrong?" she repeats louder as she steps slowly towards Jan.

The allure of her soft voice momentarily helps him to regain his composure.

"Your name's not Anjea, is it?"

Jan looks down at her athletic shaped legs that stretch down from her hemline to the flat sandals that she is wearing. He gazes back up at her face and he is unsure if the image before him is even the same sex as the nurses. He is fighting with his thoughts, one part of him insists that he pay attention to the conversation, while the other part wants to understand more about the appearance of the person talking to him.

"I don't understand. Are you okay?"

"I mean ... I'm looking for someone named Anjea," Jan says trying to cover the slowness of his responses.

"Anjea?"

"I'm sorry, I thought you might be her."

Jan can see from the look in the woman's eyes that he has made a mistake. Her eyes remind him of a picture of an animal, a tiger, that he saw in the book *The Animal Kingdom*. He is failing in his attempt to maintain a conversation and he is stunned by the beauty of the creature that is addressing him.

"I have to go," Jan states abruptly.

"No wait, follow me, Dr. Ericson."

She knows his father. For the first time, Jan wonders if he can trust the woman, but he looks at her and immediately feels at ease. He feels a sense of truth emanating from behind her eyes. She smiles, turns, and walks for about two minutes, with Jan following beside her. She enters a façade at number 1640 and then points to a seat in the front reception area.

"Have a seat, sir," the woman offers, as she heads to the other side of the room, where she sits down.

Jan begins to sweat around his neckline. He finds himself staring at the woman across the room, so he forces himself to look elsewhere. The room feels much smaller. He looks at the ceiling, then the floor but he can't look anywhere without it feeling awkward. In the silence, the woman sits gracefully across from Jan. The room is starkly decorated with white walls and one built-in cupboard on the longest wall.

"So, what I don't understand is ... I've met you before, several times, but you don't seem to recognize me."

Jan thinks that maybe he DID recognize her. He can't control his open-mouthed gaze as he looks directly at the woman's face. He notices that her features are smaller and daintier than the other adults, more like those of a young boy. Her soft appearance looks peculiarly familiar to him. He then observes how her lips are also different than any others he has seen. Without thought, he let his eyes wander down her body. Below the utilitarian design of the blue smock, Jan can sense the outline of her breasts. They are different than his, smaller yet larger. Their pert outline seems to be supported somehow and for a moment Jan wants to reach out and trace their shape. Jan feels a stiffening in his pants, followed by a feeling of guilt. His confusion is overcome by a sweet smell in the air. The aroma captivates Jan's olfactory memory and he thinks of the yellow flowers in the field near the school. He slips into a trance, where he imagines lying in the field, inhaling the floral aroma, and rolling between the plants. He finds the woman lying beside him, and a desire seizes him again, this time even stronger. A voice pulls him back to reality.

"Do you want me to call anyone? If you've forgotten, my name is Anya …"

Jan continues to perspire. His eyes quickly return to hers and sitting across from her, he forces a stilted smile. The woman is staring right back at him with a smirk. She had watched Jan take inventory of her, not unlike the way his father took inventory of him last father's day. Jan is sure that she somehow knows everything that he is thinking. If she could read his mind (like a paperback novel), then she would know that he doesn't belong here. His deception is consuming him.

".. and you are Dr. Ericson. Do you recognize me?"

Jan is trapped.

"Do you want something to drink, while you think about your answer?"

"No, I'm fine, thank you," Jan answers, finally speaking.

"That's different … an Emdee saying no to a drink and actually saying 'thank you'."

She spoke with a certain amount of sass. This only makes Jan's feelings for her grow stronger. He is strangely drawn to her personality, and he almost feels ashamed for his previous physical attraction. Still, he is sure they had met before, but of course that isn't possible.

Jan breaks free from his ogling and looks around the room. In many ways, it reminds him of his dorm room, but without beds. It is very sterile, lacking in anything that would represent an individual's personality. There is nothing on the white walls, but also nothing that really indicates any purpose for the room.

The Gemini Project

"What is this building that I'm in?" Jan blurts out to absorb the quietness.

"I think you know already."

Puzzled, Jan decides he can find the answer without embarrassment.

"Anjea, what is this building that we are in?" Jan calls out into the emptiness of the room. Anjea doesn't answer.

"Again with the Anjea. It's Anya and I live here. Where do you live?"

"I'm visiting someone who lives on level 34."

"Level 34, I think that's usually for visiting Emdees, isn't it?"

"Yes," Jan answers, letting his eyes take in the sparsity of the room. It isn't like Dr. Osler's home at all. Jan begins to wonder about the lack of photographs on the wall. There are no pictures of her with other people. No pictures of old ladies. No pictures of children.

'If she was a mother, there would probably be some pictures of her children on the wall.'

"Do you have any children?"

"Of course. I've had seven children. Five of them boys," she adds with a sense of pride. "Not really great production though … that's why I'm living on Level 21."

Anya's smirk turns into a wry smile.

"Oh, and how are they doing in school?" Jan asks trying to be polite.

"School?"

Anya's face quickly turns to resentment as she glares at Dr. Ericson. Why is he being so cruel as to ask how her children are doing in school? Is this some sort of test? She decides that she will not let him rile her, and instead she will play along.

"I don't know any of my children Dr. Ericson, I haven't seen them since they were very young."

Jan smiles and Anya gives a forced smile back. She is a nice lady and Jan wonders if his mother is as nice.

Then the definition that he read three months ago comes flooding into Jan's mind. Mother: a woman who conceives, gives birth to, or raises and nurtures a child. Anya appears to be very nurturing, but she doesn't know her children. Jan doesn't know his mother. Could Anya be his mother?

"How old are you?"

"My, my, my, you drive straight to the point don't you."

"I'm sorry. That was rude ... wasn't it?"

"It was. Is there something else you'd like to know?"

"I was really wondering ... when did you first give birth?"

"I'm not sure that's a much better question, but I had my first child about 18 years ago. Why?"

"I ..." Jan begins shyly, then becomes consumed by his excitement. "I thought maybe you might be my mother."

Anya is caught off guard by this statement. She assumes that he is probably four times her age. Why is he doing this? What did he expect to gain by such bizarre speech and behaviour. She decides she will just answer the question and see where he is going.

"You want to know if I am your mother, do you? If we dismiss the fact that I am younger than you, then what would the odds be that I am your mother. Well, there are about 500 bearers in New London, so if your mother is here ... I guess the odds are 1 in 500 that I would be your mother. But the average Pelacur has at least 10 children, so increase the odds a bit to account for my poor production. I'd say there is a 1 in 700 chance that I am your mother, provided of course that I could give birth when I was negative 80 years old."

Anya can't resist being a little sardonic as she concludes her statistical analysis. Jan is upset. He thinks about it and decides that her features don't match his, and this probably isn't his mother after all. He turns into a 17-year-old boy who just had hope taken away from him and he begins to weep. As the tears roll onto his cheeks, for the first time Anya thinks that maybe this isn't a test. Maybe this isn't even Dr. Ericson.

"How do you know who your children are?" Jan eventually asks, trying to understand why she didn't raise or nurture her children.

"I don't Dr. Ericson. If I am lucky enough to get pregnant, then I move down ten levels or so, where I get treated like a queen for twelve months. Then shortly after giving birth, I am shipped back here. After that, I am allowed to watch my children in the Crèche, but when they leave, I never see them again. Do you understand?"

The Gemini Project

Jan doesn't understand. Anya believes she is stating the obvious, but it has become clear that there is actually extraordinarily little that Dr. Ericson understands about what is going on. 'Maybe he's ill', she thinks.

"Are you sure I can't get you a drink?"

"Sure, a drink would be nice," Jan answers, trying to compose himself.

He watches as Anya gets up and goes to the built-in cabinet. She removes a tumbler from a high shelf, pours a shot and a half of Scotch and then adds a few ice cubes. She passes it to Jan, who immediately gulps it down. With half a mouthful consumed, Jan tries to stop the firewater from burning his throat. He spews some of it back out and onto his turtleneck.

"What is that?"

"Scotch on the rocks. Did you want something else?"

"No, definitely not! That's worse than java."

"Sorry. Would you rather I watered it down?"

As the half mouthful enters his system, Jan feels the light-headedness take effect.

"No ... no thanks. You're right ... it is strong stuff, I think If I drank too much of that, it would leave me baked more than a potato!"

"That's an interesting phrase. Where did you hear that one?"

Jan thinks about it. Dix was the only person who used that phrase. The pair had been close for three years but had drifted apart when Jan discovered the library. Jan felt a twinge of guilt for allowing their relationship to fade.

"My friend Dix says that all the time. He's also a student at the Corpo Academy. You'd like him. He takes some time to get used to, because he's always full on about trying to win, but once you understand that, then you'd see that he really is kind of great. I guess I miss him."

Anya, still standing, starts to pace nervously around the room.

"And does Dix have a last name?"

"Yes, it's Gémeaux. His father, Dr. Gémeaux, lives here in New London ... on level forty-something ... I think."

Anya turns abruptly and looks directly at Jan.

"I think, maybe you've been here long enough. You should leave now."

Jan feels a sense of rejection. He stares at Anya trying to understand her apparent change of attitude. What has he said to insult her? Jan rises and nods. He walks to the door. Anya follows. He feels a desire to turn around and tell her that he loves her. It's a word that he has never used before, not even before learning the truth about the renaissance. He is unsure of what type of love he feels for her, but he is sure that this is love.

They get to the door, and it hisses as it slides open. Jan is still wondering if maybe, somehow, this could be his mother. As he steps outside, he is about to turn back and tell her again, but the door hisses closed. She has turned and walked back into the building without saying another word to him.

'I'm 34 and a half,' Anya says to herself, stopping a tear from escaping the corner of her eye. 'I gave birth to my first child 18 years ago this week.'

Jan heads to the elevator and takes it to level three. He forgets all about his desire to return to the café. He goes straight to the gardening headquarters to find Elf. He wants to tell him that maybe he has finally met his mother.

"He's not here," Mr. Tuinman said from behind a row of lettuce. "He won't be here until after ten."

There is a tear welling up in Jan's eyes again.

"Okay, why do I have a grown ass man crying like a baby in my nursery?"

"I met a woman," Jan responds.

"You met a woman? Are you sure? I've never met a woman."

Jan pictures the delicate features of her face and the unusual colour of her eyes. Their familiarity made him want to reach out to touch her face. He pictures how sassy she is, full of attitude, just like …

Then it hits him. The familiarity. She is a female Dix. She is Dix's mother! Why hadn't he seen the similarity in their eyes? He smiles as he realizes and wishes he could tell Dix or even Elf.

"So did this woman tell you how to find the library then?"

"No, it's okay. I don't need the library anymore, I've got Anjea. Well, at least on the 34th level I've got Anjea."

The Gemini Project

The gardener looks intently at the visitor.

"Anjea, you say? So, you really made it to level 34, did you? And now all your questions have been answered by Anjea?"

"Well, not yet. "You have to know what to ask before you can get answers."

The gardener smiles at this philosophy.

"And you have to trust before you can be trusted," the gardener responds. "Let's say I trust you for a minute. Let's say I let you fire some questions at me, and then I give you some answers. Will you then trust me and explain why you seem to know so little, yet know so much at the same time?"

"I think I can do that."

"Okay then, let's get at it. You made it to level 34, what do you want to do next?"

"There's so much. I need to join the labour-force, but first I'd like to go to level 42."

"Good, good. The work we can arrange. If we can get through this little interview successfully, and you learn to trust me, I can give you some work. Elf can train you. As for level 42, that will be the same answer as level 34 … either you have access, or you don't. But I sincerely doubt you'll have access to 42. Do you know what class of citizen has access to level 42?"

"I'm not sure what you mean," Jan replies.

"And there it is … the jump to the hyperspace of a complete lack of comprehension. That's what I was referring to earlier. Okay, let me fill you in, and feel free to stop me if you've heard this one …

Here in New London, there are two classes of citizens: the Emdees and the Hebs. I am a Heb. We are born, we live, we die. Then there are the Emdees … there are about 400 of them. They were here before we arrived, and they'll be here after we are gone. Now don't get me wrong, I'm not jealous. On the contrary, we Hebs like our place and we live a rather good life … including 100 days of rest every year.

But I look at your skin colour and I know that you wouldn't understand what it's like to be here, and only here. I've never left the city. I've never seen the sun in my entire life. How do I know it really exists? Maybe its just part of the Outsider mythology."

The gardener stops as the boy furls his eyebrows.

"Oh ... that's right, you have no idea what an Outsider is, do you?" Tuinman continues with a hint of cynicism. He lowers his voice and speaks with reverence. "Well, sometimes, a Heb gets stupid and wants to discover what life would be like outside The Gemini System. So, they stow away on a shuttle, hide in a trash pod, or take a vent ladder to the surface. They become an Outsider, and they supposedly live in a tent-city called Superficie. But how would anyone know for sure? They've never returned, so it's all just conjecture ... the stuff that fables and myths are made of. Maybe they're alive, or maybe they fell victim to a never relenting sun that burned their skin. Either you believe in the existence of an Outsider city on the surface, or you don't, and deep down we all want to believe. But if an Outsider ever did return, it's a crime to help them. A capital crime ... you know what that is, right?"

"No," Jan replies.

"That's where you are put to death for going against The Gemini System. Your life is over, and your organs are harvested for those Emdees that can't even care for a body for a few decades.

When you look around here, you might notice that there isn't really much security required, and there is a reason for that ... there's very limited opportunities to commit a crime. There's no way to access someone else's credits and you earn enough credits to buy food, so what would the point be anyway. However, taking in a stray Outsider without reporting it is a crime. And although you carry yourself like you might be an Emdee, something tells me that you are from the outside and that scares me."

"That's why you didn't want to help me," Jan concludes, "but I'm not an Outsider. I lived at the Corpo Academy for Development. Up until four days ago, I was a student there."

"I see," the gardener contemplates. "You're from Corpo. It's starting to make sense now: your appearance, the gaps in your education ... I have a theory ... this is tied to your renaissance, isn't it?"

Jan doesn't answer.

"Okay ..." Tuinman pauses. "Tell me this ... did your father ever call you by another name?"

"Sometimes he called me ..."

"Fire," the gardener interrupts.

The Gemini Project 229

"Yes ... but how did you know ..."

"Judging by your age, I figured it was either going to be Tre, Fire or Fem," the gardener continued. "You don't need to tell me now, it's obvious. I should have seen it before. The scars around your cranium are the first clue, but the fact that Elf knows you seals the deal. You two seem to have known each other for a long time ... longer than he has been in New London. That means he must have met you before he lost his place at Corpo. All this makes me think that you've been recently renaissanced. Renaissanced at the Corpo Academy ... but you are still old ... so something must have gone wrong. Brain damage perhaps ... are you in there remembering daisy chains and laughs? Is that why you're here? Are you looking for someone on the 34th level to help you with a botched renaissance?"

Elf enters the gardening headquarters.

"Elf, just in time," the gardener says. "Mr. Jan here could use some food to strengthen him up and wash away the smell of alcohol. Would you mind taking him down to level five for something to eat, while I arrange his future?"

"But I start work shortly," Elf answers.

"Consider this a work assignment then. Where are you going to take him?"

"I'd like to go back to the French Café, if that's alright?" Jan says.

"Sounds great ... have a croissant on me," the gardener smiles.

On the way to Plaza Mayor, Elf asks Jan what a cwa-sawnt is. Jan answers that he really didn't know, then he tells Elf about the pain au chocolat.

"Sounds great," Elf says as they exit the elevator, "but let's go there for dessert. I know something else you need to try."

They walk past the café and Jan looks into the other restaurants. The sign for 'Coloured Stone' said that it is fine dining, then 'Garrison House' claims to be a gastropub, then finally they stop at 'Tommy Rockets' which is an American diner. Inside, the floor has checkerboard black and white squares, seats with luminescent red cushioning and a lot of shiny stainless steel. Elf walks up to a counter marked 'Take-Out'. Jan reads the menu and becomes interested in 'banana berry brownie pizza', while Elf orders two American cheeseburgers, fries and onion rings.

Other men are sitting inside to eat, but Jan and Elf stand at the take-out counter so Jan can watch his meal being cooked. A boy wearing a white tent-like hat flips the patties over as they sizzle on the grill. Cheese is melted on the patties, which are then placed between two halves of a bun, then smothered with at least three different sauces.

The two boys take their wrapped burgers outside and stroll towards one of Elf's gardens. Elf states that the burgers taste best hot, so they start eating as they walk. Cheese drips down Jan's chin as he tastes a delicious char-broiled cheeseburger for the first time. Elf chuckles watching Jan try to eat and walk.

"Here," Elf says, "you better sit down and eat."

The two sit down on a park bench and watch the people coming in and out of the restaurants. They look like a father and son, sharing a meal. After the burgers, Elf opens up a bag filled with French fries and onion rings.

"Now, try these …"

Jan reaches in and grabs a handful of fries, while Elf watches the restaurant activity. He notices four gendarmes heading towards the French Café. When they enter the restaurant, they immediately grab a man in green overalls and pull him outside.

"Why are they questioning Mr. Tirwedd?" Elf asks grabbing a handful of fat onion rings and motioning towards the gendarmes.

Jan looks up at the brownshirts surrounding the green overalled man. He gets a twitch in his temples.

"I told your Mr. Tuinman we were going to the café, and now men in brown shirts show up to harass a gardener at the café … I think maybe Tuinman is running a play."

"No, he wouldn't."

"Wouldn't he? Let's go find out."

Jan stands up and briskly marches toward the elevator, with Elf following. They go back up to the third level and bee-line it to the gardening headquarters.

"Surprised to see us?" Jan asks, as he enters and meets Tuinman's eyes.

Tuinman's face says that he isn't really. Tuinman isn't underestimating how intelligent Jan is.

"Tell me, Mr. Tuinman, what is the reward for turning in an Outsider? I think you left that part out of your earlier speech."

"10,000 credits," the gardener answers with a wry smile of self-satisfaction.

Jan looks at Elf. Elf's face shows his disappointment in his supervisor's betrayal.

"So, I guess when you say 'a little bit of truth goes a long way', you mean a VERY little bit of truth ... on your part. Why do you want 10,000 credits? You said you get all the credits you can use."

"Retirement, Mr. Jan. Once you amass 10,000 credits, you can stop work for life. I want to retire tomorrow, Mr. Jan."

Jan picks up a spade and steps toward Tuinman. Elf watches in horror as Jan holds up the spade to the gardener's throat and raises his voice.

"Maybe we can make your dream come true today. Maybe I will retire you right now. Do you want to learn what it really means to live and DIE?"

"Jan!" Elf urges.

Jan looks to Elf.

"Don't worry, I just want him to understand what will happen to him, if I hear that anything happens to you when I'm not here," Jan states, then turns back to the gardener. "Do you understand Tuinman?"

The gardener, now without any of his cockiness, silently nods.

"Good, now we're just about finished here. But first tell me, where do these retired people go?"

"They go to Jardin Island to live on the beach and soak in the sun," the gardener answers.

"So, they leave here, and are never seen again?" Jan questions thinking about the story of *The Fixed Period*. "You are a bigger fool than I realized. Do you honestly believe that the people that thought up this system, one that includes killing their own offspring, would include a happily-ever-after for their labour-force?"

A realization washes over Tuinman's face.

"That's right ... your fate is no better than that of a Emdee's child. This system is built on lies," Jan states, then turns to his friend. "Elf, I need to get out of here before the brownshirts come."

Jan turns and walks towards the door. Elf follows him.

"You better stay here for now," Jan says at the door, then whispers "I don't think Tuinman will be a problem now."

"But where are you going?"

"I'm getting ready to live and die Elf, but under my rules. Not Tuinman's. Not my father's. And definitely not De Visie's. But first, I need to have a conversation. I need to discuss a few things with my father and then I can start my new life."

Jan leaves the garden centre. It is time to go to level 42. He heads straight over to the elevators, still carrying the spade, and presses the down button. The down arrow lights up and Jan waits. When the elevator door opens, Jan starts to enter before he realizes that four gendarmes are exiting at the same time. Jan backs up. The brownshirts attack first, with one of them reaching for a square gun in his side holster. He pulls the trigger and wires shoot out towards Jan as he backs up.

Jan's innate sports skills still take control, and he raises the spade in time to deflect the wires. The wires wrap around the blade of the spade and Jan realizes that he had instinctively averted trouble. He then circles the other three brownshirts, allowing the wires to touch each of them. The three gendarmes convulse and fall to the ground. Jan looks at the remaining man who is still standing in front of the closed elevator door. Jan tries to rip the spade free from the wires, but it is too tangled. He drops the spade and heads towards the lone gendarme who guards the elevator door.

'Three down, one to go,' Jan thought.

The lone guard's eyes dart slightly to the left and right. Jan recognizes this movement from soccer when a player is looking to make a pass. He turns around quickly and sees four new gendarmes are approaching. Had they rushed him, they could have easily tackled him. However, the gendarmes are obviously not used to seeing violent acts, particularly ones that are directed towards them, so they approach slowly.

Jan has performed well up to this point, considering he has never fought anyone before. Once at the Academy, boxing was introduced for about a week. The boys received instructions, but before the first bout was scheduled, the sport was cancelled without any explanation. Jan wasn't disappointed in that decision as he was uncomfortable stepping into the ring and physically assaulting one of his schoolmates. Now he tries to remember the instructions as he realizes that he will have to fight for his life. As the tasered gendarmes regroup, they join the slow approach towards Jan. There are now eight of them to deal with. Jan is surrounded.

At that point, Jan thinks that the brownshirts would have done well to study *The Art of War*. Their approach is such that they are backing their enemy into a corner with no way out. Sun Tzu would have warned them that this tactic will create the fiercest of enemies as they are leaving their enemy with no choice but to attack … 'On desperate ground, fight'.

All of the gendarmes are approaching, and they each pull out a small stick that extends to triple its size. The sticks emanate blue electric sparks from the tip. The circle of gendarmes gets tighter, and Jan has eight electrical devices stretching out towards him. Jan is reading in his mind.

The Art of War, Chapter One, Laying Plans. Jan needs to come up with a strategy. He can't just take on all eight of them at once. When under attack from a large force of men, Sun Tzu stated that victory was a matter of merely dividing up their numbers. Jan first needs a one-on-one battle. He scans the men to determine who is the weakest, but they are all about the same height and build. However, one of them has taken the worst shock from the taser wires and is still looking weak in the knees. Jan has his strategy.

Gathering his strength and shifting just before the gendarmes are within striking range, Jan turns to his left and stretches out with a right hook across the chin of the weakest officer. The brownshirt falls to the ground and the motion catches the other gendarmes by surprise. A hole opens up in the circle and Jan shoots through it. Even though they had him surrounded, the gendarmes are caught off guard by his violent attack and it takes them a few seconds to start chasing after him. Jan finds himself running away from the elevator and towards the stores. He makes it to the Hardware Store before the brownshirts are able to catch up to him. Once inside, he heads down one of the aisles. He turns at the crossroad of a centre aisle, then tosses racks and supplies to the ground behind him to make the route more challenging for his pursuers.

The Art of War, Chapter Three, Attack by Strategum. Jan's path through the aisles looks random, and although he feels that he might be faster than the individual men, he also knows that he needs to stop them from surrounding him again. 'Prevent the junction of the enemy's forces', Sun Tzu had written. So, Jan zigzags down one row after another but never a row that will allow the man behind him to team up with another approaching officer. When he meets a pursuer one-on-one, he lays into them quickly, then continues on. The brownshirts' frustration with the pursuit is noticeable, and the lack of leadership becomes obvious. There are at least four men shouting out directions to the others as they try to contain Jan. Some stop to survey the situation and Jan approaches to reengage them back into the chase. On his third circle towards the front of the store, Jan has what he needed.

The Art of War, Chapter Ten, Terrain. When Jan finally circles back to the entrance, he finds one brownshirt guarding the door. This is the same gendarme that had guarded the elevator door. Jan continues to run towards the entrance and comes close enough to the man that the officer reaches out and tries to shock the perpetrator, but Jan changes direction at the last minute. Even in an older body, Jan's agility and physical skills allow him to bend his torso and avoid the electric emissions that were reaching out for him. Jan heads back inside. The frustrated officer joins the chase. Now the door is left unguarded. Why didn't the men know that Jan was going to run not fight. 'Other conditions being equal, if one force is hurled against another ten times its size, the result will be the flight of the former.'

Jan didn't need to read Sun Tzu's words to realize his options. He just has to complete one more circuit and head to the entrance. As he rounds the store, he faces three men who finally caught on to his circular pattern and are now heading towards him in the opposite direction. Jan stops and throws three hammers that he has picked up in his travels. The first hammer hits a brownshirt in the torso and the second takes one out at the knees. The third brownshirt dives into some paint cans trying to avoid the flying hardware. Jan runs down the aisle to the front of the store and sees the door again, this time without a guard.

Outside, Jan has a clear path to the elevator, but he takes a longer route through a garden, to camouflage his intentions. When he arrives at the elevator, he is out of the line of sight from the garden. He presses the down button and anxiously waits. He is still carrying some items that he picked up in the store. His shovel is also there, so he frees it from the wires and picks it up. Two partially beaten-up gendarmes are approaching the elevator just as the door opens. Jan raises the shovel up threateningly to keep the brownshirts at bay, then he backs into the elevator and presses 34. The doors close with the two men making a last-ditch effort to dive towards him. The elevator heads down.

Pressing 34 wasn't an accident. Jan pressed 34 because he knew it would work. However, he has no intention of going back to Dr. Osler's place. The arrival of the gendarmes means that he has to get to his father as soon as possible. While the elevator is in motion, he presses 42 and he can feel the blood flowing from his heart to his fingertip. 42 lights up. The elevator first opens at 34. Jan stays out of sight of the greeter, and just before the door closes, he throws the spade out. The elevator continues its ride to 42. Without realizing it, Jan has laid a trail of breadcrumbs that will mislead the brownshirts. The gardener has already reported that Jan had access to level 34 and when they check the elevator logs, sure enough it headed to that level right after the confrontation. The brownshirts head for level 34 and proceed to start a search. There are doctors on this level however, so the gendarmes will have to be delicate in their approach. This will take some time.

The elevator doors open again, and Jan exits at level 42. Three men dressed in black suits with bowties, sit behind a polished wooden counter in front of the elevator. They greet Jan as he exits, still carrying a hammer and some rope from his hardware excursion.

"Dr. Ericson," says the middle man. "Your son arrived a few days ago, and he's in your house now."

Jan looks around discreetly. This level has a smaller mall as the surrounding walls are closer to the centre. The liveries on the buildings have been styled to look like New York City brownstones. There are several gardens of various sizes throughout the mall. The air is fresher, and the light is provided by classic gas streetlights and a subtle overhead glow. This level smells of privilege.

"Great," Jan says.

Now, which way to go?

15. And the Cradle Will Rock...

Jan looks at the street sign. 'Candlewood Lane' ... there is nothing to indicate in which direction he should head. He knows he better start moving before he raises suspicion, so he invents a reason for his slow motions. He leans slightly on his right leg and proceeds to walk past the greeters with a limp.

"I've pulled a leg muscle. Could I get one of you to help me to my place?"

"Certainly sir," one of the concierge men responds.

He stands up and immediately moves to Jan's right side and puts one arm around Jan's back. Jan places a lot of weight on the greeter to convince him that his leg is in really rough shape. The greeter helps Jan and leads him 180 degrees around the elevator. This isn't the direction Jan would have selected if he had to guess. As they walk, Jan reads the name tag on the greeter's jacket. "Irving.' The man takes Jan to a garden path in front of a brownstone numbered 698. The concierge offers to help him into the house, but Jan says he'll be fine from that point. Jan walks up the path slowly, giving his assistant time to retreat.

The Gemini Project 237

Before Jan makes it inside, a voice calls out "Ericson!"

Damn, someone from this level that knows me. Time to put on another front.

"Hey," Jan says turning around slowly.

There is a man, about 21-years-old, coming out of the façade next to his father. Double damn, a neighbour.

"Are you getting excited about the big day?"

What big day? What big day?

"Oh yes," Jan responds, "my son's renaissance. Very exciting."

"Your son's renaissance ... good one!"

The neighbour laughs like he has just heard the funniest thing in his life. Jan doesn't know what he has said to amuse the man. He also doesn't know what his father and this man have in common. If he says something wrong, it won't be long before the brownshirts are at the door. But how can he make familiar conversation with a man that he doesn't know at all. He can see that the man is dressed the same as his father, wearing the customary black turtleneck.

It turns out that Jan doesn't have to worry about making conversation. His neighbour seems to talk non-stop and doesn't leave much space for a response. He is very conversant. Too conversant. At first Jan is worried that he might give himself away, but black-turtleneck doesn't need anyone else to have a conversation.

Jan hears about the pros and cons of birthing another son every five years versus every ten years. 'The more possible vessels being cultivated at the same time, the better the choices, but also the more work'. Jan also hears how his neighbour is going to revolutionize the ordinateur business in the next year by introducing a fully functional micro-organism made from pure silica. Then he learns what to do to book a trip to Jardin Island and how the journey is 'almost too good to be true'.

"Back to where it all began, I tell you it's practically religious. I can't believe you've never been there," his neighbour concludes. "Well, I've got to run. I'll drop by after your renaissance and see how you're doing."

'Of course ... it was my renaissance, not my son's ... good one!'

"I've got a great bottle of Scotch that I'm waiting for a reason to open. Talk to you soon."

"Yeah ... see you then."

Now at the front door, Jan looks at the scanner with anticipation. There is a whir as the door unlocks. Jan enters and immediately spots his favourite running shoes.

'Hello old friends.'

The inside of the brownstone is laid out similarly to Dr. Osler's house, but the capacious space is subtly opulent. Where Osler had photographs on the wall, his father has very colourful, large paintings. Jan stands silently in the front hall, looking into the house, waiting for his father to approach. No one comes. Jan still doesn't call out. Instead, he moves slowly from room to room. As he enters each room, the lights come on and Jan prepares himself to confront his father. Every room on the main floor is empty. He pauses in the living room.

"Anjea, if you're here, don't answer me, just blink the living room lights," Jan says softly.

The lights blink. The house is Anjea-equipped, and she recognizes his voice.

"Anjea, blink the living room lights if my son is home."

The lights blink again. Jan wonders if his father is upstairs, or perhaps he is hiding somewhere. Would Dr. Osler have warned Tre to expect company?

Jan quietly heads to the staircase. From the bottom of the stairs, he hears a small thud, followed by a static-like sound. As he slowly heads up, he listens to what sounds like a partially melodic tune. It is his own voice. He is singing. There is a surreal feeling hearing his own voice coming from a different room.

Once he reaches the top of the stairs, he enters the main bedroom, and smells the scent of the eucalyptus. He realizes that the sibilance is the sound of a shower. The singing voice is slightly muffled but, once in the room, Jan can hear the lyrics through the open door of the attached washroom.

> *Steve walks warily down the street,*
> *With the brim pulled way down low,*
> *Ain't no sound but the sound of his feet,*
> *Machine guns ready to go.*

Jan moves softly across the room and peers tentatively into the bathroom. The room is larger than his Corpo dorm room. The shower

The Gemini Project

is running hot, and the glass door is steamed up, but Jan can make out the shadow of his former body.

Dum, dum, dum ... Another one bites the dust.
Dum, dum, dum ... Another one bites the dust.

And another one gone, and another one gone
Another one bites the dust.

Thud.

The shower has been shut off and the singing comes to an abrupt stop. Jan scrambles back across the room and quickly ducks through the open door of the closet. He just makes it into the dressing room, as his father comes out of the steam shower, grabs a towel, and walks directly across the marble floor from the bathroom to the large mirror in the bedroom. Jan backs up and takes a motionless position between the clothes, where he can still see has father. Tre stands in front of the mirror, lightly dries himself, then drops the towel. He changes his song, mumbling the words as he wiggles in front of the mirror:

He says, "I'm sorry but I'm out of milk and coffee."
"Never mind, sugar, we can watch the early movie."

Jan realizes that he has a mediocre singing voice, but his father also has bad taste in music. He crouches down in the blackness, watching and listening. He thinks about how much he looks like his father. He also thinks about how much he now hates him. As his father gets dressed in an outfit that has been laid on the bed, Jan decides it is time to confront Trevor Ericson.

His father stands in front of the mirror again, admiring his now fully clothed physique. He gyrates to the song's chorus, thrusting his hips towards the mirror.

'Stop it! Stop it! Stop it!'

Jan comes out of the closet.

"I believe you have something of mine."

"What the hell?" Tre says spinning around.

Jan just stands there, leaning against the closet doorframe and staring at his father. He is still partially shrouded by the darkness of the closet.

"Who are you? What the fuck are you doing here?" his father snaps, as he moves to get a better look at the intruder.

Tre hadn't recognized the sound of his own voice, perhaps because it isn't in the realm of possibilities running through his mind. Jan approaches him. Two steps later, Tre realizes who the intruder is, but he still doesn't understand why he is hearing and seeing his old self. Then it sinks in.

"It's that fucker Osler ... he did this, didn't he? Well, he's going to pay for this little joke."

Then he thinks about what brain could operate his old body.

"Fire, is that you?"

"By Jove, I think you've got it. But my name is Jan, not Fire."

Jan's father realizes what Dr. Osler has done.

"So, we've swapped bodies?" Tre says rhetorically, as he nods. "That damned doctor certainly has some tricks up his sleeve. But what's the point of this little scam?"

"I wanted to see you ... to tell you that I am going to find a position working with the Hebs, and I might need your support."

"Well ... this is a bit to take in. The prodigal son returns, and it looks like you haven't been caring for my body very well," Tre says looking at the scar across Jan's face. "You're such a wildcard. I don't understand you at all. Saying things like 'By Joe, I think you've got it'."

"It's 'by Jove' ... with a vee. It's a form of saying 'by Jupiter', the Roman god of the sky ... used by Christians to avoid saying the blasphemous 'my god'."

Tre stares at him. He wonders how many useless pieces of information Jan has stored away or where he acquired this information. Of course, he has no idea that his son studied the dictionary for months and has been making regular trips to a library.

"Sure, sure. I mean, I could help you get a job working with the Hebs. First, we need to determine what your skill sets are. Let's go downstairs and work this out."

Father and son head down to the kitchen, where the father, in the son's body, grabs a pen and paper.

"Let's make an old-fashioned list. Let's start with this ... you told me before that you can read ... CAN you read?"

"Yes."

"Can you write?"

The Gemini Project 241

"I guess so ... I've never tried."

"This is interesting. I bet that Dr. Osler taught you. Let's see what else he taught you. Tell me about a book that you've read ... The Cat in the Hat, maybe?"

"Well ... the book that made me think the most so far is *Catcher in the Rye*."

"Really? Of course ... adolescent angst and alienation. Any favourite parts?"

Jan thinks about the book, and it brings him back to a late-night reading session in the library. He remembers sitting on the floor, under the light of a glow-tube, and relating to the main character, Houlden Caulfield. He found it very humourous and could relate to Caulfield's statement that he reads a lot but that he is really quite illiterate. A smile appears on his face, as he is flipping through the pages of his mind. He answers his father with the line that stuck with him the most:

> *I think that one of these days ... you're going to have to find out where you want to go. And then you've got to start going there.*

"Wow Jan ... very impressive. It sounds like you've got a photogenic memory," Tre says in an attempt to amuse and confuse, "and I should know ... I've seen it up close and personal."

At that moment, Tre grabs the longest knife from the knife rack and immediately points it towards Jan.

"Seems like you've come a long way," Tre begins, with the knife at Jan's chest. "Have you studied medicine yet? Do you know the internal organs?"

Jan retreats slowly from the kitchen to the living room, facing his approaching father as he walks backwards.

"You don't have to do this. All I want is to live a normal life."

"But I don't think I can allow that Jan. You see if you're alive, then the renaissance is flawed, and that will raise some questions. Especially, if you die from a liver disease in short order. You have to be laid to rest in order for this little scheme to work. Capiche? And don't look at me that way ... I'm not bad, I'm just drawn that way."

His father follows Jan into the living room, still pointing the long knife at his son.

"As the tongue twister goes, it's time to ask yourself: are our hours ours? And the answer for you, I'm afraid, is 'no'. Your time is up," his father states.

"This is your last chance, father. You can either help me or you will leave me no choice."

"You really are a glass-half-full kind of guy, aren't you?"

Jan looks at his father and a look of bewilderment comes over his face.

"Ahh ... I've found something that you haven't learned yet! I mean you are an optimist ... do you know what that is?"

Jan nods.

"I don't know where you get that from, because I am a pessimist ... that's why I take precautions. So, for me, the glass is not half-full ... it is half-empty."

Tre moves slowly towards Jan.

"I'm not an optimist and I'm not a pessimist ... I am a realist ... you have the wrong size of glass ... now, this really is your final chance to drop the knife."

"A realist?" Tre repeats as he deliberately looks down at the knife then back to Jan. "You are really quite funny Fire. Do you really think you can take me? I know you're having a literal out-of-body experience, but really ... I know that body and it is old. This one on the other hand, well ... you know how good this one is, don't you?"

His father lunges towards Jan, waving the knife in one broad stroke. Without a weapon for a responsive parry, Jan can only pull in his body to lessen the impact. The knife brushes across Jan's chest, cutting through the black turtleneck and drawing a surface amount of blood.

"That's just a preview of the things you're gonna get. The next one is going directly through your heart. Why don't you make this easy and just give up. It will be less painful."

"Don't say I didn't warn you," Jan states.

"Here's a new word for you ... piñata. And my question for you is ... is it more fun being the piñata or the stick? What? No answer? Well, you're the piñata and I am the stick, so you are about to find out."

His father smiles then lunges at him again, this time with the knife pointing straight in front of him.

"Anjea, lights off!" Jan shouts.

The lights immediately dim, and Jan ducks down in the darkness to avoid the knife. While he is on the floor, Jan swings his legs in a circle in front of him, knocking his father to the ground. Jan grabs the footstool that he had backed up to, then stands up and pounces on his father pinning his arms under the stool.

"Anjea, lights on!" Jan shouts.

Jan punches his father in the face as soon as the lights turn on. His father still has the knife in his hand, even though it is pinned down by the foot stool.

"I'm sorry father, did that hurt?" Jan says with a degree of sincerity.

His father is formulating an answer as Jan punches him again. Confused by the combination of sympathy and punches, then the force of Jan pressing on the footstool, Tre drops the knife. For a brief moment, Tre thinks that Jan is relaxing his hold on him, when suddenly he realizes that Jan has picked up the footstool. Too late, it comes crashing into his head. His father is unconscious.

'No quarter.'

When Tre Ericson comes to, his legs are tied to the legs of an armchair and his arms are also strapped down. He looks at his bondage.

"Where did the rope come from?"

"Oh, I ran through the Hardware store and picked a few things up on the way here. You have to 'Be Prepared' you know."

"So, you're a boy scout too, are you? Can I get a drink?"

"Yes, of course," Jan answers, reverting back to his father-son roll for a moment. He goes to the kitchen and takes a tumbler over to the tap.

"No, over there, in the cabinet, you'll find a bottle of amber liquid."

Jan returns to the living room and opens the cabinet to find several bottles of Scotch.

"Any of the ones from Islay will do," his father calls out and then he continues under his breath, "… they're all replicas anyway."

Jan reads the labels to find out which ones are from Islay. He picks up a bottle labelled 'Laphroaig' and struggles to pronounce it in his head. He glances at another one labelled 'Bruichladdich' and struggles even more.

"Anytime," his father calls out sarcastically.

Jan settles on 'Lagavulin', then pours a full tumbler of Scotch, and brings it to his father. After tasting the drink at Dix's mother's place, Jan doesn't even think about pouring himself a glass. He unties his father's left hand.

"You do a good pour," his father says seeing the size of the glass.

As Tre sips, he lets out a satisfied 'ahhh'.

"You know, you'll never get away with it. Whatever it is. Do you even have a plan? Sure, you can tie me down, but what next? You'll have to let me go and when you do, that's when the shit hits the fan … are you listening? I said … are you fucking listening to me?"

Jan says nothing. His father continues to talk and drink.

"Don't think you wouldn't do the same thing as me. Don't forget, you come from me. You have to do … what you have to do. You have to survive, that's what we were put on this planet to do."

Jan still doesn't respond.

"Are you taking any of this in? You can't fight the system. I am you, and what I see is me," Tre says as he raises his voice.

The more he drinks, the more he talks. The more he talks, the more he slurs. Questions, turn to complaints, which turn into philosophical diatribes. Eventually, his father starts to sound like he has been listening too much to Dr. Osler.

"You know you really don't deserve this body," Tre says as he admires his current form, "… you don't even understand it, or how it works. Can you point to where the spleen is or tell me what it does? I didn't think so. Have you got any idea what your lymph nodes are up to right now?"

He takes another glug of Scotch and looks his body up and down.

"You have absolutely no idea, do you? How many times a day do you think you blink?"

Jan still says nothing.

"Come on, I'd like to hear your guess."

The Gemini Project 245

"I don't know," Jan blurts out, not wanting to play along. Then eventually answers "500? 1,000?"

"Not even close. You blink 14,000 times a day ... so these eyes will shut for 23 minutes of every waking day. No ... you don't have what it takes to maintain this body on your own. Watch this ..."

Tre waits a second, takes another swig of Scotch, and then snaps his fingers.

"In that time, this body has made a million red blood cells, and they are coursing through my veins, keeping me alive ... keeping me alive, because I understand that there are enough veins to wrap around the world twice. Yes ... I understand what a great invention this body is."

Jan has never heard his father talk so much, but he has never seen him drunk before either. Tre sits silently for a moment and sips on his Scotch. When he begins to speak again, his words slur together.

"You know, there have only been four great developments in the history of man. Everyone would point to the wheel as the first invention ... that's an old story, so it's an easy one. Then of course, there is the Gutenberg press, we have that one to thank for the proliferation of Bibles."

"THANK YOU," Tre calls out sarcastically.

"Now when I was a boy, everyone talked about Alexander Graham Bell like he was the reincarnation of Gutenberg. I mean we had him elevated so high up that you couldn't say his name without saying his full name, including his middle name. Then, practically over-night, we moved on to the next idol. There are those that point to Gates and the microcomputer as Gutenberg Two, but that was just a half a platform ... a place to store your recipes or play a game to waste your day. No, the third transformational invention was the internet, so kudos to Al Gore," his father concludes as he let out a laugh.

Jan remembers seeing the *Rolling Stone* story on 'Al Gore's Grim Warning'. Maybe he could get Anjea to drown out his father by reading an article from *Rolling Stone*, maybe Anjea could find the one with Jimmy Connors the tennis player.

His father's slurring has become worse, and the tumbler of Scotch is three quarters empty. He holds the glass out and Jan refills it.

"So that brings us to invention four, the next great jump point ... and do you know what that was? Come on ... you can figure it out, it's not brain surgery. Oh wait, it is. It's the Gemini Project, the first successful brain transplant. A way for man, I mean mankind, to live on with his knowledge, not just pass it down and hope the next generation understands the information correctly."

"Anjea, can you drown out this boring speech please?" Jan finally asks.

"Sure, would you like me to play some music?"

"Yes, that would be great," Jan answers eagerly.

"What would you like to hear?"

Jan thinks about the music from the café but didn't know how to describe it. Then reverts back to *Rolling Stone*.

"Can you play something from 1980?"

"Of course, anything in particular?"

"Yes, I'd like to learn about Heavy Metal Lust. Can you play the 1980 release from Van Halen, please and thank you?"

"My pleasure. Here is the first track from the 1980 release 'Women and Children First'."

A distorted, phase-shifted guitar plays a 4/4 beat and is immediately followed by the thumping rhythms of the drums and bass. Soon the vocals blare out:

> *Well, they say it's kinda fright'nin' how this younger generation swings, You know, it's more than just some new sensation,*
>
> *Well, the kid is into losin' sleep, and he don't come home for half the week, You know, it's more than just an aggravation,*
>
> *And the cradle will rock ...*

His father has finally stopped talking. He recognizes the music but is stymied at how Jan knew to request Van Halen. And did he just say 'Heavy Metal Lust'? His father throws back another mouthful of Scotch.

'And the cradle will rock, indeed!' Jan thinks.

The music continues to blast out. Tre is relatively quiet.

'And I say Rock On.'

Jan thinks about his father, and his mood quickly turns dark. He remembers how he used to admire, worship, and even want to become

The Gemini Project 247

this man. Now, he has become his father physically, but he refuses to become like him mentally. Jan is left with a dilemma. He has to decide if he is going to execute his father or let him live. Jan knows the word: dilemma. He remembers the day he read it in the dictionary and reviewed it with Dr. Osler. 'Di' means 'two'. 'Lemma' means 'a choice or an alternative'. So, Jan ponders his two lemmas. Kill or be killed. If only there were a third lemma. Why couldn't this be a tri-lemma? Life was so much easier for Jan ... before he knew about his father's plan to escape death. His father would have had Jan killed anyway, but it would have just been the way society operated. There was no choosing required. Maybe for his father, it would have been more of a uni-lemma.

As his father starts once again to ramble on, and Van Halen continues to wail, Jan's mind moves back and forth between words and choices. Then, in a moment of clarity, he knows what he is going to do. He has found his own uni-lemma.

His father passes out.

'Baked like a potato.'

"Anjea, I'm going to cook dinner for two tonight, can you help me?"

"Of course. Would you like me to suggest a recipe?"

"That would be great."

"How about Asian Inspired Pork with a Peanut Sauce and Zucchini Ribbons."

"Sounds good. Can you get the ingredients delivered to this address and can I add an extra ingredient to the sauce?"

"Of course. We already have radishes, green onions, and chili peppers in the fridge, but I will get the other ingredients ordered immediately."

15 minutes later there is a knock on the door and Jan greets a young man dressed in a red suit and ballcap, who passes him a paper bag filled with everything required for tonight's dinner. Jan lays out all the ingredients, and then he cooks dinner with some step-by-step guidance from Anjea.

At the dining room table, his father wakes up to the smell of the peanut sauce. He is still tied to the armchair. Jan tells his father that he has already eaten, then he unties his father's arms and serves him dinner. His father's head is splitting, but a good meal is exactly what he needs. He works his way quickly through the pork dinner, making several 'm-m-m' sounds.

"That was delicious ... and you made it? You didn't make that sauce though?"

"I did make it, and I didn't follow the recipe for the sauce."

"Okay then, how did you make it?"

"I'll tell you later," Jan says controlling the conversation, "but right now I've got a couple of questions for you. Who's my mother?"

"Oh, you think you've got some attachment to your mother, do you? She's a Pelacur. I don't really know her that well ... I've just used her services a couple of dozen times."

"And where is she?" Jan asks sternly.

"She's up where we keep all the Pelacurs. Up on level twenty-something," Tre answers aggressively. "Oh sure, we could have grown you in a test tube, but it was De Visie's idea to create the procreation levels, someplace we can go make our offspring. Go visit her if you like. She's at 32 Windsor Gardens. I'm sure she'll be glad to see you."

"Maybe I'll do that. Now, tell me, how many times have you done this before? How many times have you killed your son, so you can stay alive? I'm sure you remember, after all you've taken your memory with you each time. So, how many times would that be now?"

"Fire," Tre answered, "you are so aggressive. You just need to take the time to understand ..."

Then it occurs to Ian that the gardener knew his father's nickname for him. The only information the gardener had was his Norwegian heritage, but somehow he deduced his nickname.

"You are sick," Jan says. "I already knew this system was perverse, but to be so blatant ..."

"What are you talking about now?"

"Anjea, can you count to ten in Norwegian for me," Jan requests.

"Sure ... éin, to, tre, fire, fem, seks, sju, åtte, ni, ti." Anjea answers.

"So, Tre Ericson," Jan says. "Let me introduce myself to you, it seems like you are right ... I must be Fire Ericson. So, I am your fourth renaissance?"

"Jan, it's not like ..." his father begins.

The Gemini Project 249

"Call me Fire," Jan cuts him off with attitude.

"Look, Jan …" Tre starts again tentatively, then seeing Fire's mood, he adjusts. "Fine, Fire … it's not like that. You are given a good life, the best life you can have for eighteen years. We do this out of love so you can …"

"Stop. Just stop. You don't really believe that, so stop trying to convince me. You do this so your vessel can be developed into the best vessel it can be for you on day one. You have us do the exercises to build muscle, so you don't have to. Then you do your best to run our bodies into the ground because you know you have another one lined up. Tell me, is my brother Fem already born?"

His father is fully exposed and there is little he can do to cloak the truth.

"So, what are you going to do?" Tre asks.

"Well, you asked yesterday if I have a plan … and I do, now. As you may remember, my birthday is in two days time, so I'm going to have a party … and you're invited. Oh yes, I promised you something … Anjea, can you tell my father the ingredients for the sauce from tonight's dinner, please."

"Gladly. Vinegar, sesame oil, soy sauce, chili-garlic powder, peanut butter, water and Benzodiazepine."

"Do you like a good dose of sedatives in your peanut sauce?" Fire asks, seeing his father's perplexed gaze. "It seems, as a doctor I can just order some anytime I want to. So, I had Anjea recommend the type and dose, so it would have the right effect. Then, just to be safe, I gave you a shot of Phenobarbital. Oh, and it's not your fault you didn't taste it. I made sure to put enough of the chili-garlic powder in to numb your tongue."

On schedule, Tre begins to lose consciousness.

"And don't worry, I've got seconds here for when you start to come around."

Fire reties his father's arms and then puts the rest of his plan in motion.

"Anjea, can I authorize someone to come to the 42nd level?"

"Yes. I can authorize someone for you, to have access to any level where you live or work."

"Anjea, can you contact Elf in the Gardening Headquarters?"

"Certainly. Elf Johannes in the Gardening department. What would you like to say?"

'Johannes?'

Fire realizes that he has never heard Elf's last name before.

"Ask him to come meet me at 698 Candlewood Lane on level 42 and ask him to bring a gardening waste bin. Then provide him with the required access."

16. Like Father, Like Son

Elf exits the elevator on the 42nd level pushing a large green wooden bin. He is confronted with an environment unlike anything he has ever seen. Aromatic scents and soft lighting are surrounded by the gentle sound of an orchestra playing Samuel Barber's 'Adagio for Strings'. He looks around at the large homes with lush gardens. In awe, Elf doesn't even notice the three men sitting at the counter in front of him.

"Mr. Johannes," one of the men states. "If you'd like to follow me, I'll take you to Dr. Ericson's home."

The man leads Elf to Tre Ericson's residence.

"Will you be doing some extra gardening here?" the man asks as they walk.

"I'm not sure," Elf replies.

Which is true.

"Well, if there is anything you need to complete your work, please don't hesitate to ask us," the man concludes as his arm extends to point up the path to the entrance.

The door opens and Fire walks out smiling at Elf. He recomposes himself, looks at the concierge and says, "Thank you Irving."

Inside, Elf is in awe once again. He slowly walks through the home like a patron walking through a museum. He comes to an abrupt stop when he enters the living room and sees Jan's slumped body, tied to a chair.

"Is he …"

"Dead? No. Not yet. My father is just sedated."

"So, what are we going to do?"

"This is my battle, Elf. You don't need to do anything except help me get my father down to the shuttle."

"Then where are you taking him?"

"We're going back to Corpo."

"I see. Okay …" Elf says, then he heads back outside to get the cart.

"Anjea, can you ready my shuttle to go to The Corpo Academy for Development?"

"Of course, when would you like to leave?"

"Tomorrow morning, first thing. Can you also contact Dr. Osler at the Academy?"

"Dr. William Osler of the Corpo Academy for Development. What would you like to say?"

"Tell him to prepare for tomorrow evening's renaissance as scheduled and tell him to use Nurse Banaltram for the procedure. Oh, and let him know that both patients will arrive by shuttle tomorrow afternoon."

Elf returns with the cart.

"Right, is this for what I think it's for?"

"Yes, it's to move my father down to the shuttle level. Don't worry I've got him juiced up enough to last until tomorrow. You grab his legs and I'll take his arms."

They lift Tre up and gently put him into the garden cart, where Fire reties his father's arms and legs.

"I'll go get some leaves to cover him up."

"Good idea," Fire responds.

The Gemini Project

Elf heads out to the central garden with his secateur and returns with garden scraps. He tosses leafed branches on top of the torso to camouflage it.

"Gently," Fire says. "I don't want to make any unnecessary bruises on him … I mean on me."

Once they have the greenery sufficiently covering the body, Fire offers to cook dinner for Elf.

"Anything you want, just name it."

"Okay … I'd like to have spaghetti with meatballs."

"Watch this … Anjea, can you find a recipe for spaghetti and meatballs, then order the ingredients."

"Certainly. The ingredients have been ordered and will be here in ten minutes."

"No way. What else can it do?"

"She seems to know how everything works," Fire says, "so I think it's more a question of 'what can't she do'. Anjea, will you play some music suitable to cook dinner by?"

"Here is Johann Sebastian Bach's Cello Suites BWV 1007 to 1012."

A gentle solo cello starts playing arpeggiated chords as the two boys sit at the kitchen counter and Fire tells Elf his plan. The food arrives and Anjea directs the boys as they make spaghetti for the first time. Anjea offers the boys wine, but they decline. Making the spaghetti, they are already laughing like they are tipsy. After dinner, Fire shows Elf to one guest room and then he heads to the other. At first Fire thinks he is too excited to sleep, but soon he is dreaming of walking through a large library. He finds a book titled '1984' and he sits down and begins to read. A woman's soft hands come from behind and massage his shoulders. He feels her breath on his neck, followed by a flutter of her eyelashes. He turns to look at the woman, but he can't see a face.

In the morning, Anjea gently wakes the two boys. They each have a shower in their ensuite bathrooms, then Fire gets dressed in one of the suits his father wore to father's day, and Elf gets back into his green overalls. When they see each other, they let a smile turn into a laugh. Elf stops laughing first, and his face shows a slight concern.

"You need to shave. You look like Dr. Osler after he's come back from vacation."

"Oh", Fire says. "I've never done that before …"

He returns upstairs to his father's bathroom and finds a drawer filled with shaving products. He takes out a manual razor and holds it to his throat. Without applying any shaving lotion, he gently pulls the blade up from his throat to his chin. He feels a small nip and he sees blood forming out of a straight line on his throat. This isn't going to work. He looks in the drawer again and finds a black apparatus with an on/off button. He switches it on to hear a whirl, then mows the electric device across his throat. He carefully works his way around the healing gash of the bobcat battle. This is doing the job nicely. Sometimes, maybe the new ways can be an improvement on the old ways.

Back downstairs, Fire pours out some muesli and then he fills Elf in on his trips to the library. After breakfast, Fire slips another tablet of Benzodiazepine under his father's tongue, and the boys head out. Before leaving his father's house, Fire grabs his favourite running shoes at the front door. Elf pushes the cart and Fire leads the way across the mall to the elevator. They don't speak to each other, or to the three men at the concierge desk. They board the elevator and Fire presses the number 26.

"Where are we going?" Elf asks.

"I was asking Anjea some questions last night while I was waiting for you to arrive, and she said level 26 was where the newborns reside."

"You mean … like babies?" Elf mouths slowly.

Fire nods. The elevator opens on floor 26. There are no greeters at the door but there is a sign saying Conch Street. The wide central expanse has no gardens, and all the building facades are white stone. The twosome exit the elevator and walk around the floor, Elf is pushing the garden cart. The first person they see is a woman in her early 30s, wearing a white uniform. She is heading their way. Fire looks over at Elf.

"Try not to stare."

"But she's a … she's a … she," Elf croaks.

"She's a woman. There are others on other floors … maybe even your mother."

"Doctor," the nurse says as she passes them on her way to the elevator.

The Gemini Project

"Good morning."

Once the nurse has passed, Elf turns to Fire and congratulates him on being so calm with his interaction.

"Likewise."

They continue to walk around the mall, seemingly without direction. Elf looks up and takes in the almost light purple hue to the sky.

"Jan, I've got a weird feeling about this place."

"I do too. Oh, and I go by what my father thinks of me now. Call me Fire."

Elf giggles.

"That's a silly name."

"Yeah … that's why I like it. Tell me, is your feeling about this place like it all looks sort of familiar to you?"

"Exactly … like I've been here before … but I haven't. Right?"

"I'm not sure. I've got the same feeling."

They approach the front of building 124 and see that the building is labelled 'Crèche'.

"Are we going to go in?" Elf asks.

"Not today, but soon … I think."

A sliding door whooshes and a pixie-like girl comes out of the building. She is a seven-year-old red-headed lass, wearing a green skirt with matching ribbons in her hair. This is new for both Fire and Elf … a younger version of a woman.

"Hello, who are you?" she asks as she approaches the pair.

Silence.

"Umm … I'm Elf and this is Fire," Elf finally answers.

The small girl laughs.

"Your names are funny."

"Really?" Fire says. "What's your name?"

"I'm Skye … not like the one above you, 'cause that would be silly."

Both Fire and Elf look up as she points to the purple projection with white clouds that are floating across the ceiling of Conch Street. Elf and Fire smile.

"What are you doing here?" Skye asks innocently.

She is able to remind Fire and Elf that they shouldn't be there, querying them in a way that other adults had failed to.

"We are just leaving," Fire says. "Would it be okay if we came back and visited some day?"

"I would like that ... your names are funny."

Fire and Elf start back towards the elevator.

"Bye ... see you later alligator," Elf calls out.

"In a while, crocodile," Skye answers, then laughs again.

Fire looks at Elf and can't wipe the smile from his face.

"Tuinman says that all the time," Elf says, and after a pause adds, "... what do you think will happen to her."

"I don't know Elf. As much as I now understand how things work here, there is so much that is still a mystery."

They reach the elevator and Fire presses the button.

"Perhaps she'll become a nurse ... or maybe ..."

Fire's words and darker thoughts are interrupted as the elevator doors open. As they board, they are surprised to see that there is already another doctor in the elevator. Fire looks down and sees that the doctor is heading up to level five. Elf quickly moves to the back and Fire stands beside the other passenger, then pushes the button for the shuttle level. He looks towards the man to greet him.

"Good morning, Dr. Ericson" the other doctor says, ignoring Elf.

"Good morning," Fire responds wondering if it is obvious that he doesn't know the doctor's name.

As the elevator starts to move, Fire becomes concerned that the doctor is about to start a conversation, so he decides that he will run a play-fake and speak to Elf instead. He gives Elf a leading question.

"So, what did you call those plants you put on the fifth level?" Fire asks hoping Elf will run down field for the pass.

"Lupins ... sir," Elf answers, looking at Fire.

Fire raises his eyebrows twice, in an attempt to get Elf to continue talking. Elf takes the pass.

"They are an annual plant, but they are also available as a shrub. The soft grey-green leaves are topped with towering flowers that range from blue to light purple."

Fire motions with his eyes again. This elevator ride seems exceedingly long.

"The flower shape has inspired other common names such as bluebonnets. The fruit is a pod containing several seeds which can …"

The elevator slows down, and the door opens at the fifth level.

"Ericson," the other doctor acknowledges, then he nods as he steps out of the elevator.

"Doctor," Fire responds again with the only thing he can think of.

Fire is sure he saw the other doctor turn around and do a double take, just as the doors closed.

"I had nothing left," Elf says, letting out a nervous laugh as soon as the door closes. "I just told you everything I know about lupins, and I don't really know if they are the same as bluebonnets! I'm not exactly Anjea you know?"

"That was close," Fire responds, "but I'm not sure whether he grew suspicious near the end. At least he didn't look at our plants too closely!"

Fire looks down and points at his father's uncovered hand. Elf chuckles as he watches his friend rearrange the branches. The elevator door opens again, and Fire realizes that he doesn't know which shuttle is his. As they exit the elevator, Fire scans the level but there are too many similar shuttles for him to quickly pick out his father's. A man in blue overalls approaches the elevator.

"Quickly," Elf says. "Which direction?"

Fire has no idea, but he knows if they head to the wrong shuttle, they might raise suspicion.

"I'm not sure. Follow my lead."

"Excuse me …" Fire calls out to the approaching shuttle worker.

'You can't ask him, it's a dead giveaway.' Elf thinks.

"Yes, Dr. Ericson," the worker responds.

"Could you show this boy over to my shuttle please, he needs to load some plants for me."

Fire doesn't wait for a reply, he just heads towards the whiteshirts as if he has a reason to go there before going to his shuttle.

"Certainly, Dr. Ericson," overalls responds as if he has a choice.

Fire looks back to watch where Elf is heading. Yes … that's his father's shuttle. Fire circles around and meets Elf at the rear of the shuttle. Blue-overalls has dropped the shipping compartment down at the back of the shuttle. There is a tarp in the back, so Elf attaches it, covering the top of the cart completely.

"Are we putting him in here?" Elf asks.

"I guess so. It would be less suspicious if that's what they are expecting."

"Okay by me, if it's okay by you," Elf says as he wheels the cart up a ramp and fastens it into the compartment. "What time do we leave?"

"You need to stay here. I'm playing singles from this point."

Elf nods, slightly disappointed. They close the back door and Fire enters the falcon-winged side door. He looks back and smiles at Elf. That's when it occurs to Fire that he has no idea how to control the shuttle. There are eight comfortable leather seats in a circle facing each other, but there are no controls anywhere. He doesn't even see something to close the door. Fire needs to figure this out quickly in case the elevator doctor is sending some brownshirts down to the shuttle level.

"See you soon," Elf says, and the door closes.

"We'll depart in one minute," the voice announces.

"Anjea, you're here!"

"Always."

Fire sits down in one of the tan coloured seats. The shuttle lets out a slight hiss, and Fire is prepared to leave. He doesn't realize the vehicle is already in full motion, until he feels the incline of the exit ramp. As the shuttle levels off, Fire figures he is now beside the apple orchard. He wonders if the pack is outside waiting for him. The shuttle accelerates down the blue road.

The ride is comfortable, but Fire is missing the scenery.

"Anjea, is there anyway I can see the outside?"

"Here is the 360-degree view from the external cameras. To zoom in to any point, just raise your hand and stretch your thumb and pointer finger."

The large dark panel surrounding the chairs lights up to show the outside view. Fire can see the prickly shrubbery on each side, and unconsciously he starts rubbing his legs. Soon they are at an overpass where the shuttle veers right to take a blacktop road. As he passes the junction, Fire looks at the concrete underpass and thinks 'there's one of my bedrooms'. He can't feel the shuttle slow down but looking at the side view he can tell that it does. He looks at the front view but can't see anything of note, until the shuttle reaches a hill and starts to head down towards the river.

'Youngstown.'

The shuttle passes through the river, over the bridge and heads slowly down Main St. The force of the shuttle's air is blowing sheets of water onto the front of the shop windows, giving them a much-needed wash. Next, he sees the rat-infested Stagecoach Restaurant and Fire is happy that he doesn't have to go in again. The shuttle comes to the bottom of the hill that leads out of town and it starts to pick up speed again.

After 15 minutes, Fire can see the Corpo dome coming into view. The shuttle slows down again as it arrives at the dome. An opening appears similar to a large elevator door, and the shuttle slides into the dome. It drives through a wash of green liquid that showers over the vehicle at the entrance.

"Anjea, what is that liquid that is being sprayed on us?"

"That is a mixture of neem oil, berberine and benzalkonium chloride. It is a disinfectant used to limit the entrance of viruses, bacteria, parasites, and insects that the shuttle might have picked up on the way here."

The shuttle slowly winds its way through a grass path that leads to an interlocking brick road and then heads to the lawn in front of the Administration Building. As Anjea parks the vehicle, Fire can see someone approaching.

"Dr. Primero is heading to the shuttle parking. Shall I open the doors when we stop or request him to leave?"

"You can open the doors Anjea," Fire says with confidence. It's time to see if he can pull this off,

The shuttle comes to a gentle stop and the falcon-winged door opens. Fire steps out and feels a sense of melancholy as he takes in his old school.

"Dr. Ericson, welcome to your renaissance," Primero calls out.

"Dr. Primero."

"Dr. Osler tells me that your son has made a full recovery and he'll be ready today."

"Excellent, excellent," Fire says, remembering that Jan is supposed to be in isolation.

"It's been quite a while since your last renaissance, hasn't it?"

Is this a test? Fire wasn't there for the last renaissance, so how would he know the last time his father did a brain swap. He quickly does some calculations so he can provide a sufficiently vague answer.

"I'd say it was about twenty … no, thirty years or so," Fire answers and then throws in, "… since 'To'."

"To?" Primero asked.

"Yes … éin, to, tre, fire …"

"Right, of course Tre … Norwegian."

"Exactly. So, I guess you can call me Fire now."

"Okay … Fire," Primero says laughing.

Fire has successfully amused the good doctor. From that point forward, Primero laughingly refers to Jan/Tre as Fire, not realizing that there is a joke, but the joke is on him.

"I see your shuttle is still dripping from the sanitization process," Primero states. "We had to increase the amount used this week when one of the boys appeared to have a mosquito bite … nasty little bugs those things."

Fire nods realizing that the mosquito had probably entered through the hole he made in the dome's structure behind the air conditioning units.

"Could you send someone to get Dr. Osler? There are a few things I would like to discuss before the procedure," Fire requests as they cross the grass towards Renaissance Hall. He wants rid of Primero, as he starts to worry whether he can pull off his plan.

Fire sits in the hall nervously waiting, then a smile comes across his face as Dr. Osler enters the room. The doctor sees Fire dressed in his father's clothes and thinks it is Tre Ericson … but it can't be.

"Jan?" Dr. Osler questions.

"In the flesh," Fire answers. "But you can call me Fire, it will help keep things straight and no one will know who I am?"

"Fire?"

"It's a long story."

"But what are you doing back here? What's going on?"

The Gemini Project

"Another long story, but it boils down to tonight … tonight is my renaissance, so you'll proceed as scheduled. It's time for me to get back into my old body, by getting out of this really old body."

"And the second patient?"

"Ahhh … I was hoping that you'd figure that one out yourself. We'll need one of the orderlies to get the plants from the back of the shuttle."

"That's Jan's body I hope."

Dr. Osler has the cart brought in and once the orderlies leave, he proceeds to uncover Fire's father's slumped body.

"What did you give him?"

"Benzos," Fire answers using the short form Anjea had used.

"Jan … I mean Fire, you never cease to amuse me. How much did you give him?"

"One tablet this morning, one yesterday along with a shot of Phenobarbital."

"Perfect … do I have to start worrying about my job?" Dr. Osler quips.

"No, I've got other plans."

"You'll have to tell me all about it after the renaissance. Now is there anything that you need to know from me, or is this procedure old hat to you now?"

"There's nothing I need for the operation, but I do have a personal question for you."

"Sure," Dr. Osler replies, "ask me anything."

"How did you do it? How did you make the leap to performing these operations, and I assume being a recipient as well … so taking your own son's life?"

Dr. Osler pauses. He needs to collect his own thoughts on this question, not justifications, but real truths about what brought him to this point.

"I was a brain surgeon, and a damned good one, but I had my own troubles. I was broke, lonely, and addicted. When ARP-40 hit …" Dr. Osler paused. "Do you know what that is?"

Fire shakes his head.

"It was the global pandemic that was about to wipe out mankind in 2040. There was a race between global warming, a world war, and a respiratory virus to see which one would claim the honour, and ARP-40 won. Anyway, when the pandemic hit, it hit hard and fast. That's when De Visie offered me a position in New London. It was a Hobson's Choice, if you know what that is," Dr. Osler says pausing again.

Fire shakes his head, again.

"You're getting a good education from me today ... it means take it or leave it, a choice where there really is only one option."

"A uni-lemma," Fire says.

"Sure ... a uni-lemma," Dr. Osler smiles. "My choice was to perform brain surgery in New London or die. I chose the former ... and once you've made that choice, it's easy to believe the rhetoric that the *Book of Generations* offered ... it represented a new chance for mankind. There had to be a better way than what had brought us to that point. *Generations* offered an opportunity to ensure that lessons and knowledge were truly retained, not just passed on through a generational set of Chinese whispers."

Dr. Osler is getting into his familiar amped-up speech pattern, the one where he is no longer waiting to ensure that his audience is keeping pace with him.

"I was 36 when ARP-40 plundered its way through the human population. I still had a lot of life to live and a lot of drugs to use, so I made the decision to take a surgery position in New London ... but that was the easy part," Dr. Osler says as he becomes emotional. "I was lucky enough to get my position in New London, but I had trouble getting started. I remember attempting my first transplant, I couldn't go through with it ... when it comes to being lucky, I was cursed ... Dr. Chirug had to step in for me. After that first one, I didn't have any issues ... it gradually became second nature .. routine ... just a job.

I had been there for four years and had performed three dozen renaissances, when De Visie informed me that I had a son. A woman that I met in my undergrad years at university, for want of a cliché we'll call her the 'love of my life' ... assuming of course that career, greed and drugs can't be the 'loves of your life' ... well, she had my child and she never told me. We had a falling out shortly after she became pregnant, and our lives simply proceeded on different paths. I'll never know exactly why she didn't tell me because she passed away at a very young age."

Dr. Osler pauses, not to allow Fire to come up to speed, but to swallow the truth that it was his mother that had killed Katie. Fire lets him gather his thoughts.

"It was a car accident … anyway … the pandemic hit and thanks to his data warehouse investments, De Visie knew about my son," Dr. Osler returning to his regular pace. "Some genius in his data mining group had processed DNA and produced my name as a recommended hire. The genius knew about my son and De Visie brought the boy to New London before the pandemic could claim his life. I had been set up.

You have to understand, De Visie controlled everything … and I really mean everything … still does. So, in 2044, De Visie not only let me know that I had a son, but he also told me that my son was approaching the ideal renaissance age. If I wanted to remain in the program, I had to believe in the program. Even though it was another 'take it or leave it', I still struggled. Here was a boy that I didn't know, and I would never be given the opportunity to meet. If I said no, my son would be ejected from New London, never to be seen again. If I said yes, then wouldn't a part of him live on through me? I told myself he would, and I agreed to the operation. I wanted to look down at my body and see my son. To see a little part of Katie. I wanted to look into my eyes and see hers. I know that being constantly juiced is not a good excuse for what I did, but De Visie made sure that I had access to one of his latest concoctions … Flash.

Dr. Chirug performed the surgery and when I awoke in my son's body, it didn't feel right. It didn't work for me. My addiction became worse after that, and I was permanently stoned in between surgery dates. If I were a patient, I'm not sure I would have gone under the knife if I knew that my doctor was in the condition that I was in. It was then that they transferred me to the newly constructed Corpo Academy … out of sight and out of mind … very out of mind.

I have renaissanced two more times since, using the services of the women on level 24. I'm not good with where I've wound up, but what were my alternatives? I don't believe in the Gemini System, but I can't change that. In case you haven't noticed, I am one of the oldest doctors here and I do not have a son waiting in the wings. It's been a number of decades since I went under the laser. But I can't stop working … I have too many unhealthy habits to pay for. Now does the guilt trip you've taken me on answer all your questions, or is there something else you need to know?"

"Just a couple of things ... are you juiced right now?"

"No," replies Dr. Osler routinely. "Anything else?"

"Yes ... last thing. Will I remember being in my father's body?"

"Of course. Your memories are carried with you in your brain. All of Jan's memories were with you in Tre's body, weren't they?"

"Yes, but the coaches often talked to us about muscle memory and why practice was so important, but I didn't seem to have muscle memory on my journey to New London."

"Ah, I see. Well muscle memory is more complicated. Unlike octopi, we don't have any actual brains in our limbs, so we can't really remember just using our muscles. What we have is a combination of procedural memory and muscle cells. The procedural memory is what lets you remember how to do your uneven bar routine, and the muscle cells are what you build up by repeating the routine. They stick around so you can do the routine again and again."

"So, I have my memory of how to do something, but my father's body doesn't have the muscle cells."

"Exactly. You'll remember the things you experienced in your father's body, because that type of memory sits in your brain. People think their memory is like a movie, and you just hit the play button in your mind and you get an instant replay ... but it's a lot more complicated than that. Memory storage is strangely disjointed. Your mind breaks memories into components, so your memory of today's procedure will store the date in one place, the smells in another, and my name in another. Memories are extraordinarily complex, so when you recall today, your mind has to reassemble all of the various components. When it can't, you might get that feeling of déjà vu all over again. And any one component can trigger that memory reassembly ... that's why you might not remember the layout of the Gehirn Academy ... but if you go back there, a colour or a smell might make you remember everything about it."

"That's funny, because both Elf and I had a strange feeling that we had been to level 26 before?"

"That's because you have. Both of you would have been raised in the Crèche."

The Gemini Project 265

"But neither of us had any memory of being there until we got there."

"Something brought it back to you ... the buildings, the people ..."

"The colour of the sky," Fire concludes. "But why is the memory gone in both of us?"

"The memory is very susceptible to suggestions. When you remember something, you are actually reassembling the last time you recalled it. I would swear that I watched the news of the ARP-40 outbreak at Johns Hopkins, but I wasn't even working there at the time. Somehow, I'd convinced myself that I saw it on the TV in the doctor's lounge ... but of course, I hadn't. One day, something might trigger the memory reassembly and I'll know where I was that day. So, it is possible to accidentally, or purposely, update your memory. You can do it ... and so can someone else!

De Visie used Dr. Penfield Wilder to program your memory so you can't remember anything before you arrived at the Gehirn Academy. None of the boys remember anything before that. But the idiosyncratic nature of memory makes it impossible to erase all the components of a memory. If you override your memory of my name, the date of this operation, and what we are doing here ... it can all come back when you smell the operating theatre."

"They can do that ... change our memories?"

"They can and they do ... and they're getting better at mapping memory synapses, so they are getting better at making the complete change. All of the Hebs have had their memories programmed. Now before we forget ... is there anything else you need to know?"

"No ... that's it."

"Good. Now let's get you two prepped, then I'll bring your father around to put him under again. Nurse Banaltram?" Dr. Osler calls out to the washup room where he sees her and the two orderlies scrubbing up.

The two patients are prepped while the doctor also gets ready for the procedure. Fire is wheeled back into the theatre on a gurney and this time he is on the opposite side of his father. He sits up and looks over at his father's near lifeless body.

"I think we are about to do something that will have greater ramifications than I initially anticipated, and you should understand that I am okay with that. More than okay. What's your thought regarding your father?" Dr. Osler asks.

"Stitch him up and put him back together."

"And then what?" Dr. Osler asks with a determination.

"Then I'll get him a place in the labour-force in New London. It seems I can do that … I'm a pretty big deal there."

"That's one school of thought. Another is … there is absolutely no place he can go, no place you can put him, where he won't report these events," Dr. Osler stresses. "Then you'll find yourself, back on this table and soon after that, you'll be dead. There'll be nothing to save you from his renaissance, not yours, HIS."

"I know my father is a monster and the whole system is an abyss, but I don't want to become the same as him?"

"You are nothing like him. I should know … I've stared into that same abyss for over a century. What determines who you are will not be this decision, it will be what you do with your life from that point on. Your father has zero intention of changing who he is. It is time to fight monsters Fire."

"Maybe you're right," Fire answers slowly.

"You know I'm right. It's a Hobson's choice … take it or leave it … you really have no options. He's got to go. Don't think you can bring him around and ask him how he could do this to his own flesh and blood … and you would hear some sort of recapitulation that would justify this sick system that he lives in …. that we live in. There is no El Dorado; there is no Xanadu; there is no happy ending where you and your father kiss and make up. There is just you OR him."

Outside, Fire is silent. Inside, he seethes with hatred for his father, but what did that say about him? He is angry with his father for not only wanting to kill his son, but also for making Fire have to make this decision. If he let his father die, is he any better than him? But what is the alternative? There really isn't one. It is a uni-lemma. Dr. Osler is right. If Tre survives, he will go to the authorities as soon as he is able. Fire needs to survive. He needs to prove who he is by choosing the right path after the renaissance. He needs his life to make a difference.

"Harvest him," Fire responds decisively.

"Great. I'll get nothing for his liver, though. It was going to kill him eventually anyway. This works out perfectly, now to everyone else, this will just be a Renaissance as per usual."

Fire lies down on his gurney and watches his father. There is zero compassion left. Tre has sown enough hate in Fire's heart to make the decision easier than it should have been. He can see the effects of the Benzodiazepine wearing off. Soon his father will be getting the prescribed anesthesia, and he will go back under again, this time for good. His father opens his eyes momentarily, staring at the ceiling, then closes them again. Fire wonders if he realizes what is happening.

"Now there's a good little corpo ..." Dr. Osler says as he smiles down on Trevor Ericson from the top of the gurney, "I've stimulated your preBötzinger complex which will affect your breathing patterns and your ability to speak. No matter, I think all you have to do is listen ... there's someone here who wants to talk to you."

Fire wonders if Dr. Osler really is juiced. He isn't.

"Is there anybody in there? Just nod if you can hear me," Dr. Osler jokes as he pries open Tre Ericson's eyelids. "Here's a good one for you ... knock, knock ... who's there? ... not you! What? You didn't like that one ... well here's an oldie but a goodie ... I'd rather have a bottle in front of me than a frontal lobotomy. I know you're straight faced on the outside, but I bet that one has you laughing on the inside."

Tre opens his eyes. Dr. Osler continues to amuse himself, using one hand to turn Tre's cheeks slightly towards Fire. There is a slight scowl on Tre's face. He seems to be starting to comprehend. Fire leans over towards his father and gazes down at his own body. His mind is on one side of the gurney, but his body is on the other. Fire is having the out-of-body experience that his father had spoke of.

For a brief moment, Fire wonders what his father would say if he were able to speak at this point. Would he express remorse? Would he apologize? Did he even have the capacity to hold any regret for selfishly taking the lives of his three previous sons? The answer is clear. His father would probably continue to expound his privilege. He would be angry, not at the system that allowed him to continually survive, but at Fire for trying to circumvent that system. Fire stares into his father's eyes.

"Good morning father. It's my birthday today. I thought I was going to go with you to New London, but I'm going to change my mind ...," Fire states, content with his decision.

Dr. Osler chuckles at that one. Fire waits to see whether his father is comprehending the severity of what is going to happen. He sees the look of dread enter his father's face ... his face. Tre tries to speak but can't ...

"Oh, don't get that indignant look on your face. This is nothing more than exactly what you previously planned," Dr. Osler says. "Yes, that's right. Surgery for two, but only one makes it through."

Dr. Osler can't resist and he leans back into the light.

"Oh yes, and if you think that I did you wrong, it doesn't matter to me ... but I didn't," Dr. Osler whispers into Tre's ear. "I said I'd get you into your son's body for 100,000 credits ... and I did. I never promised how long you'd be there. That's on you. Besides, now I get paid my regular fee for this operation too, and it was all your son's idea. You've got a pretty smart boy there Dr. Eriksson, you should be proud of him."

With that, Dr. Osler turns on the dial that is attached to the tube that runs into Fire's father's ear, and his father fades into darkness.

The renaissance was a success, at least from Fire's point of view. With the spinal bayonet already installed in both the brains and the body, it was one of the quickest transplants the doctor had ever performed. Fire had his old body back ... his young body. Other than a shaved head and a few bruises that he couldn't remember getting, Fire was back together. He didn't ask Dr. Osler anything concerning his father, and the doctor never offered any information.

After the morning recovery, Fire got dressed and stepped into the hall to find a waiting Dr. Primero.

"Fire," Primero said as though he had just told the world's funniest joke, "I was just coming to see you. Dr. Osler told me everything went swimmingly. How do you feel?"

"Yeah, I feel like a new man."

"Good, good," Primero responded sincerely. "Just one final step ... if you don't mind, can you stare into the financial system scanner?"

He motioned for Fire to look into an iris scanner that was set up just outside the recovery room. This step wasn't included in his

The Gemini Project

father's illegal renaissance. Fortunately, Fire understood how to use the device. A small red laser moved across Fire's eyes and then the device let out a quiet ping.

"Well, that's it ... your new body's got access to all that you own, minus our fee of course. So, I guess this means we won't see you for a few years now. How is Fem doing?"

"Fem, yes ... yes, of course ..." Fire said, discerning that he had a younger brother. "I'm going to be checking in on him real soon. I think he's real Corpo material."

The two men walked outside, and Fire was pleased when his body didn't ache as he walked down the steps of Renaissance Hall.

"Good, good. There'll be a spot here when he's ready."

"You know," Fire said, "it's amazing how quickly I've gotten used to this body. Tell me, your son doesn't attend this school though, does he?"

"No. He attends the Körper Academy on Jardin Island."

"Jardin Island, you say ..." Fire responded introspectively, "I've been told I should visit there one day."

"You haven't been yet? That's hard to believe. It really is a religious experience."

Fire looked over at the soccer pitch. He thought to himself: 'Paradise'. The boys were playing a match and Otto just scored. Dix looked to be on the same team, so Fire knew Dix would be happy ... at least for another couple of days until his father arrived for his renaissance.

"Dr. Primero, would you mind bringing Alain Gémeaux's boy over so I can have a word with him?"

Dr. Osler was just coming out of Renaissance Hall to say his goodbyes when he heard Fire's request.

"That's very unusual," Dr. Osler stressed. "The boys aren't really permitted to see you leave after a renaissance."

"I'm told Dix had been a good friend to my son, and I just want to personally thank him."

Dr. Osler looked at Primero with a shrug. Primero nodded then signaled for one of the orderlies to come over.

"Don't forget," Primero said, "when he sees you, you're Jan not Tre, so don't slip up."

'I'm neither ... I'm Fire.'

"Dix is not the brightest boy," Dr. Primero smiled. "He might not catch on even if you do make a mistake."

"I think the boys would surprise you," Dr. Osler said.

"Right then," Dr. Primero concluded, "I'll say my goodbyes and we'll catch-up soon."

Primero and Fire shook hands, then Primero headed to the Administration Building.

"What's going on Fire?" Dr. Osler asked out of the side of his mouth as he watched Primero depart.

"Nothing. I'm just thinking about what needs to change, and I thought a little discussion with my old friend might help me with my priorities."

"What are you thinking?"

"Well, I'd like to visit my mother; I'd like to find Fem, the brother that I just found out about; I'd like to get my friend Elf some care for his poorly healed leg bone; I'd like to give Dix the opportunity to skip his renaissance, and to visit his own mother; I'd like to unlock my childhood memories; I'd like to pay a visit to Dr. Primero's son on Jardin Island; and then of course, I'd like to bring down the whole fucking system."

Dr. Osler looked at the boy in disbelief. He was partially hoping that Fire was joking, but there was no laughter when he got to the punchline. The doctor grinned when he realized that this really was a list of priorities.

"So ... the Fire is going to spread?" Dr. Osler said, letting his smile show his approval. He agreed that this might be exactly what's needed at this point.

"So ... the Fire is going to burn it all down. I took my father's life, not so I could live, but so I can enact change. People in the present, understand that people in the future will want to know what happened in the past. That's why they want to continue to wipe out dangerous memories. They want to control the narrative, but I can't let that happen. No more secrets. No more hiding what's really been happening in the Gemini System. We need to rewrite our future out of respect for the past."

'Wow, that sounds like something I would say,' thought Dr. Osler, 'but I would never have had the cahonas to act on it!'

The Gemini Project

Dr. Osler believes he has done a respectable job schooling the boy in the discipline of philosophy, but he had never imagined that he would create a philosopher ... no, a prophet. Dr. Osler nodded just as the orderly returned with Dix.

Dix saw Dr. Osler first and thought he was in trouble for something. Then he saw Fire.

"Jan, you're out of confinement! I was worried about you."

Dix gave Fire a hug. It was a hard hug and Fire felt the love. Things were not as black and white as Fire had perceived them to be only a few weeks earlier. Dix was just a pawn in the system, the same as Jan had been. Fire hugged him back. It was a purposeful hug.

"I really missed you," Dix said. "I wish you didn't have to go. Otto's been acting like he's the top man since you've been sick."

Fire felt a pang of guilt for once questioning Dix's friendship. Now he could define what being a good friend was, and deep-down Dix was his friend. If Fire was going to be a good friend back, then he shouldn't be keeping secrets. There were some things that he really needed to explain to Dix.

He put one arm around his friend's shoulder and led him across the grass to the shuttle.

"Come check out the inside of this shuttle ... I've got a couple of things that I want to tell you."

17. Enlightenment

The release of *The Book of Generations* was followed by religious reform, economic reform, political reform, and legal reform. A new order was born. Anything that was in contravention to the new system was a capital crime, for which death was the one and only punishment. As a result, society had virtually wiped-out crime. Access to the neurological gateway made perjury detection infallible and had eliminated the necessity for entering a plea in courts. Limited crime meant there was little need for policing. The gendarmes, who only had the power to stun individuals, were more like hall monitors than a police force.

In New London, Dix will apologize to Elf for the injury he caused, but Elf will tell him that he calls it 'his lucky break'. The newly-formed three amigos, Dix, Elf and Fire, will get off the elevator on the 21st level, then head to 1640 Riverside Drive. Anya will be waiting outside her front door. As the boys approach, she will immediately recognize her son. Elf and Fire will stand back and let them embrace. Looking over Dix's shoulder, Fire will see that Anya managed to smile and cry at the same time.

Elf will be excited to track down his own mother, only to be disappointed when he finds out that she passed away the previous year. The pain of this thought will be dulled when he learns that he has a brother in the Gehirn Academy and a sister in the Crèche. They'll visit the 26th level, where Dix will be surprised that Fire hadn't noticed the resemblance between Elf and Skye.

Fire will be by himself when he visits Dr. Wilder to discuss memory writing. The doctor will offer Fire some pills to negate the impact of his work, but Fire will make him swallow a few before he takes them back to Dix and Elf. The boys will take the pills and as promised, childhood memories will come flooding back. Dix and Fire will remember that they used to play together at the Crèche as their mothers watched on.

Thanks to such minimal security, even on Jardin Island, De Visie's assailant will be able to walk right up to him and inject a dose of toxins to kill him instantly. The bottom block of society's Jenga tower will be removed, signalling a change is gonna come.

Fire Erikson will die, at the age of 160, in 2258. On his casket, Fire's wife will place a vintage photo that she took over 120 years prior. It will be a portrait of Fire and his mother sitting outside a tent in Superficie. In the picture, at Fire's side, will be his blue-eyed dog: Osler. His younger brother Fem, his son William, and his grandson Reilly will all attend the funeral with their wives. William will weep when someone approaches him and tells him that his father was 'a great man'.

18. Easter Eggs

32 Windsor Gardens – Fire's mother's address – The address for the home of Paddington Bear.

124 Conch Street – The address of the Crèche – The address for the ~~home~~ pineapple of SpongeBob SquarePants.

698 Candlewood Lane – Tre Ericson's address – The address for the home of Jessica Fletcher on *Murder She Wrote*.

742 Evergreen Terrace – Dr. Osler's address – The address for the home of *The Simpsons*.

1640 Riverside Drive – Anya's address – The address for the home of Emmett 'Doc' Brown in *Back to the Future*.

Angelo – Italian male name meaning *Messenger* or *Angel*.

Anya – Hungarian for *Mother*.

Anjea – The indigenous Australian goddess of Fertility.

ARP-2500 – A monophonic analog modular synthesizer built from 1970 to 1981.

Asino – Italian for *Ass*.

The Gemini Project

Banaltram – Scots Gaelic for *Nurse*.

Bartel – German male name meaning *Bright*.

Cervello – Italian for *Brain*.

Chirug – Afrikaans for *Surgeon*.

Corpo – Italian for *Body*.

De Visie – Dutch for *Vision*.

Demikhov, Dr. Vladimir – A Russian scientist and organ transplant pioneer who created a two-headed dog. True story! Google it!

Ernst, Alwin C. – Founder of the accounting firm that would become Ernst & Young.

Gehirn – German for *Brain*.

Gémeaux – French for *Gemini*.

Gemini – From Roman mythology, the singular name for the twins Castor and Pollux.

Heb – Welsh for *Have Not*.

Irving – The doorman from the movie *Crocodile Dundee*.

Jardin – French for *Garden*.

Körper – German for *Body*.

Logan's Run – A dystopian novel based on a Malthusian future society by William F. Nolan and George Clayton Johnson.

O'Flanagan, Dr. Kevin – An Irish physician who represented his country in both soccer and rugby.

Ordinateur – French for *Computer*.

Osler, Dr. William – One of the founders of Johns Hopkins Hospital, a documented white racist who also gave a speech where he quoted from *The Fixed Period* by Anthony Trollope.

Paradise – Celtic Park, home of the Glasgow Celtic football club.

Pelacur – Malay for *Prostitute*.

Penfield, Dr. Wilder – An American-Canadian Neurosurgeon who found that when the temporal lobe was stimulated it produced a combination of hallucinations, dream, and memory recollection.

Penzler, Otto – an editor of mystery fiction, and the proprietor of The Mysterious Bookshop in NYC.

Plaza Mayor – Madrid's main city square, which has hosted bullfights, markets, symphonies, soccer games and even executions.

Primero – Spanish for *First*.

Renaissance – French for *Rebirth*.

Rocco – Italian male name meaning *One who rests*.

Rossignol – French for *Nightingale*.

Síceolaí – Irish for *Psychologist*.

Sicilian Defense – A defensive chess move when White's first move is E4.

Smith, Jedediah – An American and trapper who was instrumental in the development of the American West.

Smith-Morra Gambit – A chess move used as an aggressive response to the Sicilian Defense.

Soma – The happiness-producing drug in *Brave New World*.

Superficie – Spanish for *Surface*.

The Secret of the Silver Horse – A Canadian government publication to instruct children about secrets concerning sexual abuse.

Tirwedd – Welsh for *Landscape*.

Treinador – Spanish for *Coach*.

Verwalter – German for *Caretaker*.

Wullerton – The neighbouring town, 37 miles away from Dog River in the series *Corner Gas*.

The Boys:

Dix – French for *Ten*.
Elf – Afrikaans for *Eleven*.
Fem – Norwegian for *Five*.
Fire – Norwegian for *Four*.
Jet (เจ็ด) – Thai for *Seven*.
Otto – Italian for *Eight*.
Tam (八) – Vietnamese for *Eight*.
Tre – Norwegian and Italian for *Three*.

Inspirational Lyrics:

*It's been a long; a long time comin',
But I know, A change gon' come.*

A Change is Gonna Come
Sam Cooke

The heat was hot and the ground was dry, But the air was full of sound.

A Horse With No Name
America

Well, they say it's kinda fright'nin' how this younger generation swings, You know, it's more than just some new sensation.

And the Cradle Will Rock…
Van Halen

*Ain't no sound but the sound of his feet,
Machine guns ready to go.*

Another One Bites the Dust
Queen

Remembering games and daisy chains and laughs,
Got to keep the loonies off the grass.

Brain Damage
Pink Floyd

Hello, is there anybody in there? Just nod if you can hear me.

Relax, I need some information first ... just the basic facts.
Can you show me where it hurts?

Comfortably Numb
Pink Floyd

He says, "I'm sorry but I'm out of milk and coffee."
"Never mind, sugar, we can watch the early movie."

Da Ya Think I'm Sexy
Rod Stewart

By chance, two separate glance meet,
And I am you and what I see is me.

Echoes
Pink Floyd

In just seven days, I can make you a man.

I Can Make You a Man
Tim Curry

I had a dream, we went away.
You and me, in a French Café.

French Café
The Lone Pipe

Don't surround yourself with yourself, move on back two squares,
Send an instant karma to me, initial it with loving care.

I've Seen All Good People
Yes

Just Like a Paperback Novel, the kind the drugstore sells.

If You Could Read My Mind
Gordon Lightfoot

Quand il me prends dans ses bras, Il me parle tout bas
Je vois la vie en rose

When he takes me into his arms, He speaks to me softly
I see life through rose-colored glasses

La Vie en Rose
Édith Piaf

You get a good job with good pay and you're okay.

Money
Pink Floyd

Ni le bien, qu'on m'a fait
Ne le mal, tout ça m'est bien égal!

Neither the good things people have done to me;
Nor the bad things, it's all the same to me!

Non, je ne regrette rien
Édith Piaf

That's just a preview of the things you're gonna get.

Oh What a Feeling
Crowbar

And my dear mother left me when I was quite young
When I was quite young

On the Road Again
Canned Heat

Seein' things that I may never see again
And I can't wait to get on the road again

On the Road Again
Willie Nelson

Same as it ever was, same as it ever was (letting the days go by).

Once in a Lifetime
Talking Heads

It's a dirty story of a dirty man and his clinging wife doesn't understand
His son is working for the Daily Mail

Paperback Writer
The Beatles

Well, it burned while I cried, 'Cause I heard it screaming your name.

Set Fire to the Rain
Adele

She works hard for the money, So hard for it, honey.

She Works Hard for the Money
Donna Summer

We take all kinds of pills that give us all kind of thrills
But the thrill we've never known
Is the thrill that'll gitcha when you get your picture
On the cover of the Rollin' Stone

The Cover of the Rolling Stone
Dr. Hook & the Medicine Show

'Cause when it comes to bein' lucky, she's cursed.

The First Cut is the Deepest
Cat Stevens

Spotify Playlist
https://open.spotify.com/playlist/4Z6jhKRopkm3Ptd93gJa6w?si=5b5ae54176e14170

Acknowledgements

"How did we get here?"

I wanted to write a third person novel about the future and put it in past tense. Thanks to my wonderful wife Lorraine, the text was reviewed several times. However, after she was finished her final edit and was ready to give it her seal of approval, I changed the remembrances of Dr. Osler to first person, then I decided to change the time that the protagonist spends out of body to present tense.

Any mistakes in tense, person, spelling, or fact, are on me and my fickle last-minute changes (maybe some of the factual errors are on Google)! Special thanks to the authors and musicians for the lines that I have borrowed ... by which of course I mean 'who inspired me'.

Printed in Great Britain
by Amazon